Dots

Cancer Sleuthing on the 21st Century Frontier

Clark Thomas Riley

For John Roberts (my cousin, who knows how to hold a community together — Clark

DEDICATION

My mother, Margaret Crim Riley, made sure I did my homework, and she regularly met with teachers at school in parent-teacher conferences. My father, Thomas Leslie Riley, pushed me to pursue the best education possible. My wife, Debbie, put up with so much while this work underwent its multi-decade incubation. My children, David and Sean, inspired me with their unending enthusiasm and bright curiosity. My sister-in-law, Toni Wilson Riley, generously shared her expertise on cattle breeds and other farming wisdom. My Novel Workshop Group made sure that this work was worth reading.

CONTENTS

ACKNOWLEDGMENTS

Our novel workshop group is perhaps the main reason my works have seen print. Our regular meetings foster a commitment to writing, an irresistible deadline. The camaraderie of the group instills a desire to please our fellow readers. Lucy Hoopes has contributed her critical grammarian mind. Her keen eye and grammatical thought process have been crucial for smoothing the paper-to-brain pathway. Lauren Goodsmith is one of the finest writers I have had the pleasure of knowing. Her insistence on honest relationships and proper cause and effect has relieved you, dear reader, of arduous suspensions of disbelief. She also speaks wonderful French. Alex Duvan has urged passionate relationships between the characters and is ever properly impatient with storyline *cul-de-sacs* or tangents. Margaret Rooney and Gail Mitchell were crucial finders of inconsistencies and ambiguities, most of which I hope to have squashed. Judy Tanner and Teresa Elguezabal insisted on familial authenticity in the story. Other members of our group have joined since this work was first completed and their valuable contributions to my future publications will be acknowledged when the ink and electrons of those works meet paper and screens. I am especially indebted to my editor, Elizabeth Dorcey, who found so many writing burs so that you would not have to. Her skills at polishing grammar, style, and content have been a true blessing.

1 JUST TO BE CLEAR

Before I tell you the story, let me say a few things. I'm a good investigator. I would never say this to boast. After all, it's futile, I believe, to boast about anything that's either factual or not. Facts are facts. Pride doesn't change facts. I only want to make the point that I've tried to do the best I could through all my life. I applied myself in college and earned my degrees through hard study and years of perseverance. To be sure, I was fortunate for my master's to study under the infamous Professor Stanley Kerwin at the School of Public Health of the University of North Carolina at Chapel Hill. I can vouch for his reputation as one of the most difficult and challenging educators you'll ever fear to meet. I'll also vouch that those three years were the most important stretch of learning in my life.

Since my graduation, I've served the good people of the United States as a clinical investigator with the Centers for Disease Control and Prevention. Some say I have a reputation for being meticulous. Many, my wife, Baylor, included, use the term 'obsessive.' Maybe so. I've cracked some spectacular, vexing cases. Remember the 2001 botulism outbreak in Lincoln, Nebraska? I was assigned to that case based on only five incidents above background. By the time our team finished, we had identified over 100 additional cases and traced the swarm to one small lot of contaminated catsup. Catsup. The only time catsup has ever been implicated in botulism. And from a vendor whose record is otherwise spotless.

I've got several commendations in my drawer at the office, including the CDC Director's Commendation for Public Service. So I know what I'm doing, and I do try to be diligent. It's just that some cases can be really hard and their outcome uncertain. I thought you should know. Just to be clear.

2 OUT IN THE COUNTRY

In May of 2009 I was assigned to find out why in the little town of Guthrie, Kentucky, four men in their late fifties reportedly developed Griffith's sarcoma, an extremely rare cancer characterized by a sudden explosive manifestation across many organ systems.

Griffith's had been documented only 17 times since its first formal description in the November 1977 *Journal of Internal Medicine*. Each was a solitary unrelated individual and 15 of those 17 reports were based on autopsies alone. The clinical presentation and patient notes accompanying the autopsies suggest that the disease is extremely painful and deforming.

* * *

A little after 6:30 in the morning on Tuesday, May 19th, I boarded Delta Airlines flight 1010, non-stop from Atlanta, Georgia to Nashville, Tennessee. I generally prefer to drive, even for trips of moderate distances like this one. The hassles of moving through the airport, the incessant fees and annoyances associated with airports today, and that stale feeling I have on arrival have taken all the fun out of flying for me. I remember when I was a young man walking out onto the tarmac without a scan or pat-down and boarding the plane using one of those rolling stairways minutes before the stewardesses closed the hatch. In those days "stewardess" was the normal and accepted identification for our flight attendants. I also remember the cabin crews being friendlier back then, though that could be a trick of memory.

For this trip, transportation would be travel by air. The Center's autos were all reserved by other investigators — or broken down —, and my Civic, at one 170,000 miles, was becoming too unreliable. I hoped that the rental waiting for me in Nashville was as reliable as the Civic, not like the last rental.

I don't know whether it's an obsession or a side effect of my training, but I like to take the window seat, and I almost always film a plane's takeoff and landing with my cell phone. I tell people who don't know me that it's because I enjoy the beauty of a plane lifting off the planet or gliding to a graceful landing. I know deep inside that in the event of a catastrophe, the video would be invaluable to crash investigators — hard-working, inquiring individuals like me. I can imagine their reaction. "Oh, wow! This guy was filming right when the engine mount tore off! That was an amazing stroke of luck!" I don't much believe in luck — just circumstance and preparation.

Flight 1010 proved routine and uneventful. I looked down on the receding landscape of western Georgia until we passed through the stratocumulus cloud layer. Millions of acres of fluffy water vapor can be boring, no matter how critical they are to life on Earth. Once the flight was level and we were allowed to access our carry-on items, I took the background reports from my briefcase and began to review them. The illustrations were gruesome even to my accustomed eye. The passenger to my right caught sight of some of the autopsy pictures and was clearly disturbed by them. He was an older gentleman with an expensive watch, wearing a new polo shirt without a trace of a stain. He looked to me like a successful small business owner on his way to a golf outing. The background reports could wait, I thought. I put them back in the briefcase and settled back the few degrees that the seat would allow. "I'm a doctor," I said. "We're working on a cure."

He seemed satisfied, and I knew that what I said was basically true. Griffith's is so rare that it shouldn't have been given any priority. The consensus in the medical community is that the syndrome is the result of exposure to an extreme carcinogen, and, in that case, Griffith's would be better classified as an accident, not a disease. Other than possibly uncovering a new and dangerous common carcinogen, these four cases would have escaped notice. That is, until Spence Conner at UCLA Medical Center speculated that the syndrome was the result of a new virus and that we may be on the verge of a virus-mediated pandemic of cancer. The good doctor's study was deeply flawed — small sample size, little follow-up, and no biological evidence whatsoever of a virus. Unfortunately, his speculations reached the press on a slow news week, and the "Andromeda Virus" has been front-section dithering for over a year.

The VA's automated medical reporting system algorithms spotted the cluster early and raised an alert to us before the press got wind of the occurrences. Mind you, when I say it that way, it sounds like some kind of cover-up. You can rest assured that whatever I find will be reported — with good documentation — in a reputable journal, maybe the *Journal of Internal Medicine* or *Journal of Infectious Diseases*. My core mission is to finish Dr. Conner's work for him and either lay to rest the virus theory or provide some actual evidence for it. My checked suitcase is about half-filled with sampling syringes and secure sample vials. I have my CDC badge ready for the day when that suitcase gets pulled for inspection.

We touched down in Nashville three minutes ahead of schedule, and the flight attendants thanked us for not causing any trouble during the flight. Well, they didn't actually say that, though it must have been on their minds. I stayed in my seat as most of the passengers jumped up and took their position in the aisle for 15 minutes of pointless waiting. Instead, I watched out the window while the worker bees with their specialty trucks took their well-practiced positions along the belly of the plane. Once the line in the aisle was thin and moving, I picked up my briefcase and took a comfortable stroll toward the exit.

"Thank you," I said to the flight attendants at the exit. "Where're y'all headed next?" I really am interested in their answers, and I support a theory that a pleasant conversation with someone in a service profession can have a powerful multiplier effect. It turns out that they would be flying on from Nashville to Las Vegas. I bid them a safe journey. I consider it a failure if I can't make a cashier smile at the grocery checkout. At our Safeway back home, most of the cashiers know me by name.

Stepping from the plane's cabin to the jetway, I felt warm, humid air breaching the gap between the terminal and aircraft. It would be a hot and humid Tennessee/Kentucky day. I strolled down the concourse. Even at a lazy pace, I'd still beat the bags to the baggage area. I used the walk to measure the civic engagement of the airport authority. Nashville did pretty well, highlighting their country music scene with LED displays featuring current cultural events with dates and easy-to-use contact information. There were exhibits of musical instruments and local cuisine like barbequed ribs and Jack Daniel's whiskey. OK, I realize that whiskey is not cuisine, but that's all right.

The Nashville ground crew seemed to be a bit better organized than most, for the baggage from flight 1010 was arriving just as I came to the carousel. When the machine assembly disgorged my suitcase, I spied a sticker near the lock. That's sometimes not a good sign. Once I retrieved the bag, though, I saw that it was a TSA sticker noting that the bag had been passed by inspection and verified with a national database. The sticker was next to my CDC seal and registry number. I felt better knowing that someone, somewhere was watching out for us. Smiling, I picked up the bag, and headed for the car rental booth. A suitcase half full of sampling syringes and secure vials isn't very heavy — mostly hollow, sterile plastic. As I took my samples in the following days, most would be mailed back to the Center save the last couple of days, so the suitcase wouldn't be any heavier on my return in a week or so.

There was no line at the Alamo booth. A young woman on duty cleared paperwork from her previous customer. She looked to be in her late teens or early twenties, although I find that I'm not such a good judge of younger ages anymore. She had an air of authority about her, enhanced by her crisp Alamo jacket with company logo patch and brass nameplate.

"Good morning, sir. How may I help you today?"

"Good morning, Sonya." She smiled at the sound of her name. Why do customers not use service reps' names? The service people have their names right on their uniforms and are, almost without exception, proud of their names. When I use a person's name, it opens a gate between us, and we have a camaraderie that often proves supremely valuable when dealing with the corporate ineptitude that often bedevils us both. I returned the smile. "John Parker. I should have an economy car on the list."

She flipped through the short stack of rental agreements on her desk, mine being the fourth or fifth one down. "Here we go." She retrieved the form and looked at her screen. She frowned, and her shoulders sank. "Looks like we're temporarily out of economies."

I knew that was coming.

She stole a glance to her left and right before leaning forward on the counter, speaking in a whisper. "I swear, I think they do that on purpose." She turned around and looked through the huge glass behind her and then turned back to me with a twinkle in her eyes. "It looks like Mike's just now finishing up on a nice Civic. It's more comfortable than the economy and gets better mileage. It's usually ten dollars a day more. I can mark the Civic as our substitute, if that's OK with you. That way you get it for the same price."

"That would be awesome, Sonya. Thank you." Always — always — address a customer representative by her name.

Sonya completed the paperwork, addressing the obligatory matters of insurance, damage waivers, returning with a full tank to avoid ridiculous fuel charges, and so forth. She came to the end of her list and I handed her the credit card.

"Oh, wow. Centers for Disease Control and Prevention. Are you a doctor?"

"Yes, as a matter of fact, I am."

"That's so great. I'm pre-med at Vanderbilt." She paused and moved her body back and forth in a nervous sway. "I know, you're wondering 'so why's she working at Alamo?'"

I smiled as I responded, "I worked my way through six years at Carolina manning a snack bar. You'll do well. You're obviously dedicated, and you've got initiative."

She beamed now. "So, are you here for a conference?"

"Not this time. We're following up on some patients up in Kentucky. A little research."

"That is so great, Dr. Parker. Here's your paperwork and the key and I'll have Mike drive the car up to the curb. He's almost finished. You just step over there." She pointed toward the double exit doors. "You can wait inside where it's cool. I think it's going to be a scorcher today."

I nodded. "Thank you, Sonya. Good luck in your studies. You've chosen a good field at an exciting time."

"My pleasure, Dr. Parker. Enjoy your stay." She smiled as I left. After a moment, she called out to me. "Oh, I almost forgot. Thank you for choosing Alamo!"

I gave her a thumbs-up. Always — always — address a customer representative by her name.

* * *

The signage leaving Nashville's airport was adequate. I still recall the total signage incompetence at Philadelphia that resulted in circling the airport three times at a crawl. After passing a few minor ambiguities here, I was on the highway traveling north by northwest toward Fort Campbell, Kentucky. I would not go that far, the exit for Guthrie being about eight miles shy of the state line. According to the map, I would exit Interstate 24 onto the Clarksville-Guthrie Highway, an auspicious name for the combined Tennessee Route 13 and US Highway 79. I was not going to take the direct route from the interstate to Guthrie, though. At this exit, only a few blocks toward Clarksville, Tennessee, there is a White Castle hamburger restaurant. Now "restaurant" has always seemed a bit pretentious to me. When I can, I purchase these addictive little burgers by the sack, and eat them on the way to my final destination. There aren't any White Castle restaurants in the Atlanta area, so I've made it a point to ferret them out when I travel to the cities where they do have them.

At the Kentucky state line, the road drops its Tennessee Route 13 co-identification and becomes Russellville Road and US 79, but you'll only travel two blocks into Kentucky before bearing right on Dixie Beeline Highway/US 41. I arrived in Guthrie a little after noon, satiated from the small sack of burgers. You may have never heard of Guthrie. It's a tiny town, about 1,500 souls, set in the rolling agricultural lands of Todd County, Kentucky. At first glance, it appears to be a quiet and pleasant place, undisturbed by the outer world and content to keep it that way. To the outside world, Guthrie's biggest claim to fame would be that it is the birthplace of Robert Penn Warren, for whom a birthplace museum is maintained. According to Kentucky Tourism, "The nation's first poet laureate and three-time Pulitzer Prize winner is remembered here at his home. Exhibits on the life and works of Robert Penn Warren are throughout the house. The house is furnished with period antiques. Donations are appreciated. Motorcoaches with notice. Sunday tours by appointment." Robert Penn Warren was the author of *All the King's Men*. I decided I would try to visit the museum while I was there.

* * *

On entering, I surveyed the town. The transition from rural to urban was not abrupt — a matter of density. The road added the name Park Street without notice and continued across railroad tracks beyond the Elkton Bank and Trust. I saw that they had an ATM. Good to know, just in case. I found myself already heading out into the country, passing Kentucky Street and Tennessee Street with only farmland ahead. I stopped and backed up on the road — there was no traffic — and turned right on Tennessee Street to return to town. Tennessee didn't go very far, simply curving to the right. I smiled as I found myself on Warren Avenue, though that avenue didn't have the courtesy of extending into town. I turned right on Tower Street to return to Park Street. I would later learn that a turn to the left on Tower would have taken me by the water treatment plant.

Back across the railroad, I pulled up to the post office — Guthrie, Kentucky 42234. In small rural settings, the post office is often the best place to start orienting to the community. Plus, this is where I'd be mailing my samples back to Atlanta. I noted as I walked in that there was only a single person on duty. He appeared to be in his late thirties and was busy stacking large boxes onto shelves well behind the counter. I tried to look as unhurried and relaxed as I could. He looked up at the sound of the door closing behind me.

"Howdy. Be with you in a sec'. Just gotta get these put up for tomorrow's delivery."

"No hurry," I said. "Take your time."

He returned to his stacking, finishing in about two minutes. He clapped his hands together to get the dust off and turned to me. "So what can I do for you today, sir?" His nameplate read 'Ridenour.'

"I'm in town for a few days and was looking for a place to stay. I didn't see any motels or hotels on the way in."

Mr. Ridenour chuckled. "Yeah, that's been the case for about a hundred ten years. Closest motels would be in Hopkinsville or Clarksville. Closest hotel's in Nashville."

I wrinkled my brow. "That'll do, I guess. I'd hoped to stay a little closer. Are there any bed and breakfasts in town?"

Now Ridenour laughed. "I'd say you're not from these parts. They're still called 'tourist homes' out here. Ellen Miller over on 3rd Street takes in boarders. You an English professor?"

"No, why?"

"Most of the well-dressed folks who stay here are coming to study Penn Warren history. English professors most of the time."

"Of course, of course. No. I'm from the Centers for Disease Control in Atlanta. I'm here to do a little health research."

"Ah, the government. Better watch out for Mr. Eugene Gough. He's retired and he'll talk your ear off about government regulations and taxes. Not that I have many feelings one way or t'other. In fact, I'm kinda fond of the government at times." He smiled as he tugged on his sleeve to display his Postal Service patch.

I smiled. "Me, too."

"Tell you what. I'll give Ellen a call and see if she's got room." He headed toward the phone on the wall. "What kind of health research are you doing?"

"I'm working on some cancer studies. There've been some cases of a rare cancer called Griffith's sarcoma — four in total — and I'm hoping that the victims will be willing to let me ask some questions and take some samp…"

Ridenour stopped abruptly and turned back to me, alarmed. "Was Frank Johnson one of them?"

OK, patient confidentiality is to be maintained whenever possible. I reasoned — or rationalized — that Mr. Ridenour was a postal manager, a government worker with required clearance, and he appeared to have knowledge of the matter already. I nodded.

"Oh, Lordy! He passed away yesterday. He's going to be cremated … today!"

I had a sinking feeling as Ridenour came out from behind the counter.

"He's over at Carson-Ward Funeral Home. Come on. I'll take you there. M'name's Jack, by the way."

I followed him out the door, expecting him to lock up behind us, but he kept moving. "Is it far?" I asked.

"Your luck's good for that part at least." He pointed across the street. "He's right over here if we're not too late. You got some identification?"

"Yep." I patted my pocket, feeling the badge.

We raced across the street and entered the front door of Carson-Ward. Once inside, he began to shout out, "Bill? Bill?"

Jack and I continued swiftly toward the rear of the building. We'd nearly reached the door in the back when it opened and a man emerged wearing a rubber apron and heavy rubber gloves. He pulled down a surgical mask from his face.

He frowned. "Jack Ridenour, what the devil do you think you're doing? I'm getting ready to do my duty. You're lucky the family's not here."

"Sorry, Bill. You know I wouldn't barge in if it weren't important."

Bill looked in my direction.

Jack was still catching his breath. "Bill, this is Dr. …" He turned in my direction with a quizzical look.

I pulled a card from my pocket and handed it to Bill. "Dr. John Parker, Centers for Disease Control and Prevention, Atlanta."

Bill nodded. "You're a bit late for Frank. Seems the disease controlled him."

"I'm sorry," I said respectfully. "Am I too late to gather any medical samples? With the family's permission, of course."

He shook his head. "You would have been if you'd gotten here about half an hour later. He's in the retort now, and I was getting ready to start the furnace." Bill extended his hand toward a sofa. "Please. Have a seat. Perhaps you'd like to explain yourself?"

I nodded and sat down on the sofa.

Jack spoke. "I'm heading back to the post office. I'll give Ellen a call and see what she's got. Stop back over when you're done."

I thanked him as he left. Taking a deep breath, I noticed the penetrating quiet. This was a feature I had noted many times when visiting tiny towns. Something to treasure. I looked up at Bill. Balding, with a small, neatly trimmed mustache, he wore a pressed white shirt and classic dark tie even though he was wearing rubber armor in preparation for his duties to the dead. "I'm John Parker. I'm gathering information for the CDC regarding some particular cancer cases reported from Guthrie. I'd like to respectfully get a history of the victims — and deceased — and gather a few discreet pathology and histology samples."

"Uh huh. I'm guessing you'll be wanting to see Ron Widing, Jim Dulaney, and Walt Tinley, too."

"Word gets around, I see."

"It's a small town, Doc. This cancer's hitting us hard. All four are upstanding citizens who've helped keep our town alive — well, at least three of them, anyway. They're Rotarians and good church-going folk. Not sure if that means so much to you city ..."

"I'm Baptist," I interrupted.

"Good enough. 'Nuff said. Anyway, their passing, especially all at about the same time, is going to leave a big hole. And I'm guessing the government wouldn't be involved unless they think something's afoot."

This is the part where I really have to be careful. In the past few years, a thread of distrust has woven itself into the fabric of society. It seems to be most prominent in struggling rural communities. A poorly worded explanation on my part could ignite fires of suspicion that are hard to put out. "It's just that we don't often have a chance to study this particular cancer. Have you heard of Griffith's sarcoma?"

He shook his head.

"That's not surprising. It's a very rare disease. More of a syndrome, really. It's been described for over 30 years, yet we don't know much about it — what causes it or how to treat it more effectively. My research indicates that Griffith's sarcoma is a particularly bad way to die."

Bill was nodding. "Yes. You've got that right, Doc. Unfortunately, you've got that very right." We were both quiet for a while. "Anything I can get for you, I will. I want people to have a fighting chance against this devil. What do you need?"

"For the biopsy, I'll need blood, abdominal fluid, and brain from the deceased, as well as lung for some regular tissue. I'd like to get some intact nodules if it presents the same way as the records I've reviewed."

"Oh, you'll get nodules. You can't miss those. Can I get you a container for the samples?"

I appreciated his willing cooperation. Bill's demeanor and the tone of his conversation bespoke the devastating emotional impact of the Griffith's. "Thanks, but I have a special kit for field samples in the car." I got up. "I'll be right back."

He called to me as I headed for the car. "I'll check with Faye Johnson, Frank's widow, and I'll have an apron and gloves for you."

I glanced backward. "That's very kind, Bill. Thank you." I looked at the sign as I walked to the car. The only name was William Carson. I figured that would be Bill and that the Ward partner remained as a business name only.

The Civic has a surprisingly spacious trunk for a small car. I could open my suitcase without removing it. I had packed the sampling kit so that it was accessible immediately upon opening the suitcase. The kit consists of a hard plastic case with handles. The case can be autoclaved in the event of a sample spill. It has snap mounts for 12 coring samplers, 12 syringes with needle guards, 24 sample vials, 30 triple-ridged heavy-gauge locking security bags, a roll of numbered labels, a logbook pre-numbered, an audio recorder, a disposable digital camera, a pencil, and a pen that writes even on wet surfaces. Finally, there are three sterile envelopes of latex gloves with rigorously defined chemical signatures. The vials contain preservatives for the samples on their journey to the lab. I had packed in the suitcase 12 metal-armored, lockable sample vaults that would be mailed to Atlanta inside padded Tyvek outer sleeves. NASA tested the vault assembly, and it can survive all but the most severe crashes.

I picked up the kit and headed back to the rear of the funeral home in less time than it took me to describe the contents to you. Bill was talking on the phone.

"Yes. He just got back. ... I'm sure. Hold on."

Bill handed me the phone. "It's Faye Johnson. She'd like to talk to you."

I generally prefer to meet the family of the deceased face-to-face. What I ask of them is so personal; I hate to do so over the phone. My options, however, were limited this afternoon. "Mrs. Johnson, this is John Parker. I'm truly sorry for your loss."

"Thank you, Dr. Parker. Bill tells me you'd like to do some tests on Frank's body. What did you have in mind?" Her voice sounded steady.

"I'm not sure what all Mr. Carson told you, Mrs. Johnson. I'm an investigator with the Centers for Disease Control and Prevention in Atlanta. The cancer that killed your husband is a very rare type, and we've never had a chance to study it really well. If we may be permitted to take a few tissue samples, it could greatly help us to understand the disease better."

"How much are you talking about?"

"I'd like to take about four syringes of blood and other fluids and a few snips of tissue from the body, including some of the nodules. A couple of ounces altogether. I assure you that the process will be dignified and that the samples will not be used for any other purpose without the family's written consent."

"Is that all?" She sounded relieved. I could hear her talking to someone else on her end of the line. "I'm sure Frank would have approved. He was in the Air Force, you know. Served his country. Good man. If this'll help anybody else with this hellish disease, I know he'd be all for it. I just talked with my daughter, and she agrees, too."

"Thank you, Mrs. Johnson. My lab will do our very best to find some answers with this donation. At some point while I'm here and when you're up to it, I'd like to bring some papers over explaining what we do with the samples and a little bit about our lab."

"You can call me Faye, Doc. Hold on a second." She spoke away from the phone again. "Dr. Parker, Bill mentioned you might be wanting to ask us some questions for your study. It's pretty quiet right now, but it's going to be a madhouse when family starts coming in on Thursday. For the moment, it's just me and my daughter, Sarah, here. If you don't have anything else planned, why don't you come over for dinner tonight and we can talk?"

"That's very kind. I don't want to impose. Might I bring something?"

"Oh, gracious no. We're just having chicken and some of the food the neighbors and church people have been bringing over. You can have some of Mrs. Tinley's coconut cake. It won't last long once the grandchildren get here. Come on over around 6:30. Bill'll give you directions."

I looked at my watch — 3:40. "That would be wonderful, Faye. I'll see you then."

"OK. And tell Bill that Pastor Roberts is good for the memorial service Saturday at 11."

"Yes, ma'am, I will tell him."

She hung up the phone.

I turned to Bill. "She sounds like she's holding up pretty well, considering."

Bill nodded. "Faye's a strong woman. And Sarah's a good supportive daughter. I'm sure the two of them are keeping each other distracted fussing over cleaning and getting ready for the service and company. Faye and Frank had a good marriage — comfortable's how I'd describe it — he suffered a lot with this thing. The final hours were really horrible. She was lucky to have Doc Isabel to help them through."

"Doc Isabel?"

"Yeah. You'll probably be working with her a lot while you're here. I guess technically she's not an MD-type doctor. When the rural doctor shortage got really bad about 15 years back, Kentucky had a program giving top-notch nurses most of the same authority and permissions as medical doctors. Best thing Kentucky ever did for medicine."

"Huh," I said. "That sounds really progressive. I'm surprised I hadn't heard about it before."

Bill looked forlorn, shaking his head. "Oh, between the budget cuts and the doctor lobby being all up in arms about it, the program was defunded. Damned shame. We pooled our resources here, though, and kept her on. It works for us, though it's probably not on the legal uppity-up. I hope I haven't thrown a monkey wrench into the works telling you this."

I quickly moved my fingers over my lips in a zipper motion.

"Thanks, Doc. Doc Isabel's been our guardian angel on a number of occasions."

I brought my sampling kit up to my chest. "I'm looking forward to meeting her. By the way, Faye Johnson said to tell you that Pastor ..."

"Roberts?"

"Yes, that Pastor Roberts is good for the memorial service on Saturday at 11."

Bill, sensing my desire to get on with sampling, handed me the spare rubber apron. "Good. Let's get a few mementos from Frank and send him on his way. I've got your mask and gloves. Want to do it by the book, now, don't we?"

"Thanks, Bill." I donned the heavy gauge neoprene apron. With its insulating properties, I was grateful for the air-conditioning. "I've actually got special gloves with a defined low chemical signature. We'll be looking for traces of unusual chemicals in the samples so I don't want to add anything from outside if I can help it."

"Makes sense," Bill agreed.

I put on the mask he provided and followed him toward the door.

He stopped before opening it. "Have you been in the operating end of a funeral home before, Doc?"

"Yes, sir, I'd say probably around a 150 times. And I've done over a thousand autopsies, some pretty bad."

Bill seemed satisfied. "Well, this is a pretty bad one as far as the disease goes. At least the body's fresh, so decomposition's not going to be an issue."

We walked past his preparation tables and tank of embalming fluid, a large stainless steel cask. Bill's operation looked textbook-orderly and clean. We approached the retort and oven at the very back of the building.

Bill opened his hands to the assembly. "When we added cremation services back in the 70s, Larry Ward and I had the foresight to see the obesity epidemic coming and got the largest retort they had at the time. Still there're some bodies that barely fit today. A lot of folks could put off seeing me for a while if they'd pay attention to diet and exercise. Ole Frank's got plenty of room in there, though."

I appreciated Bill's practical spin on everything. It was definitely making my job easier. Frank's body laid in repose within the firebrick box that is the retort, clothed in an opaque paper modesty gown against the possibility that family members might want one final viewing. My first glance told me that Bill would have discouraged that. I remembered a poison ivy rash I got during a camping trip when I was seven or eight. It was that memorable. Blisters on top of blisters, oozing and red on my arms and legs. That was Frank Johnson's appearance, all over. My expression must have reflected my sadness.

"I think it's like that on the inside, too," Bill said.

"I can't imagine the pain if those nodules were pressing on his nerves." I pulled up a stool, opened my case, and began to set vials in a row atop the side bricks of the retort. I took the roll of numbering tape and attached a tag to the side of each vial and then unscrewed each cap. I picked up the sheet of paper with the list of samples desired by the crew back in Atlanta. Finally, I placed my safety sharps collection bottle on the floor next to the stool. I talked to Bill while preparing my collection station. I pressed the 'Record' button on the audio recorder and began the collection. "Is Frank the first who's died from Griffith's?"

"First I've seen. Doc Isabel and I share coroner duty when there's no indication of foul play. We've seen plenty of cancers — happens in an older community like this. The report we get back from the state every year says our numbers are about normal except for the folks who worked at the Patton-Dalton plant back in the 70s."

After verifying the list and double-checking numbers on the list and on the vials, I took the first syringe and inserted the needle into Frank's left thigh and withdrew three milliliters of blood. I expelled the fluid into the first vial and dropped the syringe into the sharps bottle. Screwing the cap on the vial, I checked the label again and spoke to the recorder. "11-127-01-001, left thigh, surface clean, no alcohol used, numerous tubercles visible on the skin surface, blood drawn normally with oxygen depletion appropriate for 24 hours *post mortem*." I placed the vial securely in its slot in the shipping vault. This would be my routine for the next half hour until the list was finished. I had four undesignated vials in case I observed something unexpected. "Patton-Dalton?"

Bill watched the collecting with interest. We shared a passion for orderly methods and procedures. "Patton-Dalton Cable plant over in Hopkinsville. They took ingots of copper and extruded it into copper wire. Thousands, maybe millions of tons of wire. That part of the plant smelled like a sweaty fist full of pennies."

I smiled. "Interesting description. I know exactly that smell."

"Yeah, that wasn't the bad part. The worst smell was the coating division. After the wire was spun, they coated it with a varnish and baked it on. Part of the reason they chose this out-of-the-way corner of the state was to keep out of sight of health inspectors. Even with their lousy ventilation, the whole east side of town smelled like varnish. When you visited folks in Hopkinsville, you could still taste the varnish in your mouth when you came back home to Guthrie. On warm, windy days, you could smell it all the way out here. Made your throat burn. In the late 70s, after OSHA and EPA, the plant was shut down for good. Patton-Dalton moved their operations to China, where I guess they're paying off the local officials and poisoning the workers there. In the 20-some years they were operating in Hoptown, there were 34 cancer deaths that we know about in their workers, mostly pancreatic and liver, when statistically there should have been two. Chamber of Commerce was real upset that the feds closed the plant down — called it government meddling."

I nodded as I pushed a coring probe into Frank's liver and withdrew a sample, marbled and mottled when it should have been evenly dark red-brown.

"In the spring, you can still smell that varnish over near the old plant when they plow the fields. Frank worked at the Patton-Dalton plant from the mid-70s 'til they shut it down."

I looked up. "That's important to know. What about the other three?"

"Walt Tinley worked there for a couple of years and Ron Widing worked at the local paper, *The Kentucky New Era*, about half a mile away — downwind."

"That helps," I said. "I'll have the lab look up the components of the varnish. The culprits in those kinds of clusters are usually the solvents or pyrolysis products from the annealing ovens. Any chance we could go on-site and get some samples?"

"I'd imagine, Doc. You got a badge?"

"Absolutely," I replied.

"Well, between your badge and the sheriff's, I'd say you could open some doors. He lost a brother who worked at the plant to liver cancer."

I continued my slow routine. The multiple checks of the labels and the recording safeguarded against my losing my place or mis-identifying a sample. "That's one good place to start. If the plant closed down in the late 80s, that's an awfully long time to incubate a cancer that then shows up as a sudden eruption, especially to four different individuals almost simultaneously. The plant could have set the stage for triggering Griffith's, though. We'll check it out."

"Let me know your schedule when you can, Doc. As long as the others don't kick off in the next few days or someone doesn't do something drunk-stupid, I won't be too busy this week."

"Thanks. You said Walt, Frank, and Ron all worked at or close to the plant. What about Jim Dulaney?"

Bill sneered. "Humph, I know it's probably not fitting to say mean things about the dying; Jim Dulaney probably never got near the plant because it smelled too much like work. He couldn't catch cancer 'cause he moved too slowly. I'm sure it caught him."

I couldn't help grinning at Bill's description of Jim. "I get the picture."

"He's one of the ones who'll put this extra-wide to the test."

"I see. Was Jim friends with the other three?"

Bill thought a bit. "Not especially. Not since high school that I know of. All four of them were on the '73 football team that almost went to the state championship. None of them were particularly close after that, not even Frank and Walt."

After collecting a core of neural tissue from the brain stem, I finished my sampling by gathering a variety of the nodules in the four extra vials. I secured the shipping vault and the lid to the sharps container. I would finish hand-writing my log from the recording and the pictures I had taken from time to time during the examination and collecting. "I think that does it, Bill." I turned to Frank. "Thank you, sir. You've been a great help."

"You sure you're finished?" Bill asked.

I nodded.

"Once I start, there'll be no more samples."

"I'm finished. Final answer."

Bill walked over to a control panel, flipped a couple of switches and opened a valve to fire the furnace. He waited as the needle on the temperature gauge rose. When the needle passed 1,400 degrees, Bill flipped another switch, and the retort rolled slowly on gears into the furnace chamber. "Goodbye, old friend."

I stood at attention.

Bill watched the dials for a while. Satisfied that all was routine, he turned to me. "If you don't need anything else from me now, let's get you back to Jack over at the post office. He'll give you directions to Ellen Miller's, and she'll give you directions to Frank's place. You'll probably want to get settled in at Ellen's before dinner with Faye and Sarah. Let them know that everything is normal here and that I'll be over tomorrow afternoon for arrangements. I'm sure we'll be seeing each other a bunch of times in the next week or so. Here's my card. Let me know if there's anything you need.

I want to help beat this thing, too, Doc. Got any ideas so far?"

"Oh, yes. That's always part of the challenge. We've already got some yellow flags — Patton-Dalton, Air Force, even playing on the same team. I'll have a lot more suspects before it's over if this investigation takes a normal course. My job is to sort through it all and come up with something firm."

I put the shipping box back into my suitcase in the trunk of the Honda, keeping the sharps container separate. It was 4:30 by the time I returned to the post office. Jack was attending a customer when I walked in, so I surveyed the posters of upcoming commemorative stamps. He accepted three parcels, two for California and one for Illinois. Each was sent priority mail, insured for 500 dollars. From the banter, I guessed that the mailer was a seller on eBay or something. She had only the three parcels, all nice, clean, and professionally sealed USPS boxes with computer-printed labels. She did her business quickly and answered Jack's required postal questions before he could enumerate them.

He grinned. "Thank you, Mireese. I'll see you tomorrow?"

She nodded. "Hope so." She turned to leave. Catching sight of me, she smiled and nodded to me as well.

Jack carefully placed the parcels on a side shelf. "Daily pickup should be by in about an hour. Mireese always has an armful of packages about this time every day. She restores antique dolls. Husband left her about five years ago. He kinda left without a trace. It was rough going for the first year, but everyone got behind her and helped her through. Billy Deatherage at the bank suspended her payments due on the house so she could get on her feet. I remember the weekend she went down to the Nashville Flea Market to sell a couple of her prized antique dolls she'd restored. When she found out how much they were willing to pay and how much they liked her work, she kept her dolls and started a service. She's got her own website now and does a national business. She paid Billy all her back payments and has taken on a couple of the high school girls as apprentices."

"Wow!" I exclaimed.

"You're in the presence of very powerful women, Dr. Parker. My daughter has some good role models."

"Yes, she does."

"Did you get what you needed with Bill?"

I pointed in the direction of the car. "Yep. I'll get my voice notes transcribed tonight and have those samples ready for mailing tomorrow."

"Listen to me yammering on. I'll bet you'd like to get settled in. Ellen Miller's expecting you about now. She's got two rooms that she rents out, with separate outside doors. Rate's really good, and she cooks a great breakfast. Be sure to notice the needlework on your bedding. She does that herself and is very proud of it. She's a quilter. Even though she's 75, Ellen's quite the talker. That can be a problem for some of those English professors who're trying to concentrate on their writing, though she'll probably be a treasure trove for you. Ellen's up on all the gossip and has known almost everyone in town since birth. She's a retired teacher, mostly elementary school. She's probably taught 'em all since birth, too."

I smiled. "You've done well, young man. I'm impressed how tight the network is here. It really makes a difference for my work. I envy your being part of a community like this."

"Guess that's why we don't leave." Jack had taken out a sheet of paper and started sketching directions. "Hm. I feel ridiculous drawing a map. You're on Ewing Street here. Just hang a right out the door and another right at the first street you cross. That's 3rd Street. Ellen's place is three blocks down on the right — 304 3rd Street. Her house has a wide wraparound porch — great for sitting and watching nothing happen. You'll see pots of begonias hanging along the whole porch. Started as a single plant about 15 years ago. Can't miss it."

I thanked Jack for his great assistance. "I'll be coming back almost every day to ship out samples. What time is the first pickup?"

He chuckled. "There's only one — a little after five in the afternoon. I'm thinking you may be registering some of those packages. It'll help if you can get here by 4:30."

"Absolutely. Any way I can help in return. I'll see you tomorrow."

Jack looked up as I reached the door. "You got somewhere to eat for dinner?"

I nodded. "Faye Johnson invited me to her home with her daughter."

"Well, then, you'll eat well tonight. Tell Faye we're thinking about her."

"Will do," I assured.

I barely made it out of my parking place before I made a right onto 3rd Street. Ellen's place was obvious from a block away. I guess when Jack had said begonias, I was expecting the little pink and white flowers. Ellen's were robust hanging specimens with large glowing orange blossoms. I drove into the wide driveway and pulled up beneath a huge white oak tree. Ellen Miller was already on the porch by the time I got out of the car.

"Are you Dr. Parker?"

"Why, I am. And you must be Ms. Ellen Miller."

"Most days." She grinned. She was trim and elegant looking, her hair predominately gray with substantial surviving black interspersed. If Jack hadn't told me she was 75, I would have guessed late 50s or early 60s. I'd have to collect tips from her on avoiding aging.

"Nice begonias," I said.

"Thanks. *Begonia boliviensis.* Judy had only one pot of it in her flower shop back in the 90s. Haven't seen it anywhere else since except at Cheekwood Garden down in Nashville. It doesn't start so well as the

17

regular begonias, though I seem to have persevered." She came down the steps from her porch. "Only problem is I'm running out of room in my sun porch in the back in winter when I have to take them in."

I opened the trunk and started to take out my suitcase, and then stopped. "I should have asked first. Do you have a room available?"

"Heh, this is our lucky day. Traffic's been down with all the university cutbacks. Both rooms are open. I've got the air-conditioning on in the better room. You can stay as long as you'd like; the longer the better, actually. I like having world travelers for company. Guthrie's a wonderful place to live. But, it's like having steak every day."

I laughed as I took the suitcase and followed her around back.

"I hear you've got pieces of Frank in there," she said, pointing to the suitcase.

"Bill Carson and I took some clinical samples. They're in sterile containers, sealed and in a metal shipping case."

She looked at me. "Oh, I wasn't worried. I've been reading up on you and your folks at the epidemiological division. I know how careful you are."

I was genuinely surprised. "Did you know I was coming?"

Ellen laughed. "No, I've got internet. I Googled you. Did you know you've got almost seven pages?"

"Really? I had no idea. Any of it any good?"

"Seems so. I checked what you had to say about Griffith's sarcoma, and it seems that you and Dr. Conner at UCLA have a bit of disagreement. Sounds like you don't think it's a virus."

"Well, Mrs. Miller …"

"Ellen," she insisted.

I smiled and made a little bow. "Well, Ellen, it's not that I don't think it's a virus. He didn't present any evidence that it was a virus, and there are too many other more likely causes. That's why this is a really important opportunity. In this one small area, there are four individuals, three of whom are still alive. And, as I'm learning fast, you have a community that really knows each other. It's so important to get as big a picture as possible."

"Got any money riding on who's right?"

I grinned broadly now as she unlocked the door and handed me the key. "We don't usually do that."

"Should. Folks around here are going to see you get your answers, and I'm ready to put my money on something other than a virus. Just a gut feeling."

I looked at her quizzically. I long ago learned to listen carefully to the gut feelings of locals. Locals have good track records, better in most cases than the remote labs in the early stages of an investigation. "I hope you're right."

"We'll talk about it sometime while you're here. You go on and get freshened up. I'll get you directions to Faye's house. It'll take you less than five minutes to get to the Johnson place."

"How did you know I was going there?"

Ellen had a mischievous smile. "She called me to make sure. She said Bill would probably forget to give you directions. Was she right?"

I nodded.

"Men. Come around to the front porch about 6:10. I like to rock and read in the late afternoon. We might get a thunderstorm a little later, hot humid day like today."

I thanked her as she walked away. Her gait was strong and steady. I definitely wanted to hear how she kept in shape. Entering my room, I was immediately struck by the quilts, not only on the bed, but also hanging on the wall. The craftsmanship and originality of design were well above the norm. I'd been to a couple of quilt shows in Atlanta and one in Baltimore, and Ellen's quilts were certainly on a par with the best of the show entries.

The room was cool. I washed my hands, took the audio recorder and notebook from my suitcase, and began transcribing my audio notes. I wondered how much Ellen would wager.

Finishing my notes at quarter 'til six, I set my phone alarm for 15 minutes, removed my shoes, and lay down on the couch. Before closing my eyes for my catnap, I looked again at the beautiful quilts. There seemed no consistent theme among them, only consistent quality. I was particularly struck by one large quilt opposite my bed. The base fabric was a blend of sunset or sunrise bleeds I later learned was called skydyes, with quilted glory beams and assorted angels using a technique called appliqué. I figured it to be a church banner.

The phone alarm sounded at six. The brief period of shuteye had refreshed me sufficiently. I put my shoes back on and picked up my notepad, presentation booklets, audio recorder, and a camera — the little one that I took when I didn't expect to photograph much.

Ellen was sitting in one of her porch swings. She set down her book when she caught sight of me. "Smell the air."

I took a deep whiff. The fragrances were far different from what we had in suburban Atlanta. I had no idea what I was sniffing for.

"Thunderstorm. Have a seat."

I sat beside her. The swing faced 3rd Street across her well-kept lawn, and made a rhythmic squeak as we rocked slowly in the hot, thick air. Her porch was all wood; the floor painted a naval deck gray and the outer short wall the same white as the house. I don't know if the hook eyes for the hanging pots of begonias had been installed recently. They were evenly spaced in the ceiling of the porch from one end to the other. Ellen must have planned for this number to be final. As I surveyed the cascading plants, a hummingbird, brilliant green with an iridescent red patch beneath its beak, approached one of the flowers and began darting from one orange blossom to another.

Ellen watched me watching the bird. "I figure where the begonia grows in Bolivia, it must be pollinated by hummingbirds. I don't think our native ruby throated hummingbirds have ever been to Bolivia, though they seem to know what to do. The plant doesn't set seed until they start visiting."

"I thought you started these from cuttings."

"You listen well. Yes, they're more reliable from cuttings. The seeds are like dust, and the little seedlings don't tolerate neglect." She pointed down the porch toward town. "Those three pots were from seed. I can't tell any difference so I do only cuttings now."

"You said you smell a thunderstorm?" I asked.

"Well, the right elements for thunderstorms. When conditions are right, the soil gives off a particular fragrance. If you know any meteorologists, tell them to come here to study our thunderstorms. Tell them to stay at my place. I'll give them a discount if they can explain that smell."

I chuckled. "Will do. Speaking of which, what arrangements do I need to make? We didn't talk about that."

She watched the hummingbird visiting more flowers. "Depends on how much I like you. So far, looks like you'll get off pretty cheap. That is, the Centers will probably get off pretty cheap."

"I'll try to behave. I've got my computer and samples back in the room. I should probably lock up. Don't know when I'll be back tonight."

"We don't usually lock up around here." She looked down at my case. "Given you've got a government computer in the room, probably a good idea to lock up. I can only imagine the paperwork it would generate if your computer went missing." She picked up a sheet of paper from the end table by her swing. "I've got you a little map here. Just drive up to Park Street and go out the way you came in. You'll get to Guthrie Road, which you will take north. The Johnson place is 3.4 miles on the left. There's a row of red knockout roses along the roadside. Can't miss it. Her daughter's keeping her company at the house, and they'll argue most of the time you're there. Don't worry; that's just the way they communicate. Been that way since Sarah was two." She broke into a broad grin. "I remember a parent-teacher-student conference I had when Sarah was in third grade. Sarah needed some work on her math, and the two of them argued so that I hardly got a word in edgewise. In the end, they came up with exactly what I was going to recommend. Funny how these things work."

Ellen handed me the paper. "I can't get a read on how Faye's holding up. She's acting strong, but Frank's death's gotta hurt. They were sweethearts from before high school."

I thanked Ellen and drove out Park Street as it became Dixie Beeline

Highway again, bore east for a little before making a sharp turn north onto Guthrie Road, marker 181, just as Ellen had drawn. I noted the mileage, though I've never particularly trusted either stated distance or odometers. I needn't have worried, though, as the hedge of roses was like a bright red beacon.

Getting out of the car, I took a deep breath and tried to emulate Ellen's observation techniques. The air at Faye's home was subtly different. I was still not sure what Ellen was sensing from her soil. Here on the Johnson farm, the air was laced with a not-unpleasant fragrance of cow manure. A symphony of insect and bird sounds bombarded my ears. A more experienced naturalist would have a field day teasing apart the individual sounds.

Scanning the horizon to the west, I could see a number of towering cumulus clouds. Several could easily pass over with showers, so I rolled the windows up, leaving just a crack. That way, I shouldn't return Sonya's Honda Civic in a soggy condition. I closed the car door and walked toward their house. A barking collie greeted me on my approach. "Hey, pup," I called. Given the wag of his tail, I didn't sense any threat, merely a canine "Hello."

The front door opened. A woman perhaps in her mid-thirties emerged. "Kingsley, you leave the good doctor alone now." She had a large bone, maybe a ham bone, in her hand. At the sight of the bone, Kingsley lost all interest in me. She tossed the bone far out into the yard, and he took off after it.

She turned to me. "Dr. Parker, welcome. I hope Kingsley didn't bother you. He's very gentle, really."

I smiled. "Not a problem. We seemed to hit it off fine."

She opened the door wide and I walked in.

"I'm Sarah Meyers, Sarah Johnson Meyers, Frank and Faye's daughter."

"John Parker. I'm glad to meet you. I'm sorry for your loss."

She nodded matter-of-factly. "He's out of his misery now. The last couple of months were really bad. I guess you and Bill were the last ones to see Dad off. Thank you. I've gotta say your bedside manners are making a good impression here already."

I smelled fried chicken from the kitchen when an older woman came into the living room, drying her hands on her apron.

"Dr. Parker. We spoke on the phone. I'm Faye. I see you've met my daughter, Sarah." She turned to Sarah. "Did you offer the doctor something to drink?"

"Haven't had a chance yet, Mom."

"We've got tea, sweet tea, lemonade, water, and soft drinks." She turned to Sarah again. "Did you pick up more soft drinks from Kroger's?"

"Yes, ma'am. They're in the basement fridge, exactly like you told me."

"Don't know what you're used to in Atlanta, Doctor — Coca-Cola, I'm sure. We've got that, Sprite, root beer (especially for the grandkids), Big Red, and some others."

"Some sweet tea would be wonderful. Please call me John."

"Come on into the kitchen. It's a bit of a mess, what with getting ready for the grandkids on Thursday and my sister and niece. They'll be here tomorrow."

Out of the corner of my eye, I could see Sarah rolling her eyes.

"The house is ready, Mom. They're going to have it torn up within an hour or so of getting here anyway."

I offered, "I'm no expert on cleaning house, ma'am, but it looks good to me."

"Thank you." Faye took a glass, opened the freezer, and filled the glass with ice and then tea. "We've got sleeping bags for the kids and beds and couches enough for the grown-ups. I think my sister Jane and her daughter may have to stay over in Hopkinsville. I hate doing that. Stacy's a teenager, and I don't know how she'd feel about sleeping with the little ones."

"She's an elementary art education major, Mom. She specializes in little ones. You remember what she was like at the reunion last year."

"Well, it'll be crowded." Faye turned to me. "Stacy's studying at an art institute in Baltimore."

"MICA?" I asked.

Faye looked surprised. "Yes. That's it. You've heard of it, then?"

"Yes, ma'am. Maryland Institute College of Art — quite renowned. She must be good."

"Yes, she is. She's a painter and she's gotten several awards."

"I certainly wouldn't want to interfere. However, I think Ellen Miller has a room she hasn't let out. It would be a lot closer than Hopkinsville."

Faye looked to Sarah. "Why didn't we think of that?"

"Because, Mom, you're so frantic you had everything all planned out before you finished first talking to Aunt Jane."

Faye was nodding. "Good idea. I'll call Ellen now. Sarah, why don't you show the doctor around the place? Dinner will be on the table in 20 minutes."

"Yes, Mom."

Sarah jerked her head for me to follow out the back door. Once outside, she took a deep breath. "She's driving me nuts. Dad's death was expected, and I know she's totally throwing herself into getting everything ready so she won't have to think about missing him. I don't know if or when she might crack, but she's going about 150 percent of her usual breakneck pace. I need to be here to pick up the pieces if she loses it."

The heat outside seemed greater because we'd been in the air-conditioned house. We walked past a white gazebo in mid-yard toward the fence on the north side of the back yard.

"They've got about a 170 acres, mostly hay now. I say 'they.' I guess Mom has about 170 acres now. We used to have beef cattle until it got to be too much with Dad's sickness. She's rented out the west forty acres to Lee Sisk. He bought our Angus and takes care of the fences for her. He's made her an offer for the whole place if she's ever inclined to sell. I don't think she will be anytime soon. Still, the offer was very fair, and the two are satisfied with the rental arrangement for now. She certainly wouldn't sell to anyone else."

"Do you live around here?" I asked.

"Naw, I moved with Mike to Lexington ten years ago. He's a computer guy, and I run the office for a biotech startup in Lexington. Farming's not in my blood any more. Mom knows that and hasn't objected — which is rare. I often wonder if Dad would have decided to leave farming if things had turned out differently."

"How so?" I asked.

"Farmers get sick a lot. I know it's not the public image. Between the chemicals and the tractor fumes and working with germy animals, farmers get sick a lot."

I nodded. The epidemiological data supported that.

We turned back toward the house. Faye had come out of the house to fetch us. "Did Sarah tell you about the gazebo?"

Sarah shook her head. "No, Mom. I still think it's too much."

Faye ignored Sarah. "Frank and I loved to sit out here in the summer. He kept it up, nice and painted and all. Once he got sick, though, we pretty much let it go. I want to get it painted before Saturday, when we might have people over."

"We've discussed this, Mom. You don't have anyone lined up and no way to keep the children out of the way."

I looked over the gazebo. It was basically sound — a little peeling here and there, and the all-white finish was a little dulled. "You ought to have the kids paint it," I offered.

Faye and Sarah laughed together the same laugh.

"No, really," I insisted.

"They'd paint themselves as much as the gazebo."

I spread out my hands. "Latex paint will wash off of skin. You said Stacy's in elementary art ed. I'm guessing she'd probably get a kick out of it. What were they going to be doing?"

Faye and Sarah weren't laughing now.

Sarah spoke first. "That was actually a problem. We weren't sure what to do with the kids. As charming as Guthrie is, it's not exactly a hotbed of entertainment, and I was getting nightmare visions of five stir-crazy children and one bored teen. I think the Penn Warren House people would shoot us if we took them there … if the kids were even interested." She turned to her mother. "This could work."

Faye's hand was at her chin, finger drumming on her lips. "Maybe. I'll call Jane after supper."

"Baltimore's an hour later than here. Call her now."

"She might be out."

"Leave a message. No, wait. Aunt Jane has only a cell phone now. Call her."

"OK. Supper's ready. You two get washed up and start eating while I call."

Faye walked quickly back to the house. Sarah and I sauntered.

"Mom and Jane are just two years apart. Jane left here a little after she turned 18. She's kinda the wild one of the family — spent her twenties and thirties on the East Coast — New York, Philadelphia, Washington, Baltimore. Aunt Jane had a series of boyfriends and some older gentleman friends with various marital statuses. My cousin Stacy came along late in the game, 15 years younger than me. Stacy's a free spirit of sorts, too — very creative — though a lot more stable and reliable than Aunt Jane. You can count on Stacy to finish things."

We walked into the house and through the kitchen. The dining room table was spread with a bounty of homemade dishes. If I'd had a small helping of each, it would probably equal my usual weekly food intake.

Sarah and I took our seats at the table and waited for Faye, whom we could hear on the phone in the next room. I took a big sip of the sweet tea. It was wonderful. Sarah gazed at a family picture on the wall opposite her chair, probably taken when Sarah was in late grade school.

"Mom and Dad have always been there for us. We never wanted for anything, and knew we were loved."

"The boy in the picture? Your brother?"

"Yes, Greg. He's a banker in Nashville. I'm not sure of his exact title. It changes every few months, it seems. Even faster whenever the banks merge. Greg takes care of Mom's estate planning and everything financial. He and Laura will be here Thursday with their three. So, my two plus his three plus Stacy, and you can see it's going to be pretty crazy. Mom insists they all be part of the memorial service on Saturday. I'm just don't see how that's going to work. Maybe Greg, Bill Carson, and Pastor Roberts can talk sense into her."

Faye returned to the dining room. "Well, it's all settled nicely. Ellen's happy to put up Jane and Stacy in her second room." She turned to me. "She says you'll get a commission for your recommendation."

I laughed. "If I may ask, how much does she charge? She won't tell me."

"Nothing," Faye laughed. "Ellen retired from teaching after being part of the schools since mastodons roamed this part of Kentucky, I think. She likes the company of outsiders. She'll talk your ear off, all smart and well-informed talk, though."

"I've noticed that already," I said.

"And I got hold of Jane. She had her cell phone with her."

"Told you," Sarah smirked.

Faye wrinkled her nose. "She was in a bar in some city called Fell's Point. Stacy wasn't with her — too young — but would be picking her up and making sure she got to the airport on time. Jane was glad not to be staying in Hopkinsville — something about some bad memories. Plus Ellen Miller was one of the few teachers who could actually get through to Jane. She said she couldn't speak for Stacy, but expected Stacy would be thrilled to do some painting with the kids. Jane told me not to interfere. As if I would."

Sarah smiled and turned away.

Faye ignored her and surveyed the table. "Dr. Parker, would you be willing to say grace?"

"I would be honored." We held hands and I prayed. "Thank You, Lord, for this gathering of family and friends. Thank You for the life of Frank Johnson. Keep him in Your loving presence now and forever we beseech You. Grant us the wisdom and observation, we pray, to find the source of this dreadful disease. Give us the skills to bring comfort to those yet afflicted and to find a means to prevent and cure it. We thank You for the bounty of the food that is before us and for the loving hands that prepared it. Inspire us, Lord, to return this act of grace in our turn. In Your most precious name we pray. Amen."

Faye looked at me. "You pray like a deacon."

"Bingo. North Park Baptist Church, Atlanta," I said.

"Well, it's good to have you with us."

We passed around dishes and ate until I could barely hold any more food. Wisely, I did manage to save room for a small slice of Mrs. Tinley's coconut cake. They told me that the grandchildren and Stacy were already asking about it, and I understood why after trying it.

Faye commented on the cake. "We call it Mrs. Tinley's coconut cake, though her daughter Sharon's the one who baked it from her mom's recipe. Mrs. Tinley passed away about ten years ago. I do miss her."

After dinner, I offered to help with dishes, only to be sternly rejected, a well-worn Southern custom. We retired to the living room, where Faye had taken out the family photo album. I heard distant rolling thunder.

Faye looked up. "Sounds like rain coming. Did you roll up your windows?"

"Yes, ma'am."

We sat on the couch, Faye on one side and Sarah on the other, with the album open on the coffee table. I gave each of them a copy of our presentation brochure, which explained the purpose and function of our lab. I verified that it was OK to take notes, and so began an hour and a half of lively, far-ranging discussions of family history.

Frank was the youngest of four brothers and one sister. He grew up in Trenton, Kentucky, and attended Todd County High School, where he met Faye Hill. He was a wild and rough sort in the early high school days.

"He drank more than he should and knew several of my classmates ... in the Biblical sense."

"Mom, I'm not sure how appropriate this is."

"You're 27, and a mother of two, my daughter. I think you ought to know if you didn't already."

"I didn't," Sarah muttered.

Faye returned to her history. "Anyway, all that hormone got put to good use by Coach Tatum. Frank was a lineman for Todd County. The team almost made it to State Champion in 1973. Here's a picture of them in October of '73 — the five demons." She pointed to a yellowed clipping from the *Todd County Standard*. The five players did, indeed, look fierce.

I asked more questions about the picture as I read the caption. "Frank, Ron Widing, Jim Dulaney, Walt Tinley ... I see four of the victims here in this one photo and a fifth player. Who's Dale Liston?"

Faye's face grew solemn. "Sad story there. Dale Liston died about half a year later."

"Cancer by any chance?"

"No, suicide. Things went from normal to really bad that year. Right about the time the team was going for the championship, they pretty much fell apart. Two of them, Ron and Walt, quit the team. Coach Tatum resigned real suddenly. Just up and left the area. The team wouldn't win a game again for almost two years. Don't know. Some sort of disagreement or fight must have torn through the team. Those five had been best friends all through high school, and then they didn't have anything to do with one another. Dale was the quarterback, and was being recruited by the University of Kentucky with a football scholarship. One day the next April, they came home and he'd shot himself with his own shotgun. I'm not sure we've gotten over that yet."

Faye paused, reviewing the memories of '73 – '74. She turned the page to Frank's military days. He and Walt separately enlisted in the Air Force and were eventually, coincidentally, assigned to the same unit deactivating the Agent Orange left over from Vietnam.

I sat back in the couch. "Really? I'm glad you told me that out now. We've done a lot of study on health problems stemming from Agent Orange. I'll note it on my sample sheet and report and check if there are any markers in those tissue samples I'm sending back."

"Were you married while he was in the Air Force?" I asked.

Faye shook her head. "No. Those were the moody days. His joining up was unexpected, didn't even tell his parents, and had left for Lackland Air Force Base before most of us knew he'd done it. The Air Force and he were a good match at that point in his life. They gave him the structure and purpose he was missing here. He was a dedicated airman and made sergeant by the time his enlistment was up. The Agent Orange phase lasted about a year. After that he was assigned to Travis Air Force Base out in California, where he did diesel maintenance. The first day he got back to Guthrie in '78 after he was discharged, he came to see me and asked me out. We were married three months later." She flipped to the wedding page. We all three smiled.

Greg arrived in 1979 and Sarah in 1981. The rest of the album was filled with typical loving pictures of their family and their growing farm. I took notes at a slower pace than during the high school and Air Force pages. The last page contained pictures from their 25th wedding anniversary party in 2003.

"After '09 it got a lot harder to take pictures." Faye closed the album.

During our time with the photo album, thunder grew louder and more frequent. Though it was dark outside, I could see house lights occasionally reflecting off the raindrops spattering the windows, and thought I could hear the drumming of hail.

Faye looked out at the rain. "Nice summer storm. One just like this passed by a little while before Frank died." She bit her lip.

I waited before continuing. "I really appreciate your sharing memories. Everything you've shared is helpful in our search for the source of this killer disease. If you feel up to it, there are some standard questions I'd like to ask. As with every part of my investigation, you're under no obligation to answer; just know that your answers, no matter how trivial they may seem to you, may provide us with important clues."

Faye looked at me, composed. "I want to help."

Sarah got up, closed the album, and took it back to its home shelf.

"OK," I said, "I'm gathering from the VA records that Frank began to show symptoms of the cancer in late 2005, a little less than four years ago."

"About then. It would have been early summer 2005, about hay cutting time. He went to the doctor for his regular physical, and she said she wanted him to get some more tests. He'd had some bad rashes that spring. We'd had a nettle infestation in the far pasture and figured that was the cause at first, but it didn't go away."

I flipped through the medical notes for Frank Johnson. "That would have been Dr. Rodriguez?"

Faye nodded. "Doc Isabel. Bill Carson probably told you she's not an official MD doctor, though she's better'n any MD I've ever had. You haven't had a chance to meet her yet, have you?"

"Not yet," I replied

Sarah chimed in. "You'll like her. She's brought Guthrie health standards up quite a few notches."

"She sounds like a very valuable resource. Is she your doctor, too, Faye?"

Faye laughed. "She's everybody's doctor unless they want to go to Clarksville or Hopkinsville. She came with the state program right about 2000. Knows everybody in this half of the county."

I nodded. "I'll make an appointment. Where's her practice?"

She laughed again. "I don't think she makes appointments — doesn't have a receptionist. It's only her. The clinic's in the ground floor of the county building at the corner of Kendall and Second Streets. Just show up and wait your turn."

"Right." I made notes about visiting Doc Isabel and about the rash. "So, four or five months between seeing a rash and the diagnosis?"

"If that. When the rash didn't clear up on its own, he went to her to get an ointment, and she didn't like the looks of it then."

"When did you begin to see the little nodules?"

"That would have been the late fall. That's when he went to the VA down in Nashville. We don't have a lab nearby unless you count Jackson-Sheridan Hospital in Hopkinsville. Not too many trust them."

"Oh?" I looked up from my notes.

Sarah sneered. "Jackson-Sheridan consistently ranks down at the bottom of Kentucky hospitals and was even put on the national watch list by the hospital association. Their pharmacist a few years back was arrested for taking the insurance money for medicines, providing sugar pills, and pocketing the difference. He's not eligible for parole until around 2030."

"Yikes!" I noted their evaluations. "Did Frank use Jackson-Sheridan, and did any of the other three use Jackson-Sheridan as best you can recollect?"

Faye and Sarah looked at each other.

Faye spoke first. "Not that I know of. I know Frank wouldn't go there. That's all I know for sure."

"I've heard Mr. Widing and Mr. Tinley disparaging Jackson-Sheridan, so I don't think they'd go there, either." Sarah frowned. "Mr. Dulaney, hard to say."

"Not unless they're giving out free service." Faye shook her head.

"Uh huh, I'm getting a pretty consistent picture here. Bill Carson said that Frank and Walt worked for the Patton-Dalton Cable plant back in the 70s. Do you recall any health problems associated with that?"

"Nothing serious. Anybody who worked there had plenty of sore throats and colds compared to others. And several people there died early, including Sheriff Nolan's brother. Though the money was good, when

Frank came home every day, he reeked of the coating. Once Greg and Sarah were born, the thought of bringing all that home persuaded him to return to farming."

"Did he enjoy farming?"

Faye smiled. "Oh, yes. And he was really good at it. His diesel training in the Air Force came in handy with the machines — saved a fortune on maintenance. He ran a tight operation here and we came out ahead almost every year."

"Do you remember any episodes of sickness after Patton-Dalton?"

"Everybody gets sick from time to time, Doc." She turned to Sarah. "Memorable? I can't think of much. There was a time around 2000 or '01 when we had a rainy autumn, and Frank came down with something really nasty — coughing, even spitting up a little blood. The doctor in Clarksville — that was just before Doc Isabel got here — said it was from moldy hay. Walt Tinley came down with the same thing at the same time, so that might have been it. Walt always put up a lot of hay, too."

"You wouldn't know if Ron or Jim were afflicted the same way, would you?"

She shook her head. "Sorry. We weren't that close. The one time I do recall them all being sick was when Jim bought up some lumber down in Nashville. He got it cheap, of course, and they all intended to use the lumber for projects. They all got really sick. If they handled it much, their skin peeled off where they worked with it. Everybody liked to have killed Jim for that. Frank was laid up for about a month."

Sarah had been listening quietly from the armchair across the room. "I remember that. I remember you being scared enough that Greg and I were afraid Dad would die."

Faye nodded. "He was talking that way."

"I'm sure I'll find some records about the lumber. By any chance would you know what the preservative was?"

"Not exactly, except I think I remember that chrome, arsenic, and creosote were involved."

I groaned as I wrote furiously. "Creosote's smelly, but isn't linked to any increase in cancer. Chromated copper arsenate, on the other hand, is a classic bad actor. Looks like we'll be checking for those as well. You guys really get assaulted a lot out here, don't you? And we haven't even looked at diseases yet. So far everything you've brought up is basically poisonous. Anything else you remember?" I looked from Faye to Sarah and back again. Outside, the lightning and thunder grew close and loud.

"Like I said earlier, farming's not that healthy a living," Sarah confirmed. "Now that you ask, I don't really remember Dad being sick with colds and fevers and such."

Faye had a distant look in her eyes. "Yeah, Frank was a solid, level guy after high school and the Air Force. Dependable and even-tempered. I guess if there was anything I might have liked, he could have been more passionate."

"Mom ..."

Faye turned to her daughter. "It's true. You see all these scandals with the men screwing around all over. Your dad was pretty much the opposite. It's a wonder we had you two."

"I don't think that's the kind of information Dr. Parker's looking for," Sarah persisted.

They both turned in my direction. I tried to summon all my diplomatic skills. "Sarah, I appreciate your discomfort, and I want to make sure that I was completely clear that no one is under obligation to say anything. This is a medical inquiry only. That being said, libido is tied to hormone levels, which can be affected by environmental factors, and which can also be linked to cellular processes, including cancers. In fact, a number of cancers are characterized by increases or decreases in ... sex drive. I am only noting these facts if you're in agreement. Names will be removed from our reports and samples. Only a research number is seen outside of this little circle and is linked into the secure data systems."

They looked at each other, arguing in silence.

I waited a respectful pause. "Shall we call it a night?"

Sarah rose from her seat. "I'm going to go check on Kingsley. Knowing him, in this storm he's probably hiding in the barn."

"Take the umbrella. It's still coming down a little," Faye said.

"Yes, ma'am. Is the flashlight still by the back door?"

"Yes, but check the batteries."

"I changed them when I got here."

"Check them anyway. I don't want you tripping in the dark."

"Yes, ma'am," Sarah grumbled.

I could hear Sarah clicking on the flashlight and closing the back door.

"She's a good daughter. Being away from the farm's made her a bit of a prude. I don't blame her, though. She's got a good job and fine family up in Lexington. Farming takes a particular kind of person, especially these days."

I nodded. "She told me that you seemed OK with her occupation."

"Miss the grandkids, though. Only see them a couple of times a year. Now, where were we?"

"You were mentioning Frank's passion level."

"Yes," she chuckled. "I guess I'd always been led to believe that sex was about all men thought about."

I cringed.

"I was definitely in the 'good girl' category. Still, I was kinda looking forward to some of that. There wasn't much as it turned out. That's probably not your field of study, though, is it?"

"There's a wide range of activity." I waffled. "It varies from man to man and through different ages ..."

"Once a year?"

I remained quiet as long as I could. "That's on the low end, I think."

"Just thought you might note that."

I nodded. "Yes, I will." I noted 'low libido' on my history sheet.

I continued noting routine items like favorite foods (fried chicken), travels (not much aside from one family trip to Yellowstone in the early 90s), and regularity of routine medical checkups (once a year in the week of their anniversary).

Sarah returned just as I finished the checklist.

Faye called out, "Did you wipe your feet when you came in?"

"No, Mom, I'm tracking mud and cow poop all through the house! I brought Kingsley with me, too, and he's soaking wet."

"That's not funny."

Sarah walked in from the kitchen, shoes removed. "The rain's stopped, the temperature's dropped about 15 degrees, and Kingsley's happy to stay out there in the barn."

I gathered my notes and stood up. "Well, good folks, it has been a privilege to visit with you tonight. I appreciate your sharing your memories, and I thank you for all the information and, of course, that splendid dinner. I already know of about a dozen extra checks we'll be doing back in Atlanta. If you think of anything else that might seem relevant, or if there are any questions I can answer, please don't hesitate to call me. My card's in the lab brochure."

Faye looked up from the brochure. "Actually, John, would you be willing to say just a word at the memorial service? Let people know why you're here, maybe a little about getting checkups and all."

"I wouldn't want to detract from the service," I said. "However, it would be a classic teachable moment, and a chance to thank Frank for service beyond the grave." I was glad I had brought my dark suit.

They accompanied me to the front door. Outside, the air hung heavy with cool moisture from the storm and was laced with traces of ozone and honeysuckle. As I walked toward my car, sounds of the night grew in intensity the farther I got from the house until they were almost deafening. Looking toward the barn, I could see a giant Luna moth flitting in and out of the glare of the post light along the path to the barn. I opened the car door, turned, and waved goodbye to my hosts. They returned the wave, silhouetted by the living room lights as they stood together on their porch. They would, no doubt, return to their loving quarrels as soon as I drove off. For now, they were the very picture of family unity.

I saw two shooting stars streak across the sky moments before I ducked into the car. One can forget how beautiful the sky is far out into the country. The air, freshly scrubbed by the thunderstorm, was crystal clear; and the nearest real city, Nashville, lay 70 miles to the south. Moonrise wouldn't occur until around midnight. As I drove slowly back toward Guthrie, it struck me that I had not encountered a single oncoming car since arriving this afternoon. Perhaps Tuesday evening just doesn't require much traffic out here. My slow driving was an effort in part to avoid deer, a substantial rural hazard, and in part to perfuse the automobile with sweet honeysuckle essences. I turned off the air-conditioning and rolled down the windows to enjoy the night air in force. My 10-minute outbound drive stretched to 20 minutes inbound.

Pale ghostly vapors clung to the pastures and fields. Each farmhouse had perhaps one or two lights on poles and an occasional porch light. And everywhere were lightning bugs — thousands of lightning bugs. With global warming, they were making their appearance earlier each year.

When I arrived at Ellen's house, the lights were off, so I entered the drive slowly, doused the headlights quickly, and opened my door as gently as I could. I took out my bag with the notebooks and gear and set it on the driveway. I was about to push the door closed when a voice sounded from the darkened porch.

"Did you get plenty to eat?"

I must have jumped enough for her to see with her dark-adapted eyes.

She laughed. "Sorry, didn't mean to give you a fright. I've had the lights off to see the lightning bugs and the heat lightning and the shooting stars and the bats."

"Bats? Wonderful. I've just been watching the other things, and hadn't seen any bats."

"Come on up and set a spell. This porch faces south. Once your eyes are adjusted, you can see the bats against the sky-shine of Nashville."

Sure enough, after a few minutes I began to see them fluttering about.

"I've got bat houses in all my taller trees and on three sides of the house. Over a hundred bat families by my reckoning. At first the neighbors weren't too crazy about the idea until I asked them when they were last bitten by a mosquito in the neighborhood. About the time the bat houses went up. And when did a bat last bother them? Never. Some of them have their own bat houses now."

I sat back in the porch swing. A light breeze blew in from the yard and I could hear both high-pitched and low pitched chimes from various spots on the porch.

"I have to take the glass chimes in when the wind really picks up, like during the storm. They break. The copper-tubed chimes just go wild."

I smiled as I took in the wonders on and beyond her porch. "This is paradise."

"Yep." She turned to me. "So, have mother and daughter killed each other yet?"

I chuckled. "No. Their combat seems very ritualized, like dogs wrestling. They know where the lines are and when to stop."

"Nicely put. I was thinking after you left how Faye and Sarah seem to be one mind shared by two bodies. They check each other, watch out for one another. You were gone a lot longer than supper, even by Faye's standards. Did you take good notes?"

"Yes, ma'am." I dug my notebook from the bag and showed her the pages I had recorded. The porch was too dark to reveal any information.

"I'd say you did. I wish you'd been in my classes. You're not too old, you know. You could have been. I can tell that you haven't gotten your answer yet, though. You would have said something right off the bat."

"I'm flooded with possible answers at this point. And that's with only part of a day's work."

"Did either one give you surprising revelations?" she asked.

I smiled. "I think Sarah may have been a little uncomfortable with some of the personal things Faye was telling me. I offered to stop the interview and told her about our safeguards. Instead, Sarah went to check on Kingsley in the barn and left Faye and me to record."

Ellen's swing chain creaked against its socket. "Heh. I can hear it in my mind. You did the right thing. It could just as easily have been Faye going to the barn and leaving you with Sarah. That's their way."

"I hope I wasn't being too familiar suggesting your other room for her sister and niece."

"Oh, John, I love you for it. I can hardly wait to see them — Stacy, in particular. She's one of my water hyacinths."

"Water hyacinths? An invasive alien water weed that chokes rivers and lakes?"

She paused and looked at me with a smirk. "I do enjoy having a scientist around. They're far too rare out here. Yes, those aspects are what some people might see in water hyacinths. I see a plant with no place to set its roots through no fault of its own, but which floats above the flood and in its season produces beauty and grace. Stacy called me right after Faye called Jane. Stacy was still waiting for her mom outside a tavern. Stacy's the responsible one. I can't wait to talk to her again."

"So you know her?"

"She was my student for a year and a project for two more. That's another story for another time. It's nearly 11 my time and almost midnight yours and I'm guessing you could use some sleep."

"I know you're right, yet I don't feel tired. This is a fascinating place."

"That it is. What do you have scheduled for tomorrow?"

"I think I'll try to see Dr. Rodriguez. She seems like she'll be a really important source of information."

"Doc Isabel. Yes, you'll like her a lot."

"You're the third person who's said that, fourth if you count Faye and Sarah as two. Why does everyone think I'll like her a lot?"

Ellen ticked off points on her fingers. "She's smart, she's meticulous, she's observant, and she has a knack for putting people at ease. You listen to her and she'll save you days of work."

"Well, OK then. I'll head to her clinic first thing."

"Breakfast can be as early as eight. You can walk it off hiking to her office."

"I usually eat a light breakfast."

"Not around here."

I bade Ellen goodnight and went around the house to the sound of chimes while looking up to see the bats fluttering in and out of their bat houses on the side of Ellen's home. Though I did not think that I was tired, I was asleep in minutes.

3 RURAL MEDICINE

I awoke soon after sunrise. Since Guthrie sits near the eastern edge of the Central Time Zone, I guess it must have been around 5:30, 6 o'clock. I was surprised at how well I slept since I often sleep fitfully in new settings. Tuesday had been a busy day; and Ellen's room was quiet, well appointed, and very comfortable.

I couldn't tell what her rooms had been converted from. The construction finishing was seamless, almost as if these rooms were part of the original plans of her house.

With several things to accomplish before breakfast, I elected to do the quiet work first, before taking my shower. I opened the shipping case with Frank's samples and verified the ID numbers against my notes. I started my laptop, attached a cable, and began transferring my audio notes to the computer. I smiled — almost laughed — when I saw the name of the open wireless network — 'Ellen's Portal To The Whole Wide World.' I don't think I'd ever even heard of a network name that long. I connected and found the wireless very responsive, probably FiOS or some close equivalent. I checked my email, noting changes to the meeting calendar and a director's budget review scheduled for two weeks hence. The contrast of thinking about these urgent meetings and the epicenter-of-busyness culture at CDC headquarters, while sitting in the comfortable silence of this quilt-lined retreat, was remarkable.

My transfer of the audio finished, the info was compressed into an MP3 file that I uploaded to my server at the lab. By the time Susan, our laboratory manager, checked the upload, it would have been analyzed by voice recognition software with a text transcript ready for proofreading. I entered the sample numbers and descriptions into our online database and added at the bottom to check for chromated copper arsenate signatures as well as Agent Orange, aflatoxin, and other mold-related carcinogen markers.

My professional skepticism about viral origins continued, and a picture was beginning to emerge of a staged disease model with still no evidence of viral origins. The major exposures all seemed to have occurred in the distant past, though they could have left a predisposition that would cause a single triggering event to unleash the disease. I knew this was a stretch, requiring unusual coincidence to befall all four men. Still, Frank had been exposed to more than his fair share of chemical insults. His exposure commonality to the other patients was a bit vague, though. Live interviews might be more revealing. Three of the four had worked around the cable plant. Two of those three had worked in the Air Force with Agent Orange, and three of the four had handled contaminated lumber. The two veterans were both farmers who had serious exposure to moldy hay. All four had some common links, just in different permutations — unless my records were missing some common factors. I needed to find similar threads in all four lives since high school back in the 70s. A troubling thought crossed my mind that there could be four distinct diseases here that had just been lumped together. However, my review of the records suggested competent and independent documentation across the board.

After uploading my notes to the server and making some suggestions for Susan, I took my shower and dressed comfortably for the day. I hoped to establish a quick liaison with Dr. Rodriguez, since she would have the core records, perhaps notes not available electronically. I hoped I could work with Bill Carson and Sheriff Nolan to get in a visit to the Patton-Dalton plant site. I didn't have much of a chemical sampling kit, but I could put small artifacts from the site into the zippered plastic pouches. The same would apply to lumber samples if they were still available.

After dressing, I checked the room for anything else that I should include in my mailing and then closed the sample case, applied a CDC-traceable seal, and slipped it into the mailing enclosure with government postal franking. I disconnected from Ellen's network, put my computer to sleep, and walked out into the beauty of a glorious May morning.

The previous night's storm left the air clean and fresh. Following Ellen's teaching, I took a deep breath. At first I thought I missed familiar Atlanta smells. All I could come up with was missing car exhaust. Rather, the air here had added aromas of vegetation, soil, and moisture. As I rounded the corner of her house, I looked south toward the fields stretching to Nashville. A low fog still clung to those fields. We don't see low fogs in Atlanta very often, since the earth in the city seldom yields its moisture during the night. I remembered the haze and lightning bugs from the night before.

In the morning sunlight, Ellen's lawn sparkled with dew, another thing we don't see in Atlanta until autumn. I stepped up the stairs to the front porch. Her main door was open. When I raised my hand to knock on the frame of the outer screen door, she seemed to sense my approach.

"Door's open! Come on in!" she called.

Smiling, I walked in. Her living room, or parlor, was the picture of Victorian elegance, with fine upholstered sofa and formal chairs, walls covered with a museum array of photographs, and stands near the windows to accommodate large cascading ferns.

I journeyed through her equally elegant formal dining room toward the sounds of preparation in the kitchen. I found myself hungry because of the aromas emanating from the back. There I found a large table set for two with a full battery of country breakfast cuisine waiting — biscuits, grits, country ham, and cantaloupe slices.

"Sorry. The melon's not local. Still too early for good cantaloupe."

"Surely you're not going to apologize for anything on this table."

"OK," she laughed. "When July rolls around and we start getting the Posey County melons, you'll see." The twinkle in her eye let me know she was baiting me with 'July.'

I obliged. "I hope to have my investigation wrapped up long before then, so, alas, I'll miss the Posey County produce. My boss's given me about two weeks for this project."

Ellen frowned. "Two weeks? Not much time. Guess you'd best get moving. Izzy's expecting you this morning. She'll set you up with a desk so you can be close to the medical files."

"Izzy? Dr. Rodriguez?"

"Uh-huh," Ellen replied.

"You told her I was here?"

"No. She called 'bout an hour ago. Bill Carson called her yesterday, and she called me this morning." Ellen saw my growing look of discomfort. "Relax, Doc. Not much happens here. When a mysterious stranger from the East shows up, people notice."

I relaxed a little. "Can't say I've ever been described as 'mysterious.' Baylor would get a charge out of that. She'd call me anything other than mysterious."

We said grace, and I began a hearty country breakfast. The grits were nothing like the usual quick grits from home. These were smooth, slow-cooked with cheese and bits of country ham. The country ham itself was a taste explosion.

"Broadbent ham," she said. "Two-year-old. I won it at the Rotary Auction."

I looked up at her. "OK. You seem to have all the right answers. Tell me this. How do you eat like this and keep in such great trim?"

She thought a moment. "Sure you're not mistaking flavor for nutrients?"

I looked down at my plate. I'd already taken a second helping of almost everything.

"You got your grits — ground whole corn." She began her analysis. "Flavored with a little sharp cheddar and bits of lean ham. That's not a problem. Then there's the ham itself. Not much fat. That all gets trimmed off before curing. A bit salty, I'll grant you. You're going to be drinking about a gallon of iced tea before the day's through. Biscuits? Only a problem if you had fatty gravy. This is ham redeye gravy's only flavor and a little coffee. Cantaloupe? Not a problem. Add to that, you'll be walking to town."

Actually, I thought I'd be driving. I realized driving such a short distance would be ludicrous, and kept my earlier assumption to myself.

She finished up with satisfaction. "A country breakfast's big because it has to be. Starts early and has to get you to a country lunch."

I had no response since I had finished two servings and felt pretty good. I looked down at my coffee. "And how did you know I liked it black?"

"You were in the Navy," she replied.

I raised my eyebrows.

"It's in your CDC bio online."

"But, I might …"

"Percentage play, Doc. If I was wrong, I'd just bring out the sugar and cream."

I nodded.

"I'm not wrong, am I?" she asked.

"You must have been one awesome teacher."

She smiled as she got up and began clearing dishes. "So I'm told. And I still teach. Don't you forget that."

When I began gathering my plate and silver to help, she stopped me.

"You sit and finish your coffee. This is my kitchen and I have my ways. It's about eight. That's when Doc Isabel usually gets in. She said she's only got two people signed up for this morning. She'll take control of your life after that." Again, that twinkle in her eye.

"Yes, ma'am."

* * *

After coffee, I packed my research bag to carry everything rather than relying on multiple trips to my car. Ellen offered several times to give me written instructions, though I think she may have been up to mischief. She explained that 3rd Street dead-ended into Kendall Street. If I turned left and went all the way to the end — one block — I'd be at Elkton Bank and Trust. If I turned right and went all the way to the end — also one block — I'd arrive at Guthrie City Hall. That was the entirety of Kendall Street. Dr. Rodriguez's clinic was in the rear of City Hall. Ellen warned me not to expect a grand Civil War era courthouse.

I thanked her, picked up my bag, tucked the mailer under my arm, and walked away at a leisurely pace. This was not difficult because Guthrie had sidewalks, nice, actual, wide, well-maintained sidewalks. They were absent from suburban Atlanta, where the automobile-driven expansion of the 50s, 60s, and 70s had deemed them irrelevant. We continue to pay a high price for that arrogance. That morning I waved to half a dozen people sitting on their porches or tending flower beds. They all smiled back at the mysterious stranger from the East.

One block before reaching Kendall, I turned left on Ewing and entered the post office. It was as if time had stood still or I was in some time-warp movie, Mireese was at the counter talking to Jack.

She turned to me as she had the previous day, smiled, and nodded. This day, though, she spoke. "Good morning, Dr. Parker. Jack's been telling me about your research."

I nodded in reply. "Good morning, Mireese … I'm sorry. I didn't get your last name yesterday."

She giggled. "We were just talking about that. You know, do I need a last name around here? How many Mireeses are there in Guthrie? One. Todd County? One. Jack looked that up. I was thinking — why not just 'Mireese of Guthrie'? Postal Service wouldn't mind. Kinda great branding for my businesses. For all the grumpy federal people who insist on a longer name, I could just keep using Black after my no-good runaway poor excuse of a former husband. Thinkin' of him and taxes at the same time seems somehow right."

"Well, Mireese of Guthrie," I said, "I'm inclined to let you be who you want to be. I'm told you are quite the entrepreneur."

She turned and pointed at Jack. "He exaggerates. I get by OK."

"Not just Jack. I had dinner with Faye Johnson and Sarah last night. They both sing your praises, too."

Mireese smiled a broad smile. "Isn't that sweet. Matter of fact, I'm just heading down to Nashville to pick up her sister and niece at the airport at noon."

"Wonderful," I said. "They're staying in Ellen Miller's other room, next to mine."

"Change of plans. Jane's staying out with Faye to try and keep her calm. Good luck to Jane on that. Stacy's staying with Ellen, though. She'll be going out to the farm to work with Faye's grandkids on some project."

I nodded.

"Well, gotta go. See you later, Jack."

Jack leaned on the counter. "Yup. Drive safe. Remember the construction on the new airport garage."

She raised her hand in a dainty wave as she left the post office. I watched Jack watch her go and sensed that she was more of a friend than a simple postal customer. Once she had pulled her large van away from the parking space, he turned to me and spied my package.

"What ya got for me this fine morning, Doc?"

"One package, registered mail."

"Oh, good. I'll get to use my purple ink at last. It's been years since a registered package left this office." He rummaged in the back of several drawers before finding the security inkpad. "Got it. Anything fragile?"

"Yup."

He stopped at the unfamiliar answer. "Perishable?"

"Yup."

He eyed me with a smirk. "Hazardous?"

I nodded.

"Please don't tell me explosive."

"Ah, we're in luck there. Nothing explosive." I beamed.

"You enjoy giving the wrong answers, don't you?"

"All part of the job, unfortunately. You see I have all the needed permits in the sealable pouch for you to check, I have my numbered CDC seal, and the container will survive better than any plane would if there's an accident. It's designed for shipping high-level medical samples. It has Frank's samples in it today. I really don't think they're hazardous. It's just a routine precaution."

Jack examined the case. "Yeah. This is nice. Real nice."

"NASA helped design it. Out of maybe ten thousand shipments, we've never had a failure."

"Mireese would dig this. Make a nice laptop or tablet protector."

I shook my head. "I think they run about 500 dollars a case. Designs are in the public domain, of course."

Jack chuckled. "Bet she could get 'em down to 29.99. She's got connections, and she's awesome at haggling." He finished applying the Guthrie, Kentucky, purple stamp to all the seams. He sealed the plastic envelope and handed me my receipt. "You're good to go, Doc. Should I keep it refrigerated or anything?"

"No. Just keep the package away from excessive heat."

"You got it. Frank'll be sitting between a couple of 1700s dolls headed to the Smithsonian in Washington. Reckon he'd get a kick out of that. What are you up to today?"

"I'm on my way to see Dr. Rodriguez."

"Excellent. The two of you should hit it off. Tell her hi for me."

"Will do. See you later." I walked out the door and headed east on Park Street. I looked over at Bill Carson's place and, just beyond it, the Elkton Bank and Trust. I should have needed to use the bank's ATM for cash by now, except that no one was letting me pay for anything.

I turned right onto Kendall and walked toward the end where I'd find City Hall. Along the way I passed Judy's Flowers and Pretty Things. Her sign indicated she opened at ten on weekdays. I made a mental note to return and pick up something picturesque for Baylor, something that bespoke the quiet country atmosphere. Peering through the window, I saw books by local authors, including a large sampling of Robert Penn Warren. It looked as though Judy had a quality selection of candies, flowers, and wind chimes. Moving on, I passed Ferrell's restaurant, which was still in full breakfast swing. The younger crowd had moved on, and the clientele appeared to be older farmers and maybe some retirees catching up on local news. Depending on what Dr. Rodriguez had for me, this might be lunch headquarters for a few days.

It was good that Ellen had lowered my expectations. City Hall was indeed little more than a hall attached to the firehouse. The garage for the fire engines was a bit larger than City Hall itself, and both were built in the classic, pragmatic style of the 1950s. I continued around the building. The bricks in the wall showed a change in source where the large back section began, indicating that it was probably an add-on. The big wooden door in the middle of the back section proclaimed 'South Todd County Health Services, Isabel Rodriguez, Chief Medical Officer.' Her posted hours were eight to five, Monday through Friday, with an 'In Case of Emergency, call …' number.

I pushed open the stiff door, triggering a bell that announced my arrival and entered a fair-sized, clean, waiting room with two sofas and six chairs. Little of the furniture — all tidy and sturdy — matched. The two tables in the room sported an assortment of health pamphlets from pregnancy tips to sports safety. In lieu of art on the walls, the space was taken by a plethora of early warning signs posters — heat stroke, heart attack, cancer, and so on. The waiting room looked the model of a low-budget high-efficiency operation along the lines of the Johns Hopkins School of Public Health's model I had long admired. I could hear a conversation wrapping up on the other side of a curtain-shielded doorway.

"All right, somebody's out there. Get your clothes back on, and don't you go anywhere. We're having a talk when I get back."

I heard the door open and close, and a woman emerged from the curtain wearing a standard long white doctor's coat, her blue exam-gloved hands held out in the usual hygienic way. She wore a white scarf around her head. Her face was pleasant save for a trace of annoyance that vanished when she saw me.

"Ah, Dr. Parker, I presume?" She nodded gracefully.

"Dr. Rodriguez," I returned with a polite bow.

She smiled and raised a blue finger in the air. "We'll talk about that. Make yourself comfortable. I'm finishing up with a patient right now. It might take a little while — 20 minutes tops. Next appointment's at 11:30. If anyone drops in before I'm finished here, tell 'em to come back around ten."

"Will do." Given her name, I guess I had expected a darker blend of skin tones and perhaps a pleasant Hispanic accent. Dr. Rodriguez's heritage seemed more northern European with a routine Midwestern accent.

She snapped off her exam gloves in practiced fashion, turned, and began moving the curtain aside. She stopped and turned her head to me. "If you've got tender ears, you might want to cover them or step outside. I'm about to have a serious heart-to-heart with a young woman who's just had a very close brush with maternity."

I nodded and she disappeared behind the curtain again, closing the inner door.

Dr. Rodriguez began in scolding tones. "Anna Virginia Barker, I'm not going to ask you what you were thinking because you clearly were not thinking with your head. You were just luck-of-nature separated from being pregnant. I know you've got more sense in your level head than this. I taught your sex-ed class, if you'll recall. I remember you got a perfect score on the test, so I know that you know the drill. When that farm boy of yours puts his plow in your fertile field, he's planting seeds. You know that. I know you know that. What were you two trying to do?"

A long silence ensued before the girl's defensive reply came, "It wasn't his fault."

"Excuse me. He's a responsible adult, too."

The girl came back with more force. "It was my idea. Chris didn't plan this. He wasn't the one."

"I'm sorry, Gina. I may be a little behind in my medical reading, though only by a week or so. Last I checked, it takes two people to have productive sex without extraordinary medical intervention. It is not as if you held your farm boy down and forced him to make sweet love to you."

At this point, the usual script called for the young girl to protest. Dr. Rodriguez expected the same, I presume. Instead, silence flooded the room, first for a long time, and then for an uncomfortably long time.

At last, I heard Dr. Rodriguez say, her tone changed from stern motherly to inquisitive, "Did you?"

After many more seconds, the young woman answered, quiet and hesitant, "Kinda ... yes."

I clamped my hand over my mouth to keep from laughing out loud. I was left to imagine the good doctor's reaction in the examining room.

With composure, Isabel queried her patient. "I already know more than I wanted. Do you love Chris?"

"Yes."

"No, do you love him for the long-term?"

"Absolutely."

"Do you love him enough to put both of your long-term interests ahead of the passion of the moment?"

I could hear that Gina was crying now. "Why do you keep asking me? You know I do. I made a mistake, OK? I didn't want anyone to get hurt."

I imagined Dr. Rodriguez hugging the young girl as she switched to comfort mode. "It's OK. It's OK. I just wanted to make sure we were clear on the seriousness of what happened. I want to see both of you happy. Chris has got to finish at UK. You have to do what you're going to do to get ready for a full and joyful life. While someday that life will include children, now's not the time for either of you. We've all got great hopes and expectations for the two of you. I want to be the first to throw rice at your wedding."

I heard Gina sniff back tears. "Bird seed."

Isabel half laughed, half giggled. "Right. I forgot. I want to be the first to throw bird seed at your wedding." She probably had handed the girl a tissue. I heard someone blow their nose.

"OK. So we need a plan. You're an adult in just about every respect. I know now that you've sampled the sublime joys of womanhood, so we need to get you some protection in case you find yourself in the passionate situation again. Knowing you as I do, I'm sure you have a preferred method of birth control in mind. I'm happy to give you the necessary prescription, but …" — she paused for earnestness — "I want you to have a long, honest talk with your mom first."

"What?"

"That's right. You're of an age where you don't need her permission and the law says I don't have to require that. You just need to talk to her. Trust me. You'll thank me for this in short order."

"But …"

"Gina. She loves you. She brought you up right. She has a lot to say to you."

"Oh, man!"

"I'll be at the game Friday night. That should give both of you some quality time."

"You'll be over this afternoon, right?" Gina asked.

"Quality time, Gina. Wait until your grandpa's sleeping. You have to believe me. It'll be the best six hours you've ever spent."

"Six hours!?"

"Just kidding."

"Not funny."

I heard the door open, and they emerged from the curtain. Anna Virginia Barker – Gina – was the classic *Progressive Farmer* cover girl. She wore blue jeans and a plaid shirt. Her sun-bleached strawberry-blonde hair curled tightly, and her upper cheeks were spangled with freckles. I stood up when they entered the waiting room. As Gina caught sight of me, she turned at once to Dr. Rodriguez.

"Gina, meet my good friend, Dr. John Parker. He's come all the way from the Centers for Disease Control and Prevention in Atlanta to study what caused the cancers in your grandpa and Mr. Johnson." Isabel turned to me. "Walt is Gina's grandpa."

"Does he have a cure?" Gina asked.

"Anna Virginia, the man is standing right in front of you. He's a world expert on finding the causes of diseases. Unless he's unlike any other scientist I've ever met, he's more than eager to talk about his work. You should ask him yourself."

Gina turned to me. "Can you cure Grandpa?" In her sky blue eyes I saw desperation.

"I wish I could. I'm told the disease is pretty far along, and I sense that time is running out. The very reason I'm here is that we don't know even a little about what causes it. I'm here to find out and I'll do anything I can. I have to be honest with you; this is a serious disease."

She nodded sadly. "I knew that, I guess. I just hope that if I ask often enough, the answer will change." I could see a wave of determination wash over her. "I've got to go. We're putting in new fencing on the north pasture." She turned to Isabel. "You're still coming by at one?"

"Yes, ma'am. Is it OK if Dr. Parker comes along, and asks Grandpa some questions?"

"Definitely! Grandpa'd probably love that. Other than José and Pastor Roberts, he's only had women to talk to of late. See you this afternoon, Dr. Parker."

Gina pulled on the outer door.

"And what will you do between now and Friday night?" Dr. Rodriguez's motherly voice returned.

Gina rolled her eyes and answered with exaggerated weariness. "Talk to my mother."

"Very good." She waved goodbye.

As soon as the girl was out the door, Isabel slumped her shoulders and let out a deep breath. "I swear, God must have a select troop of angels like Special Forces to watch after teenagers. They can get into so much trouble so fast, it's a wonder the species survives."

"You seem to handle them rather well based on the single example I've just seen."

"Well, Gina's a special favorite of mine. We all need for people like her and her Chris to do well. They're our brightest hopes for the future. In a way, we can't afford for them to screw up."

"You seem to be confident that she'll have that conversation."

"Oh, she will. I know her. She couldn't lie to save herself. And I know Sharon — Sharon Barker's her mom — has wanted to talk with Gina for a long time. You see, Sharon married Curt Barker when she was only 18. Gina was born very premature — like three months premature."

"Whoa," I said, "that's amazing. She seems to have come through it fine."

Isabel nodded. "Yes. Eight pounds, seven ounces. They'd been married only five and a half months."

"I see."

"Gina knows that at the cerebral level, though they need to talk. Sharon's a good mom, though not the happiest of creatures. Curt was killed in a shop accident when Gina was five. She doesn't remember much about him. Other than Chris, her grandpa is the real love of her life. She's ready and yet not ready to lose him. The two of them see eye to eye on most things. You were out at Faye's place last night, right?"

"Uh huh," I acknowledged.

"Did Faye and Sarah argue any?"

I grinned.

"Thought so. Well, Gina Barker and Walt Tinley are like that a little. She's pretty progressive. He's a little set in his ways. Still, he knows she's right about most things. She learns like a mental vacuum cleaner and researches everything. He'll argue with her, only to the point she starts getting doubts. Then he gives in. Much less rancorous than Faye and Sarah; you'll see. Thanks for being honest with Gina, by the way. I kinda took a risk there. The last thing she needs is false hope."

"I try to be honest with people. I've always found them to be pretty resilient, and while they might not like some of the answers, they won't resent the truth."

"Well, she's a strong one in so many of ways. Stubborn and determined, too. I once saw her carry a calf — a 100-pound calf — across the pasture in a driving rain to get it into the barn. Yeah, she's strong in so many ways. Holding Chris down is not a stretch by any means." She was nodding. She finished with a quick jerk of the head. "Now, you're not here to talk about teenagers, are you?" She put out her hand. "Dr. Parker, I'm Isabel Rodriguez. Welcome to Guthrie."

I clasped her hand. "John Parker from Atlanta."

"Well, John, by necessity, we operate pretty informally around here. You can call me 'Izzy' if I can call you John. It's been 'Doc Isabel' to most of my patients for over ten years. Although I didn't start that, if it keeps a few more on their meds or off their feet for a few days, I don't rightly think I'm gonna fight it."

I nodded. "You've got a nice clean-looking practice here. What's your background?"

"Bachelor's and master's in nursing from Old Dominion back in the 90s." She pointed to a diploma on the wall. "A couple of years clinical experience in Norfolk, and then this spot opened with Kentucky's Rural Medicine Initiative. Been here ever since."

"I didn't know Old Dominion had a nursing program."

She shook her head. "They don't — anymore. I was in the last year of the program. They couldn't afford the upkeep and competition from UVa. Pity."

"Yes, I can imagine a good program costs a pretty penny. Bill Carson was telling me about the Kentucky program being discontinued. That's so sad."

"Yup. Makes my job harder every day. And those bastards in KMA — Kentucky Medical Association — don't give a damn, except to keep their monopoly on caregiving. They know that no MD's going to come out here for the wages and hours we face. They just can't stand to see a viable practice without an MD leading." She wrinkled her brow. "Sorry to get on my high horse, John. It's frustrating."

"I feel for you. It's no comfort that Kentucky's not alone. Nationwide, there're probably 20,000 communities without primary care. I know it costs lives and livelihoods."

She shrugged. "It is what it is. Well, you didn't come in here to talk about teenagers and probably not to listen to my whining either. You're here for the cancers. How can I help?"

I smiled. "You're right, though I am interested in the other topics, too. The cancers are my priority. I'm here to gather all the information I can so we can try to pinpoint the cause or causes. I've had all the VA records for a couple of weeks. I had a chance to get samples from Frank — with permission — and I've had a long talk with Faye Johnson and their daughter."

"Any conclusions?"

I shook my head. "Only that I'm sensing lives surrounded by carcinogens. I've only had a chance to look at Frank's case so far, and I've filled out a second page of agents to check for."

"You think they're still being exposed to carcinogens?"

"Not necessarily. Each agent is at the root of a different cancer. We can look for specific DNA signatures."

"If you know so much about all these cancers, what's so interesting about ours?"

"You've seen lots of cancers before, I'm sure." I said.

"Yup."

"Have you ever seen other cancers present such a complete and sudden presentation?"

"Good point." Isabel nodded.

"Most of the Griffith's cases have come to light in the last two years. I'm pretty sure that's a result of better reporting, and the cases came up in a rather well-covered conference."

She grinned. "Let me guess: we're talking about Dr. Spence Conner."

I raised my hand and rubbed the stiff muscles at the base of my neck. "This is getting a little creepy. I've done work in small towns before — not this small — so I know that word can get around pretty fast. Guthrie seems to take it to an extreme. Is there something here I don't know about?"

"John, John, John, we're just making the best use of the communication technologies we've got. Ellen's probably our biggest driving force." She looked at me. "You ever read up on prairie dog research?"

I laughed. "No, not really. Not much. I know there was a case of plague associated with a prairie dog sold as a pet, though that was a decade or more ago. What about prairie dogs?"

She sat down and motioned for me to have a seat. "Well, Ellen and I were listening to an NPR story about how they communicate. Of course you know they're not dogs; just great big ground squirrels. And they have these big colonies out in the middle of nowhere. So prairie dogs would seem about the perfect meal for all kinds of hungry coyotes and hawks and ferrets. Those colonies would look like a wholesale meat locker to the carnivores. But the prairie dogs are organized. They always have someone assigned to lookout duty, and they've developed a chatter language to tell each other when something's coming. On the radio, the reporter slowed down the little squeaks and whistles, and you could hear the difference between a harmless cow or human researcher walking through their colony and a canine or raptor. And they adapted fast to changes in the visitors."

"I see. I guess I've been designated a cow or human researcher. Given the questions I'm asking, I'm a bit uncomfortable that no one's so much as asked for an ID or made any checks."

She folded her arms. "Not that you've seen. Ellen's pulled up your work — even your picture — off the CDC website. Jack and Bill and Faye have all cross-checked their encounters with you. Then, of course, there's always the question of what the heck would be worth stealing out here. Look, if we had any questions, Sheriff Nolan could always pull up your vast criminal records."

"OK, then. I'll just enjoy the head start this gives me. I have the VA and federal records of four individuals with symptoms matching Griffith's sarcoma. Are there any other cases you know of or suspect?"

"Nope. Just those four. And I'm sure I would have heard about any others."

"Do you have any medical records beyond the electronic databases?"

Isabel tucked her chin and looked at me with large brown eyes, almost flirty. "Do I have records? John, you're not in Atlanta any more. We looked at the cost of some electronic records systems a couple of years back. Even the cheaper ones would cost as much as a new police car. Oh, we've got paper. Lots and lots of paper. We set you up a temporary office here in the building. Nothing fancy; at least you've got a phone, a desk, and as much privacy as anyone's going to get around here. Let me show you."

Isabel got up and opened a side door into a hallway and then opened the door to my "office." True to her word, the room had a desk, a phone, and a chair. On the desk were four neatly arranged stacks of documents, each organized into multiple dark brown folders.

"Thank you."

"There's coffee and tea in my office. Just a little K-cup maker — it's actually pretty good. Beats the mess of grounds. I provide it myself, so a donation of fifty cents a cup will cover the little K-cups."

"Again, thank you."

"My pleasure. Now I've gotta get ready for my next patient — taking some stitches out, I hope. He thought he could bone a chicken."

I frowned. "That shouldn't have been so difficult."

"Is if the chicken's still frozen."

I chuckled as she prepared to leave me to my work. I had to ask, "Would Sheriff Nolan actually pull up my records for you?"

Isabel crossed her arms. "Five parking tickets. Three in Atlanta, two in Lincoln, Nebraska. All paid online, on time. John, let's just say they won't even let you visit the Museum of Great Criminal Minds."

I stood there dumbfounded. I tried to remember what the third ticket in Atlanta was for.

Isabel nodded. "Prairie dogs, John. Prairie dogs." She turned and went back into the clinic.

I set up my laptop and for the next few hours pored over her files. It didn't take long to remember why we moved to electronic records. Tasks that would have taken seconds online each required 10 to 15 minutes of searching and transcription. The lag was no fault of Isabel's. Her notes on the appropriate forms were generous and written in a clear hand — much more legible than mine would have been. Much of the information would be appropriate and valuable for the national database. If I had brought a mobile hot spot, I could have connected that way. I saw an ethernet plug, but hadn't brought a cable. I got up and left the office, checking the handle to make sure I didn't lock myself out. I walked down the hall to an open office near the front entrance. The woman at the desk looked up. "Dr. Parker, how can I help you?"

"You know me?" I stopped and shook my head. "Of course you know me. Seems everybody knows me. I was just wondering if it would be possible to use one of your network connections. I didn't bring a cable, though." The name plaque on her desk proclaimed "Liz Kelm — Administrator."

"Oh, those plugs don't work. We took out the last ethernet routers about a year ago."

She must have seen my disappointed look.

Liz reached for a notepad. "We put in WiFi. We don't broadcast the ID, so the teenagers don't clog the network. I presume your computer's got wireless. Here's the ID and password. 'Broadband' is kind of a euphemism. Let me know if you're going to be doing any big uploads or downloads. And don't expect much speed around five. That's when we back up to the state system." She handed me the paper with ID and password.

"That's very kind. I'll remember. My connection was plenty fast this morning."

Liz shook her head. "Yeah. Well, Ellen pays an extra 30 a month for her connection. The City Council in its wisdom doesn't think police and fire high-speed communication are worth an extra 360 a year. Of course, I didn't say that."

"Say what?" I grinned.

"Good man," she affirmed.

I returned to "my" office and began uploading my notes. The wireless connection was more than adequate for my simple text entries.

Around noon Isabel appeared at the door. "If you're hungry, Ferrell's is the place for lunch. It's no Ruth's Chris or even Applebee's, for that matter. It's good comfort food if your arteries can take it. Ferrell's is it for anything within reasonable walking distance. After that, you've got sandwich and pizza carryouts down by the Clarksville road intersection."

"What do you usually do?" I asked.

"I bring a sandwich and fruit. I take a long walk by myself to work off any stress."

"I'll check out Ferrell's."

"Be back here around ten 'til one, and we'll go out and visit with Walt."

"Yes, ma'am."

She smiled and returned to lock up the clinic.

My one block travel to the café led past brick buildings from the early twentieth century. Most were empty. Historical markers outnumbered inhabited buildings. One building had a sagging brick wall. It appeared that some renovation had been started, though the weeds growing between the bricks piled alongside and the photo-degraded caution tape bespoke a project delayed or abandoned.

Ferrell's had many lunchtime customers — not crowded. I took an empty stool at the counter. Their menu took me back to my childhood — grilled cheese, hamburgers — even fried bologna, which I ordered. As the meal cooked, I fielded questions about 'the cancers.' Was it 'catching'? Why so many? Was it because of the big Conrad-Mattlock Agro farm to the north? I learned in short order that the Conrad-Mattlock Agro operation was a sore point with this crowd. I had often seen such distrust between small farm communities and Big Agra. I did my best to answer their questions without raising either false hopes or alarms, expressing my appreciation for the cooperation I'd gotten and my hope that something good would come of the research.

The fried bologna sandwich exceeded my expectations — tasty, served with fries and a pickle. Today was enjoyable, though I knew it would be dangerous to come here every day. I was halfway finished with my meal when a distinguished gentleman approached me. Unlike the other patrons, he was dressed in a jacket and bow tie. His thin gray hair added to the elegance. His build suggested he was a regular at Ferrell's.

He looked me over. "You must be the government agent sent to check up on us."

I extended my hand. "Mr. Eugene Gough, I presume." It was my first chance to turn the tables on the familiarity of the natives.

Local tradition was strong, and he was honor-bound to shake my hand.

"John Parker, Centers for Disease Control and Prevention, Atlanta. Pleased to make your acquaintance, sir."

"You're pretty far from home, son. Why does the federal government think it can do a better job out here than our own people?"

I wasn't sure of his agenda, other than he didn't like the federal government. "Better job?"

He frowned. "Taking care of the sick and dying. That's our job. The community. The people."

I nodded. "True. I didn't come out here to take care of the sick or the dying. You have that in good hands."

"Then what's your angle?" he asked.

I finished the sandwich, dipped a French fry in catsup, stalling while I ate it. "I study diseases, Mr. Gough. My team and I find out what causes diseases when no one else can. We figure out the causes and report them so everyone knows."

He finished my sentence in his own way. "... thereby transferring the local responsibilities to Washington."

"Atlanta."

"You think this is funny, son?"

I extended my hand to encourage him to take the empty stool next to me, which he did. The CDC doesn't often draw the ire of citizens who were otherwise irritated with the national government. I had encountered a few. "Just a little, sir. It reminded me of a day I had back in the Navy. But that's another story for another time. Did you know that the Centers for Disease Control was founded during World War II as the Office of National Defense Malaria Control Activities?"

He eyed me with suspicion.

"Just thought you might be interested in some of our past. I understand you're a high school history teacher over in Hopkinsville."

"Retired."

"Ah. Well, the Centers were founded to combat malaria in the South. The disease was debilitating the population so much, it was dragging on the war effort. The South did not have the resources to mount an effort to eradicate the disease or control the mosquitoes. It takes a great deal of coordination and research to deal with communicable diseases like malaria, polio, and influenza. The cost savings of fighting pestilence across the nation rather than piecemeal — if that's even possible — was and is dramatic. So, I guess Guthrie could do the research to find the cause of Griffith's sarcoma. It'll cost you about five million to set up the labs and hire the people. And every other community that's affected by Griffith's will have to do the same. As far as we know now, that would be about 18 county governments or — let me do the math — 90 million dollars, assuming it's not a virus-borne epidemic. My lab should be able to get to the root of the disease in a couple of months if our past history is any indication. We should be able to find the answer for under 200,00 including travel, and it will be reported in a Public Health Advisory that every clinic gets, and that report will be available online. It's a choice to make. Seems to me a pretty clear case of a more perfect union." I didn't mention that the Public Health Advisories were available online for the whole world to benefit, because that benefit doesn't often help in these arguments.

Mr. Gough pursed his lips and scratched his chin. "You're a slick fellow."

I continued with my fries. "I get time to think about it traveling. I'm guessing that you're in favor of national defense."

"For the most part," he conceded.

"I'd suggest we fall more into that category than whatever irritating agency you might have had in mind. We in the U.S. Public Health Service are, in fact, one branch of the Uniformed Services. In time of war, I wear a uniform — Lieutenant Commander Parker." I continued with my fries while Mr. Gough mulled over whether to continue arguing. The waitress brought him coffee.

"I got an A in high school history," I offered.

He was having a hard time suppressing a grin by this point. "Bet you were the teacher's pet."

"Eh, I've been accused of that. Long ago."

Mr. Gough and I talked about other things, the farm and the war. He got up after a while. We shook hands and he left without grumbling. I noticed he didn't pay for the coffee.

Cheryl, our waitress, came over to me. "Can I get you anything else?"

I smiled. "I'm good."

"That was pretty impressive," she said.

"What?" I asked.

"You talking with Mr. Gough. I've never seen anyone hold their own against him."

I looked out the front window. The man was no longer in sight. "Oh, I don't think there was any 'against.' I don't think he knew why I was here, or what I did."

Cheryl chuckled as she tore off my bill and placed it face down beside my plate. "Uh-huh."

I paid and left a tip that would cover Mr. Gough's coffee as well. I imagined that Mr. Gough enjoyed free coffee from time to time.

When I got back to the clinic, Isabel was finishing a discussion with her patient, a woman in her 50s or 60s. She handed the woman a slip of paper. "This prescription will take care of the soreness. Take the tablets on a full stomach, now. If you don't, they'll make you queasy. All right?"

The woman nodded. She turned from Dr. Rodriguez to me. "Hello, Dr. Parker. Doc Isabel was telling me about your work. We're all praying for you to find an answer."

"Thanks. We need all the help we can get."

The woman thanked the doctor and put the slip in her purse. I held the door for her as she left.

Isabel finished her notes on the patient record and began to tidy up. "Give me a couple of minutes and we'll be off to see Walt."

"Anything I can help with?"

"No, just want to get things put away before we head out. Did you have a good lunch?"

"Very enjoyable. Good comfort food. I met Mr. Gough."

Isabel laughed. "Lucky you. Need any first aid before we leave the clinic?"

"Oh, it's nothing I haven't encountered before. It helps that I'm a PHS officer. I left out the part that we're an agency of the Department of Health and Human Services."

She pulled shut the door to her office and checked that it was locked. "Smart." She checked the back door and we went outside. She pointed to her pearl-gray Prius. "Hop in. I'll drop you off at Ellen's when we're done. Or back here if it doesn't take long out at Walt's."

"Thanks." I picked up my sample kit that I had brought with me.

As we drove out into the farmlands, Isabel filled me in on some of the details. I had studied Walt Tinley's records first, since we would be seeing him that day, so I knew the clinical details. She filled me in on the personal side. Walt, like Frank Johnson, had grown up in Todd County. They were good friends in high school and did a lot together, including Future Farmers and football. Both were cattle farmers. Both had daughters who were not interested in continuing the farming tradition.

Their family similarities diverged when Sharon's husband died in the shop accident. She and her infant daughter moved back with her folks for economic reasons. Little Gina proved an avid and capable farm girl, and Gina and Sharon stayed on in the small cottage on the Tinley farm. Mrs. Tinley — Susan Bea, though everyone always called her Mrs. Tinley — developed pneumonia after getting the flu about ten years ago. She died suddenly. Walt was devastated. It was hard to say what might have become of him had he not focused on his responsibilities to Gina and her mom. "You've met Gina. She had to grow up really fast, and she did. Kind of a shame that she missed so much of being a regular girl. That comes out from time to time. While she and Chris are the same age, she's had to take time off high school, so she's a class behind him now. He's heading off to UK this fall. Between that and Walt's decline, she's feeling the pressure. Not that she'll show it. She just throws herself into the work. That's easy to do on a farm the size of theirs."

We had traveled about ten miles north and east. I hadn't paid close attention until we turned off the main road and onto ever-smaller roads until we came to the driveway of the Tinley farm. I heard the crunch of gravel that I had not heard in many years as we drove slowly to the house. An enthusiastic black Labrador retriever came bounding to the car as Isabel opened the door.

She bent down to greet the canine, his tail wagging so hard that it moved his whole body. "Jason, Jason, how's my buddy? Huh?"

Jason was well trained. He did not jump, and relished her petting. He came over to me without barking. I was pleased to see that being a friend of Isabel was enough for me to be accepted. "Hi, Jason. You're a good dog, aren't you?" After receiving a pat on the head from me, he dashed off to the house giving a couple of announcement barks.

Gina appeared at the screen door. "Hey, Dr. Isabel, Dr. Parker. Come on in." She held the door for us. "Can I get you something to drink?"

Isabel smiled. "Thanks, maybe after we're finished."

"A little something would be nice if you're having something. Thank you," I replied. The saltiness of the lunch still lingered.

"Would you like some sweet tea?"

"That would be spectacular," I said.

"I made some fresh tea for lunch." She waved her hand toward the back of the house. "Grandpa's out in the sunroom. Go ahead on back. I'll be there in a minute."

Gina headed to the kitchen as we made our way through the house, an older Victorian home furnished in pleasant country style more like the Johnsons' ranch house than Ellen's city home. The sunroom lived up to its name, bright and cheery. Several large ferns sat near the edge, and the furniture included steel-framed patio furniture with heavy padding. Several of the windows were open to let in May breezes.

Walt Tinley reclined on a chaise lounge with a blanket covering him. He looked very tired, far older than his chronological age. He exhibited the same nodules as Frank, maybe not so prominent.

"Doc, Dr. Parker. So good of you to come out. Did my granddaughter offer you something to drink?"

Isabel leaned over and patted him on the hand. "You know she did, Walt. You brought her up right. She must have told you that Dr. Parker's come from Atlanta to see you. Is that OK?"

He wrinkled his brow. "Oh, yes." He looked at me. "Gina tells me you're from the Centers for Disease Control. We don't often get visitors of that stature around here. Are you enjoying your stay?"

I am forever impressed with the sense of hospitality I find in the heartland. Despite his obvious suffering, Walt's focus was on the guest. "I am indeed, sir. Folks have been friendly and helpful beyond my wildest dreams."

"Did you get to visit the Penn Warren house? He was the first poet laureate of the United States, you know."

"I walked by his house this morning. I haven't had time to stop in yet. I absolutely will."

Gina appeared in the doorway with two glasses of tea. She handed me one and set the other one on the table next to her grandfather's chair. "Do you need privacy?"

I looked around at the three of them. "For my part, I'll just have a few questions and would like to draw some blood if that's OK after Dr. Rodriguez does what she's come for."

Walt began to laugh, which caused him to cough. After the coughing subsided, he grinned and looked at Isabel. "Dr. Rodriguez. We haven't heard that for a while, have we?"

She smiled. "Nope. Funny how you fall into a groove. 'Doc Isabel' sounds about right, doesn't it?"

He nodded.

Isabel opened her bag and brought out her stethoscope and blood pressure cuff. "Have you been taking those meds regularly?"

"Oh, yeah. You know Gina won't let me skip those. She's a tough nurse. No nonsense. No siree." He turned with a grin. Gina leaned on the doorframe, a kind smirk on her face. I noticed that her arms were scuffed from her morning work.

He watched Gina as Isabel took his vital signs.

Isabel said, "Well, Walt, you're doing about as good as might be expected. Good thing your granddaughter's kept after you. Those pills may have given you an extra season or so to be with her."

"Then it's worth it."

"Are they still upsetting your stomach?"

"Not so much. Not after you gave me that other stuff to go with them."

Isabel nodded. "Yeah, that's new. Makes a big difference if we can make the medicine go down easier and stay down. OK if Doc Parker draws a little blood now?"

"Let Gina do it," Walt said.

I raised my eyebrows. Isabel looked at me and nodded.

Walt turned again to Gina. "She's got a gentle and steady touch. She's the only one Ferdinand will let stick him."

I drew out two vials and a syringe from my kit. "Ferdinand?"

Gina pulled up a chair beside Walt, watching as I assembled the blood-drawing gear. "He's my bull."

Walt grinned, gazing at his granddaughter. "Kentucky State Fair Grand Champion 2008 bull, registered Limousin, finest steer ever. She picked his parents and was there to assist his birthing."

Gina tucked her head under his praise, blushing.

Walt continued, "And the meanest cuss we've had on this farm."

Gina rolled her eyes. "Is not. He's just a big baby, and he has his ways and doesn't care for people interfering. If you're nice to him, he's gentle as a lamb."

"That's not what José says." Walt seemed in a teasing mood.

"Well, José doesn't have patience with Ferdinand. And José doesn't talk with him."

"Maybe Ferdinand doesn't understand Spanish."

Gina's eyes flashed. "We've had this conversation, Grandpa. Ferdinand understands Spanish, too. I'm almost as fluent as José, and I can converse either way."

Walt turned to me. "That's true. She and José get to talking, and they'll switch back and forth between English and Spanish so fast you lose track."

Gina insisted, "You have to talk to Ferdinand."

I set out the final items — gauze and alcohol rubs. "Does he talk back?"

She looked at me and nodded. I think she expected skepticism, so I let her know my genuine interest. "Yes, he does, in his way. Not with his voice. I think it takes too much energy for a bull to vocalize. He'll turn his head or snort, and I'll know what he's thinking. He comes up to me at the fence, and I'll ask him about the cows. He'll turn to each one as I say her name."

"Except Daisy," Walt chuckled a little so as not to stir up the coughing again.

Gina chuckled in return. "Right, except Daisy. The two of them don't get along. Something happened. I'm not sure what — he was limping for a couple of weeks. When I ask him about Daisy, he doesn't look in her direction. He just looks down."

I laughed. "Amazing. I've heard of communications with many different animals, including cattle. You're the first I've met in person, though, who practices it with cattle."

Gina donned the gloves from my kit, picked up a swab, applied the tourniquet, and handed Walt the rubber ball to squeeze. "Yeah, well, he's the only one with much brains. The cows ... not so much." She swabbed Walt's arm. "Go ahead and start squeezing." She picked up a syringe. "So, Grandpa, tell Dr. Parker what breeds we've had here."

He turned to me. "In the late 70s, we had standard Herefords. They gave us a good run. In the 80s, we added Angus. That was when the craze in the restaurants started. We also tried some Aubrac, just for fun. But they don't do well in our heat. We're too far south for them."

I watched with admiration as Gina went about her tasks. She worked with deft hands, finding the vein on the first stick and withdrawing the needle with a smooth, practiced motion.

Walt made only a flicker of a wince as she stuck him and kept talking. "In the 90s, we kept the Angus and added Shorthorns, which were OK. When Gina really got into the operation, she wanted Limousin. I think she just liked their color."

Gina grinned.

"Not only did she want Limousin, which is an expensive breed, she wanted to raise 'em organic, which is hugely expensive."

"And how has that worked out, Grandpa?" She smiled with pride.

He smiled back. "We're the most profitable farm in the tri-county area. We're even more profitable per acre than the damned Conrad-Mattlock Agro."

She nodded. "Restaurants pay a big premium for certified organic. Conrad-Mattlock Agro is stuck so they can't make a profit unless they can ship by the trainload. And Conrad-Mattlock Agro can lose a whole field if a part breaks on one of their big machines at the wrong time. José and I have things covered on the animal end. Chris provides the organic grain and hay." She looked up at Isabel. "Someone has a field out on Boulder Road and lets us cut hay in return for maintaining her property. Too generous, though it sure makes us profitable."

Isabel folded her arms.

Gina turned to Walt. "You left out the Longhorns again."

Walt's expression darkened. "Yeah. I wish I could forever. That was a stupid, romantic idea just before the Angus. Ornery, finicky, and not all that much meat for the amount of pasture they took. I have nothing good to say about Longhorns. Texas can keep 'em, and good riddance."

We all laughed. Even Walt, though it started his coughing again.

I had labeled the samples as Gina handed them to me. I opened my case and began packing the vials. "Your technique is impressive, Gina. Have you thought about medicine?"

She nodded. "I am in medicine. Cattle; not human. I like my patients with four legs. I've taken all the certification classes at the community college and the state diagnostic lab over in Hopkinsville. I have my license for private farm veterinary. Doc Isabel taught me what more I needed to attend to Grandpa. Mom has a thing about needles, so I'm 'it' between Doc's visits."

"Fair enough. You've also got a wonderful bedside manner. I can see how you and Ferdinand must get along." I looked at Walt. "I know drawing the blood isn't too bad. Still, it's not painless."

She grinned. "Oh, you get Grandpa talking about his cattle and it blocks the pain pretty good. Right, Grandpa?"

He nodded. "You betcha."

I closed my case. If things went without any hitches, I'd be able to get the samples to Jack at the post office in time for today's pickup.

Gina turned to Isabel. "Can I ask you some questions?"

"Sure."

"In the kitchen, maybe. Girl stuff." Gina pointed toward the inside. They both rose, leaving Walt and me alone.

"Your granddaughter is an amazing woman, Mr. Tinley."

"Yup. As fine as they come. I feel bad that she's missed so much school looking after me."

"I sense she doesn't mind. Though I haven't known her very long, she seems the kind who loves to 'do,' to care for things. She immerses herself in the tasks like it's not work, just life."

Walt nodded. "Well put. You've got a keen eye and ear, Doc. For all the downsides of dying, I know the world's a better place for leaving it in Gina's hands." He grew quiet. "And Chris, too. Have you met Chris?"

"No, sir. Not yet, though I've heard a bit about him from Doc Isabel. All good."

"Yeah. He's like Ferdinand — tough and strong when he has to be; gentle and loving with Gina."

I felt, as Walt grew quiet again that he wanted to talk.

"I hear you're a church man, Dr. Parker."

"Yes, sir. I'm a deacon in my church, North Park Baptist in Atlanta."

He nodded, pondering his words. "Do you believe in judgment?"

I get questions like this more often than you might think. The question often starts as more of an argument, since people often assume my science background would be at odds with my faith. Straightening that out, I've had some good discussions over the years. "Yes, sir, I'd have to say I do. Now, you're asking a pretty loaded question, of course. There're all those 'it-depends-on-what-you-mean-by' parts to the answer."

"Good. You're a thoughtful fellow, so I can be direct. Do you think that something really bad, really evil, that someone did in their youth will damn them to Hell for all eternity?"

I folded my hands on the case in my lap. "Wow, that is pretty direct. Here's what I'm thinking. When I look at all the actions in the 'evil' categories, I see that they're all behaviors with consequences; bad consequences for our lives and for those around us. Sometimes people get caught up in images of a punishing God or loving God and leave out the part about the proscriptions in scriptures being warnings. I don't see them as arbitrary rules. And the rules laid out in the Hebrew scriptures are so consistent in their harmony with modern medical practices — derived independent of scripture — that I see judgment as a natural consequence of ignoring the proscriptions. Does that make sense?"

Walt nodded again.

"On the other hand, I don't often see anything that looks like the hand of a vengeful God touching someone unlinked to physical cause and effect."

"Hmmm."

In the ensuing quiet, I heard the faint rustling of leaves beyond the open window. "Same goes for repentance and forgiveness. They have powerful healing properties for everybody. Ever hear Jesus referred to as 'The Great Physician'?"

"Yeah." Walt pondered my answer. "I've seen the hand of God punishing. Too much to be coincidences." He had a far-away look in his eyes.

"Want to talk about it?"

We heard Isabel and Gina returning. Walt turned to me. "Yeah. Maybe later. Let me check my calendar." He grinned. "I'll give you a call. Promise."

I guess we must have looked pretty somber when the women returned, all smiles and happy.

Isabel offered that they hadn't been gone that long. "We do have to get going for now. I've got two more patients to see this afternoon."

We made our goodbyes to Walt. He squeezed my hand as we shook hands. Gina went with us through the house toward the front door.

"Is there anything you can do for Grandpa, Dr. Parker?"

I rubbed my chin, stalling for some thinking time, and then put my hand on her shoulder. "Doc Isabel has provided everything medical we know of, as good as anything we'd have in Atlanta or any other major center. He's gotten much better attention than in any other rural setting I've ever been to. Your grandpa doesn't have much time. We don't know the cause, and we don't know the cure for this hideous affliction." I lifted the sample case a little way up. "These donations should go a long way toward helping us find those answers. For now, he's getting ready to let go. Talking to him while you were out, I can tell that he is so very, very proud of you."

Tears began to stream down Gina's face.

I continued, "The best thing you can do for Grandpa now is to show him where you're going. If he likes it there in the sunroom, bring your pictures there, your ribbons, and your trophies. Confirm to him the value of the legacy he's given you. That will mean more to him than all the medicine in the world. You'll be glad you did. OK?"

She nodded quickly, while biting her lip.

"He said he thought he might like to talk about faith matters with me." I reached into my pocket. "Here's my card. There's my cell phone number on it. For anything physical medical, call Doc Isabel. She's his doctor, and she's doing everything just as she should." I took my hand off of her shoulder and followed Isabel onto the front porch.

Midway down the steps, Gina whispered through the screen door, "How long?"

Isabel and I exchanged glances.

She turned to Gina. "Not long. Make every hour count."

Gina remained at the door while we walked to the car. Just as we reached it, I heard the crunch of gravel near the road. I looked up to see a large, dark red Ford pickup piled high with bales of hay coming down the drive toward us.

A faint smile crossed Isabel's lips. "That would be Chris. As usual, his timing couldn't be better."

The truck slowed to a stop beside us. I figured that he was accustomed to slowing to prevent a dust storm on the gravel stretch. The rain of the previous night had prevented the dust that day.

"Hey, Doc, Dr. Parker." He got out and bounded around the truck, extending his hand to me. Chris was tall and good looking, of strong build. Under his closely cropped hair, he had a friendly, gentle face. "How's Mr. Tinley?"

Isabel offered her assessment. "He's comfortable. Gina's taking good care of him, of course. He's getting pretty weak, though."

"Except when he's talking cattle," I said.

Chris laughed. "I'll bet. Didn't have to try too hard to get him started there."

Isabel shook her head. "Nope. Anyway, Gina's going to be super relieved to see you. The next few days could get rough. She'll need to summon all the strength she's got. She's going to need someone to lean on."

"She's got me," Chris assured.

"I know." Isabel gave him a hug and then pointed toward the house, where Gina had just come out of the door and was creeping down the steps.

We got into the car and headed for the road. I turned around in my seat to watch. Gina flung her arms around Chris and buried her head in his broad shoulder. He enfolded her in his embrace and they remained at the house end of the drive as we reached the road and drove out of sight.

I turned back to watch the road ahead. "She has a lot to face, doesn't she?"

Isabel was calm, almost stoic. "Yes, though she'll be fine. As painful as it's going to be, she'll land on her feet and emerge on the other side stronger. I'm certain of that. She won't have much time to be sad. Farms don't let you linger. And she doesn't know it yet that when Walt passes, Gina becomes one of the wealthiest women in the county."

I turned to Isabel, inquisitive.

"George Boone, their family lawyer, told me that Walt's will leaves the whole operation to Gina. That's the main farm and several big parcels they've rented out to tenant farmers."

"Not to his daughter, Sharon, Gina's mom?"

"Nope. It goes straight to Gina."

"I'd think that could cause some difficulties."

Isabel smiled. "Not in this case. Sharon also told me. I'm pretty sure it was her idea in the first place. Like I said earlier, Sharon wants nothing to do with farming. And she doesn't have the same organizational bent that Gina has. She's quite content being an assistant branch manager over in Hopkinsville. Knowing Gina as I do, Sharon will be well looked after. Walt's will specifies that the cottage is Sharon's should Gina ever sell the farm, though I don't see Gina selling any time before the Second Coming. She's mindful of every blade of grass on that property."

Isabel continued her historical tour of the county as we drove back to town, pointing out who owned what and who was related to whom. I returned to "my office" a little before three, giving me plenty of time to get the new samples documented and ready for shipping.

I locked the case and applied the CDC seal. At the post office, Jack seemed glad to see me. Besides Mireese's packages from this morning, mine was the only outgoing parcel. I asked him about the Patton-Dalton plant, and he suggested I talk to Sheriff Nolan.

Returning to City Hall, I stopped to greet Liz, who introduced me to Curtis Nolan. He wore his uniform with authority. During our conversation he switched effortlessly between me and about a dozen calls that came in.

"Yeah, we're all lucky that damn' company's gone. Once they saw the lawsuits coming, they moved their headquarters overseas. Today it'd cost more to sue them than you're ever going to get back. You say you'd like some samples from there? I've got a Pennyrile Emergency Services meeting tomorrow at noon in Hopkinsville and nothing particular in the morning. We can go over and I'll give you the fifty-cent tour. I hear that Brian Kingsbury's company's going to be cleaning up the place next year and turning it into warehousing. He's got his work cut out for him, so he's looking to get one of those professional remediation companies out of Chicago or Saint Louis to do the cleanup. What time would you like to head out?"

I smiled. "You tell me what's good for you. I still have my Navy sleep perspective. The clock is only a guide."

He took a call about an abandoned vehicle and returned to me. "Let's leave here about 8:30, then. I'll give the Christian County sheriff a call when we get close, and he'll send someone to unlock. I find surprise visits are often more useful. Bring your car. No telling how long my meeting might go. That'll give you the freedom to knock around Hopkinsville and head back when it suits you."

I thanked him and returned to my office to continue researching the files. By now I was entering Isabel's records into the standard national database. Her documentation was thorough and specific and would be useful, without a doubt. I felt the frustration of knowing, perhaps more than the victims here in Guthrie, that there was nothing I could do to save them, even if I found the cause that day. The only things I had in abundance were suspects — mold, industrial chemicals, outlawed lumber treatments. It was a wonder that more people weren't sick. I pondered whether I should solicit samples from healthy relatives who should have been exposed to similar risk factors. Such requests are rare and can cause considerable community stress. I needed to concentrate on finding some commonality among the four. I would have the first metals-in-blood analysis for Frank and Walt by Friday. On Monday afternoon or Tuesday I would be getting some of the first genetic analyses from the lab.

I found it challenging to suppress my aversion to Conner's viral origin theory. Though there was no evidence yet to suggest a viral origin and plenty of alternate candidates, there was nothing to negate it either. I just had to await the genetics.

By 5:30 I was feeling the fatigue of a long, thoughtful day. I looked at the pile of records. I was about a third of the way through. I couldn't continue because my typing skills plummet as I get tired. Even a single misspelling can make a record irretrievable. Our software engineers had developed prototypes of search algorithms that would compensate for such errors, but those upgrades weren't ready for prime time. I tidied the files, closed my laptop, and put it back in its case, and locked my office.

I left through the Health Services office. Isabel was at her desk, entering notes. "I need to get you some kind of grant to let you go electronic. It would save you a tremendous amount of time in the long run."

She smiled. "You do that, John. I've applied for about 20 over the years. At first, they were all turned down because other areas had more severe needs. Of late, we're getting rejected because there's no MD on staff."

"Sorry," I replied.

"In the meantime I'll keep my records the old-fashioned way. Were you able to read my writing?"

"Your penmanship is exquisite."

"See? You wouldn't have that with an MD."

I sat down in the patient chair in front of her desk. "Hey, I'm on your side in all this. With the growing demand for quality medical care, the degree requirements are going to have to be relaxed. That's inevitable. We both know it won't happen without a political fight the likes of which we've never seen."

"Right. You're right. Sorry. On a different topic, have you found anything interesting?"

"Oh, yes. Nothing you haven't noted. First feedback from Atlanta by the end of the week. Do you have any thoughts that might not be in the records? You have your finger on the pulse here after all. Anything peculiar say five to eight years ago? Given the course of the disease, that's about when it would have been initiated."

She thought for a moment. "You know, when you get so busy, the years kinda blur together. I'd only been here about five years at that point."

"If you think of anything, let me know. In the meantime, I'll be in Hopkinsville tomorrow checking out the Patton-Dalton site. Maybe I can check out the *New Era* archives."

"Ah, so you've met Sheriff Nolan."

"Uh huh. He seems on top of things. He's giving me a tour of the plant."

"Good. You'll like him. He's way better than his predecessor. Sometimes people stay in one job too long. That was ole Carl. Holdover from the Wyatt Earp days. Carl and I didn't get along from the get-go. Curtis is a different story. Solid professional to the core. Yeah, you'll like him."

I stood up to leave. "Thank you again for all your help. Too many times I almost have to pry information from communities. I don't guess I've ever been anywhere so cooperative as here."

"The community would like to take vengeance on this disease. Don't worry. We'll help you."

With that, I left the office and strolled back to Ellen's. As I walked up the drive on the way to my room, I spotted a young woman sitting in the porch swing. As I approached, she got up and leaned on the railing. Her hair was cropped in a pixie cut, a splash of pink on one side. I could make out a dainty piece of cheek jewelry on the other side.

"Hello. You must be Dr. Parker."

I smiled. "Yes, ma'am. And you must be Stacy Coudron."

"Wow, word gets 'round fast here."

"You have no idea. I hear you attend MICA. Your school has quite the reputation."

"So they say. I just graduated, so I hope that reputation will land me a job, especially with the economy like it is. Hey, Ellen tells me you're a medical detective."

I rocked back and forth, enjoying the description. "I guess that'd be a romantic way of describing it. I'm an epidemiologist with the CDC in Atlanta."

"Well, Baltimore has Hopkins. I guess you're familiar with that."

"Of course. We work with the School of Public Health there. I've visited Hopkins maybe 20 times over the years. Awesome place. I guess you flew out of Baltimore. Pleasant trip, I hope."

"Other than getting Mom to the airport on time, yeah."

I smiled. "If I remember — Jane?"

"Ew, you're good."

"Is she here?" I asked.

"Mireese took her out to Aunt Faye's. They're stopping to pick up some things on the way. In the push to get her out the door, she forgot about half her stuff. I'm just enjoying some quiet time with Mrs. Miller."

"I hear she was your teacher."

"Uh huh. Best ever. She's the main reason I'm in art education."

"You enjoy it?" I inquired.

"Love it. There's nothing I'd rather do. That and painting."

"I hope you don't mind. I suggested to your aunt and cousin that you might like to help paint their gazebo. I know it's not high art and you might not have planned anything for your visit."

"Oh, so you're the one who suggested that. Thank you, thank you, thank you. I was afraid I was going to have to spend a week listening to Mom and Aunt Faye trying to control each other. You may have saved me … and them, too. They can get pretty intense."

I chuckled. "So what sort of excitement do you have tonight?"

"Mrs. Miller's getting supper ready. I think you're joining us. She's put out three place settings."

"I don't know. We hadn't discussed it, and my plans were a blank."

About that time Ellen came out onto the porch, drying her hands on a dishtowel. "Well, Dr. Parker, I see you've met your new neighbor. Isn't she a charmer?"

"Yes, ma'am. We were just talking about Baltimore."

Ellen nodded. "Dinner's about ready. Will you join us? I've got enough for three."

"I'd be honored. Let me put my gear away, and I'll be right back."

I stowed my computer in the room and washed up. By the time I entered the house, Ellen and Stacy were already inside. I followed their voices to a side room.

I found myself in Ellen's quilting room. Shelves lined one side, replete with a rainbow of fabrics, bundles of batting, and a small library of quilting books. The opposing wall displayed a gallery of finished quilts, many with designs I had never seen, along with traditional patterns. Ellen and Stacy stood beside a large table with colorful blocks of cloth laid out in a pattern.

"You like?" Stacy opened her arms to the assembly.

"You sure we should ask a man?" Ellen adopted a skeptical look.

"You be nice now. If he notices, we've accomplished what we wanted."

I smiled as I examined the design. "The colors are pleasing. It kinda draws you to what I presume is your upper right corner, like you're walking out of some cold woods into a sunrise."

Ellen looked at Stacy, smiling, though she talked to me. "Stacy suggested those blues at the bottom left to give that corner a cold feel. Used color theory to pick the exact shade. I never got that far in my art education. We'll keep the blues for sure. Guess the teacher becomes the student at some point, eh?"

I smiled in turn. "Happens to me all the time. What's the piece called?"

"'By the Dawn's Early Light.'" Ellen turned off the light on her sewing machine and unplugged her iron. As I surveyed the work, I began to see other images— a dark barn and a path emerging from the darkness and brightening toward the sunrise. Some smaller elements suggested farm animals.

"This is complex. You could study it for a long time."

"That's the idea," Stacy giggled.

We left the quilting room and moved to the kitchen. After our blessing, we shared roast with potatoes and green beans. Stacy exuded the maturity of an only child of a single parent, a single parent who had not matured. Though she never said it, it was obvious that many financial and household responsibilities had fallen on her at an early age. Still, she kept a sharp and quirky sense of humor, and was a good conversationalist.

"Your Aunt Faye said you'd be part of Uncle Frank's service."

"Yup. I'm glad she's letting me. I owe it to him. Ms. Miller and I are working on our part."

Ellen interrupted. "I think that's all he needs to know. Give him some plausible deniability."

Stacy agreed, "Good point."

We went on to talk about Stacy's days in Ellen's class, how she had arrived shy and alone, a city girl eight years old dropped into the middle of a very rural community. She emerged from her shyness and thrived with the supportive protection of the Johnsons and Ellen's classroom. Stacy's curiosity about all things mechanical put her in good standing with the boys and she discovered her natural love of art under Ms. Miller.

"It's hard to believe I was here for only two years. Seemed like most of my life."

Ellen got up and brought over dessert, a glazed strawberry pie with fresh whipped cream. "You tend to remember the good times. That would favor your years here, I suspect."

"Oh, yeah." Stacy then turned to me. "Ms. Miller tells me you're going to Hopkinsville tomorrow."

"Uh huh. The sheriff and I are going to check out the plant where your Uncle Frank and Mr. Tinley worked. I need to get some samples."

"You think they got cancer from working there?"

"I think we need to check that out. These cases are putting all my training to the test. Right now I'm just hearing about the clues. There's tedious analysis to be done before we reach a conclusion. And I'm not ruling anything out."

"Except a virus." Stacy ate her pie slowly, savoring each bite.

I looked at Ellen. "I'm not ruling anything out. Even a virus, though that's not high on my probability list." I turned back to Stacy. "All the tissue samples I take will be analyzed for infectious agents, so let's hope it's not a virus."

"Yeah? Why not?" Stacy asked.

"Because if the cancers have been caused by a virus, then hundreds, maybe thousands of people in the community have been exposed to it."

After I broached that grim possibility, we changed the subject to Stacy's art. She had dabbled in many forms, even winning an award for her costume work. Her favorite medium was paint, though. She fetched her tablet and showed me her portfolio as Ellen cleared the table and loaded the dishwasher. In general, I dreaded art students' works. My experiences were that they tended to be dark and grumpy and "made a statement" at the expense of being enjoyable. Stacy's work favored brightness and levity. I was drawn in particular to a series of children's cartoon figures, sassy little girls and mischievous little boys.

"These are great! Have you considered selling some of these?"

She looked over at what I was viewing. "In fact, those were commissioned. My instructor put me in touch with a children's book author who needed an illustrator. I drew the whole book for royalties, since he didn't have much money up front. Good thing, too. That got Mom and me through the winter of '09. His book won a Caldecott. They don't have a separate category for art, though our share of the royalties will keep coming for a long time."

"Wow!" I looked at Stacy with newfound admiration. Her family trials and busy life did not appear to have taken a toll on her. She possessed an air of contentment, her face unlined by worry.

The three of us continued talking around the table for a long time. Her portfolio included a number of pictures with her school children. My favorite picture was of her with about 20 paint-spattered kids in front of an enormous wall painting of the battle of Fort McHenry, part of a Baltimore City Public Schools project. The thought of the logistics of completing that project with all those children was exhausting, yet the photo showed triumph, Stacy's and the children's arms all in the air.

Before I knew it, the clock was striking ten. I made my apologies and left them to their service planning. Neither seemed the least bit tired. I got ready for bed, expecting that I would fall asleep right away. Instead, I found myself pondering one of the loose ends of the day. I couldn't fall asleep for quite some time. I kept remembering Walt's words to me before Isabel and Gina returned from the kitchen. He said, "I've seen the hand of God punishing. Too much to be coincidences." I needed to talk to him to see what he meant.

4 MODERN INDUSTRY

I awoke soon after sunrise. Since Guthrie sits near the eastern edge of the Central Time Zone, I guess it must have been around 5:30, 6 o'clock. Though it had taken me some time to fall asleep, still I woke up eager to get the day going. I looked afresh at the quilts decorating my room, informed by the previous night's introduction to Ellen's fabric storytelling. The large skydyes work had become my favorite, and I studied it for a while after I had dressed and before I left the room. The quilted angels were gathered into working groups, both male and female angels. Across the top were several clusters singing, each with a choir director angel. Others flitted about on other assignments. I smiled to see one group of kitchen angels washing celestial dishes. My heart warmed to this group, because I was on the dishwashing crew of our church.

All the angels were dressed in white save one in the lower center. A cluster of female angels gathered around a smaller angel with a red striped shirt and jeans, perhaps a new arrival. I smiled as I stepped out into the humid morning air. Despite the busyness in its detail, Ellen's quilt had an overall coherence that overrode the activities portrayed.

I didn't want to presume that breakfast would be provided every day. As soon as I rounded the corner in the front, I saw Ellen tending her begonias along the front porch, pinching back errant growths and spent blossoms.

"Good morning, Dr. Parker."

"Good morning, Ms. Miller."

"OK. Enough of that for one day. Hope you slept well."

"I did."

"I made a cinnamon coffee cake for breakfast. Old family recipe."

"Thank you," I replied. "Did you get any sleep? Looked like you and Stacy were doing quite a bit of planning work when I left, and it was already late."

"Oh my yes. We were charged. Lots to do, and she's a doer."

I looked around and saw no sign of Stacy. "You must have worn her out. Guess she's sleeping in."

"Oh, then you would be wrong, John. She got up an hour before you. She's already eaten and is on her way to Clarksville to get supplies for the gazebo."

"Really?" I glanced about and realized Ellen's car was gone from the driveway. "I feel a bit responsible for that project. Think she'd let me donate some to cover the costs?"

"I'll take your contribution. I gave her my credit card with an authorizing note in case anyone gives her a hard time, which I doubt. As you've seen, she can be a charmer."

"You really trust her. Your car, your credit card."

"In my business, teaching, you learn to recognize the good ones and the bad ones pretty fast. She'll be taking the paint and things straight to Faye's to start working with the kids. I'll betcha she comes back tonight with the receipts all arranged in an envelope and totaled on the front with pictures on her phone of the progress they've made. She had to be that way to survive with her mother." Ellen shook her head. "Anyway, I'll let you go halvsies with me if you'd like. She's pretty frugal, so I can't imagine it will be too much."

"That's more than fair," I confirmed.

We had our breakfast of coffee cake and oranges. We went over my plans of the day in Hopkinsville. Ellen suggested some restaurants there for lunch and dinner. "I'll give Dee Ferguson a call at the *New Era*. She'll make sure you have access to the back issues and have someone to talk to you about Ron Widing. How long do you think you'll be at the old Patton-Dalton place?"

"If there're no obstacles, I'd say an hour and a half, two hours."

"I'll tell her about one o'clock, then. That'll give you time for snags. If everything runs smoothly, you can spend some time in Trail of Tears Park or the Pennyrile Museum downtown."

I thanked her, picked up my computer and camera gear, checked the sample kits in the trunk, and drove to City Hall. I walked in to the sounds of argument coming from Sheriff Nolan's office. I looked to Liz Kelm.

She shook her head. "Party A's cow broke its leg in a hole in Party B's pasture and Party A is demanding compensation. Party B says that Party A should have fixed the fence six months ago and says the cow was trespassing and is keeping the cow."

I scratched my head. "Without any other information, I think B would be in the right."

"Uh huh, this round." She looked at the clock. "That's what Curt will tell them in about three minutes. Next week it'll be something else."

"Seems an odd thing for a sheriff to be handling."

"Maybe. They blow off steam here, and it takes much less time for us than going to court."

I heard the sheriff break into the argument. A moment of silence followed, then a dual "OK."

The two sullen parties left his office and exited the building without a word. Sheriff Nolan appeared in his doorway. He leaned on the wall, looking very tired for that early hour.

"Liz, please call Ellen to see if she would come out of retirement just once to teach a remedial kindergarten class."

Liz nodded.

"Sorry, Doc. Some parts of the job they didn't warn me about. Shall we get a move on before they start eating paste?"

I followed the sheriff out of the door and drove behind him the half hour to the outskirts of Hopkinsville. We turned off Pembroke Road and drove over a railroad track to a block-long assembly of buildings. I could already smell the acrid bite of organic lacquers. We pulled into a parking lot alongside a Christian County Sheriff's car. A uniformed officer leaned on the car and talked with a stocky gentleman in a white shirt holding a clipboard. By the time I got out of the car, the three men were shaking hands and laughing. The parking lot had a number of cars and trucks with "National Remediation Group" on their sides.

As I approached the men, Sheriff Nolan reached out his arm to me and made introductions. "Brian, Robert, I'd like you to meet Dr. John Parker from the Centers for Disease Control and Prevention in Atlanta. John, this is Robert Majors. He's sheriff in this neck of the woods. And this here's Brian Kingsbury, the owner of all this."

I saw a worried look on Brian Kingsbury's face.

"Not to worry, Mr. Kingsbury. This isn't an inspection or investigation of the plant *per se*. This is more a historic mission, more like archaeology."

He seemed a bit relieved, though not altogether convinced. "Forgive me — for my part, I'm hoping you don't find anything new. The conversion is already six months behind. The first firm gave up after a month." He nodded in the direction of the trucks. "This crew has a national reputation." He pulled a brochure from his clipboard and handed it to me.

I looked over the write-up. "Ah, yes, I know these people. They did the chromium cleanup in Baltimore and PCBs in Times Beach, Missouri. You must be paying a pretty penny for them. It'll be worth it, though, because they set the standard for the industry. I'm just glad we got here when we did. After National's finished, there shouldn't be anything worth sampling. That seems to be happening to me pretty often here."

"I'm relieved to hear that, Dr. Parker. Do you need us to help or to stay out of your way?" Brian asked.

I shook my head. "If all goes well, we'll just slip in, get our samples, and get out. Thanks, anyway. I'll let you know right away if we find anything you should know about. I think you're in good hands."

Sheriff Nolan put his hands on Brian's shoulder. "Better to get bad news early, Brian."

I sighed. "I'm predicting no new bad news."

Brian motioned in the direction of an open door. "Then have at it, Doc."

Curtis and I started walking toward the building. "Hold on, Doc," he said. "Let me get something." He jogged back to his car and returned with two chemical respirators.

I frowned. "I don't think we'll need those."

"You haven't been in there. Suit yourself."

He handed me one of the units. I held onto it along with my kit. We entered the dim, cavernous interior, lit by windows along the top level and a few hanging lamps. The former factory floor was studded with bolts that had once secured wire-spinning machinery. It was as if a bulldozer had come through and ripped the machines off their foundations and carried them off. I was already finding it hard to breathe, so I set down my case and put on my respirator. "Right."

Sheriff Nolan gave me a brief tour of what had once been on the floor. Though his mask muffled his voice, I understood. I took pictures along the way. At last, we arrived at what were once the hardening ovens, their sides still coated with flows of lacquer. The ovens were built with concrete bases that would have been unprofitable to move. After documenting their appearance, I took a razor blade and collected scrapings into vials, speaking slowly into my recorder. I wasn't sure that my audio notes would be easy to interpret and knew the lab back in Atlanta was going to have a field day with me when I returned. I found scraps of wire and scooped up various oozing material along the way. We proceeded to a former chemical storage area. Surveying the floor with its spill and goop-filled crevasses, I felt relief that I had started my career well after this kind of hazardous dump had been outlawed.

With two-thirds of my containers filled, I turned to the sheriff. "Unless you know of some other areas I should see, I'm good to go."

He motioned and we walked to the exit at the far end of the building. I pulled off my mask as we emerged. "Thanks for the breathing apparatus. I had no idea."

"Yeah. Walt, Frank, and my brother all worked in there without masks. Those execs better hope to hell they never meet me alone." His jaw clenched.

We left the building near the trucks. The remediation teams were suiting up to begin work. I talked with the team leaders about what they'd be looking for and how they planned to dispose of what they found. One of the advances they incorporated in their services was a high-temperature, forced oxygen furnace to render the recovered organics into carbon dioxide and heavy metals into recyclable oxides. Even the cleanup suits would be incinerated.

I held my sleeve up to my nose. The odor clung to my clothing.

"You'll want to have Ellen throw that in the wash when you get back. Otherwise, it'll hang on for weeks."

I nodded. "Thanks."

"OK, I've got my meeting. You know your way around?"

"Yeah. Ellen gave me a map. Even marked places I should visit."

He grinned. "Bet she did. Have a good time. Or productive. Or both."

I handed back the respirator. He put the gear in his trunk and drove off. I looked around the parking lot as I returned to my car. I saw Brian Kingsbury talking with the lead supervisor of the remediation team. Waving, I called out, "Thanks."

He gave a little salute, and smiled.

The sample gathering had been successful from beginning to end, so it was too early for lunch, yet too late to do any serious sightseeing in Hopkinsville. I drove around the town to get a sense of it. In small town America, there is an awkward size — too large to be satisfied with rural hub status, too small to host a stable cadre of permanent industries. At present, Hopkinsville boasted several distribution centers, a bowling ball manufacturer, and a branch of a regional college. The old tobacco warehouses were long-shuttered, and a number of buildings were on their fourth or fifth owners.

I sat down for lunch at the Main Street Café just before noon. Their food was good and prices reasonable. My attendant, a student at the local college, was working on her degree in medical technology. We had a good conversation about the future of medicine, until customers began to arrive a little after noon. I wished her well, and, on her recommendation, I was treated to pork chops from local swine farmers and a fresh vegetable medley.

I had just gotten in the door at the *Kentucky New Era* when I heard "Dr. Parker!" A charming woman greeted me. "I'm Dee Ferguson. Ellen said to expect you. You're right on time. She said you were interested in several things, including the Patton-Dalton plant. We've got most of the issues around the time of the closing digitized. Let me know if you need copies of the files or printouts. The papers from the mid-70s haven't been digitized yet, so Tracey's fixed up a quiet spot for you to go over them. I'm afraid we're a little behind the times on that."

"Mid-70s?"

"Ellen said you'd be wanting to see the October '73 through May '74 papers."

I frowned. "Any idea why?"

"No, she just said you'd be wanting to see those."

"OK, thank you." I didn't remember Ellen saying anything specific; just figured I must have mentioned something.

Dee led me to the archive room for the paper. I thanked her again and seated myself at the table with my notepad and voice recorder. I began by pulling up issues from the 1990s, when talk began of closing the cable plant. The earliest mentions were in connection with a surprise inspection by the EPA in September 1994. Two days after that inspection, the town got news that the fines would be in excess of five million dollars, a mind-boggling sum in those days. The rest of September and October 1994 featured daily meetings of civic and business groups organizing to fight the levies. In mid-October, EPA released the full report detailing the deaths linked to the plant. The company had up to that time been pretty skillful hiding the health costs. That EPA report seemed to split the community so that by Thanksgiving most of the civic groups had left the pro-plant coalition and begun to demand more information from Patton-Dalton. Three churches called for the plant's closing. By February 1995, the company announced it would be pulling out, which it did by summer of that year despite the efforts of the Chamber of Commerce. Their closing was complete and the building stripped of resources by August '95. It would sit empty until Brian Kingsbury's Standard Mill Supply bought it in January 2008 to use as a regional supply distribution center for industrial machinery.

Though I had learned little about the specifics of the chemical exposure, I had a sinking feeling that there might be many more cases of Griffith's sarcoma than the four I was investigating. Tracing the records in Hopkinsville would take time and many more connections.

I took a break from my note taking and chatted with the staff. Most knew Ron Widing and were saddened by his condition. They described him as a loner — friendly, not gregarious. Everyone praised his integrity and his reporting. He was the reporter perhaps most responsible for uncovering the conditions at Patton-Dalton. His reporting would have gotten him fired by the conservative owners of the paper, had not the tide turned against the plant before they could push him out, and his reporting brought several awards to the paper. Ron never married. One of the older staff wondered whether he was perhaps gay — not a very safe status even today in that community — while most said he just didn't fancy the company of others. The words *sad* and *melancholy* came up often.

I returned to my research, checking out all I could about Ron Widing. I read a number of his pieces, which were insightful, to say the least. Around 2001 he left his full-time position at the paper to concentrate on writing. He moved to Guthrie and contributed occasional articles, mostly historical pieces, until he revealed his cancer in 2009.

The *New Era* staff's feelings toward Ron were more admiration than affection.

I started on the '73 issues around four in the afternoon. I was surprised how jarring it felt to read the papers as if for the first time. The lunar missions had ended, and few realized there would be no follow-up. The Soviet Union and international communism were the bad guys of the day, while opposition to the war in Vietnam was reaching a peak. The attitude of the conservative small-town paper stood in marked contrast to the classic established eastern papers. Watergate was becoming a major topic, though Nixon's resignation was almost a year away. I scanned the papers, trying to avoid getting bogged down in the fascinating minutiae of the times. I started with Monday, October 1, and breezed through until Saturday, October 20, in the sports section, an area of the papers I seldom entered. There, on the first page of the sports section, were Dale Liston, Frank Johnson, Ron Widing, Jim Dulaney, and Walt Tinley, the "five demons." The picture appeared to be the same that Faye Johnson showed me from the *Todd County Standard*. Of course, while the *Todd County Standard* praised their team's victory of the previous night, Hopkinsville was mourning the loss.

I read the article covering the game. The Todd County team's performance seemed excellent, though probably not legendary. I took my time on this issue, reviewing it again from cover to cover, even the back, on which the comics resided. It had been a while since I had seen so many comics. The front page was filled with Watergate matters. I realized that this was the Saturday of the "Saturday Night Massacre," when Nixon's legal team resigned or was fired *en masse*. There were stories about that year's tobacco prices, a missing local girl, Friday night disturbances in the Durrett's Avenue neighborhood, and the opening of the Sydney Opera House. The number one song was *Midnight Train To Georgia* by Gladys Knight. The Israelis and Egyptians were fighting in the Sinai, and the OPEC oil embargo commenced. It was almost five by the time I looked up from the paper. I went to see Dee, who was preparing to leave. We agreed I should come back. I didn't have specific plans for the next day, except I needed to finish the Guthrie medical records. She said there would be no problem setting aside the pile of paper until the next week. I thanked her and we exchanged phone numbers.

I left the *New Era* and drove back to Guthrie. It was a little after five in western Kentucky. Back in Atlanta, an hour ahead, it was still rush hour. I was the only one on the road most of the trip. I mulled over the details of that long-ago Saturday, three years before I was born.

Pulling into Ellen's driveway a little after six, I saw that her car was still gone. I left my case in my car and walked onto the front porch. I called through the screen door, "Hello."

Ellen answered, "Hello, John. How were your adventures in Hoptown?"

"Quiet, productive."

I walked through the house back to the kitchen, where Ellen was frying chicken. She began sniffing the air once I entered the room.

"I can tell you spent some time at Patton-Dalton."

I lifted my sleeve and took a sniff. "Guess I didn't notice once I left the plant. Is it that bad? Everyone I met must have smelled it except me."

She chuckled. "It wouldn't be like folks to bring it up. It can't be good for you. Why don't you wash up and change before dinner. We'll get your things in the wash and get that chemical smell out. Back when the plant was active, we'd have that stench here in Guthrie some days when the wind was just so."

"Thanks. I'll do that. I took quite a few samples to send back to the lab. Pretty grim."

"Dinner'll be ready in about half an hour. Come back after your shower and have a seat so you can tell me about the newspaper. I haven't been over there in months."

I went back outside and around the house, stopping by the car to retrieve my sample case. Now that my sense of smell was returning to normal, I noticed the odor in the car and rolled down the windows to air it out.

Ellen must have anticipated the chemicals clinging to my clothing. A white plastic bag, perfect for a laundry bag, had been placed on the bed. On most trips, I traveled with ten days' worth of clothing, assuming I'd be back in Atlanta in that amount of time. I seldom needed to deal with laundry in the field. I still expected to be back within ten days, though the growing trove of samples and the list of suspect agents meant I was going to have to speed up my work or let the lab know I'd be here longer.

The shower felt good. I noticed the soap didn't lather so much as soap did in Atlanta. Western Kentucky is a limestone region, and the water is hard compared to Atlanta, where the ground water travels through granite. Thinking about it, I realized this was one of the few health positives I had encountered so far. Calcium-rich water correlated with lower risks for heart disease and osteoporosis, at least when you strip out the risk factors of diet. I had dined on more comfort food in the past two days than I ate in a normal month.

I placed my clothes in the white bag and returned with it to the kitchen.

She glanced at the bag. "Go ahead and take those to the laundry room. It's just on the other side of my studio. Even though you're a man, I sense I may be able to trust you with my washing machine. Use double detergent, and I'd recommend hot or at least warm setting. Cold water won't get the smell out. I've never been a fan of cold wash for anything other than quilting fabric, anyway.

I smiled as I headed to the laundry room. The epidemiologist in me wasn't fond of cold wash either, just for different reasons.

Ellen's laundry room was indeed a full-sized room, not just a closet. Shelves in the room sported an assortment of specialty soaps for quilting fabrics and even boxes of dyes. I long ago learned that quilters occupied the top technological tier of the fabric arts community, and it was obvious that Ellen was a major player in those ranks.

I stopped in her studio on my way back to the kitchen. The quilt top from last night was in the process of being sewn together. It appeared that Stacy's design suggestions were all incorporated. I stood for a while admiring the design. It was, indeed, beautiful, the craftsmanship superb. Yet something about the design felt uncomfortable, edgy. Knowing those two, that was intentional.

In the kitchen Ellen was placing dinner on the table. I saw three settings.

"I haven't heard from Stacy since early this morning," she offered. "I suspect she'll eat with the kids at Faye's, though I fixed a little extra in case she comes back hungry."

After the blessing, we dined on fried chicken, corn, and fresh-baked cornbread.

I began briefing her on my findings of the day. "Dee Ferguson sends her greetings. I take it you two go way back."

"Yes, indeed. We've been best friends since we were youngsters." She smiled. "Which has been a long, long time. She started with the *New Era* contributing articles to the women's section back in the 60s when the *New Era* was the main way people got their news. When you think about it, that was a big responsibility way out here before multi-channel television and the internet. Back then, we could get CBS and ABC television — NBC, too, if you lived on a high hill. That was it for TV. WHOP was the local AM station. No FM. If you wanted a worldview, you might listen to WSM from Nashville. Otherwise, your news came through the *New Era*, which you read cover to cover. For certain, the Woods family, the owners back then, would be considered right-wing aristocrats today, but who knew back then? The *New Era* was the source for all that most people knew. Dee's always been pretty progressive, and she hid it pretty well to get along and stay employed. When the paper was sold to the national chain, and so many of the senior people couldn't adapt, she hung in there and is at the top now. We spent long nights talking during those times."

I nodded, remembering the editorials in the archives I reviewed. "Thanks for recommending me to them. Everything was ready when I arrived, even the stories about the football team. Don't know if it will provide many clues to the disease, given how long ago that was. So far, though, the football team's the only thing I've found in common among the four. I've never encountered team sports as a carcinogen."

She shook her head as she took a second helping of corn. "You never know."

I continued. "It was eerie reading the stories of the day. All of the international stories — OPEC, the mining of Haiphong Harbor, the first mentions of Watergate — seemed so isolated on that day, and yet the events all turned out so important. Hard to connect the dots when they're so few and so fresh. Wish I knew the local history. The same would apply to those stories, too."

She nodded.

After the main meal we had fresh peach ice cream with peaches on top.

"I froze those last summer. You'll love the local peaches. There's nothing like a warm, tree-ripened peach."

I smiled. "I live in Georgia, the Peach State."

Ellen laughed. "Yes, of course. You must get your fill of them."

I grew reflective. "Truth be told, I haven't had real Georgia peaches in a long, long time. I've been so busy; I haven't even seen peach trees in fruit for … I don't remember how long. Baylor went with some of the church women to pick peaches a couple of summers ago. They canned most of them as a group project, and we also had fresh peaches for a week."

"John, you've got to lighten up. Life is passing you by, you know. As good as you are and as important as the work is that you do, you're missing life in the process."

We remained quiet for some time. She was right, of course.

Ellen and I sat on the porch after dinner. The orange blossoms of her *Begonia boliviensis* glowed in the sunset. I typed notes into my laptop, looking up from time to time at the changing hues of dusk. Ellen read a novel, getting up to turn on the porch lights when it got too dark to read by natural light.

Stacy drove in about 9:30. We both laughed as she came up the front steps. She was spattered and streaked with paint, even in her hair.

She grinned. "Oh, you should see the kids. I'd say they're pretty well color-coded. And they'll sleep well tonight. I worked their little butts off."

"You hungry?" Ellen got up from her seat.

"Even though I had dinner with them, I wouldn't mind a little snack." She followed Ellen into the house.

"Were you able to finish?" Ellen asked.

"Just about. We'll have a little touch-up to do in the morning. I'm going back so we can work on their parts while Mom and Aunt Faye go down to Nashville for some shopping for Mom's outfit for Saturday. All right if I borrow your car again?" Their voices trailed off as they went to the kitchen.

I continued entering my notes and emailed a copy to the lab before shutting down the computer. I got up and walked to the edge of the porch, looking southward to the glow of Nashville and heat lightning on the horizon. I would need to remember to roll up my car windows.

5 GAME NIGHT

I awoke soon after sunrise. Since Guthrie sits near the eastern edge of the Central Time Zone, I guess it must have been around 5:30, 6 o'clock. Despite the heavier than normal amount of driving I had been doing, I felt rested and eager to get on with my investigation. I completed my notes the previous night and the Patton-Dalton samples were ready to ship. Between my time inside the plant and my laundry, I was pretty sure I had a bead on at least three of the four cases. The puzzle was more that there were so few cases of Griffith's. Given the technology, reporting, and political climate of those times, it was possible that many cases were unreported, at least in a way that would trigger a hotspot investigation.

Fortunately for the investigation, cancers triggered by the suspect chemicals are rather constant in their genetic signature. Frank's samples from Tuesday would have been put in for overnight analysis Thursday if the lab wasn't too backed up. I resolved to call Susan once I got to the Guthrie medical office.

By 6:30 I had showered and dressed and was ready for the day. I figured it was too early even for Ellen, so I stepped out of my room and quietly closed the door. The morning haze and humidity lent softness to everything. I decided to take a walk around the block, starting westward, since I had not gone that way yet. I eased down the driveway until I heard the front door open and shut.

"See you tonight, Ms. Miller!" Stacy called behind her. She bounded down the front steps, keys sounding in her hands. She broke into a wide smile when she saw me. "Yo, Doctor P! Up pretty early for a city boy."

I laughed. "And you're not a city girl?"

"Nope. I'm adopted. I'm off to Aunt Faye's. Going to be a busy day." She unlocked Ellen's car. "See you at the game tonight."

"Game?"

"Football. It's Friday"

I looked surprisèd. "Seems too warm for football."

She shook her head. "Not American football — football. The teams here play soccer during the summer to keep in shape for the winter season of American football. There'll be as many people watching tonight as at a regular season game."

"I didn't know about it."

"Well, ya gotta come out. Otherwise you'd be the only one in town not there."

"OK, then."

"Gotta go. Ellen will be glad to see you in there. She figured you wouldn't be up for another hour or so. She fixed goetta for breakfast — a yummy sausage and oats dish from Cincinnati. It's good, you'll love it."

Stacy got into the car and drove off. I turned back to the house and announced my presence. Ellen was indeed glad to see me early. We enjoyed the breakfast, the first time I'd eaten goetta since an investigation in Cincinnati several years ago, where goetta was a local delicacy. We talked about a wide range of topics.

"I heard Stacy say something last night about working with the kids on their parts?"

Ellen smiled as she cleared the dishes. "And that's all you need to know for now. Like we said, best to maintain plausible deniability. She's still the fearless little girl I remember, just with a lot more experience and energy now. You'll see soon enough."

"She said she'd see me at the game tonight. I didn't know about the game."

"Right. We shouldn't assume you know all about the local customs. We'll be playing Trigg County tonight. Should be a good game. You'll probably see a higher score than usual if you're familiar with soccer. I'm not sure if we have stronger men on the field or our goalies aren't as good. We need to play a more experienced team sometime."

"Soccer's kind of new as a regular sport out here, isn't it?"

"I guess so. It was Doc Isabel's idea. The game keeps the team sharp during the off-football season and cuts down on the make-up training getting ready for the fall season. Since we began soccer, we've had regular winning seasons. Winning hadn't been the norm since the '73 team. That's a long drought."

"What time is the game?" I asked.

"6:30."

"I'll be sure to get an early dinner."

She chuckled. "We all eat at the game. Mireese runs the concessions with Ferrell's. It's all classy. I remember when the Doc first got soccer going, the old timers thought it was silly — too 'frou-frou.' Now it's a point of pride, and we're seeing two-phase football popping up in high schools across the state. Puts the kids in the program at an advantage over some of the better schools, too."

I finished my goetta and coffee, picked up my samples, and headed to the office by way of the post office. Jack was waiting for me.

"What body parts have we got today, Doc?"

"None today. Pretty boring for a change — chemical contamination samples from the Patton-Dalton plant. I guess we should say hazardous, though I doubt even that."

"You think that's what gave 'em the cancer?"

"Don't know. While the chemicals are suspect, it seems there should have been other cases."

"Several people from around here who worked at the plant died from cancer. Sheriff's brother, for instance."

I nodded. "Do you happen to know if the others presented the same way? Did they have all those bumps?"

Jack thought for a moment. "No, I don't think so. I've been out to see Frank and Walt. Their cancer's pretty creepy. The others didn't have the blisters and bumps. I would have remembered that."

We finished the package paperwork; I thanked Jack and then walked over to the office. Isabel was having a conversation with a small boy, perhaps four or five years old. His hand sported a fresh bandage. A woman, I guessed his mother, looked on with a relieved smile.

Isabel lectured him, "All right, now, you're going to keep that bandage on for a couple of days. Right?"

The child nodded.

"And you're not going to pick at the bandage so we don't have to glue it on. Right?"

He nodded with more enthusiasm.

"And if your mom tells you to stay away from the stove, you're going to …?" Isabel reached out and gently lifted his chin, pointing his face to hers.

"Stay away from the stove," he replied with all the seriousness he could muster.

Isabel smiled. "Right answer, Timmy. OK, give me a hug and you guys can be on your way."

The boy hugged her.

"You want an adventure book?" Isabel asked.

He nodded.

She handed him a small comic book, an educational book for small children the Public Health Service had produced for young readers and pre-readers. I admired the creative teaching of these little books and had often wondered if they were well received by children. This little boy seemed eager enough.

Isabel straightened up as the boy took his adventure book to a seat in the waiting room. She adjusted her headscarf and turned to Timmy's mother. "He'll be fine. Might be red for a day, maybe a small blister or two. He'll be back to full speed in two days. The bandage is as much to keep the ointment off your furniture as it is for his hand. Knowing Timmy, I doubt the bandage will last the day."

The mother took a deep breath. "Thank you so much. I feel so bad about this."

"No, no, you can't hover over him every second. You wouldn't want to. You got him here right away. He learned in a way he won't forget that the stove is hot and that you listen to your mom."

The mother gathered her things and motioned for Timmy to follow her. "Well, thanks again. I hope we won't be seeing you medically for a while."

"Is he going into kindergarten this fall?"

The mother nodded.

"Make an appointment in early August for his preschool exam."

"OK," the mom agreed.

They left the office as Isabel made notes in her patient records.

"Morning, Dr. Parker."

"Morning, Dr. Rodriguez."

She scowled and shook her head. "Morning, John."

"Morning, Isabel," I replied with a grin.

She smiled in return.

My cell phone rang. I took it from my pocket, saw "Susan" on caller ID, and answered it. "Susan, you beat me to the phone by a matter of minutes. How are things in beautiful Atlanta?"

Isabel grinned as she continued with her notes.

"John, Mike wants to know if there was any possibility of contamination with the Frank Johnson samples. Any strange chemicals from the embalming process?"

I sat down in a chair in the room. "No, Bill Carson runs a textbook operation. Besides, the body wasn't embalmed. It was just being prepared for cremation."

The phone was quiet. I imagined Susan talking with Mike. "I'm putting him on so he can tell you what he found."

"Dr. Parker, this is Mike. I put the samples into all the analyses you asked for. When I got the results back from the mass spec lab, the peaks on the chart were really tiny. I went back to the lab, and they looked at it and said something out of the usual range was pulling the normalization off. The tech guy pulled up the data, and sure enough, there was a spike down at eight."

"Eight?"

"Yes, sir. Eight."

"Beryllium?"

Isabel looked up from her notes and cocked her head to listen.

"Yes, sir," Mike continued, "the tech guy said he'd seen it only a couple of times, once after an accident at the Savannah nuclear research center. He said it's not a good thing to be exposed to."

"I guess it wouldn't be. Beryllium's so rare I don't even remember its epidemiology. I'll have to look into that. Do you have any genetics back?"

"Yes, sir. Unfortunately, the beryllium thing took up my time yesterday, so I only got to glance over the results. I saw several flags. I'll give you a call this afternoon after I have a chance to go over the results. We got the Walt Tinley samples yesterday, and they're in process now."

"Thanks, Mike. Anything else?"

"Not yet. Let me check with Susan. No, nothing from her, either."

"Thanks for the update. I'll look forward to your call. I just put some chemical samples into the mail. You should get them tomorrow."

"Saturday?"

I thought a moment. "Sorry. Monday. I sent them registered mail, not express. Does the mass spec lab operate on the weekend?"

"No."

"Right. No need to change it then. Add beryllium to the substances of interest for the chemical samples."

"Yes, sir."

"Thank you, Mike. And thank Susan. Talk to you later."

I put the phone back in my pocket and looked to Isabel. "That was strange. The samples I sent back to the lab contained beryllium."

"Beryllium? Haven't heard that in a long time. Isn't that what kills Superman?" she asked.

I smiled. "I think that would be Kryptonite. Beryllium's a very light element, atomic number four, atomic weight eight. Our mass spectroscopy lab picked it up. I recall it's used in some special copper alloys and in the atomic industry because it doesn't absorb much radiation. The little window in your x-ray machine is made of beryllium. I seem to recall that it's a class-1 carcinogen, so we'll need to find out where he might have been exposed."

"Frank worked out in the Pacific when he was in the Air Force. It was at one of those old nuclear test sites," she offered.

"True. Still, I doubt it has a dwell time in the body that long."

Isabel continued, "What about the lumber treatment?"

"Beryllium would be forbidden for lumber treatment. And unlikely, too — it's expensive. Chromated copper arsenate is also forbidden. I need to find some lumber samples from that batch."

"I'll be paying Ron Widing a visit this afternoon, and I'm sure you'll want to talk to him, too. He's not doing well, so you'd best ask your questions while you can. He was starting a project with that lumber, though

I don't think he got it underway before they all found out it was contaminated. There may be some set aside in his shed."

I nodded.

"I've got him on the schedule for two o'clock. We'll leave here around 1:30. Take your car too 'cause I'll need to go home to get my uniform before the game."

"You play soccer?"

She giggled, a pleasant, throaty giggle. "No, I'm the sideline medical staff. You've got two teams of strong, heavy young men coming at each other at high velocity without padding. Things happen. You can be my assistant. Good chance to get to know your new community."

"'My' community?"

She smiled.

An older gentleman with the sun-bronzed look of a farmer entered the clinic. He moved slowly with stiff, dignified grace.

"Mornin', Doc."

"Good morning, Mr. Adams. How are we today?"

"Between the damned bugs tryin' to eat my corn before it's grown and the guv'ment taxin' away what the bugs don't eat, I could be better."

He looked to me and smiled, his face crinkling into a hundred wisdom lines. "I ain't complainin'. I'm 85. I've survived the damned Nazis at Normandy, the Communists, the Democrats, the Republicans, drought, and tornados. Hell, it'll take a lot more'n bugs and taxes to get me down." He thrust his hand forward. "Johnnie Adams, sir. I reckon you must be Dr. Parker."

"I am, sir. Are you the Johnnie Adams of Riverbend Farm?"

He turned to Isabel, still smiling. "You been tellin' him all our secrets?"

She shook her head. "Not a word, Mr. Adams." She looked at me.

I chuckled. "Lucky guess. I imagine you've heard I've been researching the cancer that's attacking Frank, Walt, Ron, and Jim. Yesterday, my research took me to the papers from back in the 70s, including their football days. I remember seeing that Johnnie Adams of Riverbend Farm was one of the team sponsors. Did I put that together right?"

Mr. Adams turned to Isabel. "He's good. He's real good."

She smiled. "That he is."

He frowned. "Damned shame about that team. They were right on the edge — could'a gone all the way to the state championship. Three near-perfect years and then in October '73, just fell apart."

"I'm coming to appreciate what a blow that was to the community. What happened?"

He shook his head. "Damned if I know. A lot of folks think it was the coach. I can't tell what's true or not. Reggie Tatum — Coach Tatum — must have pushed those kids pretty hard. In the six or eight years he was there, they went from permanent losers to almost state champions. Other folks think it might be drugs of some kind. Jim, it wouldn't surprise me. Ron, maybe. Not Frank or Walt, and definitely not Dale Liston. Mind you, those were hard-drinkin' kids. They say ole Sheriff Cox had DUI tickets preprinted with their names. He'd let 'em go as long as we were winnin.'"

His face grew sad as he stared at the floor. "That was a damned miserable year, Dr. Parker. The team fallin' apart was more of a final blow. Even I'll admit Washington was in a worse mess then than it is now. And you had the little girl disappearin', and the war, and the oil — almost went broke that harvest payin' for gas for my tractor."

He turned back to me, folding his arms so that each hand grasped the opposite elbow. "You got some new treatment for arthritis?"

Isabel retrieved his folder from the small pile on her desk. "Mr. Adams has osteoarthritis. While it bothers him, he's got less than you might expect for an 85-year-old crusty curmudgeon. I've got him on celecoxib and duloxetine. Last time, you told me that helped a lot."

Mr. Adams nodded. "True. I get around a lot better. I still feel it, most often in the mornin'. I want it fixed."

"Dr. Rodriguez is following the best and proven recommendations. There's a lot of good research going on. You just hold on 'til 90. There may be some new treatments to try by then. We don't even know if they're safe in rats yet."

He glanced back and forth between the two of us and then nodded. "I can do that."

I smiled, shook his hand again, and wished him well.

Returning to "my" office, I saw that Isabel had added folders of some of the family members to my desk. I had constructed a timeline for each of the four men on my computer and had flagged notes for several events across their medical histories. I was eager to get the genetics results. Knowing as we did the stage of the disease and the synchronized progression of the two patients I had examined, I was pretty sure I could backtrack to the time of onset, perhaps within a month or two. I had redlined four items from their records. Starting in June of 2005, she had entered long narratives about their exposure to the lumber. She saw all four displaying severe rashes and noted her thoughts by July that the rashes could have been caused by Jim Dulaney's illegal lumber. In November 2006, they had all received flu shots. In January 2006, she had recommended senior vitamins to all four. Then, in October 2007, all four began displaying the first nodules of what would become Griffith's sarcoma. At first, she identified them as warts, which would be consistent with what we know of the disease. Her first referral to the VA hospital was in May '06. There was nothing in the records that I could connect with beryllium exposure, though I wasn't sure how that would present. The patient notes kept by Isabel's predecessors were not so meticulous. Walt Tinley's record from a Dr. Baxter in Clarksville, Tennessee, was the only one to mention the moldy hay and then only as "Hay allergy: prescribed Benadryl" on April 7, 2001.

I spent the morning comparing the spouses' and children's records to those of the men. Faye Johnson and Sharon Barker had received flu shots within a few days of Frank and Walt. Donna Dulaney's record noted, "refused" for the flu shot. Isabel had recommended senior women's vitamins to Faye in January 2007. There were no other common elements that I could see in any of the records. Gina Barker's chart was typical of a young farm girl. The family records had very little overlap with those of the four men. That was good news both for the families and for my investigation.

About a quarter 'til noon, Dr. Rodriguez appeared in the doorway. "Amazing. You're still awake."

"Oh, it's riveting reading. Intense plot, colorful characters. Should be a best-seller."

She smiled. "Is the writing clear?"

I nodded. "Yes. I meant to compliment your style. Both clear and very thorough. I found a couple of commonalities. They're long shots. I don't suppose you kept records of the lot numbers of the flu vaccines, did you?"

"Oh, ye of little faith. Of course I have those."

"Wow! The flu shots were one of the few things they had in common in your records. You recommended vitamins, though I doubt the men would have told you what they purchased."

"No, I gave them sample bottles to get 'em started."

"Common brand?" I asked.

"No, it was some generic brand that was trying to break into the market. Senior medicine's a growth industry — I don't need to tell you that. The guys didn't like that brand. You'd have to check with them what they went with after that — if they did."

"I don't see much in common with the relatives. That's good, I think." I smiled. "I saw that Donna Dulaney refused the flu shot. Is she anti-vaccine?"

Isabel rolled her eyes. "No, she's Donna." She shook her head. "I'll get the vaccine records."

She was back in about a minute with another folder. It contained page after page of vaccine lot number stickers removed from the vaccine vials with the names of the recipients penned beside them and dates given.

I looked up at her. "This is fabulous. Outside the military, very few doctors have kept such records."

She folded her arms, grinning with pride. "Like the bumper sticker says, 'Nurses do it better.'"

I nodded in agreement.

"Hey, I'm going for a walk and a bite to eat," she said. "I'd like to head out to Ron Widing's about one. Will you be ready to follow me?"

"I will. I'm working my way down Ferrell's menu. I think it's a hamburger today. If things go well, I should wrap up the investigation before my arteries give out."

She turned to go. "Hmmm."

Lunch was indeed hamburgers, well prepared, with fresh-cut potato fries. Most of the conversation in the café was centered on the game coming up that night. Though I knew little about the teams or the players, I was impressed with the sophistication of their soccer analysis. The only familiar name was Chris Waddail, on whom they seemed to be pinning their hopes.

I left my customary tip and was making my way to the door when Mary, my server, caught up with me. "You know, you don't need to leave a tip. It's not done much around here."

I rubbed my hand on my chin. "It's a tradition of mine. As long as it's not offensive, I consider it a courtesy, like 'please,' 'thank you,' 'sir,' and 'ma'am.'"

She smiled. "Oh, it's not offensive at all. Just wanted you to know it wasn't required or anything."

I thanked her for the good cooking and made my way back to the office. Isabel was packing her doctor bag. She looked up. "I'll be ready in about 15 minutes if you want to go get your car."

I turned around and headed to Ellen's. I found her weeding a row of peonies when I arrived.

She looked up. "Good thing the peonies last as long as they do. I planted this row back in the 60s to use on Memorial Days to decorate the graves. With the warming over the years, the flowering's moved up almost ten days. If this keeps up, in another ten years or so I'll have to go with something else. Pity. Peonies are a good Decoration Day flower. Generous with their blooms, and they smell pretty good. This is an old variety that doesn't get mildew."

I nodded. "Bet it makes a nice table decoration, too."

"Oh, no, they attract ants, which dine on the natural wax that covers the buds. The flowers are full of ants. When I cut the flowers, I put them in a bucket of water, and they're in the car only long enough to get them to the cemetery. I'll have ants in the car for a month after that."

I examined one of the blossoms. Sure enough, it was full of ants.

"So, John, what are you up to this afternoon?"

"Dr. Rodriguez and I are on our way to see Ron Widing. I'm dropping by to get my car. I'm following her, since she'll be going home to get ready for the game."

"Oh, good. I have something for you to take to Ron." She got up stiffly from her weeding. "That used to be easier. Do yourself a favor, John. Stay young. It's much better."

I smiled and nodded. "I'll try."

"You do that." She headed into the house and emerged a few minutes later with a small canning jar containing some preserves.

"It's pear honey. I made it last fall. It's one of his favorites. I don't reckon he's got much of an appetite, still this might cheer him up a little." There was sadness in her face. "Ron's a good man. He's always been a champion for the truth, and I admire that. You tell him I said so."

"I promise."

I placed the pear honey on the passenger seat, waved goodbye, and drove back to the clinic. Isabel was waiting beside her Prius. As I drove up, she approached my open window.

"Just follow me. We'll be heading by the water treatment plant and out Hadenville Road about ten miles. You have a GPS in your car?"

"Yes, ma'am."

"Knowing you, you won't need it, though I wouldn't want you wandering around out in the wilderness. Not much cell phone reception out there, and, as you know, your GPS works off the towers."

She got into her car and I followed. Isabel was a cautious driver and I had no trouble keeping up. I made a mental note of distinctive landmarks for the trip back. About ten miles from town, we turned into a narrow drive with weedy banks on both sides. At the end of the drive, a small, unremarkable cottage stood in a clearing. The quality of the grass suggested irregular mowing. A small tractor was parked near an outbuilding beyond the cottage. Vines growing around the rear tire told a tale of plans deferred. The outbuilding was larger than a shed, smaller than a full barn. Perhaps I might find some of the suspect lumber inside. I would ask.

Isabel set her bag on the ground and adjusted her headscarf. "His nursing aide's name is Roberta. She's one of my favorites; competent, reliable, and a good record-keeper."

Isabel knocked on the door.

Roberta opened it. She was a slender black woman, perhaps mid-thirties. "Hey, sweetie. Good to see you. And you brought the new doctor with you." She extended her hand to me. "Roberta Bussell, Dr. Parker. Pleased to meet you."

I shook her hand, a strong grip. "The pleasure is mine. You come with highest recommendations."

She smiled a wide smile. "We do what we do. Ron's been expecting you two. Come on back."

I sensed what I've come to call "the smell of death" there. I had not noticed it at Faye's or at the Tinleys'. I suspect Gina kept Walt's place open, bright, and aired. Ron's place was darker and more closed up. Maybe the essence of death was a combination of ointments and the smell of humans who can't move about as much as they'd like. I always felt a sense of foreboding in the presence of that smell.

We followed Roberta into the bedroom, where Ron managed a smile as he struggled to sit up. "Doc Isabel, good to see you again. And I see you brought the big guns with you."

I turned to look behind me and he laughed. Ron's laugh brought on a coughing fit, as it had with Walt. I made a mental note to be sensitive to that.

"I'm sorry," I said.

Ron waved his hand. The coughing subsided. "Not to worry. Humor's a scarce commodity these days."

His condition was as bad as — maybe even worse than — Walt's. Nodules above his right eye had almost forced it closed. Isabel donned gloves and began taking his vital signs — blood pressure, temperature, pulse. He turned to her and smiled. Then he turned to me.

"You bring any new tools for the doc?"

"No, sir, I'm afraid I didn't. Dr. Rodriguez has kept up on all the current research, even some treatments I hadn't heard about. You're getting state-of-the-art care."

"Good." He eased back on the pillows. "And we three get the finest caregivers to see us off, eh?"

I guess the confusion showed on my face.

"Frank had Faye fussing over him. Walt has Gina and Sharon. I've got Roberta. And we all three have the doc." He smiled and closed his eyes for a moment. Opening them again, he looked at me with a mischievous smile. "You thought I forgot Jim, didn't you? You haven't visited him yet, I'll bet? Some people leave in the presence of a little bit of heaven, others in a corner of hell."

I looked up to see Isabel shaking her head. She struggled for tactful phrasing. "Jim Dulaney's family doesn't … display the warmth you'd like to see under the circumstances."

"Warmth? He'd feel more warmth from garter snakes. No, I've got it good — given the alternatives." He reached out and took Roberta's hand.

As Isabel finished her examination, our conversation drifted to the night's soccer game. Ron gave me a player-by-player analysis of the Todd County team. He was predicting a two-goal victory over Trigg County.

Isabel grinned. "I'd play that bet, John. Ron's never wrong." She finished repacking her bag. "Speaking of which, I need to get on home and get some rest before the evening festivities. You be able to find your way back, Dr. Parker? I can leave you two to talk if you'd like."

"I'll be fine. I'd like that, if it's OK with Ron."

He seemed eager. "That'd be great."

Isabel talked over some changes in Ron's medication with Roberta as they left together.

Ron grew serious. He lowered his voice. "Yeah, old Jim's getting an early taste of hell. Justice, I reckon."

I felt uneasy. "I'm still getting to know the people behind the disease. Jim Dulaney doesn't seem to have a lot of friends. I sense a lot of hostility whenever his name comes up."

"Hmmm." He closed his eyes and took a deep breath before proceeding. "Faye tells me you're a Baptist, a deacon."

I raised my eyebrows.

"She came out yesterday afternoon with Jane. I had a real crush on Jane back in high school. She was a wild one. They brought me a chicken potpie. While my appetite's not what it used to be, that pie was so good."

"I can imagine. I had dinner with Faye and Sarah Tuesday night," I said.

"Lucky you. Anyway, as a Baptist you've got to have thoughts about judgment, divine retribution."

"I do, quite often since I've been here. It seems to be a topic on a lot of people's minds. My training and predisposition is to look for cause and effect and link them. You've got causes in spades out here. I know for certain that causes, effects, and divine guidance are often indistinguishable."

He looked at me in silence for a while. "I wish I'd had you as a Sunday school teacher way back when. While I was never very religious, I respect anyone who's serious about religion and thoughtful. Since this damned cancer, I've spent a lot more time thinking about the big picture. Samuel Johnson was right about impending death concentrating the mind."

I nodded. "Yes. In his example, I think it was an impending hanging."

"Still a death sentence, a judgment," Ron continued.

"I've been gathering a lot of information on the possible causes of the sarcoma that the four of you have. I've found carcinogens in your air stretching back to the 60s, biological carcinogens in moldy hay, and maybe in lumber. I haven't found any evidence for viruses; still I haven't ruled them out. I was going to ask you if you had any of that contaminated lumber still around and, if so, could I get a sample. All four of you were exposed to those cancer-causing agents in some combination. Still, I've got this gut feeling that I'm missing something. You spent your life putting these kinds of stories together. Do you think I'm missing something?"

"Heh." A look of disgust moved over his face. "Those reeking boards are still stacked up in the shed. You're welcome to all of it. And you're right: we've all been exposed to more than our fair share of poisons. So has everybody else. We're the only ones who got the disease. Just the four of us. All four at the same time. I'll give coincidence some role in some things; not this."

"I'm listening," I said.

"Are you an MD doctor or a PhD doctor?

"Both, as a matter of fact. PhD in epidemiology, MD as well."

"Fair enough. You're one of my doctors, then. We both know the importance of patient confidentiality and protecting sources." He took a deep breath and exhaled slowly. "I'm not quite ready. I'm writing everything down. It's on the computer, just not finished."

"What're you writing down? If you've got something that might help the community avoid this cancer, I'd like to know. We'd all like to know."

He smiled a wistful smile. "Naw, that's not it. You might say it's more a sports piece, a dark sports piece. What happens to people when winning is everything, when winning's the only thing. It's a story of betrayal and manipulation."

"The '73 team?" I asked.

"You don't miss much."

"I learned a long time ago that the devil's in the detail. The reason CDC sent me here was to find a common link among the four of you so that we know how to avoid Griffith's in the future. The four of you have precious little in common. The '73 team's one of them. The lumber is another. Given the progression of every cancer we know, 1973 is too far back to be a direct cause. The team is one of the few bonds you have other than the lumber."

Ron sighed. "I don't mean to be difficult. And you have my word; I wouldn't keep anything from you if it affected the health of the community. I'm not that kind."

I nodded. "That's what Ellen Miller says."

He smiled. "Thank God for people like Ellen. She's good. She could have done big things in a place that appreciated her — maybe national prominence. Instead, she chose to do good here. That's special." He thought for a bit and then looked at me. "I'm not avoiding your question, Doc. There are people involved in my final story. Living people. Living people who will be hurt by crushing disappointment at the failures of those they loved and still love. Like I said, it's on my computer, just not finished. And it won't change what you can report 'cause you're not going to put anything in your report about divine retribution." He looked at me with a penetrating stare. "Are you?"

I stared back at him and took a deep breath. "I've never listed divine retribution as the root cause of any disease. I've never had a reason to. If I find that's the cause in the end, though, I promise that's what I'll put in my report."

"Then you're a man of integrity. Tell you what. If I don't get the piece finished before I go, I'll leave the notes to you. If I finish, you get to see the first draft. If not, I'll make sure Roberta gives you what I have."

I sensed he wasn't going to reveal anything more for now. I reached for the jar at the base of my chair. "Speaking of Ellen Miller, I have something from her for you." I handed him the jar of preserves.

He beamed. "Ah, pear honey. Now this is good stuff. Thick and super sweet and aromatic. Being a bachelor, I don't eat so well. The last few days have been good, really good, though. Thank her for me when you get back. Tell her it made my day."

"I will do that," I promised. "All right if I draw a little blood?"

He nodded and I made quick work of the sampling, explaining what I was doing as I went along. He seemed genuinely interested the whole process, including my precautions against contamination. After I finished, he closed his eyes as he rested his head on the pillow. "I won't be able to make Frank's funeral I think. Memorial service I guess to be technical. You'll be going, won't you?"

"Yes, sir," I replied.

"It isn't fair of me to ask you. I'm just running out of options. Tell Jane I love her. Present tense. Promise me you'll tell her. My life's full of regrets. That's gotta be my biggest, that I never told her. Stupid thing to not do."

"I promise," I vowed.

"Thank you. Thank you for coming out here. Thank you for bringing Ellen's pear honey. Thank you for listening. And thank you for trying to fight to protect us from disease and pestilence. Don't know if many people appreciate what you do. But I know."

I heard Roberta walking through the house heading our way. I patted his hand. "It is an honor, a true honor."

Roberta entered the room. She spied the jar he held in his hand and smiled. "Looks like you got more food presents from your lady admirers." She turned to me. "Did you two have fun talkin' old times?"

I nodded. "Yes, ma'am."

"Roberta, Doc Parker's going to get some of that lumber out in the barn before he goes."

She made a face. "Why would you want that smelly old stuff? It's nasty."

I explained, "That's why I want some samples. We need to check whether it's related to the cancers."

"I see. Well, let me get you some plastic to wrap it up in. You don't want to be handlin' it."

"Thanks. That sounds like a good idea. I've got gloves in the car."

"Good. Ron told me how he got blisters just hauling it from Jim's truck to the barn. Nasty stuff. Nasty."

I rose, thanked Ron, and prepared to follow Roberta to get some plastic sheeting.

As I reached the door, Ron spoke. "Doc?"

I turned and waited.

"Find Coach Tatum. He vanished in '74. Bet he hasn't been exposed to any of the things we've been exposed to. Bet he's got the cancer, too. Do it."

"I will. You have my word."

He closed his eyes and I followed Roberta. We rummaged in a small room in the front of the house.

"Ron was going to make this into a guest room. Never got around to it. Got the paint and ... ah, here's what I was lookin' for ... plastic to put down on the floor while he painted."

We stopped by my car to get some gloves and then headed to the barn. I began to smell the creosote while still 20 feet or so from the building. Though the structure was quite open, the air inside hung heavy with a powerful chemical odor. An abandoned power saw lay on the ground amid some small cut pieces, another project abandoned and now irrelevant.

Roberta held out a portion of the plastic sheeting, and I gathered several small chunks of wood and scooped up some of the sawdust to place in the plastic. We left the barn as soon as we could.

Outside, I wrapped the samples, rolling them in layers of the sheeting. "I see what you mean by 'nasty.' I'll use that word in my report."

"Yes. When the time comes to clear all this out, they'll need to get those people in space suits to clean it up," Roberta said.

"I think you're right. Seems a lot of that happening out here. The space suit guys were over at the old Patton-Dalton place in Hopkinsville yesterday."

"Hmmmm. My mama told me about that place. More nasty."

I agreed. Back at the car, I retrieved some medical tape and secured the plastic. I put the lumber in the trunk, hoping the odor wouldn't leak out enough to smell up the car.

I thanked Roberta for her help and for looking after Ron Widing so well.

"He deserves looking after, Dr. Parker. Our church's prayin' for him. We've moved our prayers from him gettin' better to him havin' a peaceful passin'. I can tell he's ready. Only thing keeps him goin' is he wants to finish one last story. I've seen that before a lot. Waitin' for a weddin', waitin' for a gran'child to be born, waitin' for a child to get back from service. One last thing to hold on for. He's ready otherwise."

I gave her a hug, thanked her again, got into the car and headed back to town. I drove with care, checking off the distinct landmarks in reverse order as I returned, an old tire turned inside out and painted white acting as a giant flower pot, a mound of stones cleared from a field and piled near the road, and the field at the edge of town with the billboard reading "Bring Back the Gold Standard."

I stopped by the clinic. Isabel's car was not there. I processed Ron's samples so that I could get them to the post office before the daily pickup. I made it there with only a few minutes to spare. I continued on to Ellen's and parked. Her row of peonies was now weeded, the pulled weeds wilting as mulch. I figured Ellen wouldn't go for packaged mulch if local plant debris were available. As I observed the bed, I heard the front door open. Ellen descended the steps, flower clippers in hand.

"How's Ron?"

"Hmmmm. I was about to say not bad. That wouldn't be true. Ron's in really bad shape. He's just not letting the disease defeat him. He's enjoyed the visits he's been getting and thanks you so much for the pear honey. Faye and Jane brought him a chicken potpie yesterday."

Ellen grinned.

"He and Jane were an item back in high school?"

She dropped her grin. "No. Wish they had been. Things would have been better for both. I think he was getting up the courage to approach her in '73 when everything fell apart. When she ran off, they lost track of each other. Pity."

"Ron and I talked about many things. He's had a lot of time to think," I suggested

"He always was a thoughtful one," she agreed.

"Ron said I should find Coach Tatum. Though he was being very cryptic, he believes Coach Tatum has the cancer too. He wouldn't say why."

"Reggie Tatum was never one of my favorite persons. We came at life from very different angles. For him, the game was everything. He didn't care for the arts or English — 'sissy stuff.' We didn't have a lot of direct contact. In '73 he was coaching high school and I was teaching fourth grade. We were both on the Board of Education advisory committee. He always ranted about English teachers holding his players back. Even though the standards weren't what they are today, you could lose a player to grades. After an afternoon of practicing with Coach Tatum, a young man didn't have the energy to work on a paper about *Canterbury Tales*. Those boys followed him faithfully, too. If they performed, he made them believe they were invincible.

"Those attitudes got him and his team in trouble. I know of ..." — she paused to tally — "... at least four times that he was called before the Board. Twice — once in fall of '71 and again in the summer of '72 — players collapsed of heat stroke during some of his full-uniform practices. Pete Massey died as a result. Reggie didn't even attend the funeral. I've never forgiven him for that." I could see Ellen's grip tighten on the flower clippers.

"While the Board gave him a pass on the '71 incident, they couldn't sweep it under the rug after Pete's death. Several of his players were convicted of rape. In the '60s and '70s, the 'boys will be boys' defense still went a long way. Still, he'd beefed them up to the point that the rapes could be pretty violent. In the end, what put an end to the rapes was when the mayor of Russellville's daughter had her jaw broken when she tried to resist one of his players. Russellville's in Logan County, so they weren't giving any passes. Reggie had defended that young man two other times. The coach turned on him during that trial, and the young man committed suicide in jail."

"Was that Dale Liston? I thought he died at home."

She shook her head. "No. Dale was two years later, after the coach had blown town."

"Wow!" I was almost speechless. "I'm beginning to see why the players aren't talking about him. Where did he go?"

Ellen shrugged. "No one knows. The Todd County team had been steam-rolling the other teams for three years and then just crashed in October of 1973. On Monday of the first or second week of November, Coach Tatum didn't show up at the high school. People called to the house and went out to check. His wife said he'd packed up for a conference that morning and left, though there were no conferences scheduled that anyone knew of. The sheriff later found out he'd withdrawn about 7,000 dollars the Friday before from a slush fund he kept at the Elkton Bank. They didn't have Saturday hours in those days. 7,000 went a long way back then. Credit cards were just becoming commonplace, and he didn't have one. He didn't take his checkbook, either. All in all, it was pretty clear he didn't want to be found."

"Why didn't he want to be found?" I asked.

She shook her head. "Beats me. Ole Sheriff Cox did a sort of investigation — interviewed the high school staff and players. No one much wanted to talk. I think Reggie had terrorized too many of them by that point. It was like a curtain of silence fell over his disappearance. It's a big world out there. Plenty of places to hide. If a person doesn't want to be found, they can vanish if they're clever. Seems he was clever enough."

We stood watching the peony bed in silence for some time. "Ellen, Ron said that I should find him, that he is somehow linked to the cancer."

She turned to face me. I noticed for the first time that she had ice-blue eyes. "If Ron Widing told me I should check anything out, I'd do it," she confirmed.

"OK. I'll start some queries."

"Talk to Doc Isabel. She's already tried."

"I thought she only came here about ten years ago."

Ellen nodded. "True. You know how she is about her records. Some of her patients, even those getting on in years, still feel the effects of playing under Reggie Tatum. She'd like to know what he did to them, what he might have given them. She's done her best to find him. Unfortunately for her, the trail's pretty cold by now. Fortunate for him, though."

"I'll talk to her. I have access to tools she wouldn't be able to access."

"Good."

We watched the peonies a while longer. They didn't seem to have grown any more. It was approaching 5:30. I turned to her. "I should get a bite to eat before the game."

She waved her hands in dismissal. "Like I told you this morning, you'll want to eat at the game. Mireese takes all of that wonderful heart attack food that Ferrell's makes and transforms it onto a whole higher plane." She grinned. "You're not going to find any other food places open anyway on game night."

"Got it. Can I give you a lift? I'm less likely to get lost that way."

"You haven't gotten lost since you've been here. You're getting a feel for the place. Thanks for the offer. I need to pick up Miss Ledbetter and Shirley. The high school's right on Main Street just before you get to downtown Elkton. You must have passed it coming back from Hopkinsville."

I smiled at her use of the word "downtown" applied to Elkton. "Yes, I think I did notice the high school. What time should I be there?"

"The Rebels take the field at seven. There's always plenty going on by 6:30. The doc gets there about 6, 6:15, so you might want to get washed up and head on over there. I hear you're her intern tonight." She grinned. "That's a good thing. Get to know all the juicy goings-on behind the scenes. Lotta' history at a football game."

I started toward my room before remembering the lumber beside my specimen case in the trunk of the car. I called to Ellen, who was almost at the front door. "I brought back some lumber samples from Ron Widing's place. I don't think I want to take 'em into my room, and I don't want to leave them in the car, either, or out where they might get damp."

She turned from the door and came to the edge of her porch facing the driveway. "No, I guess you wouldn't want them in the house. Can you put them just inside the garage? The side door for the garage isn't locked. It's empty right now. Stacy's still got the car. She'll be back any minute so we can pick up the other ladies. As long as it's not in the main path tonight, it'll be fine."

"Thank you."

She waved and headed back into the house while I took the plastic-wrapped, stinking wood from the trunk to the garage. The interior of her garage was neat, as I expected, sparse except for a dresser in the back, set atop some newspapers, perhaps in preparation for refinishing. The far wall sported a long neat rack with hoes, rakes, and shovels. Below the tools were several bags of organic fertilizers, each bag resting in a separate plastic bin. The interior of her garage was the very picture of well-researched simplicity.

I laid the package against the wall just to the left of the door, closed the door, and went to my room. I had taken specimens from Ron as we talked. I would not have time to pack them now, and I could take care of that after the game if I still had the energy, or else in the morning. I opened my suitcase and took out my white lab coat. Isabel had not mentioned what I should wear. I could always leave it in the car if it was out of place.

I left my room and got to the car just as Stacy drove into the driveway. She flashed a broad, happy smile when she saw me. She was at least as paint-speckled as the previous night.

"Hey, Doctor P. Lookin' good!"

"You, too. You're pretty well decorated."

She turned her head from side to side so that I could see her cheeks. I could see then that some of the marks were intentional.

She grinned. "We were practicing."

"Practicing what?"

"You'll see." She reached into Ellen's car and pulled out a bright red tee shirt with "Rebels" emblazoned on it. "It's game night! I've gotta' get ready. I'm the driver tonight."

"I heard. I'll see you there," I shouted.

Stacy ran to the house and bounded up the steps. She possessed a powerful beauty and grace that complemented her powerful positive attitude.

It took me a mere 15 minutes to reach the high school. Several students in orange vests were on station directing traffic. I slowed nearing the drive into the school and rolled down my window as a student approached. "I'm Dr. Parker. I'm —"

"Yes, sir, Doc Isabel said to expect you. There's a spot reserved for you over there by her Prius. It's got a traffic cone with your name on it."

I smiled. "Thank you." Though I thought I was on the early side of early, the lot was already filling up. Isabel stood beside her car talking on her cell phone. I was glad I had brought my coat, as I saw she was wearing hers. I parked, got out, and put on my coat just as she was finishing on the phone.

"Oh, good. You brought your uniform. I forgot to mention that." She examined the Centers for Disease Control and Prevention embroidered patch on my coat. "Nice. Very classy."

I nodded. "It opens doors, sometimes."

She smiled. "Tell me about it. Just like my black bag." She hefted her tor's bag. "Ever notice they come only in black?"

We followed the crowd streaming toward the field, a wonderful blend of young people and old. Many of the younger ones dressed right to the edge of modesty, some of the older fans arrived with coat and tie. The excitement was something I hadn't felt in many years. I could smell the smoke of grills and hear in the distance the sound of a marching band practicing.

Isabel pointed to a pair of large tents. "Hungry?"

"Absolutely!"

"Tent on the right is hamburgers, hot dogs, other boring things. Let's head to the tent on the left."

We were third in line. There were no menu signs, no prices. I heard the first customer order chateaubriand. I turned to Isabel, who was grinning.

"They modify it a little so you don't need a knife and fork."

The next two ordered combinations of chateaubriand and duck à l'orange.

I shook my head. "I am not believing this."

We arrived at the front of the line. I recognized Mary from today's lunch.

She smiled an excited smile. "Hey, M'reesey, it's Doc Parker!"

Mireese looked up from her grill and eyed my coat. "Hey, Dr. Parker! Looking good. Welcome to our humble snack shack."

"I'm dumbfounded. How do you pull this off?"

Mireese and Mary switched positions. Mireese came over to us. "Mary, I think the Docs would like the duck tonight. I had this idea a couple of years ago, and we're developing it so we can franchise it. I realized it doesn't take that much more work to fix something great than it does to do the other stuff. We just had to make some changes to the recipe to stretch out the timing." She tossed her head toward the tent on the right. "We fix various classics and dice them a little so they work in a wrap. I've got a little better grade of wrap so that it doesn't dilute the flavor of the main meal. The wrap goes in an aluminum foil holder that can be recycled. You get a nickel off desserts if you turn in the foil. I get about 97 percent recycling that way and no cleanup. I think we've got most of the kinks worked out and should be able to expand next year."

Mary returned with two foil-enclosed wraps, handing one to Isabel and one to me. I got out my wallet. Mireese waved me off. "On the house for our honored guest."

I nodded. Spying a tip jar, I inserted a 20.

Mary giggled. "He does that at the café, too!" She put two sweet teas down on the counter.

We picked up our drinks. Mireese looked into a bin and called to Mary, "Oh, love, we're low on ice. We could use another two bags from the truck."

"No problem." Mary took off her apron, turned and gave Mireese a firm kiss on the lips, and ran through the approaching crowd toward the parking lot.

We strolled toward the field. Isabel waited a minute or so, eating her duck. "Not what you expected? Does that offend your Baptist sensibilities?"

I scowled. "No. I'm not with that branch of Baptists. Also no, it wasn't what I expected. I've met Mireese a couple of times at the post office — Mireese of Guthrie."

"Uh huh. Then you no doubt noticed that Jack is rather fond of her."

"I may have sensed that," I acknowledged.

"Mireese and Jack have been best buds since high school. She and he might have gotten married except for a tragic choice on her part."

"Mr. Black?"

"Yup. Joe Black is what is clinically known as an idiot. He and Mireese let their hormones get the best of them and they eloped. It wasn't long, though, before ole Joe discovered that she likes women, too. She was quite happy to share. It freaked him out, though. Now, I had always heard that men like the multiple choice tests." She looked at me with a mischievous grin.

I shook my head. "No comment."

Isabel laughed. "Anyway, Joe Black skedaddled for parts unknown, leaving Mireese with a mortgage and a pile of credit card debt."

"Ah, yes, Jack told me about that. The community rallied around her — the doll business. He didn't mention the rest of the story."

"Well, meanwhile Jack and Kathy fell in love and got married. They have a daughter, Brittany — a real cutey and smart as a tack. Jack's an awesome dad and model husband. Mireese and Mary met when Mary was working for Mireese on the dolls. They've been partners for going on four years. I don't see Kentucky letting them marry anytime soon, though they're a good example of why marrying makes sense regardless."

We arrived at the team bench and sat down to finish our meal. "I might have expected some community opposition."

"Well, you'd be right … in part. Some folks didn't approve; some folks thought it OK. Most people around here live by an 'ain't none of my business' philosophy. A little earlier, I asked if it offended your Baptist sensibilities. I apologize. That wasn't fair. Mireese and Mary are both Baptists, and their church is very supportive. I remember the pastor, John Roberts — you'll be meeting him tomorrow at the memorial service — during a revival a couple of years back. The church brought in a Louisville pastor of some note. The first night he preached a real hellfire and damnation sermon, laying into the gay community something fierce. Mireese and Mary were in the congregation that night. The second night, no one showed up — no one. Pastor Roberts paid the guy what they had contracted and told him to leave. The third night, John Roberts preached on love, forgiveness, and community. I think that revival had record attendance. Even though I'm not a big adherent, I've called Guthrie Baptist my home church ever since.

"So there you have it. Jack still has a crush on Mireese. Kathy's well aware of that and is still great friends with Mireese. And Joe is somewhere else being an idiot, no doubt."

I smiled as I finished the wrap and drank my tea. Fans continued to stream into the stadium, and the seats were filling up. The marching band took the field and performed a series of maneuvers while playing a medley of marching themes. Six Todd County cheerleaders led the home crowd in all the classic cheers. One young woman in particular, second from the right, stood out. She was tanned to a professional grade and epitomized the term 'buxom.' Her long black hair swooshed and swayed with the rhythm of the chants. I could swear her uniform was tighter by several inches than the others.

"Lovely to look at, dangerous to hold." Isabel had been watching me. "Enchanted by number two there, Doc Parker?"

I don't know if I blushed or not. I seldom do. "Uh, she seems more mature than the others, more … developed."

Isabel clasped her hands to her chest in a mock swoon. "Oh, Dr. Parker, you are so observant! No wonder the diseases don't stand a chance when you're around." When she finished laughing, she explained, "That would be 'J.B.' — Jessie Belle — Jessie Belle Dulaney."

"Jessie Belle? You're kidding. Is that her given name?"

"Yup. We have Donna Dulaney to thank for that. She named her and she trained her. I think Donna figured that if the mom couldn't conquer all the men of the world, her daughter would."

"So Jessie Belle is Jim Dulaney's daughter?"

"Maybe. Though, knowing Donna, I wouldn't bet my life on it. If morality has a genetic component, I say she's his daughter."

The marching band finished their pre-game performance and began forming for the National Anthem. The cheerleaders ran off the field. I spied Gina Barker on the sidelines near the portal where the players would emerge to take the field. Approaching the sidelines, J.B. veered off course and slammed into Gina with her shoulder. In the blink of an eye, a phalanx of high school girls and boys intervened to keep the two separated.

"Whoa!" I exclaimed.

Isabel shook her head. "Did I mention that there's serious bad blood between Gina and J.B.? I'll tell you about it in a minute."

We all rose as a four-flag color guard marched toward the band, wheeled, and lowered the Kentucky, the Todd County, and the high school flags. We sang the national anthem with enough enthusiasm to match the volume of the band. After the last line, the Kentucky flag was raised, and the crowd sang "My Old Kentucky Home" with the same familiarity and strength.

The band entered into a complex exit march as Isabel continued. "J.B.

made it her high school goal to 'do' everyone on the football team. Everyone." She paused as the band left the field and the players ran out from both sides, forming two facing walls. Coaches and referees began walking toward the center between the two sides. Isabel reached into the side pocket of her medical coat and pulled out a whistle on a lanyard like her own. "Here. Put this on and follow me." We fell in behind the referees in the midst of remarkable silence.

The head referee gave his standard spiel about sportsmanship and enforcement of the rules, finishing with "and if you hear a whistle from either Dr. Rodriguez or Dr. Parker, both teams will take a knee immediately. If either team continues play after a medical whistle, they forfeit the game, then and there." He took a silver dollar from his pocket and flipped the coin. It landed tails up. Trigg County took initial possession, and we moved to the sidelines.

"So, like I was saying, J.B. set out to have sex with everyone on the team. And she was well on her way to completion until she hit several snags. One was the team student manager, Bruce. Turns out, he's gay and I'm guessing interested in the same boys as she was, but without the aggression. And the other was Chris. Chris is totally loyal to Gina and wouldn't have anything to do with J.B. And so the feud between J.B. and Gina began.

"Sometimes I almost wish the two met without their protective crowd. J.B. doesn't know whom she's dealing with. I was the medical rep when the high school rodeo team went to the National High School Rodeo championships in Wyoming. I watched little Gina chase down, lasso, and tie up a 230-pound calf in 8.7 seconds. The world record is about six seconds. J.B.'s nowhere near 230. If the two of them ever went head to head, it wouldn't be pretty for J.B."

The ball was in motion and I was impressed by what I saw. The teams were serious about their game.

Between cheers for the Todd County team, Isabel continued her sordid saga. "Now, by junior year, J.B. figured she was falling behind. She couldn't get Bruce and portrayed him in her circles as a 'sub-male' who didn't count. She couldn't get Chris, so she tried convincing her cadre that Chris was gay. Of course, no one bought that. While she couldn't get Chris, what she *could* get was gonorrhea. To make up for lost time, she engaged in some of the riskiest behavior I've ever heard tell. By mid-junior-year when I first found out about it, she and half the team were infested with clap. I shut the team down for almost two months."

I was stunned enough that I wasn't sure what to say. "Did you get pushback or support from the coach?"

She looked at me with raised eyebrows. "You remember I said her goal was to do *everyone* on the team?"

"Oh, no."

"Yeah. You talk about awkward. I had to tell a man in his late forties that he needed to get his wife into the clinic for testing. He did. You bet he did! He knew his job was on the line."

I shook my head. "Job on the line? I would have thought it a lot bigger than that. What he did must have been illegal."

"Yeah, well, in this one particular instance, luck was on his side, sort of. First, the cheerleaders weren't under the football program. They fall under Ms. Adams, the tennis coach. So he didn't have any authority over J.B. Second, she failed two grades over the years and was 19 at the time. So she wasn't a minor … in any state. Third, she boasted to a number of people, including myself, about 'draining his balls twice.' So their sex was documented consensual. While their conduct was immoral — a term I seldom use — it was not illegal."

"But …" — I was exasperated — "surely the school board couldn't allow this kind of behavior."

She turned her head from me. "That's where it gets even more complicated. There's a lot of gray area in all this. Even in a small community like Todd County, secrets can stay buried for a long time. Knowing those secrets can give you a lot of leverage. You heard what the ref said." She raised her lanyard. "These whistles rule. You bet your ass I'm not going to get any guff from the coach for my calls. As a result, we have the safest program in the state. The team gets intense coaching on social responsibility; and any drug, alcohol, or sex misbehavior is dealt with immediately and constructively. I have mixed feelings about the ethics sometimes. I have to look at the big picture. You're free to disagree. Just be thoughtful about it."

I watched the game while trying to process all these new revelations. At the half, the score was tied one to one. As the players left the field and the marching band and cheerleaders moved on to take their place, Gina came running to the bench to talk to Isabel.

"Doc, you were right! Mom and I had about the best talk we've had in … I don't know how long. And you were pretty close on that six-hour joke. We talked from the time Grandpa fell asleep until almost midnight."

"And?" Isabel spread out her hands.

"Mom thinks that Chris and I are responsible enough to make those decisions, and she supports us."

Isabel smiled. "Well, you earned that trust. I was pretty sure I knew what the outcome would be. I think I know the three of you pretty well." Isabel reached into the front pocket of her coat and pulled out a small folded sheet of paper and handed it to Gina. "Be responsible; be loving. You know I expect that of you."

Gina blushed as she stuffed the paper, unopened, into her shirt pocket.

She hugged Isabel and then raced back to the sidelines.

Isabel turned back to see me smiling. "A very different outcome with a very different back story. Yeah, much as I hate to see them grow up at times, it feels good when they grow up right."

"And you're sure that Gina was telling the truth about talking to her mother," I said.

"Like I told you the day we met, Gina couldn't lie to save herself. Besides, Sharon called this morning to thank me for getting Gina to talk to her. I think with all that's been going on in Sharon's life, with Walt leaving the scene, and all the changes that's going to bring, their talk was a rare bright spot."

After the halftime show, the players returned to the field with a more aggressive play than the first half. Penalties came early in the second half and piled up fast. After ten minutes of play, Chris scored a goal for Todd County, bringing the home crowd to their feet. At the 11-minute mark, one of the larger Trigg County players looked back for the ball to be passed to him. He plowed into Chris at a full run with enough force that we could hear the collisions almost as a crack.

Isabel and I were both on our feet, blowing our whistles as we ran onto the field. The referees likewise sounded their whistles and both teams dropped with their knees to the ground.

We both arrived at Chris's side at the same time. The player who had collided with him spoke up. "I didn't see him. I just turned my head for a second to see the ball."

Isabel reassured the player as she knelt beside Chris. "We know. We saw. It was an accident. These things happen. You just stay there and let us concentrate on him." She turned back to the Trigg County Player. "Are you OK?"

The Trigg County player nodded.

Chris took a deep breath and exhaled slowly. "Oh man. That was brutal."

I cautioned him. "Don't move. Don't even think about moving. How bad does it hurt?"

"It was a stabbing pain when we hit, but it doesn't feel so bad now. Kinda weird."

I asked Isabel for a needle. "I'm not a neurologist, though I know a good bit about neural anatomy from studying encephalitis." I turned to Chris. "Tell me if you feel this." I pricked him with the needle around his ankle. He didn't respond. "Anything?"

"No."

I stuck him again near the top of his thigh. "How about that?"

"No, sir."

Again I stuck him near the lowest rib.

"Ow!"

I moved my hand slowly under his back and felt the contours without putting any pressure on his back. By now, the referees had sent both teams back to their benches, and Sheriff Nolan had joined us.

I looked back and forth between Isabel and the sheriff. "Where's the nearest complete shock trauma center?"

Curtis offered, "Vanderbilt, Nashville."

I frowned. "Jeez. That's 70 plus miles away." I turned to Chris. "All right, young man, you appear to have a very serious injury to your spine. I'm sure it can be treated. We just want to get you to hospital as quickly and as motion-free as we can."

I looked up. "Sheriff Nolan, is it possible to call in an airlift, and will they take him to Vandy?"

"Yes to both. One of the Highway Patrol medical choppers is stationed at the Russellville barracks. I'll make the call." He ran to his car parked near the south end of the stadium.

I pulled out my cell phone and scrolled through the 'H' list. "I have a friend at Vanderbilt who's an awesome neurosurgeon."

The phone answered. "Charlie Hamor."

"Charlie, this is John Parker."

"John, good to hear from you! I was thinking of giving you a call. What's up?"

"I'm up in Elkton, Kentucky, at a soccer game. There's been a collision and one of the players is hard down. I did a field prick test and checked the external contour. Looks like maybe a rupture around one of the lumbar vertebrae. We're sending him down your way by helo unless you have a better recommendation."

"I'll be there to meet the bird. You owe me a lecture on encephalitis."

"You patch him back to full service and you've got whatever you want."

Sheriff Nolan returned at a run. "The helo was in 'ready-ten.' It should be airborne by now. It'll take only five or ten minutes."

Isabel looked down at Chris. "Help's on the way, bubba. How're you doing?"

He put on a brave face. "OK, I guess. Am I going to be paralyzed?"

Isabel turned to me.

"Not with Dr. Hamor on the case. He was a military surgeon during Desert Storm — legendary. Just stay calm for now. We only need to get you to him without doing any more damage."

Isabel turned to the sheriff. "Should I ride with him, or would John be a better choice?"

He shook his head. "It's pretty tight in the patient compartment and they have an EMT. What they'd prefer is a family member who can give consent and handle details once he's at the hospital."

She looked to Chris. "Where're your mom and dad?"

He sighed. "No go. They're with Rob visiting colleges. They won't be back until Sunday night."

"Any other relatives here tonight?"

"No, ma'am."

She looked up, biting her lip. After a moment's thought, her scowl disappeared, and she scanned the crowd near the locker room entrance. I followed her outstretched arm and pointing finger to see Gina, her hands to her mouth in anxious worry.

Gina pointed her fingers at her chest as if to ask, "Me?"

Isabel swished her hand and Gina raced onto the field.

"Is he OK?" Gina asked, tears welling in her eyes.

Isabel reached up and cradled Gina's face, "Pay attention to me, Mrs. Waddail. I don't have much time to explain what you have to do. We're sending Chris to Vanderbilt to get put back together, and the hospital will need next of kin to consent to all the medical stuff when Chris is out under anesthesia, which he will be part of the time. Are we clear, Mrs. Waddail?"

Gina nodded, her face all seriousness.

I turned to Sheriff Nolan. "Go over to the bench and get about six of the strongest members of the team. When we lift him onto the medical carrier, it'll be like handling a cracked egg. We need strong hands we can trust."

"Got it." Curtis headed toward the sidelines.

Isabel continued her instructions. "OK, Mrs. Waddail, Chris's got some damage to the lower spine. It could be serious. Doc Parker's got a buddy, ..." She turned to me.

"Dr. Charles Hamor, a world-class neurosurgeon, best of the best," I said.

"So, Dr. Hamor's going to meet you guys down in Nashville. He knows you're coming."

Gina glanced in the direction of the county ambulance. "Shouldn't we be getting going?"

"You're not going by ambulance, Mrs. Waddail. Doc Parker says the ride wouldn't be a good idea. The state helicopter's on its way. You ever ride in a helicopter?"

"No, ma'am." Gina shook her head.

"Well, it'll be tight and noisy. You just concentrate on keeping your husband absolutely still. Are you hearing me? Absolutely still, Mrs. Waddail."

By now, the field lights were on. I could see tears in Gina's eyes reflecting the lights.

Isabel released her, and Gina transformed with authority, looking down at Chris. "OK, Bud. You heard what the docs said. One move and I'll slug you as soon as you're better. You got that?"

Chris grinned. "Yes, ma'am."

Gina looked up. "What if they don't believe me, Doc? What if they ask for ID?"

Isabel hesitated a mere fraction of a second. "You're newlyweds. You're changing your name, but haven't had time to get a new license, what with all the work on the farm." She thought some more. Looking down at her hand, Isabel slipped off her rings and put them on Gina's hand. "It'd be more romantic if Chris did it. He's not moving, though. Keep your hand visible. Just be casual. People see what they want to see."

Gina looked at her hand and smiled.

I could hear the soft "whup, whup, whup" of the helicopter in the distance. "OK, we're going to stay here with Chris. When the helo comes in to land, there'll be a strong wind from the rotors. Get anything loose into your pockets. And close your eyes when it first lands. It'll kick up a lot of dust and debris, papers, that sort of thing."

Isabel turned to Gina with urgency. "Give me your 'script, Mrs. Waddail."

Gina reached into her shirt pocket and handed the prescription paper to Isabel. I watched as Isabel penned "Waddail" after "Gina Barker." She handed it back to Gina. "In the unlikely event they have doubts, just flash that and ask if the pharmacy's open. It's ridiculous, I know, but you're distraught. Got it, Mrs. Waddail?"

"Yes, ma'am."

I watched as the running lights of the aircraft grew closer. Isabel tightened her headscarf. We were at about the American football 23-yard line, so the helicopter had plenty of room to set down midfield. I positioned myself to block the rotor wash, and Gina placed her hand over Chris's eyes. As the EMT crewman emerged from the craft with a metal mesh stretcher, Sheriff Nolan headed in our direction with six husky players.

I was a little miffed that the EMT approached me rather than going to Isabel. We both had the same uniform. Still, it was no time to grumble; there was work to be done. He wrote on his clipboard as I shouted above the helicopter's rotors. "Male, 18, collision during soccer game. Apparent dislocated spinal cord or rupture around one of the lumbar vertebrae. Patient failed a prick test below the lumbar nerves. Cursory exam supports a dislocation. Patient has been kept immobile since the accident. Transport to Vanderbilt Medical Center. Dr. Charles Hamor will meet you at the helo pad. Anything else?"

"Any next of kin who can accompany him?"

"His wife, Gina. We've given her instructions on keeping him still."

He nodded. We completed his records with my name and cell number while designating Dr. Rodriguez as the doctor of record.

Satisfied, the EMT closed his flight notes and placed the stretcher at Chris's head. He talked to the players and spaced them alongside Chris. He and the players lifted Chris with admirable grace, placing him on the palette. The EMT fastened Chris with restraining straps.

Chris spoke to one of the players, a redhead with ruddy complexion. "All right, Bill, you've got it. Number Seven seems distracted, and the kid who ran into me should be, too. You'll be able to run around them. Concentrate. OK?"

"Aye, aye, Captain," Bill saluted.

The team lifted the stretcher, carried it to the helicopter, and secured it inside. With the team returning to the sidelines, the EMT briefed Gina and handed her ear-protection gear. He climbed in first and helped her board. Once the door closed, the helicopter powered up, rose from the field, and disappeared to the south, leaving the three of us alone on the field.

Sheriff Nolan was first to speak. "Wow, that was impressive!"

We turned and started walking toward the Todd County bench.

"What? The helo or the lies?" Isabel laughed.

"You did the right thing," I said. "I think we can tolerate some misinformation if it keeps Chris from paralysis. But I distinctly remember you saying she can't lie to save herself."

"That's still true, John," Isabel insisted. "She can't. But to save Chris or any member of her family, she'd lie to the face of God. And God would believe her. Gina would breathe for Chris if she could to keep him still. He's not moving."

Sheriff Nolan chuckled. "Aw, it wasn't a lie. It was just the truth ... told early."

We laughed, and Isabel pointed to Coach Nelson. "Play ball!"

I did my best to concentrate on the remaining game. Bill, I learned, was the team's co-captain and was true to his charge from Chris. Todd County racked up another two goals in short order.

"It was impressive how you constructed such a consistent backstory on the fly," I said.

Her eyes were on the field. "Working out here on the frontier with all the people and institutions opposing me, I have to improvise. I don't have a lot of alternatives. It's a fragile make-believe world. One little block gets knocked out of place, and the whole system comes crashing down around me. It'd be a lot easier if there were a *bona fide* doctor here — if he'd come."

Uncomfortable, I turned to see her looking at me with unaccustomed seriousness.

"Is Chris really going to be all right?" she asked.

I nodded. "I think you know by now that I won't raise false hopes. I know his injury is severe. Twenty years ago, I would have predicted a lifetime of disability. With today's tools and techniques, a lot of which Charlie's team developed, I'd put all my money on a full recovery. And I'm not a betting man."

"Thank you, John. Thank you."

* * *

The two goals right after Chris's evacuation would be the last of the game, a final score of four to one, Todd County.

Isabel and I sauntered back to our cars, meeting dozens of members of the community along the way.

I shook my head. "Guess Ron was wrong about the score."

She laughed. "That doesn't happen often. He's pleased, no doubt." We arrived at the parking lot. "I'll head on down to Nashville and keep Gina company. I know that place pretty well. I'm guessing Chris's in surgery now. He ought to be getting out of the O.R. a little after I get down there."

"Want some company?" I offered.

"Naw. I could use a little solitude. Thanks, though. I'm sure Gina's called her mom; still I'll talk with Sharon on my way down. If she needs any help with Walt, I'll give you a call, OK?"

"Absolutely!"

"Get some rest yourself. Tomorrow's going to be a long day, with the memorial service and all."

She drove off into the night and I returned to Guthrie. As I expected, Ellen was waiting on the porch.

"Do we know how to stage exciting games or what, John?" she teased.

I chuckled. "You didn't need to do all that on my account."

"I understand you all married Gina and Chris out on the field."

"How did you … never mind. I don't think it was official."

"Don't know, John. In several societies, the shamans can do that. We owe those two kids a big wedding some day, though. We'll keep tonight unofficial."

I climbed up the stairs to the porch and sat in the porch swing, watching lightning bugs and bats, listening to a dozen or so species of crickets, katydids, and other creatures of the night.

I opened the conversation. "It was clever of Isabel to give Gina her rings. Isabel doesn't seem the married type. I didn't notice her rings before."

"Men seldom notice … unless they're on the prowl. Your inattention speaks well of you in this case."

"I sense Dr. Rodriguez is a very complex person. Really, really smart. A survivor."

Ellen closed her eyes as she rocked. "That she is."

A car pulled into the driveway, the first car in the neighborhood since I got to Ellen's. Stacy emerged from the car and stepped up to the porch.

"Hey, Doctor P, hey Ms. Miller, exciting game, huh?"

"Yes, it was. I'm sure Chris will be fine," I said to answer the obvious next question.

"Good. That was pretty awesome with the helicopter and all. Kinda like aliens swooping in and carrying Gina and Chris off to some mother ship."

"A little more benign, I hope," I said.

"Yeah, well, we almost had another casualty for you earlier," she said.

"Oh?"

"Yeah. When J.B. started getting in Gina's business on the sidelines. I was part of Gina's posse, and I was about ready to deck J.B. myself. What a bitch!"

"Thank you for your restraint," I offered.

"So what's Gina doing with Chris down in Nashville?"

"I'd guess she's signing papers and giving the go-ahead to doctors," I suggested.

"She could get in trouble for that, couldn't she? Like fraud and jail."

"Not likely," I said. "Even if someone raised an objection, Ms. Miller has a shaman defense prepared."

Ellen chuckled. "No one will ever know. By the way, Stacy, where did you go after the game?"

"I checked on my platoon. They're camped out in Aunt Faye's living room. We moved the chairs and made tents with blankets for the little ones. I left them with orders to get a good night's sleep for tomorrow's mission. They're having Aunt Faye's waffles for breakfast so they'll be good to go. As for myself, I'm going to hit the sack, too. We've packed an awful lot into this day."

We took our leave of Ellen. After returning to my room and washing up, I fell asleep almost immediately.

6 WARRIOR'S FAREWELL

I jolted awake at the sound of my phone and fumbled for the device until I held it. At 3:27, caller ID showed "Charles Hamor."

Charlie started before I could say anything. "Top o' the morning, John. Figured you wouldn't mind some good news."

I laughed. "Always on call for good news, Charlie. What've we got?"

"You called the lumbar region right. Chris had a dislocation between the L1 and L2 vertebrae. There was very little tearing of the cord — compression for the most part. We got his bones realigned without incident. I injected a new corticosteroid cocktail we developed to keep the swelling down. This new cocktail has fewer side effects, and includes a healthy dose of neural growth factor factors to mend the tear. I'd guess he'll experience some enhanced sensitivity for the next month or so while his new nerves grow. I stabilized the L1 and L2 interface with a couple of collagen elastic bands around the arches to keep them from shifting while they heal. The bands will resorb after a few weeks when he'll be up and about. I told his wife he'd have to lay off the sports for about a year. She seems like a good enforcer."

I was elated. "That she is, Charlie, that she is. I can't thank you enough."

I heard him chuckle. "Oh, yes you can. Make sure you've got two weeks cleared for lectures this fall. I'll send you the dates."

"Consider it done," I agreed.

"You know, John, Chris is one lucky kid to have had you right there, right then. If anyone had tried to get him to stand up, which people often do, the whole cord could have severed, and he'd have been in a world of shit. As it is, he'll be immobile for a few days, then some bed rest. I'll send you the records when I get 'em written up. Meanwhile my people will bring Mrs. Waddail up to speed on home therapy."

"Just give the records to Dr. Rodriguez. She's his physician." I said.

"Hmmm."

"Yes?" I queried, suspicious of his tone.

"She seemed to see you as the physician," Charlie responded.

"Gina's had a long night, Charlie. She's distraught," I explained.

"I'm not talking about Mrs. Waddail, I'm talking about Dr. Rodriguez."

"Oh."

"You know, John, we've known each other for a long time. Though you're a brilliant epidemiologist, community medicine is just as important and can reach even more people sometimes. I've seen you in action before. You're good at it. You shouldn't dismiss changing venues from time to time."

"You're sounding like my wife."

"Heh, I've known Baylor as long as I've known you. She's a smart lady."

"You have anything more for me other than career advice at 3:30 in the morning, Charlie?"

"Nope, not at the moment. I'm going to clean up and head home. Just hope no idiot's driving drunk at this hour. I'm planning to take the kids to Cherokee Park later this morning, and I don't want to be putting some yahoo back together instead. Gina and the doc are sleeping in the patient chairs in Chris's room so they'll be there when he wakes up. The doc says they need to get back to Guthrie for a memorial service later this morning. Good night, John."

"Good night, Charlie."

Thoughts of rural medicine swam in my head as I drifted back to sleep. I needed to call Baylor in the morning for a reality check.

* * *

For the first time since arriving, I woke up to my alarm. I showered, pondering the conversation with Charlie and earlier with Isabel. Community medicine, rural medicine in particular, had been neglected and disregarded for so long, it was approaching Third World status in many states. As an epidemiologist, I saw once-rare diseases erupting into regional epidemics in the absence of monitoring and coordination. The intrusion of big agri-business with its chemical- and antibiotic-laden practices was setting the stage for catastrophic new diseases while suppressing the very warning systems on which we relied. It was a troubling set of thoughts to start the day.

It was fortunate that I walked out into a bright, clear Guthrie morning. The sun, half an hour farther along than previous mornings when I woke up on my own before the clock, shone in a cloudless blue sky. Ellen's grounds were awash in bright colors devoid of pastels. As I rounded the front corner of the house, the Crayola-orange *Begonia boliviense* hosted at least three hummingbirds flitting from blossom to blossom. I ascended the steps to her open door and went in.

"Good morning."

"Morning, John," came her voice from the kitchen.

I made my way in, finding a plate with generous helpings of scrambled eggs, bacon, biscuits, and cantaloupe.

"Nothing fancy this morning. In fact, I'll be leaving you on your own in a bit. Gotta get over to the church to help get things ready for the service. Starts at 11, though you'll want to get there about 10:30 to meet people. You don't have to worry about a seat — they've got a spot for you on the second row, since you're going to be saying a few words. I've seen you in action enough that I don't need to say it — just keep it simple."

"Yes, ma'am. I've presented many, many times to Rotary and Kiwanis, even elementary school classes."

"I thought so. Just checking."

"Good idea. I got good news early this morning about Chris. Charlie Hamor expects a full recovery."

"So I heard," Ellen said.

I smiled. "Of course you did. Tell me what you heard."

Ellen gave me a mischievous smirk. "Well, Chris woke up about five this morning. Gina and the doc have been fussing over him ever since — lucky boy in that regard. Your friend Charlie gave them copies of all the medical charts. Doc Isabel explained what little that Gina didn't know already, Gina called Sharon, and Sharon called me about half an hour ago. Sharon didn't have the technical details down, so why don't you fill me in?"

"Dr. Hamor did the surgery. He found that two of the vertebrae near the bottom of the spine had gotten knocked out of alignment — disconnected, in fact. There was only a little damage to the spinal cord itself — nothing that he thinks can't be fixed. Dr. Hamor repositioned the bones, put in the medical equivalents of rubber bands to hold the bones in place, and put in the proper medication to prevent further damage and help the nerves re-knit."

She smiled. "Nice explanation, John. You'll do fine this morning, though you did leave out the part about how if you hadn't been there to guide everyone, Chris could have been crippled for life." She turned to me as I ate quietly. She continued, "I'm heading out now. Put the dishes in the sink. Don't even think about doing them. I have my own way, and I know just where everything is placed. Pull the door to on your way out. It's not locked and don't lock it. Stacy might need to drop in. She went out to Faye's about 5:30."

"Yes, ma'am."

"You got all that?" Ellen persisted.

"Yes, ma'am. Dishes in the sink. Do not wash, under penalty of death. Front door closed, not locked in case Stacy comes roaring through."

"Good. No wonder you're good at what you do. You listen. Your wife is a lucky woman, I reckon."

"I try."

Ellen left and I enjoyed a quiet meal. I stacked my dishes in her sink. It was tempting to wash them anyway. Still, I sensed she was serious about leaving them alone. I verified that the front door was not locked before I pulled it to. I sat on the porch swing and listened for sounds. From time to time a distant car or truck sound would intrude — blocks away — though for the most part I heard only the sounds of nature.

I called Baylor at 7:30, 8:30 Atlanta time.

"Hey, lover boy, you been out carousing all night?"

I laughed. "Only if getting a spinal cord injury down to Nashville counts as carousing."

"Oh, dear!" she exclaimed.

"He'll be OK. Charlie Hamor met the helicopter and fixed the kid up in best Charlie style."

"Ah, how is Charlie?" she asked. I could hear her soft smile.

"Great as ever. Also, the same troublemaker, as ever. I think he's trying to recruit me to work here. Rural practice. Same old Charlie." I waited for her response a while.

"I got your postcards and the book. Seems like a really peaceful place, nice place," she murmured.

"I'm finding a lot about the darker underbelly as I work the case."

"Ah, yes, dark underbelly. Good thing we don't have that here in Atlanta," she intoned.

"You're mocking me. Am I sensing wanderlust in my lover?"

"We've talked about this John, about what it would be without the stress and noise. Imagine the clean air, the dew, the walk to work."

Sitting on Ellen's porch, I was not imagining it; I was experiencing it. "The work of the lab is important."

"Yup, you're right. That's why you have to fight tooth and nail every two years for funding."

"Someone's sounding a little down."

"Your book arrived the same day we got notice they were laying off two more staff. They promised last year there'd be no more layoffs. I made it to the post office just in time to get your package because of traffic on 285. It was not a good day. I looked through the book several times. At first I wished you were here; then I so wished I were there. I miss you."

"I miss you, too. Promise I'll get things wrapped up as soon as I can. Everyone's being so cooperative. I've got some good leads and a ton of data. I expect to have the causes pretty well narrowed down by Tuesday," I assured.

"Don't know how you do it, John. I do know that you're right most of the time. What sort of fun stuff do you have planned for today?"

"A memorial service for one of the men at 11," I replied.

"Oh, sorry."

"I think it's going to be a celebration. The faith community's strong here. The man's niece from Baltimore has something planned for the service. Ms. Miller and Stacy won't let me in on what it is — big secret. Knowing Stacy, it should be different."

"Well, give my best to the families. I'm going over to the garden center to get some perennials. Dobbins is having a post-bloom sale on peonies."

I didn't want to bring up the size of the peony bed she could have here. "Enjoy your planting. I'll call you Sunday night. I'm sending you some country ham in the mail. It's fully cured, doesn't need refrigeration —very salty, so a little goes a long way."

"Sounds like it would be good in green beans," she suggested.

"Yes, as a matter of fact. Hey, I love you." I kissed her through the phone.

"Love you, too. Hurry home."

I returned to my room to work on my greetings for the service. I tried to link Frank's service to his country to the cooperation I was getting from the community. I flipped through some of the clippings and papers Faye had lent me. I reviewed Frank's Air Force service, yet kept coming back to the full page featuring The Five Demons of Todd County High and wondered what it was like to be so isolated from the rest of the world's problems, embargoes, and wars. I saw again in the paper the haunting picture of the missing local girl, Jennifer Collins.

Putting the finishing touches on my remarks at about 9:30, I read them aloud a number of times until I could recite them from memory. I timed the words to about two minutes, smiling as I kept in mind the grade Ms. Miller would give me. I think I was looking at a "B," maybe "B+." Once I approached the point of diminishing returns, I got dressed in my Sunday suit. I had learned long ago that when investigations involve deaths, I should bring a suit appropriate to funerals.

I realized how well I had come to understand Ellen when I went to print my remarks and set up a printer on my computer without even thinking about it. Of course she had a printer, and of course it was on the network. Charlie and Baylor were on to something — the place was growing on me.

At a little after ten, I left the room and entered the house to pick up my draft copy. I didn't remember seeing a printer. The logical place for one would be near her sewing area, and there it was. I picked up the papers, left the door closed and unlocked, and walked down the driveway, making a right turn onto Third Street. Guthrie Baptist Church was only three blocks from Ellen's house. Cars were arriving, with parking already extending to two blocks from the church. As people emerged from their cars, they greeted me by name. Just behind the church, a group of men were having their last smoke before the service. Kentucky still had one of the highest smoking rates in the country — with the accompanying grim health statistics. One consolation was the composition of the smokers here. In days gone by, the group would have represented a cross-section of the men of the community. Today, there were no 20-somethings or 30-somethings in the group. Most sported well-grayed — or very little — hair.

I smiled as they instinctively tried to hide their cigarettes when catching sight of me. Today was not a day for lectures on smoking. We exchanged greetings, and I moved on toward the front door of the church, where I could hear an organ playing traditional prelude music inside while the summer chorus of cicadas was just starting with the warming day outside. Two teenagers, a boy and girl from the church youth group, flanked the front door handing out the order of service.

"Good morning, Dr. Parker."

I smiled. "Good morning. Thank you."

I admired the solid early-twentieth century church architecture of dark varnished wooden beams rising to the high vaulted ceiling. I checked my watch. At 10:30, the sanctuary was almost half filled. Off to the left, I saw Isabel talking with several women. The room was awash, almost festive, with floral arrangements. At the very front, I saw that the altar table was draped in white linen rather than black and that an urn was centered on the table. Flags flanked either side of the altar, one the U.S. flag and the other a military flag, maybe Air Force. The family sat in the second row. Beside Faye sat a woman in black, I guessed Stacy's mom, Jane Coudron. Though I couldn't yet hear Sarah's words, it looked as if she was issuing stern behavior instructions to her two children.

Sarah looked up and saw me as I eased down the aisle. She left her seat and dashed up to me. "Oh good. You're here. Thank you. Thank you so much for everything."

I smiled and nodded. I reached out to shake her hand; she hugged me instead.

"It's only a few words. No problem. I'm honored to be here."

She shook her head. "No, not just that. Everything." She paused. "Do you have plans after the reception?"

I hadn't looked at the order of service yet. Post-service receptions were the norm. "None as yet."

"Good. Would you join us out at the farm? We're having a get-together with family and a few friends. You need to see the gazebo."

"The gazebo?"

"It was your suggestion to have Stacy get the kids to help paint the gazebo, and it took Mom's mind off her worries. You've gotta see what they did!"

I glanced at the children and almost laughed. Now I could see patches of paint in their hair. I was surprised at first to see paint on their faces, too, only to realize that the face paint was intentional; what looked like chevrons and hash marks on their cheeks. I looked around for Stacy, as this had to be her doing. She was not to be found. I turned to Sarah. "I'd be honored and delighted."

"You still know the way out to the farm?" Sarah asked.

"Yes, ma'am."

"Good. We'll see you there." She returned to her seat beside her mother, and then moved between her two children, who had been poking one another.

While I talked with Sarah, Gina had approached from the side. I turned to her and smiled.

"Dr. Parker …" She had wanted to say something formal, I guessed, but was overcome. She broke into tears and hugged me. "Thank you!"

I patted her on the back. "It's OK. Dr. Hamor talked to me this morning. He said Chris is going to be OK."

She regained her composure in a few moments. She nodded. "I know. He gave me all the details and instructions. He also told me how close to disaster it was. Do you believe in angels, Dr. Parker?"

I chuckled. "I think so, depending on what you mean by angels. I haven't seen the Christmas card kind. Mind you, those aren't all that biblical anyway."

"Well, Dr. Hamor and Doc Isabel both said that you're an angel."

"They're too kind. I'm just glad Chris is going to be all right. Were you able to reach his folks?"

"Yes, sir. They came back straight to the hospital." She looked around. "They'll be here soon. Chris's brother is down there now staying with him. We'll all go back to Vanderbilt right after the reception. Dr. Hamor said Chris will be down at the hospital for a couple of days, maybe a week, and then rehab."

Isabel finished talking and came over to us. "Did my sleepover buddy give you all the details?"

"I'm getting details from all over. Ellen gave me a play-by-play just before she left this morning."

Isabel laughed. She turned to Gina and held out her hand.

"What?" Gina asked.

Isabel looked at the rings on Gina's hand and smiled.

"Darn. I was getting used to them. They fit so well."

"All in due time, 'Mrs. Waddail.'"

With a soft smile, Gina removed the rings and handed them to Isabel. "Thanks, Doc."

The organist launched a more formal piece, signaling the start of the service. I found my designated seat alongside Isabel and Ellen. Turning around to survey the congregation, I saw that it wouldn't have mattered what I wore that morning. The congregation's attire ranged from full dress formal to farm overalls. They represented a spectrum of the community from elders to toddlers. Many families sat with their children. If that represented the church's membership, it was a healthy sign.

In the front, the door on the left side opened. Two men and a woman entered. I recognized one of the men from Faye's photographs as Mike Meyers, Sarah's husband. The woman would be Frank's sister. I didn't recognize the other man. The order of service listed Sam Gallant, one of Frank's fellow Rotarians.

Stacy entered next. Her expression was more serious than I had seen before. Still her cheeks sported painting similar to the children's. She smiled as she caught sight of me. The cheek markings appeared to be a good rendition of a major's rank. She stood out from the others with her dark blue slacks, crisp light blue long-sleeved shirt and black tie. A crisp blue uniform jacket draped over her arm. I wondered what the congregation would think of her unorthodox appearance.

Pastor Roberts and the associate pastor entered last and took their seats on the platform. Pastor Roberts opened with an invocation and greetings to family and friends. He read the Ecclesiastes passage about a time for everything, concluding that now was the time to draw around Faye's family and remember the life of Frank Johnson.

Next, Sam Gallant rose and echoed the theme of drawing close to the Johnsons. Sam was a soft-spoken man. Though he and the others were long prepared for Frank's passing, it was clear that the loss weighed on him. As Sam listed Frank's accomplishments and involvements, I was reminded of the critical roles that individuals — good individuals — of necessity played in small communities. We sang "Shall We Gather at the River."

Frank's sister, Amelia Bennett, read the "love passage" from Corinthians. She talked about her big brother and about the mischief he would get into as a boy. She mentioned his football days in brief and about how he grew disillusioned with sports and entered the Air Force. She related how the military experience had changed his life, given him focus. Amelia told of how she had hoped that Frank would marry Faye since Frank was in the sixth grade. We sang "Be Thou My Vision."

Mike gave greetings on behalf of the family, reminding the congregants of the lunchtime reception after the service. He read a passage from Matthew about the joy of a servant whom the master finds at work when the master returns. I noted again how duty was an assumption in this place. It was not dreaded or questioned. We sang "Holy, Holy, Holy," and it was my turn.

"Good morning. I am John Parker. I bring you personal greetings from North Park Baptist Church in Atlanta. If you come to visit our fair city, we will extend to you the same love and warmth that you have extended to me here. I bring you warm wishes from my wife, Baylor, who extends her prayers for you in this time of loss. And I bring you greetings from the Centers for Disease Control and Prevention, where we struggle to find the causes and cures for the diseases that afflict us." I had spotted Eugene Gough earlier. I glanced at him. He was smiling — a pleasant smile, not sarcastic.

"In my sojourn with you, I have learned so much about Frank Johnson, about his service and life among you. I admire him and I wish that I had known him earlier. I was one of the last two people to see him; and even then, with the blessings of his wonderful family, he was serving me and he was serving his fellow countrymen with the medical information he provided through medical samples. You see, we fight an enemy that is small, hidden, and stealthy. When the enemy wins, it is because it has evaded our defenses and overcome our natural ability to fight.

"Through the past two centuries, we've learned about some of the diseases that kill us and disable us before our times. Bacteria we have in large measure conquered. Viruses are just now yielding to our understanding. So, the big battlefield is cancer. Cancer is the battlefield on which Frank died, though not before leaving clues to the disease that overcame him. We do not yet know how Frank contracted this rare cancer, though we now have clues we didn't have before. Even as we meet to celebrate his life and mourn his loss, our laboratory is analyzing those samples for every bit of information we can get from them. Be assured we will not stop until we have found the reason for the cancer, a remedy if we can catch it earlier in others, and steps we can recommend to others to prevent its occurrence again.

"I know that many of you are concerned, as all reasonable people would be, that this cancer may spread. I am cautious enough to never rule anything out. Still, you should find some small comfort in knowing that I've found no evidence of any infectious disease and plenty of known and controllable hazards that are most likely at the heart of this particular cancer." I turned to the urn. "You can thank Frank Johnson's last gift for that knowledge. Thank you, sir, for your service to the end."

I returned to my seat. I turned to Ellen and raised my eyebrows.

She smiled. "B plus, A minus. We'll talk later."

Relieved, I smiled and leaned back in the pew as Stacy stepped forward, the last person in the order of service before the unspecified recessional. She would deliver the benediction. Stacy did not move to the pulpit, instead standing on the platform between the pulpit and the altar. I could see that she was wearing a wireless microphone like we used back at North Park.

"Hi. My name is Stacy, Stacy Coudron. Some of you remember me. I'll warn you in advance that I may have trouble with part of this, even though

I've practiced. Ms. Miller said to expect that, and I'm OK with it.

"I never knew my biological father. I don't even know who he is. I grew up with a tough and loving mother, and I thank her for all she did. Those were hard times, and there came a point when Mom could not bear the load she faced. It was then that I met my real dad." She turned to the urn and then back to the congregation. "I met Uncle Frank. When Mom could not take care of me, or even herself, Uncle Frank and Aunt Faye just appeared and took me in. I had only heard of them — never met them. Without conditions or asking anything, they took a troubled fourth grader and moved her from the big city to the farm. Every single thing that was familiar to me was gone. My mother, my friends, the streets, the schools … all gone.

"In the place of all that, I found a father any kid could only dream of. He fixed my room just the way I liked it. He walked to the bus stop with me. He made sure I was in Ms. Miller's class." She turned again to the urn, and then raised her eyes skyward. "Thank you for that, Uncle Frank."

She was streaming tears by then. "What I remember so vividly that it colors my dreams to this day was how he showed me the beauty and wonder of the farm and all its dimensions. When he mowed the hay in the rolling pasture, he would let me ride on the back of the tractor. As we mowed, we stirred up all the grasshoppers and other bugs. A cloud of swallows always followed us, swooping and soaring, feasting on the bugs. I loved those birds, so free and full of life. Uncle Frank always smiled when I ran through the back yard, my arms stretched out, swooping and soaring as best I could while still bound to the earth. He showed me the corners of the barn where the barn swallows nested — our secret spot. And he taught me how to observe them without disturbing them.

"I loved those birds, Uncle Frank. When I was 16, long after returning to Baltimore, where swallows are scarce, I told Mom I wanted to get a tattoo." Stacy began to unbutton her right sleeve. "At first she said no, but — after quite a bit of arguing — she at last said OK; only if I got my grades up. Uncle Frank, from that time forward, I got straight As." She rolled her sleeve up. "See, Uncle Frank, swallows." She turned around, displaying the tattoos on her right arm — a flight of swallows swooping and soaring up and down. She rolled her sleeve back down and rebuttoned it. She turned back to the urn and then looked skyward. "I also have a tattoo of their nest in a secret spot, and I won't be sharing that."

She stepped over to her seat, retrieved the jacket, and put it on. She turned to Faye. "He was a trim guy, wasn't he? It fits pretty good." She was wearing Frank's Air Force uniform jacket. She bowed her head as she buttoned the front. "So now we say goodbye to a hero. You know him for all he has been in your lives. You know him for his proud service. I know him as my dad — Uncle Frank." She turned to the urn one last time and saluted crisply. "Well done, good and faithful servant."

She then wheeled to the family and barked out, "Assemble the troops!" The grandchildren came forward and stood in a line of review in front of Stacy, the oldest at the center. Mike came up and stood just behind the line. "Sergeant Meyers, Sergeant Bennett, strike the colors!" The two older children marched to the stands and hoisted their respective flags. Mike went to the altar and lifted the urn. The congregation rose. As the children paraded the flags up the aisle, Mike fell in behind with the urn. The organist launched into a spirited "Off We Go Into the Wild Blue Yonder," the Air Force song. The younger grandchildren followed, reaching out their hands for Faye, Sarah, Amelia, and the others as they recessed from the sanctuary. Stacy brought up the rear.

We all turned to watch them parade out. I could see universal weeping in response to her eulogy. For the first time, and one of only three times, I saw tears in Isabel's eyes. I turned to Ellen. I couldn't trust my voice, saying only, "Water hyacinth."

Ellen just nodded.

The entire congregation relocated to the fellowship hall and the reception. Of course, the term "reception" didn't do it justice. The tables were heaped with comfort food — chicken, ham, casseroles, vegetables, and so forth. I spied a separate table with cakes and pies — a feast of epic proportions. I smiled at the din of conversation. By the time I got my plate, Stacy and the children were well into their meal. I saw that the flags were standing on either side of a sturdy small table hosting the urn. Gina was seated beside Stacy, and they were deep in animated conversation. A small cluster of young men tried to get Stacy's attention, while she was more occupied with her young cousins.

I tried to find a quiet spot to sit and eat, but everyone had things to say to me, either questions about the cancer or asking about Chris. I made my way at length to Stacy's table.

"Yo, Doctor P! How'd we do?"

"Spectacular. I don't think I've ever seen a better, cleaner use of symbols in a memorial service. Well done, young lady. Baltimore's lucky to have you."

"Turns out, I'm extending my stay here. I'm helping out Damsel In Distress." She pointed with her thumb to Gina.

Gina turned to me. "She says she can still use the mowing machine, so we're going to be gathering the feed while Chris is out of action."

One of Stacy's youngest cousins whispered in her ear, and Stacy pointed toward the bathroom. Stacy returned to me. "So, you coming out to the house?"

"Yes, ma'am. Your aunt invited me."

"Good. We're having a special ceremony at sunset. You can be a stand-in for ole 'Mrs. Waddail' while she skips down to Nashville. Nice save, by the way, Doctor P."

"I just made a few suggestions. Dr. Hamor and his team deserve the credit."

"Uh huh."

I left them to talk and made my way around the reception, meeting people, putting faces with names I had heard over the past few days. About an hour passed before the crowd thinned and I made my way back to Ellen's. Before leaving the reception, I offered to help with dishes, since that was my accustomed task back in Atlanta. The crew would hear nothing of it. Sarah told me to show up around five for festivities at the farm. That gave me enough time for a short nap.

I took off my shoes and lay back on the bed, soft and cool. I glanced again at the big quilt with all the angels. I smiled once more at the kitchen angels and the choir angels. I think that I met them all during the service that day. I realized that this hanging was different from most of Ellen's quilts. It involved appliqué as opposed to her normal bold patterned piecework. Plenty of individual angels, all in whites and gold sewn on piece by piece — all save that lone figure in the lower center, the little angel in stripes and jeans.

I fell asleep and slept unbroken until my alarm sounded at 4:30. Once outside, I checked around for Ellen or Stacy and found that the car was gone. I drove out to the Johnson farm and almost laughed as I approached, realizing afresh that I needed to re-calibrate my expectations of "small gathering." About two dozen cars were parked in the drive and along the road. I parked, got out, and headed toward the house. Kingsley came bounding out to greet me. "Kingsley, old buddy! How's it going?" He recognized me and urged me to follow him around the house rather than to the front door. I could hear voices in the back, so I followed. Rounding the back corner, I smiled as I caught sight of the reason why Sarah so wanted me to come out.

The peeling whitish structure had been transformed with all the colors I had seen in Stacy's hair. The base color of bright white had been restored as a background while the slats in the rails alternated red, white, blue, red, white, and blue. The individual posts sported military rank insignia while jets flew on the flat spaces just below the roof. Each panel below the railing contained the name of one of the grandchildren, with their handprints beside their names. In the center of the platform, Frank's urn rested on a small table.

As I stood admiring the work, Faye approached from the side and stood with me.

"Isn't it marvelous? Frank loved her like his own. He'd be so thrilled."

I nodded. "Looks like the feeling was mutual. I think he earned it."

She smiled a mischievous smile. "Wait 'til you see what happens at sunset."

I was glad, in a way, that Ellen did not have a scale in my room. I'm sure that I had gained an alarming number of pounds in the first five days of my stay. Between the house and the gazebo, a picnic table was spread with dishes left over from the memorial service reception, and a menagerie of chairs was arranged in groups around the yard. Though I wasn't hungry, I took a plate with a piece of chicken, mashed potatoes, and green beans anyway. I saw that a few pieces were left of what appeared to be Mrs. Tinley's coconut cake and decided to leave them for the children.

I sat in a folding chair and listened to stories as I nibbled my way through dinner. Children zoomed about the yard, coming up to Stacy from time to time — she seemed to be their "go-to" person. Jane Coudron filled in details about how Stacy came to live with the Johnsons. Jane suffered from major depression after a series of failed relationships. It was fortunate that she understood the seriousness of her condition, and that she reached out to her sister, Faye. Stacy became part of the Johnson family from the age of 8 until she was 14. I sensed that Jane and Stacy related more as friends than as a traditional mother-daughter pair.

Everyone was interested in how the research was progressing. Isabel arrived as I began to explain the purposes of the samples I had taken. She assembled a plate and joined the circle, sitting next to Sarah. I felt a little uncomfortable discussing my work. It seemed as though we should be talking more about Frank, though maybe they were tired of that for now.

"We start with the idea that there is maybe one or just a few causes for a disease. In the case of bacteria, fungi, or viruses, we have standard methods to detect them and can identify them in just hours or days."

"You said in the service you didn't think it was an infection that caused the cancer. How do you know? It might be something new," someone asked.

Ellen smiled at the question as she listened for my answer.

"We don't know for absolute certainty. The way this cancer presents — the way it looks and develops — doesn't fit the pattern of a cancer caused by an infection. There are cancers caused by viruses, of course — HPV, HIV, and Kaposi's sarcoma come right to mind. We've studied those kinds of cancers for well over 50 years, and it just doesn't fit. All the samples I've sent back will still be checked for 'germs.' We certainly wouldn't want to be surprised by something like a new HIV. Still, I'm seeing a lot of things that are more often the causes of cancer, things like industrial chemicals and the chemical byproducts of molds and such. Because we have four cases of a rare cancer occurring at about the same time in a small community, I expect all four of your men were exposed to something bad about five or six years ago. I've sent back samples from Frank and Walt and Ron so far and have some results back from the tests on Frank's workup. There were some puzzling developments there, so I still have work to do."

"Puzzling?" the questioner asked.

"His blood work showed the presence of a rare metal called beryllium. Beryllium's so rare that it gets our attention right away. We'll see if it shows up in the other samples. I want to know the source of that for certain. The cancer would have started several years ago. If it was caused by a short-term exposure to chemicals, those chemicals may be long ago flushed from the body. What I'm most anxious to see are the DNA tests."

"Like on CSI?" Jane asked.

I smiled. "Yeah, sort of. DNA is the recipe book for how our bodies work. In the case of cancers, something has gone wrong with the recipe." I pointed to the last piece of Mrs. Tinley's coconut cake on the table. "Let's say that you followed a recipe for the cake without thinking about it and the copy of the recipe you got had a typo — a 'C' or cup of baking powder instead of a 'T' or tablespoon of baking powder."

Everyone laughed. This was one of my favorite teaching examples.

"Right. It would be a disaster for the cake. Well, it's the same with DNA. A mistake can be disastrous. In the case of cancers, the mistake is in the instructions that tell cells when to stop dividing. We know enough about the code now that we can find the typos and that knowledge can help us pinpoint the original causes. Very powerful. Some of the techniques we use today didn't even exist a few years ago when these cancers would have started."

"Can you cure the others, then?" Faye queried.

I paused to compose my answer. Isabel stopped eating and watched me.

"I wish we could. I wish we could move that fast, but the disease has progressed so far. Everyone here has done everything they could. With a hundred cancers, there may be a hundred treatments. And this is a rare one. We don't even know what the cause is yet. The reason I'm here is to find that cause so we can find a cure. If there is any comfort so far, it would be that they all four contracted the disease at about the same time and no one else has shown any symptoms in those years." I extended my hand in Isabel's direction. "Dr. Rodriguez is as observant a health-care professional as I've ever met in all the decades of my work. Her records have been a gold mine of information for me. She would have seen it if more cases were brewing."

Isabel lowered her head. I had not meant to cause any embarrassment. Everyone was nodding in agreement, though.

"Anyway, I will begin to have a flood of results starting Monday. I'll keep everyone posted."

I was relieved to see Sarah's son — Sergeant Meyers — take the last piece of Mrs. Tinley's coconut cake, thereby removing the temptation. As we continued to discuss how the CDC identified diseases, Faye got up and went into the house. She returned a few minutes later with another coconut cake. Though the CDC had long ago clarified the causes of weight gain and atherosclerosis, the cure would remain elusive as long as there was Mrs. Tinley's coconut cake.

As the sun approached the horizon, Stacy got up and went over to a large bell mounted on a post at the edge of the lawn. Between the church reception and the farm gathering, she had changed her clothes and wore a draping dark purple dress with long flowing sleeves, almost theatrical in appearance. She rang the loud bell, bringing the children's play to a stop. Faye walked over and stood beside her as Mike went to the gazebo and retrieved the urn. Sarah opened the gate that led into the pasture.

Stacy's young cousins encircled her, and the adults gathered just outside that circle.

Stacy took command. "OK, troops, we have one last mission today, and it's a super important one that only we can carry out. When Uncle Frank — Grandpa Frank — knew he wasn't going to make it, he told us that he didn't want his body buried in the ground. He was really, really clear about that. He said he wanted what was left of his body, the clean dry ashes in this jar, to be scattered across the land that he loved. That way, his body will always be part of the farm. That's what he wanted and that's just what we're going to do, by golly.

"Uncle Mike will give each of us two little fists full of ashes. We'll take off into the field or some special place in the yard and let them go. Scatter them with joy. Uncle Frank was a good uncle, a good father and grandfather; this was his wish. This would make him happy. So sing or dance or fly or just jump up and down. When you have accomplished your mission, come back to the rose garden, and Aunt Faye will rinse your hands into the roses so nothing is wasted."

Stacy paused and looked at the children, listening to her instructions with rapt attention. I was impressed.

She stiffened. "Are we ready?"

The children shouted back with one voice, loud and clear, "Yes, ma'am!"

Under her supervision, Mike dispensed a portion of the ashes into waiting hands starting with the older boys. As each received her or his share, they raced off into fields, arms extended like fighter jets. They made jet sounds as they scissored back and forth, releasing a thin stream of ashes while they ran until the ashes were exhausted. The girls took charge of the youngest children and strode into the field, dispensing their portions on selected flowers. One of the youngest children tossed her load into the air and I watched the tiny cloud, backlit by the sunset, drift in the still air until it settled among the grasses and clover.

Mike handed the urn to Stacy, who poured for the adults. They walked to their spots to place their ashes, Mike and Sarah to the field, now aglow in sunset orange tones, Jane toward the barn, Amelia to an apple tree, and Faye to the rose garden.

Stacy looked to me, her face streaked with tears. "Can you hold this for me and pour?" I accepted the urn and shook most of the remaining contents into her hands.

She slipped off her shoes and ran straight toward the setting sun to a rise in the pasture. Silhouetted against the sun, she ran and danced and swirled. From time to time, she leapt into the air, spinning as she rose, her purple sleeves streaming with the dance. In the backlight, I could see grasshoppers jumping out of the way and, as if on cue, swallows swooping in to take advantage of the grasshoppers. At last she flung the ashes with a loud cry. "Fly!"

Isabel and I were alone with the urn. We watched Stacy return, spent. After rinsing into the rose bed, she came over to us.

"OK, your turn."

Though I had not expected the honor, it seemed appropriate. I handed Stacy the urn and she allocated half of what remained to me. She turned to Isabel, who shook her head.

"I'm not family," she whispered.

Stacy was somber in her reply. "You were with Uncle Frank as he died. You were the last one to see him alive, just like Doc P was the last to see him in his body. If you don't feel comfortable, I'll understand. Still, I do think it's right." After a moment, Isabel extended her hands and received the last of the ashes. We walked into the field as Stacy took the urn to be rinsed onto the roses.

I continued to the rise where Stacy had danced while Isabel continued on beyond the rise toward the pond at the bottom of the field.

I looked at the ashes in my hand, gravel-like, and gray. "Well, Frank, we meet again. Sorry for the circumstances," I said as I raised my eyes to the people assembled. "Looks like you've left quite the good legacy. I admire your whole family, and want to thank you in particular for what you did for Stacy. You transformed that eight-year-old into a powerful young woman who has made, and will make, you proud. And thank you for your service to your country. Rest in peace."

I raised my hands and let the ashes fall in a slow stream into the vegetation. I brushed my hands through the grass before turning back to the house. Glancing over my shoulder, I saw Isabel seated on a concrete bench beneath an old weeping willow tree beside the pond. Her head was bowed, her hands in front of her, cradling the ashes. I debated whether to go down to talk to her. I sensed a desire on her part to be alone, so I decided I would check back later.

Returning to the crowd in the back yard, I helped Mike setting up citronella torches to chase the bugs away. I took a seat and listened to "Frank stories." Sarah told about how she almost missed her junior prom because her dad had picked up her dress in Hopkinsville and he put it in the open back of the pickup he was driving. When he got home, the box with her dress was missing. They retraced the route back at full speed, spotting it at last alongside the road just three miles out of Hopkinsville. The dress was in perfect condition in its box and Sarah made it to the prom on time, but Frank apologized for the event the rest of his life.

Amelia told about how she had set up Frank's first date with Faye, and how Faye had heard his name as "Hank" rather than "Frank" and so she called him Hank for the whole date. Frank couldn't figure out how to correct her without embarrassing her, so he remained "Hank" for almost a week.

When Stacy was 11, she had decided she wanted a zebra. Uncle Frank explained that they didn't domesticate well, like horses. He returned from Rotary one afternoon to find that Stacy had painted black stripes on their white horse. He laughed so hard he said that his ribs hurt for several days.

As dusk deepened into night, the yard filled with lightning bugs. Amelia's youngest granddaughter, Clare, ran up to Stacy with a jar of six or seven of the flashing insects. Clare beamed.

"Hey, Lady Clare, look what you got." Stacy smiled.

"How do they work, Stacy?"

"You mean the lights?"

Clare nodded vigorously.

"I have no idea, Lady Clare. However, there's someone here who would know." She pointed to me. "Bet Dr. Parker knows."

Clare walked over to me and presented the jar without saying anything.

"I see you have some lightning bugs, Lady Clare. Take a look on the inside of the jar here. See the tail where they flash?"

She nodded.

"Well, in their bodies, they have little sacks of chemicals — juices. And when they want to flash, they squeeze those sacks, the chemicals mix together, and ... presto ... it makes light!"

She grinned at the explanation. I looked up to see Stacy and Ellen both smiling as well.

"So, Lady Clare, what are you going to do with the lightning bugs?"

"Cousin Jacob said that if you squeeze them onto your skin, your skin will glow too."

I frowned a gentle frown. "Well, yes, that's true. Then the lightning bug dies, though. It's sort of tearing their bodies in two."

Clare gave a horrified look, her eyes wide and mouth open. "That's awful!" She returned to Stacy.

"He's right, Lady Clare. I remember Uncle Frank telling me not to hurt them. He also said that lightning bugs ate mosquitoes." Stacy looked up at me for confirmation, and I nodded. "So what we always did was we watched them for a while and then let them go. That way, everyone was happy."

Clare agreed. "Let's let them go now."

"You sure?" Stacy asked.

"Yes." Clare handed Stacy the jar.

Stacy unscrewed the lid. "OK, Lady Clare. Now watch. It's fun how they take off." The insects performed as Stacy narrated. "They climb up to the highest spot. See? Then they spread their wings to check them out. And — poof — off they go into the night."

Clare jerked her head to watch the insects fly away. She was beaming again, and turned to run back into the yard.

"Hey, Lady Clare, don't you want your jar?" Stacy called.

Clare turned back on the run. "No. You can keep it. I'm going to fly with the lightning bugs."

Stacy smiled as she reseated the lid on the jar. "I tried that, too. I climbed up on the fence." She pointed to a spot in the pasture fence. "Even if it didn't work, it wasn't far to fall." She turned to me. "Another nice save there, Doctor P. The lightning bugs thank you from the bottom of their tiny butts. You know, she was right. You'd be a great doctor for here."

"Who said that?" I asked.

"Doc Isabel. She was tellin' Gina you'd make a great doctor for here."

"Well, that was kind of her. I take it as a high compliment, because she is a top-flight professional. Guthrie is lucky to have her. I hope they know that. Speaking of which, she hasn't come back from the field. It's been a long time. I think I better check on her."

Ellen spoke. "She left a while ago. I saw her coming back from the pond and went to talk to her. She just needs a little time alone."

Stacy stretched her arms and rubbed her knees. "Yeah, she seemed pretty shook up. Maybe I shouldn't have pushed her on the ashes thing."

Ellen shook her head. "No. That was the absolute right thing to do, totally appropriate. That's not it. Frank was her first patient to die before his time."

"Really?" I said.

"Yup. She's had some of the old folks pass on; never one Frank's age."

Stacy leaned back in her chair. "Wow!"

After a somber pause, they resumed telling Frank stories. Around 9:30 everyone began bringing dishes into the house, tidying up the yard, and getting the children ready for bed. While they wouldn't let me help with the dishes, they were pleased to have Mike and me get the chairs and torches back into the house.

I made my thank-yous and left about ten o'clock. The children were camped out on blankets and sleeping bags in the living room. As I left, Stacy and Ellen were doing a round-robin bedtime story. Each would take the narrative for a while and end with a difficult transition to challenge the other. The children laughed at the resulting mayhem of a story.

I eased back to Ellen's through the deserted countryside, watching the lightning bugs and reflecting on the spirit of community. I guessed that most of the children would remember for the rest of their lives the day they scattered their grandfather's ashes in the field in Guthrie. I hoped that Isabel would not take Frank's death too personally for too long. There is always a balance between patient care and the inevitable forces of nature.

7 THE APPOINTMENT

"So at that point, you had no idea what was causing the cancers," she persisted.

A good physician treasures a blunt patient, as long as they are kind and honest, as was the case here.

I wagged my finger. "That is not true. You cut me to the quick. I had nailed the causes by Saturday night. It's just that there were too many competing explanations that would have been just as valid. Plus, even though I had the agents identified — among many more possibilities, to be sure — I did not have the triggering event."

I saw the patient's skeptical look as I continued, "You see, in my field ... hmmm, I keep saying that, don't I ... in the field of epidemiology, the causative agent is only half the story. You visit a community where dozens of people have come down with food poisoning symptoms, for instance. It takes a day or two at most to identify *botulinum* and rule out other organisms or poisons. That's just battle one. Then you have to find out where it comes from. And over the years, I've almost always found a single source, most often an obscure piece of equipment or someone without proper training. That's the hard part because you need to rely on people's memory and honesty to give a full picture of where they've been and what they've done so that you can sort out the overlaps."

"Yeah. On Saturday night, you still didn't know."

I folded my arms and smiled. "Have you ever hunted for four-leaf clovers?"

"Sure. I've found lots of them," she asserted with pride.

"And it's easy to find them, isn't it? After all, they're right there in plain sight."

"No. You've got to look real hard. I'm good at it," she said.

"Is it easy to help someone else find them?"

"No way! It'll drive the other person nuts."
I kept my arms folded and smiled.
"OK. I get your point. You win this round." She surrendered.
"Thank you. Now hop up on the table, please."

8 RESPECTFUL OMNIVORE

I awoke soon after sunrise. Since Guthrie sits near the eastern edge of the Central Time Zone, I guess it must have been around 5:30, 6 o'clock. Though Saturday had been a busy and emotional day, I slept well. My experiences in the memorial service and surrounding events left me eager to attend Sunday service. I knew that Ellen could recommend a Sunday School class to attend. I resolved that I would not conduct my business asking questions while there, though I knew from experience that there would be questions for me from others.

I showered and shaved, and put on a shirt that would go well on its own or with a more formal jacket. I'd check with Ellen as to the most appropriate attire. Then I composed a long email to Baylor describing the service, the reception, and the gathering at Faye's. I didn't mention Isabel's comments relayed to me by Stacy.

I walked out into the morning around quarter 'til seven. The piercing blue sky was half-filled with fluffy cumulus clouds. If the day turned hot, we could expect afternoon thundershowers.

I didn't want to presume that Ellen was up. I wasn't even sure whether she attended church or, if so, which one. Should have asked earlier. I strolled along her peony bed. If we did live here, Baylor would have a huge bed of peonies. Ellen's were a uniform shell pink, no doubt originating from a single division long ago. Baylor had told me about the newer varieties, which had a much wider range of colors, and many had different forms. Unfortunately, the newer varieties often mildewed, having been bred more for appearance than disease resistance. Perhaps the breeders would turn their attention to that someday as they were now with roses. Alas, there were a lot more rose breeders than peony breeders.

I was approaching the end of the bed when I heard the front door open, and turned to see Ellen on the porch.

"Are you hungry? Breakfast is almost on the table."

"Yes, ma'am. I was just admiring your flowers."

"Your wife would love it here. Peonies do well even if they are blooming earlier."

I turned and walked back toward the house, not remembering telling Ellen that Baylor liked peonies. Breakfast started with some of the most flavorful patty sausages I had ever tasted.

"This is Broadbent sausage. I suspect it's stronger than you're used to," she said.

"It's wonderful!" I assured her.

She brought a small bowl of biscuits to the table along with a jar of sorghum molasses.

"Old man Taylor out on the Russellville road still runs a sorghum press — just for friends. He told me a few years back he was going to get out of sorghum because no one was buying his grain at a reasonable price. Then Gina started taking all that he'd produce for her Limousin cattle, since old man Taylor doesn't spray his crop with anything. He's kinda set for life there. And the rest of us get fresh sorghum molasses every fall. Nice arrangement."

I savored breakfast. "I was going to Guthrie Baptist this morning unless you have a better recommendation. I saw on the sign that Sunday School's at nine."

"Good choice — that's my church. They're thoughtful people. You'd enjoy the young adults class. They have 15 to 20 in that class on a typical Sunday and the discussions can get pretty spirited."

"What's the customary dress?"

She surveyed what I was wearing. "Oh, you're fine. Almost overdressed. They'll still give you a little out-of-towner credit. No one wears a tie in summer any more. If you get there between quarter of nine and nine o'clock, you'll have plenty of time to chat and get to know everyone a little better. I'll drive out about 8:30, only because I need to go out and get Miss Ledbetter and Shirley."

I finished breakfast and got ready for church, taking my paper Bible rather than the electronic tablet. The three blocks zipped by, and I arrived for class about 20 minutes early. I helped set up coffee while I talked with the teacher, a young lawyer with a practice in Hopkinsville.

The class was studying a book about justice, focusing on incarceration. That day's lesson dealt with forgiveness of crimes. The passage was in the eighth chapter of John, the one about a woman who had been caught in adultery brought to Jesus. It's a fertile passage for discussion and a bit of an anomaly. The same story appears in Luke, though in a different part of Jesus's ministry. Historically, the passage is not well anchored in the scriptures. Some very old documents have it, some don't. The story is all the more layered by virtue of the woman being brought before Jesus with no mention of the man involved. These details we had studied back at North Park, and I was pleased to find them well known here, too. One of the challenges of traveling around the country is avoiding prejudiced assumptions about the education of the locale. Ellen's description of the class as "thoughtful" was spot-on.

My input was welcomed, and I reflected on the open-ended finale of "I do not condemn you either. Go, and from now on do not sin any more." My division at CDC doesn't do any specific work with prisons. Still, other parts of the Center were becoming aware of the health consequences of our nation's extraordinary incarceration rates. Prisons were costing the country over a hundred billion dollars a year, while the entire CDC budget, including the Agency for Toxic Substances and Disease Registry, was a little over ten billion.

We went on to discuss enforcement of biblical laws today, including those laws requiring stoning for violations such as adultery and male homosexual behavior. As predicted, the discussions were spirited; we had made little progress moving through the book by the time the class ended.

I sat with Isabel and Ellen during the service, as I had Saturday morning. The sermon topic had been changed from the scheduled lectionary topic to the passage from Matthew centered on "Well done, good and faithful servant." I was all the more impressed that Pastor Roberts did not shy away from exploring the fact that the original context might well have referred to a slave rather than a paid servant. The rest I had gotten since coming to Guthrie allowed me to stay alert throughout the sermon.

After the service ended, Isabel asked if I had plans for the afternoon. I had none.

She continued. "I was thinking of going up to Pennyrile Lake and wondered if you and Ellen might want to join me. It'll be a good mental health break after this week."

Ellen declined. "If I didn't have duty at the Home this afternoon, I'd love to go." She turned to me. "You'd love it up there. It's a nice trip."

We left after talking with several congregants. Isabel checked to make sure a couple of her patients were taking their medications and I answered a few more cancer questions. She drove north and westward through Hopkinsville, where we stopped for lunch at a café with superb barbeque.

Pennyrile Lake is located in a Kentucky State Resort Park within the Pennyrile State Forest. Isabel explained that "Pennyrile" might be a corruption of pennyroyal, a pungent herb found in the dry, acidic woods of the area. Pennyroyal has some alleged medicinal properties, and is also a proven mosquito repellent. She said she knew of several patches of Pennyroyal in the park. It was not uncommon.

Throughout the drive, she pointed to the homes of several patients, giving me a synopsis of the maladies that afflicted the citizens of Christian County, Kentucky.

"So even though you're with the Todd County health service, you have patients over here in Christian County, too?"

She smiled. "The lines get blurry. For the most part, they're relatives of my Todd County charges who don't trust the Hopkinsville medicine. They'll travel a ways or wait to avoid a trip to Jackson-Sheridan. Too many horror stories."

"I saw that as a theme in the records. What's with Jackson-Sheridan?"

She frowned. "They're a locally owned for-profit hospital — very for-profit. They cut corners and don't have a national organization to answer to. They do whatever they must to qualify for Medicare payments — no more. Their marks for just about any quality measure are pretty poor. Anyone with the wherewithal goes to Vanderbilt. You'll recall we didn't consider sending Chris to Jackson-Sheridan, even though it was a fraction of the distance. For one thing, they don't have a helicopter landing spot because it would open them up to too many more state inspection requirements."

"So your patients drive an extra 20 miles to avoid Hopkinsville?"

"Uh huh. Or I sometimes do house calls."

"That's a lot of time for you, then."

She pondered for a moment. "I don't think about the time."

We entered the State Forest with its cool, dark woods. Northwestern Christian County is hilly — much more so than the rolling meadows of southern Todd County. Once inside the State Park, we followed signs to the boat docks. We parked and got out. Pennyrile Lake is not very large, perhaps 10 to 20 acres formed behind a dam at the northern end. It's nestled below steep cliffs and ledges, shrouded in deep woods. The lake was a peaceful place, and I could understand why Isabel retreated here for refuge.

"Let's find you some pennyroyal." I followed her on a trail from the boat dock area along the cliffs on the west side of the lake. The view from the cliffs was beautiful. A few visitors had rented paddleboats and were cruising the lake. Though there was a landing for putting fishing boats into the water, I didn't see any fishermen today.

She saw me surveying the water. "You fish?"

I shook my head. "I've never taken it up. We've got some great lakes in Georgia, and I have several friends who are devoted fishermen. It's just too much for me to get everything together to go from urban Atlanta out to where the fish are."

"Yeah, I hear you. I'm happy to see them break surface from time to time." We climbed a little farther. "Ah, here we are."

She found a small patch, perhaps a little moister than the surrounding ground. In the dappled shade, I saw perhaps a dozen small plants of the mint family.

"Run your hands along the plants, and then smell your hands."

I complied. The fragrance was a piercing mix of wintergreen and other essences.

"Oh, that's nice," I said, "I recognize several things in there that would repel mosquitoes."

"They say the pioneers would gather it and put the dried plants in pillows and beddings. This area once had some malaria, so I guess the pennyroyal helped. Gained enough respect that it gave its name to the region."

I reflected on my conversation with Mr. Gough about CDC and malaria. I took a small side sprig and put it in my pocket, leaving the rest in peace. We turned back and followed the trail along sandstone outcrops back to the boat landing.

"Want to go sailing?"

I grinned. "I thought I'd had enough sailing in my Navy days, though these waters look pretty calm. Sounds like fun."

A teenaged boy manned the boat concession. I reached for my wallet.

She put up her hand. "No, I've got it."

"Well, I'll pick up this or the gas. Take your pick."

She waved me on to pay for the rental. The paddleboats were ten dollars for the first two hours, so I think I got the better end of the deal. The operation was must have been subsidized by the state. The attendant handed each of us a personal floatation device and directed us to Boat 7.

We cast off onto the lake. From the vantage point of a small paddleboat, the lake seemed much larger than it would appear on a map.

"I love this spot. When I've had a bad week, which seems to be pretty often of late, I'll come up here by myself, and just drift for hours. It's self-service during the week early in the season and sometimes I'm the only one on the lake. I think I get an idea of why Jesus tried to get away on the lake."

"Sea of Galilee?" I offered.

"Yeah, that's one name. The Romans called it Lake Tiberias, I guess after one of their emperors."

"Right. Emperor Tiberius — different spelling, ironically. Kinneret and Lake of Genesaret were other names. It figures in a lot of cultures there, even today. It's one of the biggest freshwater bodies in the area. I visited there once."

She seemed quite interested. "Oh, yeah? Medical business or tourist?"

"A little of both. CDC partnered with the Israeli health ministry on studying the eye disease, schistosomiasis. They have a very effective effort controlling it. CDC paid my way to the conference there, and I picked up lodging so I could stay an extra week. I visited a lot of the sites, including

Magdala, Mary's home."

"The hooker?" she asked.

"No, I don't think so. Actually, I'm a little surprised you'd see her that way."

Isabel shook her head. "Sorry. I do know better. I guess I was testing you. I don't know why I do that, John. You've shown yourself to be honorable and scholarly in every way. I guess I've just been looking over my shoulder for so long, it's become a habit. You won't find Mary mistaken for a hooker in our church — we know better."

"I thought so. She is an interesting and intriguing woman. Don't know anything about her past or her religious training. She leaves a lot for our imaginations."

"And conspiracy theories." Isabel giggled.

We were adrift in the middle of the lake.

"Let me show you a couple of my favorite places here. You paddle. I'll steer."

I churned the water as Isabel guided the boat toward one of the steeper rock faces.

"OK. Stop."

We drifted to a stop about 15 feet from the wall of sandstone.

"I like this place so much in mid- to late summer. Turtles will sun themselves on the branches at the water's edge, and they'll just watch you if you approach slow enough and don't get too close. And water snakes will perch in the branches of the shrubs growing out from the rocks. When they spot a fish down below, they'll plunge straight down." We paused in the spot for a while. There were no turtles or snakes that day. "Too early. You'll have to come back in August." She pointed to the shallow end of the lake. "Let's head down there."

"While I'd love to see them then, I'm hoping to finish up in a few days."

"Pity. We could use a good doctor here — you know that."

"The people have a good doctor here. I think you're letting outside forces get to you. The community will protect and support you as long as you continue. There's always a way."

She stared straight ahead at the patch of greenery we were approaching. "OK. Stop."

We drifted toward a wide patch of emergent vegetation, the huge round leaves of the native lotus. I had seen the pink species in water gardens in Atlanta; never the native yellow species. It was impressive up close.

She stared at the plants. "There's always a way, but sometimes I get so tired. I said Jesus liked to get away on the lake. I feel for Him, even though I'm no Jesus. Can you imagine how tired he must have been? He tried to heal people. He was always surrounded by people wanting more and more from him. He worked outside the system. The system hated him and tried at every turn to stop him, killing him in the end."

"I guess it's small comfort he won in the end."

"Yeah, what a price. And I'm not Jesus. I don't have his backup. I can't even heal myself." She caressed the left side of her scarf. "Some day, they'll come swooping in on the clinic and it'll be all over. Just like that." Her voice bespoke more sorrow and resignation than anger. She turned to me. "That's why we need someone with credentials."

"I have a mission that serves a lot of people. I'm not the doctor you're looking for," I protested.

She laughed at the cinematic reference. "You'd do so well here. You'd love it. Baylor would love it, too."

I was getting irritated. "I'm not here on a recruitment visit. And, to be honest, I'm not sure why everyone thinks they know what Baylor would like."

She turned away toward the lotuses and gave a soft chuckle.

It was then that I realized that they did know Baylor more than I had imagined. "Has someone been talking to my wife?"

Isabel kept staring at the lotuses. I leaned back in my seat of the paddleboat, puzzled that I was not upset by the emerging revelation. As I struggled for a response, Isabel's cell phone buzzed.

"At least Jesus didn't have a cell phone." She looked at the text message on her device. "Oh, no." She hung her head and handed me the phone. The caller was "Gina" with the message "it's time."

We both paddled as she turned the boat around and we sped to the dock. We turned in our flotation collars and got in the car for the trip back to Guthrie.

Isabel was very quiet on the way.

"I meant what I said the other night. You've done everything anyone could do for Walt. Believe me. I know these diseases. You've gone to the limits for him."

She savored my words for a while as we raced across the flattening terrain. "I know what you're saying in my head. In my heart, he's mine. He's my responsibility. And it pains me that he's dying. Like Frank and Ron, Walt is a good man and he's dying. I'm feeling that loss very much. Good men like Walt shouldn't die so early.

I sat quietly. She had not mentioned Jim Dulaney, the only one I hadn't met because of his distance from Guthrie. It did not seem like the time to discuss Jim. I had heard enough to know that he was in a different part of people's hearts from the other three.

About a mile from Guthrie, Isabel turned to me. "I'm going to drop you off at Ellen's. Do you remember the way to Walt's place?"

"Yes."

"OK. You get your sampling stuff and head out there in a half hour or so. I'll get my doctor stuff and go out right away. Once word gets out, it'll get crowded at the farm."

She let me out in front of Ellen's house. Ellen's car was gone from the driveway. I went up the porch and tried the front door — it was locked. I walked around the back, reminding myself that I was a peripheral player in the drama unfolding. I understood the community enough to know that Ellen, with Stacy, were already at the farm with Gina and Sharon.

Isabel was not the only one feeling her limitations. Walt and I were going to have a talk about his thoughts on judgment. I couldn't be sure what 'it's time' meant, though Isabel felt an urgency. I sensed that Walt would have his answers without our talk.

In my room I put away my Sunday suit, gathered my sampling kit, and drove out to the farm, correcting a single wrong turn after about half a city block. When I arrived, I found Gina's truck, Ellen's and Isabel's cars, and another car I presumed was Sharon's. I parked off to the side of the drive and got out. Jason crept up to me — not bounding.

"Hey, Jason," I said.

He approached, his tail wagging slow and low, and he whimpered rather than barked. Jason knew something was wrong.

I reached down and patted his head. "Don't worry, Jason. We're going to take care of Gina. You can do your part later." He escorted me in silence to the front porch.

Despite my resistance, I was indeed integrating into the community. I opened the front door and walked in unannounced, made my way through the living room and dining room, and proceeded to the sun porch.

Walt's body lay flat in repose on the chaise lounge with a blanket covering him. Gina sat in a chair at his side, weeping. Isabel stood behind her, Isabel's hand on Gina's shoulder. Isabel's cheeks were streaked with tears. Sharon sat in another chair, staring into the room, Ellen at her side. Stacy stood against the wall on the other side of the room, her arms crossed, her expression stern. When she saw me enter the room, Stacy nodded in recognition. I set down my case beside the sofa and walked over to stand next to Stacy. The room remained silent, save for the ticking of a clock. On the table by the chaise lounge, I could see a trove of awards and pictures that Gina had placed — the farm, state competitions, Ferdinand, and Chris. Those would have been some of the last images that Walt had enjoyed.

After a long while, Gina turned and looked around the room. She caught sight of me. "Thank you for coming, Dr. Parker. Grandpa enjoyed talking with you so much the other day. I just wish you guys had met earlier."

"I'm so sorry," I offered, "even in our little bit of time together, we had a lot to talk about."

She looked exhausted. "Did you bring your kit?"

I nodded and retrieved it, walking over to Walt's body. Gina didn't move from her seat.

I sat down beside her. "Is it OK for me to begin?"

"I'll do it. Grandpa would have wanted me to do it." Though weary, she was in command.

I looked up at Isabel who nodded. I laid out the sample vials and syringes. I opened the sharps bag to receive the used syringes, and went over what I needed from each sample. With each instruction, she nodded. I handed her a pair of latex gloves and she put them on.

Gina took the first syringe. The tears had welled up in her eyes and were falling fast. Her lips quivered. She paused, took a deep breath, and went to work, once more in full control as she recited, "In the late 70s we had standard Herefords. They gave us a good run. In the 80s, we added Angus. That was when the craze in the restaurants started. We also tried some Aubrac, just for fun. But they don't do well in our heat. We're too far south for them."

As she had on my prior visit, Gina went about her tasks with efficiency. As she talked, she concentrated in a most professional manner. "In the 90s, we kept the Angus and added Shorthorns, which were OK. When I really got into the operation, I wanted Limousin. He thought I just liked their color, which was partly true. Certified organic."

She turned to me. "One of the last things he said to me was that I was right about the organic." She sniffed back her tears. "You needed a brain core and liver sample."

"I can do that for you if you'd like."

She shook her head. "No, my job. He can't feel it now. It needs to be done right. We test all the cattle we sell to check for BSE and hepatitis."

I handed her the coring tube. I knew from much experience that taking the sample took considerable strength. She took the tube, positioned it, and began the sample. "And I didn't forget about the Longhorns. That was a quaint, romantic idea just before the Angus. Ornery, finicky, and not all that much meat for the amount of pasture they took. We have nothing good to say about Longhorns. Texas can keep 'em and good riddance. We will forget the Longhorns from this day forward."

She bagged the core sample and handed it to me. "Do you need anything else?"

"No. You did him proud. He can rest in peace knowing you can handle anything."

She began sobbing hard as she removed the gloves. She stood up and looked around the room. "I wish Chris were here."

Stacy left her position at the wall, strode to Gina, and wrapped her arms around her. Stacy turned Gina away from the rest of us, and swished one hand back and forth indicating we should leave. I assembled my case and left with the others. Stacy stayed behind, embracing Gina as she sobbed.

Isabel, Sharon, and Ellen walked toward the kitchen while I strode out onto the front porch. Bill Carson had just arrived and was walking up the steps.

I nodded and he nodded in return. "Sharon, Doc Isabel, and Ellen are in the kitchen. You should see them first. Stacy and Gina are on the sun porch with Walt's body. I'm guessing Stacy will let you guys know when the timing is right."

"Thanks, Doc, I appreciate the heads up. Walt was a good man. I'm glad you got to meet him while he was still alive."

I nodded.

Bill opened the front door. "Damned shame. Damned shame."

I sat down on one of the lower steps; appreciating the courage it took for Gina to complete those samples. While I felt drained, I couldn't begin to imagine her state.

Jason approached me, still whining, still wagging his tail low and slow. He came in close, watching my eyes, and laid his chin on my knee.

I rubbed his head. I didn't have a dog — no time with my schedules — yet I knew what felt good to dogs. I scratched behind his ears. "You know what's going on, don't you? Gina's OK. You know. Jason, she's going to need you a lot in the next few days. She's going to need all the companionship she can get."

Jason raised his eyebrows. He lifted his head off my knee and backed up. He turned as if to go, looking back to me. His tail wagged more strongly. I watched him a bit longer. He came toward me, paused, and then turned away again, watching me behind him.

"You want to go for a walk?"

His wagging grew more intense. I moved the sample case to the side of the steps and stood up. Jason walked forward a few steps; only to look back to be sure I followed. An air of normality seemed to come over him as I followed across the yard toward the pasture fence, where I saw a massive Limousin steer. Ferdinand, no doubt.

Back in Atlanta, dogs were walked on leashes. Here, Jason was lord of the manor, leading me with a gentle trot. He would pause from time to time if he got too far ahead of me. And he was leading me straight to the fence beside the bull.

Knowing little of farming, I'd never felt threatened by an animal, other than an occasional mean dog. Still, I felt a definite unease as we approached Ferdinand. My first impression was of his size — taller than I was by a head and rippling with muscle. He stood his ground and watched my approach. As we neared the fence, Ferdinand lowered his head and snorted what I guessed was a warning. I was almost entering his personal space. I slowed my approach. Jason noticed and came back to urge me on. When Ferdinand snorted again, Jason came alongside me, pressed his side against my leg, and faced the bull. Jason gave a throaty greeting, alternating his gaze between Ferdinand and me. The bull fell silent and raised his enormous head to look me over.

"Hello, Ferdinand."

Jason left my side and walked to the fence, putting his paws on the wire to gain as much height as he could. I advanced to join him.

I put out my hand, and Ferdinand approached. I was making a critical assumption that bulls don't bite. I didn't know that, though I didn't recall hearing of anyone's being treated for cow bites. I have since become aware of a few occurrences. In Jason's presence I felt safe. I stroked Ferdinand's head and neck. I didn't know what to expect — maybe soft and fatty, but his hide was rock-hard beneath his short hair.

I looked down to Jason to see if he approved. He changed position, as if nervous, between sitting and standing. Again he switched his attention between Ferdinand and me. I began to understand.

I continued to stroke the bull's head. "Well, Ferdinand, I guess I'm the one who has to tell you. Walt died." The bull backed away and turned his head toward the house. I felt a cold shiver come over me. Gina was totally right. Ferdinand lowered his head and snorted, not at me.

"Gina's OK. She has people around her helping. She'll be out to see you as soon as she can."

Jason left my side and moved to the fence, putting his nose through the mesh. Ferdinand snorted again, very soft.

"Gina will still be here. Stacy's helping her while Chris is away. Chris will be back in a few weeks." Ferdinand turned to scan the driveway. "Chris isn't here now. He'll be back."

Jason left the fence and turned toward the house. His tail wagged in its normal way, and he turned in my direction, his tongue hanging out.

"Well, Ferdinand, I think I have to go. Good to meet you. Sorry it was under these circumstances." I left the fence and followed Jason as best I could. I wondered if I was experiencing some delusion until I heard the sound rolling across the meadows. I turned back to see Ferdinand, his face to the sky, bellowing over and over. The chill returned. That day was the first time I had ever interpreted between species. It would not be my last, and while I'm still not quite a vegetarian, I pause before I eat meat to ponder the life contained therein.

Back at the porch, I sat on the front steps in silence for perhaps 20 minutes. I heard the front door open and close, and heard the sound of heavy shoes coming down the steps. Bill Carson sat beside me.

"You want to give me a hand in a while? We'll get the body onto the stretcher and into the hearse."

"Sure. No problem. Whatever you need."

Bill was a professional — calm and proper, an island of serenity in times of chaos. "The women are getting together an outfit for the viewing. I injected some relaxants around his face. I'm glad I was able to get here before *rigor mortis* set in."

I turned to Bill, appreciating the details he had to consider.

"Ya' know, Doc, I hate this disease. I really do. I'm used to death — it's my business after all. Has been all my life I guess. This one's different. This disease is cruel. It reaches out and hurts its victims. I see it in the faces of the deceased — a terror, a fear. Sarah told me that Frank was sobbing as he died. Walt, the same. Most of the folk who come my way have died, peaceful in their sleep or suddenly in a crash. Not with this disease. The last moments are painful, scary. I hate this disease."

My mind raced with explanations. Given the profusion of nodules, it didn't take much to imagine them pressing on nerves, causing excruciating pain. Bill seemed to be talking about more than physical pain. Reactions like fear came from specific areas of the brain. I didn't know of any cancer that targeted specific areas of the brain. Perhaps this was just one more possible anomaly associated with Griffith's sarcoma. Walt was not in unusual pain that I could tell when I visited on Friday, though he was clearly dying.

I gazed out across the yard to the pasture. Jason rested in the sun a few yards from our perch. Ferdinand stood motionless beyond the fence. "Yeah, this cancer's getting to me, too. The epidemiologist in me is always worrying about the bad diseases we don't yet understand. Some day, something like this will turn out to be contagious and virulent. I'm pretty sure this one isn't, some day ...."

"Like smallpox or the Black Death?" Bill asked.

"Yeah." I turned to make sure I wasn't giving Bill the wrong impression. "Still, this isn't that day. Whatever it is, the problem is serious. Everything points to it being limited and local — seems to point to an environmental factor. With the quality of the samples I've gotten, I should have some answers in a few days. I've got several probable causes, maybe all of them. I just need to make sure I'm not missing anything."

Bill seemed reassured.

"Will Walt be cremated?" I asked.

"No. Traditional burial here on the farm. We went over plans starting about a year ago."

I nodded. "Let me know if you see anything out of the ordinary when you prep the body."

"Right."

I heard the door behind us. Jason rose from his spot in the grass and approached the porch. I looked around to see Gina.

"Mr. Carson, Mom and Ms. Miller and the Doc have everything

together for you."

Bill got up and went inside while Gina held the door open for him. She came down the steps and sat where Bill had been. Jason walked over to her and put his head in her lap as she scratched behind his ears. The silence of a farm is a beautiful thing, inconceivable to most urban dwellers.

"I've got to tell Ferdinand."

I stared at the ground before me. "I hope I wasn't out of place … I've already told him."

She looked at me with a look of amused surprise.

"It was Jason's idea," I offered.

The dog wagged his tail at the mention of his name.

She hugged Jason. "That was very kind. Ole Jason's looking out for me, aren't you?" She bent over and rested her head on Jason's head. "How'd Ferdinand take it?"

"You know, before Friday, I would have thought this conversation ludicrous. It's not. I'd say he's taking it pretty hard. He seemed relieved to hear that you were OK and that Chris would be back soon."

She looked out to the pasture. "Thanks, doc. It's best he heard it from you. I'd have been a wreck telling him. So he let you get close? He's not one for strangers."

"I had an escort to make introductions," I said, pointing to Jason.

She giggled. "I should go out and see him. Not much I can do inside right now." She got up and started walking toward the pasture. "Jason, where's your ball?"

Jason bounded around the corner of the house, returning with a red rubber ball, which he dropped at her feet. She heaved the ball high into the air and proceeded in ball-throws toward Ferdinand. The bull was waiting for her at the fence. She climbed over, and he lowered his head as she flung her arms around him.

I watched the scene and murmured, "You'll be OK."

More cars began arriving. Friends and neighbors got out and most headed toward the house. I stood on the porch and greeted them, some of whom I'd seen, some I hadn't, many with food. They all knew my name. Some of the crowd were teens and younger. They headed toward Gina, and soon a small crowd gathered at the fence around Ferdinand. They took turns throwing the ball for Jason. I couldn't hear the conversations — didn't need to.

After a while, Bill appeared at the door. "Ready to give me a hand?"

I followed him through the house, which had become a beehive of activity. We entered the sunroom and he closed the door. A stretcher with wheels stood beside Walt, a large black body bag lay open on the stretcher.

Bill pointed to Walt. "You take the feet. I'll get the shoulders. We just lift him and center him on the bag. On my count — one, two, three."

We lifted the body from the chair in one smooth motion. The long ordeal with the cancer had left him a fraction of the weight I figured he would have been before the disease. Bill arranged the body with dignity and folded Walt's arms across each other. After zipping the bag closed, we trundled the assembly out the back door of the sunroom to Bill's hearse, which he had positioned just outside, the back door of the hearse opened.

The stretcher slid into the back of the hearse, and Bill strapped the body down with a series of modified seat belts. He closed the back. "Thanks, Doc."

"A pleasure," I said out of habit. "That didn't sound right."

"Oh, it's fine, really. I know the feeling. When you don't know what you can do, you do what you can. That's the way things should work." He shook my hand. "I'll let Sharon and Gina know I'm on my way."

"Gina's up at the pasture with her friends and Ferdinand."

Bill nodded. "Good. You can tell her, if you don't mind. I'll let Stacy know, too." He returned inside.

I made my way around the side of the house. The Tinley home was a classic farmhouse, vintage 1920s or '30s. Unlike Ron Widing's place, this house showed good and consistent maintenance. No peeling paint, no loose anything. Hydrangea bushes lined the side of the house. Several raised beds of annuals lay a few feet farther from the house — marigolds, zinnias, and snapdragons as best I could tell. Baylor would know.

Rounding the next corner into the front yard, I saw the teenagers returning from the fence in a gaggle. Several boys had taken over playing ball with Jason, who seemed not the least bit tired of the game. Gina leaned into one of her girlfriends as they walked back. I nodded greetings.

Gina gave a little wave. "Hey, Doc. We just went up to talk to Ferdinand. He's going to be OK." She turned to her friends. "I think you met most of these guys at the game. Can't imagine you'd remember all their names. Anna and Christina are going to spend the night here tonight. We're going to make pizzas."

I smiled. "Sounds like a lot of fun."

I heard the front door slam and looked to see Stacy skipping down the steps. "Yo, D.I.D. I told your mom what you had in mind. She's cool with it."

One of the girls leaned over to Gina. "D.I.D.?"

"Damsel In Distress. It's a long story." Gina then called to Stacy. "Thanks! I'll let Mr. Carson know."

"Mr. Carson asked me to let you know he was on his way back," I said.

She nodded. "That's fine. We've got time. The service isn't 'til Wednesday."

Stacy joined the crowd. "Hey, Doctor P, are you by any chance heading back soon?"

"I think so, unless there's anything I can do here. Why?" I asked.

She put her finger in the air as she often did when explaining her plans. "Ms. Miller and Doc Isabel are going to be here for a while helping Sharon. I want to get started on Ferdinand's vestments. I could use a ride back to the house."

I raised my eyebrows. "OK … I can leave anytime."

"Cool. Thanks, Doc." She turned to Gina. "You got a tape measure handy?"

"Yeah. What are you going to do with it?"

"I need to measure Ferdy."

Gina smiled. "You best let me do that. He's had a rough day, and I don't want him too weirded out."

Gina, Stacy, and the four other girls walked toward the house. Stacy turned back to me as she walked and called out, "We'll just be about 15 more minutes."

I waved an OK.

The boys returned to their cars and headed away down the drive. Jason trotted over and dropped his ball at my feet. We played fetch while the young women made the circuit from drive to house to fence. Gina climbed over and took measurements, which Stacy recorded on a pad of paper while the other girls watched and conversed. Ferdinand stood still throughout the process.

I strode over to the porch while continuing the game of fetch. I picked up my sample case and returned to the car to wait for Stacy. She was true to her word and finished in a short while. We got into the car and headed back to Guthrie. She was absorbed in producing sketches at first. After a mile or so, she looked up to take in the countryside. "Ya' know, it's going to be rough on Sharon taking on running the farm. Gina's afraid she might sell it."

"I'm sure things will work out."

Stacy was quiet for too long. I turned to see her staring at me.

"What?" I asked.

"You know something, don't you?"

"I just said that things will work out."

Her finger was in the air again. "Yeah, the way you said it. Back at the house, while I was helping Ms. Miller and the Doc and Gina's mom, they were talking to each other like in code. They didn't want me to know something about what's up for Gina, and they thought I wouldn't notice they were trying to keep something from me. Ha!"

I glanced at Stacy. She stared straight ahead looking very frustrated.

I reminded her, "Even if I knew something, I couldn't tell anyone. Patient confidentiality."

She turned to me and grinned. "She's not your patient."

I concentrated on the road. I was sure that information shared among physicians bound them all to the same standards. What unsettled me in her response was that I had begun to see Gina and the others as my patients. "I'm sure that things will work out and that they'll work out well for Gina and her mom. That's all."

She shook her head. "You'd make a lousy poker player."

I was a lousy poker player. "We're changing the topic. What's with the vestments?"

She giggled, satisfied, and began flipping through her sketches. "While Sharon didn't care much one way or another about the funeral, Gina wanted to do something special. They're burying him on the farm. There's a family cemetery out somewhere in a corner of their spread. That's where Mrs. Tinley's buried, the one whose coconut cake you like so much."

I wondered how she remembered that.

"Mr. Carson's going to take care of all the usual viewings and casket and all, until the final service, which will be at the house — out in the yard, if it doesn't rain. And it's supposed to be clear for the rest of the week. At the end of the service, Gina will have an ox cart hooked up to Ferdinand. Chris was going to be the lead pallbearer, and he won't be out of Vanderbilt Hospital until Friday. I'm taking his spot, with the football team as backup. We'll put the casket on a cart, and Ferdinand will pull it to the cemetery. I've seen pictures of ancient cultures' burials where the casket was borne on an ox cart. The bulls were decorated just like the celebrating mourners. That's why I'm making something to drape over him. Also to pad him from the yoke."

I admired her matter-of-fact confidence. "What could possibly go wrong?" I murmured.

"Hey, Gina's already talking to Ferdinand about it. She'll be leading him herself, and he gets along with her friends, for the most part. You don't think she can pull it off?"

I thought for a moment. "If anyone could ..."

We could see the tower of Guthrie's grain elevator ahead. Stacy appeared lost in thought. "You got this cancer thing solved yet?"

I smiled. "I'm getting there. This 'cancer thing' is complicated. I'm most of the way through Doc Isabel's patient records. My interviews aren't turning up much new now, so I think I have most of the facts in hand. The samples should give the final answer. My lab is looking for the kinds of genetic markers associated with all the chemical exposures the four of them experienced. It may turn out to be a combination of a toxic brew of chemicals."

"So you're still convinced it's not a virus or something."

"I never said that. The lab is looking for those kinds of markers, too. I've still got a few loose ends to tie up."

"Loose ends?"

"Well, I haven't seen Jim Dulaney yet."

"Ugh."

"That's the same sort of reaction I get from just about everyone. What's with Jim Dulaney, anyway?"

"He's a selfish, crude, rude, boorish, scheming, thoughtless, careless, fat, slovenly jerk," she recited, anger growing with each adjective.

"I see."

"And that's just what I remember from when I lived here. From the snippets I've heard since I came back, he hasn't changed, even with the cancer."

"OK. I guess I'll find out tomorrow. Doc Isabel and I are scheduled to see him in the afternoon, late."

"Oh, that should be fun," she almost laughed.

"How so?"

"Doc Isabel and Donna Dulaney are always at each other's throats, a lot like Gina and J.B. I'm not sure how or when it started … it's like a territorial fight between two she-tigers." Stacy laughed as she thought. "I heard that Donna calls Doc Isabel a Mexican Muslim terrorist."

"A what?"

"It's Isabel Rodriguez. You'll know when you meet Donna — you'll absolutely know — that she couldn't abide any immigrants. So Donna's convinced herself that Doc Isabel's Mexican. Those are the only immigrants she can come up with. The Doc doesn't have the traditional Mexican look — no matter. The other thing is the Doc's scarves. Donna's convinced that the Doc wears them because she's Muslim."

I shook my head. "Wow! 'Mexican Muslim terrorist.' Where does the terrorist come in?"

"Duh! In Donna's mind, Muslim and terrorist are interchangeable. She's sure that Isabel injected Jim with something to give him the cancer."

"Why?"

"I have no idea. I'm not about to try to figure out Donna's thinking. I'm not sure I'd want to. Good luck on that tomorrow." Stacy shook her head.

"I'd wondered about the scarves, too. She says they're to cover up a nasty scar, doesn't seem to want to talk much about it."

"Yeah, I've heard different stories, most often that she had some bicycle accident when she was little. Her mom was a fundamentalist type, who was opposed to medicine, and she wanted only faith healing for little Isabel, and it was only partly effective. I've never seen her without the scarf. I'm guessing it's pretty bad."

"She's had a lot to deal with in life, hasn't she?" I offered.

"Yeah."

"I'm going back to the *New Era* tomorrow to finish up researching the

1973 football team. There seemed to be a link in Walt's mind between the disease and that team. The fact that all four cases were on that team is a peculiar coincidence. Ron Widing felt the same."

Stacy rolled her eyes. "Oh, man, that's a topic we stayed away from when I lived here. We always spoke of Coach Tatum like he was the Devil."

"Did you meet him?"

"Oh, no. He was long gone by the time I arrived here. According to the grownups, the team always gave their all for him. They were taking him — *him* — to the state championships. And then something happened. As kids, we never found out, of course. That didn't stop us from making up back-stories to explain it. When grownups leave a vacuum, kids will do what they can to fill it. I try to sort out those stories now, and it's tough to tease the facts from the legends. Safe to say, though, Coach Tatum was another jerk."

I nodded. "Those were tumultuous times. At the same time, there was a missing little girl."

"Oh, yeah. Jennifer Collins. You can bet that scared us kids. She goes out of the house one evening in her red striped shirt and jeans and is never seen again. All they ever found was a bloody shirt. The boys in our class guessed that she was eaten by wolves. Fish and Wildlife was thinking of reintroducing wolves into the Land Between the Lakes, like they did with elk and bison. They never did — too much opposition from farmers. That didn't stop us from imagining. Some said she was attacked by a soldier from Fort Campbell. Soldiers were just beginning to return from Vietnam back then with what we now call PTSD. We never knew the true story. Her murder was always used to scare us kids into behaving."

"Wow!"

I pulled into Ellen's driveway and we got out. Stacy headed to the front porch.

I called to her. "It's locked."

She reached into her pocket and pulled something out. "Key."

I chuckled. I was not the only one being woven into the community.

I lifted the sample case from the trunk of the car and headed to my room. I was anxious for Monday's report on the sample analyses of what I had sent so far. The current samples wouldn't leave Guthrie until Monday afternoon. I thought of checking with Jack to see if there was an earlier pickup in Hopkinsville or Nashville. It would take a day off the analysis. If things broke right, I would be finished with my data gathering by Tuesday. That would be my normal, professional schedule. I found myself not wanting to leave Tuesday night because it would mean missing Walt's funeral. I felt conflicted about wanting to stay.

I tried throwing myself into writing my report while dealing with too much self-distraction. I finished a rough draft, which I should review again before uploading. I decided to take a walk instead. Ellen had not yet returned. I imagined she would fix a quick dinner for us, and nothing was open in Guthrie on a Sunday night. I wasn't all that hungry. My walk took me past the City Hall building. I took my key, went in, and sat in my office, flipping through the records I had not yet examined. I kept them neat, since I didn't have the concentration to take notes that evening. I was just trying to get a sense of the flow of lives over the four decades of records.

About eight in the evening, I heard the clinic doors open, first the outside and then the one to the hall with my office.

Isabel came to the doorway. "Talk about dedication."

"No, I couldn't concentrate on my work back at Ellen's, and I was walking and just decided to stop in. Not a lot else going on in town as best I can tell."

She giggled. "Yeah. It does get pretty quiet around here. Ellen said if I saw you to let you know she's going to have a late snack around 8:30, 9 o'clock. I'm going over once I get my stuff stowed. We want to see what Stacy's up to."

"May I ask you a personal question?" I queried.

"Sure. Ask away."

"I've been wondering — why do you always wear a scarf?"

She shook her head, smiling. "I was wondering how long it would take you to ask. Most little kids ask on their first visit. Yet, with all your attention to detail, it's been almost a week."

I nodded. "I felt uncomfortable asking. Now I feel bad for not asking."

"Oh, don't. It's interesting what people will or won't ask about. My scarves are one of the most obvious things about my outward appearance, yet the topic seems off-limits. Why is that?"

I rubbed my chin. "I guess some people think it's a religious or cultural requirement and don't have the background to discuss those topics without looking foolish. Some people think the scarf covers up an injury and are afraid the subject might be painful."

"And no one thinks that I might just like scarves?"

I chuckled. "I guess not, myself included. I have no idea why I didn't assume that; I didn't. Maybe they're so rare these days. I remember my grandmother wore scarves. Lot of people did back in the 'fifties and earlier. They're just rare today."

"Granted. You're right on count two. My scarves cover a pretty scary injury, though there is one person who's convinced herself it's a religious thing. Good ole Donna decided the scarf means I'm Muslim. For her, that's a big bad wolf image even if she's never met a Muslim. She's also convinced I'm Mexican because of my name. Her understanding of the world comes straight out of her mind unchecked and unfiltered. I tried in the early days to straighten her out. That didn't work. To tell the truth, these days I'd just as soon annoy her. I pepper my conversations with phrases like 'God willing' or 'it is written' using a Hispanic-sounding accent when I'm around her. I can tell it drives her up the wall. I know that's unprofessional. José, Gina's ranch hand, says my accent's pathetic, still it's enough."

"I see. So what is the actual story?"

"My mom told me — I have no memory of it — that I was in a horrible bike accident when I was little. She said I skidded off the road and hit my head on a rock. For several days, she didn't know if I'd live or die. Yet, she didn't take me to a hospital. She was a certified religious fanatic and believed in the power of prayer to heal. Fortunately, she also had a little medical training and she kept the wounds well dressed. While I survived, I have only the haziest memories of life before about ten years old. The impact ripped off a lot of my left cheek and my left ear still isn't fully attached. In my teen years, it was pretty painful — both physical and emotional pain. Now, as you can imagine, other kids can be so cruel about deformities like mine. My mom home-schooled me to protect me for the rest of elementary school. And high school was unbearable some days. I liked people — I really am a people person. It's just that the high school world was too mean. My only accepting friends were in our youth group at church. They carved out a special safe and welcoming space for me and I am grateful beyond words to this day. They're the ones who inspired me to go into medicine."

"Are your injuries beyond restorative surgery?"

"By the time I was able to understand about plastic surgery, the scar tissue had made any procedures like that difficult. We were living in southeastern Missouri, which is still not a great place for specialized medicine. Besides, my mom was both poor and didn't trust the medical community … or insurance, or helping agencies, or just about anything else. So I guess surgery was never an option. I suppose I could be mad about that — wouldn't change anything. Instead, I wear scarves. They're my trademarks around here. They give me almost the same authority as the black bag and stethoscope.

"Judy, the lady who own the gift shop, is always finding cute or pretty designs and giving them to me; so sweet. When the little ones ask, I tell them an abbreviated version of my story and they can accept that. A lot of times, they'll ask if it hurts and I tell them not any more. Then I ask them what color I should wear and that's what I wear the next time I see them. Kind of a test to see if they remember their choices."

"Do they?" I asked.

She smiled. "Of course!"

"I'm sorry for what you've gone through. I admire your perseverance. It can't have been pleasant."

"Yeah. Well, my life as I remember it seems to have started with coming out of the fog of the trauma and has been just one long series of disappointments for the most part. My mom and I were forced together by the circumstances early on. It could be tough at times. We were different kinds of people — she was withdrawn and suspicious of everything and everybody. I was a little social butterfly — just with part of my face that would scare Frankenstein's monster. Her religion was kind of a received mysticism. I was the analytical type. We never were all that close despite being bound together. Weird.

"My grades and all were good enough that I got into Old Dominion nursing school. Ever notice how some people are drawn to their fields by family circumstances? Of course, Virginia was half a continent away. The distance helped me get some perspective on my life. I called her often when I was in school. One Saturday in my sophomore year, I called and there was no answer. I called every few hours into Sunday morning. At last, I called the Missouri police from my dorm in Virginia. They found her dead. She'd been dead for several days. She had come down with the flu. Did she tell me? No. Did she get any medical help? Of course not, and there is not the slightest chance she would have gotten vaccinated. I don't know if I ever grieved over her death. By then, I was numbed to these events. I finished up my degree, worked a series of internships, and tried to reconstruct my life, in particular the part before the scar."

I looked at Isabel quizzically.

"Mom was always vague about my childhood. She wouldn't tell me about my father. She didn't leave behind much of a paper trail so I spent vacations trying to unearth her past as well, like where the Rodriguez name came from since I never sensed it was her maiden name. It was on one of those searches that I was led to western Kentucky and stumbled on the job opening here. So, this is where I set down roots and this is home. This is where I'm happy."

"Wow. I'm in awe."

"Ya do what ya have to do. All those experiences have given me an appreciation for those who try against the odds. Guess that's part of why I'll do anything to help Gina, and why I butt heads so hard with people like Donna and J.B. I can't abide people who squander their good fortune."

I nodded. "I'm beginning to understand."

She smiled. "And, of course, you can't ask about my love life. You're too gentle and sensitive to go there. I've had a few boyfriends. I just haven't met anyone who can deal with the scars for very long and I don't see much likelihood of finding such a person out here. The statistics get in the way."

"Sorry."

"Oh, don't be. I'm on a mission here and it helps to have focus." She leaned on the doorway, seeming lost in thought. Then she started and looked at her watch. "It's almost nine. Ellen's got to be wondering where we are. I'll meet you over there." Isabel turned and was gone.

I closed the file folder I had been looking at, turned out the lights, locked up the doors, and headed to Ellen's. In the solitude of the walk through the safe Guthrie night, I reflected on all the new information I had just received. I could not imagine how I would have turned out under the same circumstances. I wondered if there was just something in the fiber of some individuals that drove them to prevail over the odds. People like Isabel, like Gina, ... like Stacy. The water hyacinths.

Ellen's house glowed with the warm light of lamps in the rooms. I could smell chili as I climbed the steps and I could hear the women talking inside. I smiled and walked in. The kitchen was deserted. Chili had been prepared in a slow cooker. A single empty bowl and spoon sat on the counter next to the cooker and next to them, a smaller bowl with some grated cheese remaining. A sleeve of crackers lay open by the cooker.

I dished out a portion of chili and placed the bowl at my usual spot at the table to cool. I walked through the house back to the sewing room. The big table in the center of the room sported the developing structure of Ferdinand's vestments.

Stacy perched on the back of a chair. "Hey, Doctor P! Did you realize how few attachment points there are on a bull? It's not like pin the tail on the donkey ... which probably wouldn't work with a real donkey anyway."

I grinned. "I have to be honest, I've never given it much thought. My guy instincts would lead me to suggest duct tape."

She pointed her finger in the air. "We thought of that. It might work going on. We're not sure about coming off. So far, out best candidate is something like Velcro. A coarse grade of Velcro in the form of a belt should hold it in place without irritating Ferdy."

I nodded. "That should work."

Stacy eased herself down from the chair, picked up her sketchpad, and handed it to Ellen.

Ellen explained. "In its basic form, the vestment is just a fitted sheet, fitted for a bull. It would attach to the yoke back where Ferdinand can't see it. We don't want him too curious about it. The Velcro or whatever would hold by friction. We would place that at Ferdinand's widest spot, just above where the fabric begins to drape. The ornamentation can be changed. If this works, ..." She turned to Stacy, who was getting ready to interject, and held up her hand. Ellen continued, "... which, of course, it will, then we could use it on other occasions. Maybe a wedding some day."

Ellen handed me the sketch pad.

"Oh, my. This is nice. Not just the design — the artwork itself. That's awesome. And very finished given you've only been working on it a few hours."

She smiled. "Thanks."

Isabel surveyed the assembly on the table. "Stacy'll present the plan to Gina tomorrow morning and take another look at Ferdinand. If all goes well, she can get the fabric tomorrow. I don't think we'd have some of this in Hopkinsville, so she and Ellen might head off to Hancock Fabrics in Paducah or down to Nashville."

Stacy looked over the table. "With a little luck and not too much sleep, I should have it ready to fit Tuesday morning. The service's on Wednesday, so there's just a little bit of margin."

We stood around the table for a while, looking at the parts of the design that had already been laid out. After a while, Ellen looked over at me. "Go get yourself some chili. It's in the pot in the kitchen."

"Thanks. I did. It's out on the table. I didn't want to bring it in here," I replied.

"Oh, that's fine — we did," Ellen said.

I looked around the room. "I'd be afraid of spilling it."

She waved her hand. "I don't worry about it. I have a whole arsenal of stain removers. You accumulate that if you're a serious quilter."

I retrieved my dinner from the kitchen and we talked for an hour or so about plans for the coming days.

"I'll get today's samples down to the post office. Then I want to go back to the *New Era* tomorrow morning and finish my research there. By late morning, I should be getting a lot of results back from Atlanta. I think I'm getting close to the actual causes. I just need to find for sure where it or they came from." I turned to Isabel. "Any chance I could meet with Jim Dulaney?"

She grimaced. "You're in luck on the Dulaney item. I have an encounter with him tomorrow at one. I'll be checking on his meds and pain management and I'd love it if you'd come along. I have this strange feeling Donna won't be quite as hostile with a male presence on site. I need to test J.B. for any recurrence of the STDs, though she spends as little time at the house as she can get away with."

"That would be perfect. Should I meet you in town? Time might be a little tight."

"I'll mark up a map. They're way out in the sticks on Pilot Rock Road. Their place is out beyond the reach of the cell towers so make any calls you need before you head out. And follow the map and directions I give you. Most GPSs don't have the roads right out there."

"Yes, ma'am."

Isabel chuckled and turned to the other two. "His wife's got him trained well, don't you think?"

Ellen and Stacy grinned and nodded.

Ellen raised her hand. "You're out of luck with the post office, though. Tomorrow is Memorial Day. The post office is closed."

"Oh, right. I lost track of the days. I guess that means no *New Era* tomorrow."

Ellen shook her head. "Dee Ferguson's keen to get this case closed." She looked at her watch. "A little late now. I'll text her in the morning. I'm pretty sure she'll get you in."

I thanked her, made my goodbyes for the night, and took the empty bowl back to the kitchen. I placed it in the sink, being careful not to wash it per instructions, and headed to my room.

Sunday had been a very long day and I felt exhausted. Just before I turned in, I looked again at the angel quilt. As was no doubt intention of design, my eyes were drawn again to the one odd angel, the little angel in stripes and jeans. As I observed the tiny figure, my conversation in the car with Stacy came back to me and a chill ran down my spine. I had a lot of questions for Ellen in the morning.

9 DEVILS AND ANGELS

I slept fitfully for the first time since arriving and woke up a bit before sunrise unable to return to sleep. Today was day seven of my visit and I would have most of my answers by the end of the day. Or not. I had forgotten about the Memorial Day holiday and wasn't sure if Mike would be giving me a call from the lab about sample results. He and I had talked about "results on Monday" — today — and he didn't say anything to the contrary. Mike often checked in for an hour or so on holidays, though I had no right to expect that of him.

Though samples from Walt were ready to go, it would be tomorrow before I could ship them. I had already sent the first samples from the living Walt last week. Some of those results would be ready if Mike called.

I would be interviewing the last victim this afternoon and I was beginning to sense that case might hold the key. Within the disparate group, Jim Dulaney supplied the one thing that all of the men seemed to share in common — the contaminated lumber. The chemicals were of the right type, the concentrations were in range, given my experience at Ron Widing's place, and the exposures would have been in the right time frame. My most nagging doubt derived from the assumption that no one else had developed Griffith's sarcoma after being exposed to Jim's lumber. That was a fragile assumption, to say the least. While Doc Isabel was a marvel at documentation, not everyone came to see her. I also had no idea how much of the lumber Jim had acquired and sold or how many people had been exposed.

While the Patton-Dalton plant would have been a good candidate 15 or 20 years ago, too much time had elapsed when the cases emerged. Perhaps working at or near the plant had set the stage for the disease to be triggered at a later date. The one person missing from my Patton-Dalton scenario

154

was Jim Dulaney. Still, he may have had a connection to the plant that no one noted. I needed to talk to him. If it turned out that he had any significant exposure at the wiring plant, then the pieces would fall together— a pre-cancer laid down by exposure at Patton-Dalton and then activated decades later by exposure to high levels of chromated copper arsenate in creosote.

The more I thought about the possibility of the disease being set up and awaiting a trigger, the better I felt. I still had beryllium and moldy hay to worry about. If they were only in Frank's and Walt's samples, and the beryllium only in Frank's, then I could remove them. Of course, if Jim had no contact with the plant, then I was bereft of a solution. My hopes rested on the outlier of the group.

I had questions for Ellen about Jennifer Collins, but I learned long ago not to go off target. Most communities have dark underbellies that can consume a lifetime of investigation.

I had showered and shaved and was ready to go by about ten 'til six. I elected to do the rest of my thinking on a walk around the block since I didn't want to disturb Ellen this early. That concern evaporated as I walked around to the front of the house. I could hear water splashing. I turned the corner to see Ellen watering her begonias with a water-breaking nozzle.

She caught sight of me. "Oh good. You're up early. I got a text back from Dee. She's going to be stopping by the *New Era* about 8:30 on her way to the Hopkinsville Memorial Day ceremonies. She'll let you in and you can have some quiet time with the skeleton holiday crew as long as you need. Dee said they left all your material together on the side table."

"Thank you." I climbed the steps to the porch and watched her finishing her watering.

"These little devils are thirsty. I'm guessing it must be wet in Bolivia where they come from. They get droopy if they dry out. Fortunately, they're what are called caudex plants — a fat stem close to the ground that stores water. Some people collect just caudex plants. I don't have the patience except for this begonia." She finished the last plant, switched off the nozzle, went to the side to turn off the faucet, and then returned to release the pressure in the hose. Ellen noticed me watching her procedure. "Keeps the hose from bursting under the pressure. Only time I've lost a hose is when I left it out during a freeze. I'm sure Baylor knows all about that."

"You seem to know so much about Baylor."

She nodded without reply.

I followed her through the house to the kitchen. My place was set and breakfast was awaiting preparation by the stove.

"Do you like French toast?" Ellen asked.

"I do — haven't had it in a long time. It's always been a favorite."

She turned the burner on low, added a dollop of butter, dipped the bread on both sides and began frying the toast. "These eggs come from Faye Johnson. She keeps a few chickens in the back of her barn, the one where Stacy's swallows live. Though she's rented out most of her acreage, the barn is special and not too much work for her, given that it's almost empty."

The kitchen filled with the fragrance of toast and a touch of vanilla in the syrup. I had come to look forward to Ellen's breakfasts every day. "I can't tell you how much I've enjoyed my stay here. With just a little luck, I should have my answers by the end of the day. If Jim Dulaney's interview goes well, I should be able to pinpoint the cause of the sarcoma."

"Still no virus, right?"

"Not yet. That seems important to you," I said.

"I've got fifty bucks riding on it," she replied, looking up from the stove with a grin.

I raised my eyebrows. "I don't remember agreeing to that bet."

"You're getting old. Memory's the first thing to go."

We both laughed.

Ellen cut cantaloupe and set a plate before me. The French toast was ready soon after that. She served it with butter and syrup on the side.

"It shouldn't take me more than an hour or so to finish checking the papers. I need to get a few dates and any names associated with the Patton-Dalton plant, with particular attention to the days when the guys would have been working there or around there. I'll be checking to see if Jim Dulaney had anything to do with the plant."

She laughed in dismissal. "I doubt he would have gotten anywhere near it. Too much like work."

"Still, if he did any contracting for any business there for more than a few days, it would have given him some exposure. That would support my theory."

She nodded.

"I also was going to check out a crime case from back then. It doesn't have anything to do with the investigation, and I can't spend any real time on it. Still, it's bothered me. Do you remember the disappearance of Jennifer Collins?"

Ellen sat down, almost deflated. "She was one of my students when she disappeared."

"I'm sorry. I didn't mean to bring you any pain."

"No. It's OK. I've dealt with it as best I can. I wish people like you had been around back then. You would've solved the case, even with the bumbling people we had on it at the time. It was one of several things for which I could never forgive Sheriff Cox. Ole Carl didn't take it seriously enough. He even made her parents out as suspects. I knew them. I knew them well. They were model parents and as loving as the day is long. I do wish you could have met Jennifer. She was the kind of little girl you knew right away would change the world. She was so smart and chatty. When I brought up something new in class, she'd be an expert on it by the next morning — and that was in the days before the internet. And she was so funny. That little low laugh of hers."

"She's the little new angel in the quilt in my room, isn't she?"

Ellen nodded, tears rolling down her cheeks.

"Did they solve the disappearance?"

She shook her head. "Never found her body. They did find her little shirt all soaked in blood by the side of the road. Between what was on the shirt and what was on the ground, Ole Carl figured she died on the spot. He never came up with a motive, never called in the search dogs, never brought in the Kentucky and Tennessee state police. He was lazy, just lazy, and justice was not served." Her tears had given way to a drier anger. Ellen sat for a few minutes, and then started as she remembered the toast. "Close one there. It'll be fine — a little crispy on the edge."

"So the Jennifer Collins case went to the cold case files? Did Sheriff Nolan pursue anything?"

"I don't think so. By the time we troublemakers got rid of Ole Carl, it had been a good five years since Jennifer vanished. Curtis came on staff after a gap of about seven months and went on duty in the late 70s right at the height of the pot wars."

"Pot wars?"

"Kentucky bottom lands were about the perfect place for growing marijuana. The soil is rich, access limited — easy for growers to secure their plots. That was in the days before all those fancy high-yield varieties they grow under lights in the Pacific Northwest, and before the Mexican drug cartels ruled the borders. By the time the federal government got serious about domestic crops, Kentucky had quite an above-ground underground economy tied up in the crop, and Curtis walked right into it. So an old missing person case, as horrible as it was, never made the list of important projects. Pity. I'll bet he could have solved it." She folded her arms, keeping a close watch on a third batch of toast.

The memories had to be painful for Ellen. I decided not to pursue the matter for the time being. Still, she had a little more to say.

"Sometimes I think it's worse when no body's found. As grisly as it would have been, at least the story would end. The Collinses left the area after a few years. She was their only child at the time. I do get a Christmas card from them every year. They have a son and daughter now. The younger one just got married. We troublemakers would walk the woods and fields for years looking for disturbed earth or any traces of Jennifer — any little clue. I guess I was getting pretty obsessed."

"Who were the 'troublemakers'?"

"Right. There's history here, isn't there. Several of my fellow teachers, Pastor Roberts, and Mr. Gough."

"Eugene Gough?"

She chuckled. "Yeah. Beneath that gruff exterior — way beneath — is a soul committed to justice. He can surprise you at times. Ron Widing joined us several years later after he got back from college. He's the only one who ever came up with anything — a sock that she was wearing that night, weathered by many years ... still recognizable. That was all we ever found. When Doc Isabel arrived, she woke me up to how it was eating me alive and taking away what I could give to other children. She's more than just a medical doctor, you know — much more. At last, we agreed to set up a headstone in the cemetery to honor Jennifer. The troublemakers all pitched in, and we had a proper memorial service at the monument. I still take flowers in a Mason jar to put on the stone. Doc said I was being morbid, so I told her she could have the flowers. I was going to leave them anyway. I can be stubborn."

I smiled.

"I take the flowers in the morning and come back in the afternoon to retrieve the jar. It's a little ritual between us." Her spirits seemed to pick up. She smiled as she turned the toast. "More?"

"Just one. Thank you again for all that you've done for me. I think this may be the most personal case I've ever investigated."

She nodded.

I praised the breakfast and picked up my notes for the morning. I realized that I had left one notebook at the office and left to pick it up before heading to Hopkinsville. Sheriff Nolan was in the office, and I greeted him. "No rest for the weary."

"Just a few things to pick up for the service at the cemetery. I'm kinda the senior law enforcement type here, and a veteran, so I'm in charge of the 21 gun salute while they play taps."

I nodded and began to walk toward my office. Before going, I paused and turned. "One of the things I'm seeing alongside my official research is a story about a little girl disappearing back in the 70s."

Curtis looked up. "The Jennifer Collins case?"

"Yeah. I understand that was one of the things that got Sheriff Cox ... relieved."

"You could say that. One damned sloppy piece of police work. He couldn't get away with that kind of crap today. I often wish I had the manpower to re-open the case. We've still got the evidence in the locker, and that's one of the few things they did right."

"So you still have medical evidence?"

"Yes, sir, and it's all properly sealed and tagged and everything. There's just no time."

"I don't want to take too much of your time. Still, it's bothered me since I first saw the story. Ellen was saying there was lots of blood. Were DNA samples ever sent to the national database?"

He scratched his head. "Don't know. I doubt it. I put the stuff in the evidence vault a couple of years after I got here; that was before DNA evidence was in vogue. Never thought about it, I guess."

I nodded. "Someday something's going to turn up — bone fragments, a grave, some items of clothing stashed in a basement, even a person with amnesia — and DNA in the database could be crucial. I've got submission bags in my kit. It's surprising how often forensic samples result from my work. I could send a small sample in to the national laboratory if you've got a few minutes to let me take a sample sometime before I head back to Atlanta. It's all official and I could save you the time looking up the procedures."

Curtis looked at his watch. "I'm well ahead of schedule. Go get your sample bags, and we'll do it all official, then. Thank you. I'll rest easier knowing we've done something, no matter how small."

I went to the car and returned with sample bags and forms. I watched as he prepared a spot on a stainless steel table, swabbing it clean with sterile gauze and then wiping the evidence bag in like manner with a separate swab.

"You were well-trained. Compliments on your technique," I said.

He smiled. "Thanks. Part of our forensic certification. Kentucky did a big upgrade of procedures about a decade ago. While we're not perfect, we've cut our cold cases by better than 60 percent."

"Well done." I opened a package of sterile scissors, donned some clean gloves, and slid the shirt part of the way out of its bag. My heart ached as I recognized the red stripes I had seen in the quilt and had heard about from Stacy. Only a bit of the pattern showed around the massive brown bloodstain. "Hmmm, she didn't linger long on or in the shirt. There aren't any clots that I see."

I snipped tiny samples of the bloodied cloth and placed them in a bag. I cut a small section from one of the few areas without blood to serve as a baseline and placed it in a separate bag. I then returned the shirt to its home and resealed the bag with evidence tape as Curtis watched.

As I sat down and began filling in my form from the notes in the evidence file, Isabel's footsteps sounded coming down the hall.

She stopped in the doorway. "What're you rascals doing here on a holiday?"

"Doc Parker's getting some evidence from one of our cold cases to submit to the FBI database."

When she looked down and saw the shirt, she raised her hands to her face. "Oh, God!" She sat down.

Curtis went over to her. "You OK, Doc?"

She moved her hand from her face to hold the scarf on the side of her head. "I'm sorry. It's one thing to talk to Ellen about that little girl all these years. To see her shirt, her actual shirt … hurts. It's too real. Why are you doing this?"

I looked up from my writing. "It's a loose end. It has nothing to do with my investigation here, but the story's in the background. I don't think there's anything else I can do about it. This is something I can do. Maybe, in part, I'm doing it for Ellen. Someday, something will turn up, and there can be closure. Entering a proper sample might help. And it's on my own time, just like with Chris. As Bill Carson said, 'When you don't know what you can do, you do what you can. That's the way things should work.'"

Isabel had calmed down by that point and was wiping tears from her eyes. "You're a good man, John Parker. I wish you'd been here for them back then."

I smiled. "I was in grade school. And DNA analysis didn't exist."

She shrugged. "You still would have done the right things, whatever they were back then — as Curtis would have." She took several deep breaths to further regain her composure. "You ready to spoil your afternoon?"

I laughed. "I don't often jump at an opportunity like that. Still, I'm ready to go for it. I'll be heading from here back to the *New Era*, and should be back about 12:30."

"See you at the Dulaney place. Unless something's changed, Jim's circling the drain, and it might be your only live encounter with him. I'm counting on your being my bodyguard out there."

"Bad dogs?" I asked.

She smirked. "Sort of — Donna. She and I get into a shouting match about every other time. Let's hope your being there does actually calm her down."

"Jim's the only one I haven't met, and he may have some critical information for me."

"Great. One o'clock. There. Don't forget the map, and don't forget to make any calls before you get out of range."

"Right. Map's in the car." I turned to my samples, placing the sample bags in the folded submission form and enclosing all of that in the padded mailer. Sheriff Nolan returned the case material to his vault, I gathered all my gear, and we left the evidence room.

The sheriff got into his car to head for the cemetery. Isabel opened up her office and began working on case notes. I placed the DNA envelope into a case for safekeeping until I could get to the post office, and I began my drive to Hopkinsville.

My phone rang just outside of Guthrie. Though I know as well as anyone that you shouldn't talk on the phone while driving, I answered it anyway. "John Parker."

"Hey, Doc, it's Mike."

"You should be relaxing, young man. It's a holiday."

"Yeah, yeah. I will. I wanted to check on a few things before we go on our picnic out to Lake Lanier. Your last samples got here Saturday, and I was able to get them on. I have the results."

"You're too dedicated. And ...?"

"Consistent across the board. All three."

I was elated. "Yes! Chromated copper arsenate in creosote in that hideous lumber. I'll be visiting the vendor this afternoon. Thank you so much."

"And the beryllium."

"Say what?"

"All three of your victims have measurable beryllium. The relatives do not. Not a trace."

When my mind begins to race, I know to stop driving. I pulled into the parking lot of the Amish grocery. "Similar concentrations?"

"Within 20 percent. I took the liberty of doing duplicates. It's no fluke. The DNA damage is not consistent with benzene or acrolein in the wire plant's lacquers. It is consistent at several loci with the chromium, arsenic, and beryllium. Those loci also overlap for aflatoxin B, so your moldy hay may still play a role. Ms. Barker's blood had just-detectable traces of aflatoxin, about what you'd expect in a farmer. Not enough to worry about. Still, it was consistent."

"I had discounted the beryllium. That's not like me. I'm down two patients. I should have asked Walt about beryllium. I'll be seeing the last patient this afternoon, and I'll get back to the third as soon as possible. I have to find out where that's coming from."

There was a short silence on the line. "Do you hear what you're saying, Doc?"

"What?"

"Patients. You're calling them patients."

"You're right; I am. I need to get this wrapped up and get out of here while I still can. Thanks so much for letting me know. Now get out of the lab and get some rest."

"Yes, sir." He hung up the phone.

My mind was occupied for the rest of the trip to the *New Era* with figuring out where I'd missed their exposure to beryllium. It's seldom encountered and should have shown up in my checks. Frank's exposure was somewhat plausible from his Air Force experiences, even though that was well outside of any time frame I could accept. There was nothing in the histories of Walt or Ron to suggest exposure. I was relieved that none of the other relatives had the element. At least it wasn't a contaminated water source or common contaminated food supply. I should have asked Mike about beryllium in the Patton-Dalton samples, though he would have said something if beryllium were in those samples, and he didn't. Beryllium compounds wouldn't be volatile, so that wouldn't be consistent with Ron Widing.

More to the point, the Patton-Dalton plant had been shuttered for decades. While damage might be in the genes, detectable concentrations of the metal just wouldn't persist that long. Unless Jim Dulaney or Ron Widing could provide an explanation, my departure was going to be delayed.

I pulled in at the *Kentucky New Era* and checked my watch — 8:20. Given all that I had accomplished that morning, I was close to schedule. Dee arrived a few minutes later. She opened the door and greeted two of the reporters, letting them know what I'd be doing and telling them to get me anything I needed. I thanked her, she left, and I went about reading stories of the bygone days of the mid-70s.

The desk where I'd been working before was undisturbed. I opened my folder and began taking notes. I reviewed subsequent pages for several Fridays. After the game of October 19h, everything fell apart. The team never came close to winning again that year. I jumped forward into November until I reached Tuesday the 13th. The headline told of Coach Reggie Tatum's disappearance the previous day. The story matched Ellen's narrative. I hoped that I would have a memory like hers when I was her age. The coach's wife had been questioned, as well as all of his associates and relatives. I checked the front sections going forward. Nothing of substance was reported aside from the suspicious — though legal — withdrawal from his bank account. I perused every issue of the *New Era* from mid-October through to the end of December. I found no further direct clues about Coach Tatum.

There were plenty of stories about Jennifer Collins's disappearance and a rising chorus of people angry with Sheriff Cox. I even found an editorial in late November calling for him to resign over the bungled investigations. His rebuttal the next week had numerous "[expletive deleted]" entries. By the end of December, neither Coach Tatum nor Jennifer Collins was a newsmaker. I knew from the present that Sheriff Cox would remain for another five years and that the mystery around the young girl's disappearance would remain unsolved.

I finished my checks earlier than I expected, so I spent about an hour just leafing through every page, enjoying the old ads and the tone of the times. I saw help-wanted openings at the Patton-Dalton plant and news of impending expansion. Editorials were particularly harsh regarding those protesting the Vietnam War. Support was strong for Fort Campbell, and there was no mention of anything we would call PTSD today. I finished the last issue of 1973 with a story speculating on whose baby would be the first of 1974. Closing the last issue, I moved the stack to the reshelving table. I knew not to do that myself. I found one reporter and let her know that I was finished and would be leaving.

Once I got into the car, I reviewed Isabel's map. It was a route traced on a photocopy with annotations about inaccurate road locations and non-obvious turning points. Several had exclamation points for emphasis. The Dulaney place was on Pilot Rock Road in the northern part of Todd County, which meant I'd be traveling south to Guthrie and then north from there. I got out my map of the area, and was not impressed by the match between my map and Isabel's. Given her warning about the inaccuracies of the GPS maps, I decided to play it safe and return to Guthrie. The distances were not that great, after all.

Before I started, I took the opportunity to call Baylor. She was off for Memorial Day and had slept late. We exchanged "I miss you." I found out a little about how Ellen knew so much. Baylor had called me twice when I had turned my cell phone off, both times at the Tinley farm. When I didn't answer, she called Ellen. The two of them talked — talked for several hours. Baylor had plenty of questions for me, including why I hadn't mentioned Ellen's peonies. She wanted to know how much weight I had put on, and if I was getting exercise to compensate. We talked for about half an hour before we phone-kissed and I drove away from Hopkinsville.

I've long been intrigued by our adaptability to changes of scale. When I looked at the map and saw the extra driving, I perceived it to be a very long way around. Yet the total extra driving time was less than a third the time that I would take one way to or from the lab and my home in Atlanta. By the time that I had driven the roundabout way, I had driven farther from Guthrie than the Johnsons, the Tinleys, or Ron Widing lived. The farther I drove, the more I found myself slowing down. The lanes were narrower, the curves tighter, and the road rougher than anything I'd experienced in the last week. I didn't know the exact geological name of the area I was traversing, so I thought of it as the "Pennyrile Highlands." Gone were the gentle rolling fields to the south. I drove surrounded by sandstone outcrops and thick woods. What pastures I passed were small and surrounded by woodlots. Twice I needed to brake for deer and once for a family of raccoons. While watching for wildlife, I twice missed Isabel's marked turns. As she and Curtis had warned, the GPS was useless — it showed me driving in a stream. I slowed further so that I could pay attention to the hand-drawn map, shedding my desire to go faster. There was no traffic. I had not seen another car on the road in 15 miles.

At last, as I approached the end of my map run, I saw Isabel's car up ahead, parked on a gravel pull-off across from the driveway that was my goal. When I was about half a city block away, she pulled out from the side and drove across the road into that driveway. Maintenance-wise, this place was more akin to Ron Widing's home than the other two, only worse. I didn't sense any effort to repair the broken fences or sagging outbuildings. I followed Isabel to the end of the drive and parked in a way that we could leave in any order.

The best of the out buildings was, or had become, a garage for a clean looking newer model car. To the side of the building, a large pickup truck deteriorated in the open. It may have once been dark red, now an ugly rust color. A set of disintegrating yellow letters once proclaimed 'Dulaney Lumber – finest products at the lowest price.' There were no vines growing around it, and the tires were inflated, so I guessed that it still ran. A warm front had moved in, and the heat and humidity made their presence felt. I could hear the low buzz of some early-season cicadas. Otherwise, all was still and quiet. As we approached the front porch, Isabel lagged a few steps behind me, and I braced for an unpleasant encounter. The porch itself could have used a good coat of paint several years ago. Now it would need some board replacement as well. Along the margins, the wood was frayed and crumbling. From the corner of my eye I caught a glimpse of something scurrying under the porch. No foundation plantings graced the dwelling save an overgrown hydrangea on the left side.

I looked to Isabel, expecting her to knock on the door and introduce me. The doorbell hung useless from the molding with exposed wires. I remembered a renovator friend back in Atlanta once describe a project he was looking into: "First step, trim with a bulldozer." I thought that's what Rich would be saying here. Instead of stepping up to the door, Isabel held out her hand for me to proceed.

My knock was answered by a loud "Who is it?"

"Dr. John Parker."

The door swung open. A woman, rather well dressed, looked me over. Her hair was done up high and a cigarette dangled from her hand. Layers of makeup could not disguise the passage of time. "Yeah?"

"My name is John Parker. I'm a doctor from the Centers for Disease Control and Prevention in Atlanta. Dr. Rodriguez offered to let me accompany her on her rounds. I'm investigating the cancer that's cropped up out here. Are you Mrs. Dulaney?"

"Yeah, unfortunately I am. And don't expect me to be bowing to some do-gooder government program to 'improve our lot' out here." She punctuated the "improve our lot" with her fingers making quote marks. Ashes fell from her cigarette to the floor covering, which at some point in the past must have been a light carpet. "We take care of our own just fine without Big Brother's interference."

"No, ma'am, I'm not bringing any programs. I'm just investigating the cancer your husband has, trying to find out what's causing it. With your permission, I'd just like to ask a few questions and collect a few specimens."

"And how much do we get paid for this?"

I scratched my head. "The CDC doesn't pay for information or samples. It's for the common good."

"Typical government attitude." She turned and walked into the room. "Take, take, take, and expect us to be glad to give, give, give." Isabel and I followed her. At the center of the room, Donna wheeled and pointed at Isabel. "Did I say you could come in?"

Dr. Rodriguez adopted a placid air. "It's the last Monday of the month. I have Jim's pain meds. If you'd prefer, I can just leave and take them back with me."

Donna shook her head vigorously. "Oh, hell no. I don't want another week of him hollerin'."

Isabel paused a moment. The conversations seemed at a standstill. "Shall I start?"

"Do what you need to do. Just be quick about it. I've got an appointment in town at five."

I heard a deep moan from another room.

Isabel turned to me. "Let me get him fixed up and you can come visit." She left in the direction of the moan.

I would have expected an invitation to have a seat. No invitation was forthcoming.

"You watch out for that girl, mister." Donna's eyes narrowed.

I lowered my eyebrows and didn't say anything.

"That girl's a goddamned Muslim come to spread terror here."

I put on a skeptical face. "I thought she was Baptist, though Muslims do worship the same God."

"That's just an act. I'll bet when she's out of sight she practices all those pagan Muslim rituals. She acts out being a Baptist in public for cover."

"I see. How do you know this?"

Donna took out another cigarette and lit it. She took a deep draw and exhaled smoke. "Isn't it obvious? Look at that headpiece, that hedge thing."

"Hijab?" I offered.

"Whatever. If you're going to be an American, then dress like an American."

"I think she wears her scarf to cover a scar."

"Who told you that? Did she? Have you seen a scar?"

I shook my head.

"And her name. 'Isabel Rodriguez?' What kind of American name is that?"

I pursed my lips before replying. "I've never associated 'Rodriguez' with Muslim, though it could be, I guess. I think of 'Rodriguez' as Hispanic."

"Hispanic! Oh, aren't we all fancy politically correct. Mexican is more like it. I'll bet she'd have a hard time coming up with her birth certificate."

I wasn't going to get in an argument with Donna about birth certificates. Isabel would have needed one to get into Old Dominion or to get a driver's license. I didn't sense that factual explanations would carry the day with Donna.

"And where do you think she gets all these drugs?" Donna continued.

"She's a doctor?" I half queried, half answered.

Donna lifted her finger in the air. "She's a nurse. She's just a damned nurse. She even admitted that to me."

"Nurses can prescribe medicine. Nursing is one of several professions that can be licensed."

She looked annoyed. "Well, she shouldn't be. Anyway, have you seen her license?"

I thought a moment, remembering the wall behind Isabel's desk. "Yes." That wasn't altogether correct. I'd seen her Old Dominion nursing diploma and remembered our conversations about the difficulties in getting pain medications.

"Well, I still don't trust her. If we had a sheriff with balls, he'd be investigating her. She's got lil' Curtis wrapped around her finger. If Carl Cox were still on the job, you can bet he'd get to the bottom of this."

I just nodded.

"You know, she's been trying to ruin our family since she got here. Even my daughter can't escape. J.B. had a damned good chance of going to college on a cheerleading scholarship until Nurse Rodriguez had to go sticking her nose into the private lives of J.B. and a couple of fellas she was fucking!"

I assumed she was talking about the football team and coach and the STDs. "Uh, she's required by law to investigate that sort of thing."

She shook her head. "I should have figured a government agent would take her side. You impose your damned rules on people like us just to keep us down. We should be free to use whatever talents we've got to get ahead. That's the American way. That's freedom."

I tried to appear as neutral as I could.

She got up and began pacing. "It's not easy living in this place, you know. I left my last husband for Jimmy when he found out this land was sitting on top of a fortune in oil. It still is, but the price has dropped so much and the damned government regulations have gotten so expensive that the oil companies won't drill here anymore. I'd have left his sorry ass, except the prenup he made me sign would leave me penniless. Looks like I might still wind up that way unless they do something about the price of American crude. It's a sad state of affairs when it's cheaper to get our oil from those damned Muslim A-rabs than from hard-working Americans."

The casual blending of religions, races, and nationalities was making me dizzy. Mercifully, Isabel emerged from Jim's room.

"I've upped the dosage of his pain regimen. He should sleep a little better. As I said last time, you've got to change his sheets daily. It doesn't look as though they've been changed in a week."

"That's too much lifting for me. He's a heavy slob. You know that."

"Then get some help. He's going to get sepsis. That's as much a threat to you and J.B. as it is to him," Isabel insisted.

"You mind your own business. I'll handle this my way. And J.B. hasn't been here in a month. She's staying with …" Donna paused as Isabel looked up from her notes. "… someplace else."

Isabel returned to her notes, finished, and closed her folder. "Change the sheets — daily — unless you want me to have the health inspectors out here."

Donna remained silent as she folded her arms.

Isabel turned to me. "The patient is waiting for you, Dr. Parker."

I went into the room with Isabel following. Donna remained behind, alone in the living room. Jim lay in bed in a dim, airless room. I had expected an obese man from others' descriptions, including Donna's a few minutes earlier. The cancer had taken its toll. Loose folds of skin hung from his frame, while Jim's body had withered to perhaps 70 or 80 pounds.

"Ah, the government doctor. Here to harvest my organs?" he spoke, a bit above a whisper.

I managed a smile. "No, sir. We don't do that where I work."

He shrugged. "Just as well. They ain't worth much now anyway."

"I'm from the Centers for Disease Control and Prevention in Atlanta. I'm trying to unravel why you four came down with this particular cancer. It's pretty rare and we'd like to make sure we know where it comes from."

"Rare? Any money in it? Like rare coins." Jim perked up.

I chuckled. "No, 'fraid not. Your wife asked about the same thing. The knowledge is for the common good."

He had a faraway look in his eyes. "Guess there's a first time for everything, huh?"

"How so?" I asked.

"I know what people think of me. Do they think I don't know? I had plans for when I was rich. Giving lavish gifts, getting buildings named after me. People would whisper, 'There's Jim Dulaney. He gave the such and such.' Didn't happen, though."

I nodded a respectful nod. "Maybe your heirs will do that for you. Your wife says this land sits on oil. Maybe she'll name things in your honor."

He looked at me for a moment and then turned away. "Yeah, maybe."

"If I may, I'd like to ask you a few questions and take a few samples."

"Samples? You mean blood, right?" he croaked.

"Yes, sir. That's all I'm equipped to take here."

"Is it going to hurt?"

"You'll feel a stick. Like a flu shot," I replied.

"You doctors all like to stick us with needles, don't you?"

"We like the end results. If there were an easier way, we'd do it. I'm pretty good at the stick. If you'd rather, Dr. Rodriguez might be willing to do the blood drawing."

"Nah. She's had her turn for today. Wouldn't be fair to deprive you of yours."

I placed my sample case on the bed and began my preparations. "Do you remember a load of lumber a few years ago that was preserved with chromated copper arsenate in creosote? Nasty, smelly stuff?"

"Oh, yeah. That's what they're blaming for this, aren't they?"

"I don't know about blame. We don't allow that preservative anymore because of a high risk of cancer. Your three companions in this disease were also exposed to the lumber. And I just got back analysis from our laboratory in Atlanta that shows that the cancer is consistent with exposure to chromated copper arsenate in creosote. I've also been taking blood samples from people who were around them then, and they've been clear. I know it's been a while, and you must've sold a lot of lumber. Any chance you remember who else you sold it to?"

"Humph. Lumber business isn't as lucrative as people think. I got that stinking stuff from a wholesaler down in Nashville at a steal — or so I thought. Turns out that con artist had gotten it on the black market — Mexico, China, some place like that. Once the first load arrived, I tried selling it to our local contractors. They took one sniff and wouldn't have anything to do with it. The contractors said it was against the law. I offered 'em big discounts, and they still wouldn't touch it. When I cancelled the rest of the deal, that Nashville bastard said I'd still have to pay him or he'd sue. I was able to deliver it to Frank and Walt and Ron before they had a chance to smell it. Once they did, they made me haul it all back. That is, Faye made me haul back Frank's load. Seems it gave him hives or something. And Gina made me take back Walt's load." He looked at me wide-eyed. "You do *not* want to mess with Gina Barker."

I nodded. "No, sir. I've already learned that. So nobody had any long exposure to the lumber except Ron?"

"I put Ron's load in his barn. He was going to put an extension on his house. Never got to it."

I was troubled. "So if I get this right, no one except maybe you had any long exposure to the chemicals."

"Yeah. And the whole rotten deal wound up costing me about five grand," he complained.

"No one else got the lumber?"

"I'm tellin' you, no. I hauled it myself to the old quarry. Maybe you should check with the skunks and possums out there." Jim seemed annoyed at my persistence.

"OK. I'm glad we had this conversation. Did you ever have any dealings with beryllium?"

"Who?" he asked.

I shook my head. "Not who, what. It's a metal. Sometimes used in paints or special metal alloys. It occurs most often in nuclear power or research. It's sometimes found in fine paints. Ever see beryllium in any ingredients?"

He shook his head. "If you're talking money, you're in the wrong part of the country, fella. I did lumber and lumber supplies. Not much paint. For metal, you'd need to go to Nashville. This ain't your swanky East Coast."

"Right." I had prepared my syringes and sample vials. As I looked at his arm, I saw numerous sores. The alcohol swab would be painful. I couldn't add any novocaine or benzocaine, because they would interfere with the analysis. I turned to Isabel.

"I told Donna to use the lotion. Obviously she didn't."

I recalled Ron's evaluation of his situation versus Jim's. Roberta, Faye, and Gina took good care of their men.

"Well, Mr. Dulaney, this is going to sting a little more than I wanted. On the positive side, the alcohol will help the healing."

"Somehow, I'm not sure that's a big consideration. Doc Isabel says there's not much time left. You know any different?"

"I've been here a week and haven't seen the doctor be wrong about anything. I'm sorry."

"Yeah, well … I guess do your doctor stuff. Sure there's no money in it?"

"Pretty sure. I'll double-check though. Take a deep breath."

I swabbed with the alcohol pad. He winced, and put up with the pain. I worked as quickly as I could. "There. That's it. These samples will go to Atlanta tomorrow, and I'll have results back by Thursday."

I heard Isabel's cell phone, even though she had it on vibrate. She retrieved it from her bag and looked at the message. "I need to check this text as long as the signal holds. Might take a while. I'll meet you outside."

Jim watched as she got up to leave. "Say goodbye to the Wicked Witch of the West on your way out."

Isabel turned and smiled as she shook her head. "You are naughty, sir." She exited the room. I could hear some muffled sharp exchange with Donna as she left the house.

Jim was still watching the door. "Those two are just like mean old she-cats. It's a wonder they haven't killed each other." He turned back to me. "Got anything more for me? Maybe some cards or good bourbon? I don't have much going on right now."

"Well, sir, I think you may have extended my stay here a bit. I thought I had the answers this morning. You've kinda knocked the chocks out from under them. As far as you know, no one else in the community has come down with this cancer or anything else like it?"

"No. This is small town. You'd hear about it. Nothing stays secret for long. Almost nothing."

"Did you ever work at the Patton-Dalton plant in Hopkinsville?"

"Shoot, no. That was a hellish place to work. Pay wasn't very good, either. Wasn't much going on in the area then, so it had one of the bigger payrolls."

"Never did any contract work for them?"

"Nope. They contracted everything construction-wise from Nashville or Cincinnati. Why are you interested in the old wire plant?" he asked.

"I'm trying to find some link between you and the other three. Your disease is rare. We're not talking about one in a million. We're talking about only 17 cases ever reported — in the whole world. To have four cases appear together and timed about the same is just way too much to be coincidence. I've spent the past week trying to find a link. I thought I had it: the preservative in the lumber and the beryllium. They're potent carcinogens. Now I see that the three of you were not exposed to that much of the preservative, and I still have no idea where the beryllium comes in. The four of you have traveled very different paths since high school. I can't see going back to Atlanta with an empty case, but the only item I still have for you guys in common was when you were part of the five demons back in '73. That was forty years ago."

I watched him grow very still and quiet.

"Something happened back then, didn't it?" I said. "Every time I bring it up, people shut down. Of the five demons, one committed suicide and the other four have a super-rare cancer. And Ron Widing said something odd to me Friday. He bet me that Coach Tatum would have the cancer too. Any idea why he would think that?"

Jim seemed reticent now. "You'd have to ask Ron. He's more the intellectual type than the rest of us. Thinks too much."

"Did Coach Tatum give the five of you something? 'Five Demons' sounds like quite a transformation from the four men I've met. Seems like a strange coincidence that the team came apart about the same time he disappeared."

His face was stern. "I've spent forty years trying to get Reggie Tatum out of my head. I don't want to spend my final hours on Earth thinking about him."

"I'm sorry. I'm just trying to get to the root cause of this cancer. Forty years is a long time for it to incubate — unheard of, to tell the truth. If he gave you something that's responsible for this cancer forty years later, I need to know."

"I don't want to talk about it and won't — even if I'm the last man standing. Promise me this. If you ever find Reggie Tatum, you fill that needle of yours with poison and stick it right into his black heart."

Jim was adamant. "You need to go now. I want to rest. My wife's going to be heading in to town soon. Maybe thinks she's going to screw someone, though I reckon those days are over. Maybe blackmail? I'm through."

I gathered my case and notes. I thanked him for giving the samples and the information and gave him my card in case he remembered something or wanted to talk more about anything. I asked if there was anything more I could do for him, expecting it would have something to do with money.

"Ever do paternity tests?" he asked.

"Not myself. Our lab has those capabilities, though. Why?"

"I've always wondered about ... naw. Never mind."

I bid Jim Dulaney good day, thanked Donna in passing, and walked out into the heat and humidity. Isabel was leaning on her car, arms folded, sullen.

She perked up as I approached. "Get what you came for?"

"I suppose, and so much more. I think I'm about back at square one. Even with the genetic evidence, the lumber preservative is looking weak now. And I still have no idea where beryllium comes in. And I keep coming back to the football team. That's a really thin lead. I think there're things I can check out back at the office."

"Good. Because I'd like to get out of here before she calls in drone strikes on me," she said, looking toward the house, where Donna was watching us through a dirty window.

"Did you get your phone call made?"

"No. I can sometimes receive a text out here. I can't get an actual voice connection. There's nothing out here."

I nodded.

"Including oil," she whispered.

"Huh?"

"Donna's stayed with him because she doesn't want to be out of his will. There's no oil. He knows that, and hasn't told her. I remember a few years back I treated one of the oil company men who was out here doing the geological surveys. Everything came up empty around here. He said that was to be expected, that they just needed to complete their maps. The nearest oil pockets are fifty miles north." She opened the door to her car and got in.

"So this land is ... ?"

"Worthless except as a wildlife refuge. I'm not going to spoil her surprise. See you at the office."

She closed the door and drove off. I followed a minute later. Tomorrow, I would send the remaining samples to Atlanta and would see about a follow-up visit with Ron Widing. Frank and Walt were gone and Jim wasn't going to talk again for a while. Ron seemed to be my last hope.

I remembered the turns rather well, still needing to concentrate to keep my speed down. Traffic out here was infrequent enough that gravel accumulated on the road, making some of the turns treacherous.

I arrived back in Guthrie after about half an hour of concentrated driving. I stopped first at the office and brought in my sample case and notes. I finished typing my notes into the database and then packed and sealed my sample case for mailing in the morning. I was logging in to the master database when Isabel arrived.

"Enjoy your visit?" she asked.

I smiled. "It lived up to its billing. Challenging pair."

"Trio. J.B.'s just as bad; maybe worse," she offered.

"Ouch!"

"You heard what Donna said about J.B.'s not being around, about living somewhere else?" she asked.

"Uh huh."

"I'm betting there will be medical consequences." She stood in the doorway shaking her head before turning to me. "And what are you up to?"

"I'm doing a database search. Looking for Reggie Tatum."

"Yeah, we did a lot of that a while back. All the state and interstate databases. You're not going to find anything. He covered his tracks really well."

I continued to enter all the information I had. "This is a little more high-octane. I'm on the national cross-agency search board."

"I don't remember that one. At least not by name," she said.

"I doubt you used this one. It gives me access across Department of Justice, Defense, Homeland Security, everything. It's important for doing a complete job and will be critical if we ever have a terrorist incident like a biological attack."

"Need any help?" she offered.

"No. Much as I'd like it, this is all pretty sensitive access. I have to have a top secret clearance just to log on."

"Wow! I didn't know you had a clearance," she said.

"Access to these searches is not something we talk about very often. The privacy concerns are enormous. That's why I get a security review every year. Those of us in the program have access to almost every bit of digitized information on every person in the country and millions of others. This is the database that DOJ can use to wipe out a person's existence for things like the witness protection program."

"So how will this find Coach Tatum when our other searches failed?"

"Well, it might not find him. It does search many more databases than any civilian searches. And the software is sophisticated, using some very high-order algorithms. There. I just entered all the information from your records and the system's doing the first cursory search, which should come back right about … now. And as expected, nothing more than his last known address in Elkton."

She shrugged. "Worth a try, I guess."

"Now it asks if I want to do a Level 2 search. That will take several hours to several days. I'll get an email letting me know if any results have come back and I can log in again and see what's in my bucket."

She turned to leave. "Well, happy fishing. Let me know if there's anything more you need from me. There are plenty of people who'd like to get their hands — or a noose — around his neck."

I chuckled. "That's part of the reason they restrict access to the databases." I watched the log-off and then remembered a question. "Any chance I could see Ron Widing in the morning?"

"I'm sure he'd be glad to see you. I'll give Roberta a call."

I stowed the remaining file folders and gathered my hardware. I was in the unaccustomed position of coming to the end of my data with the case falling apart rather than coming together.

I said goodnight to Isabel and drove the short distance to Ellen's. She and Stacy were hard at work on Ferdinand's vestments. They asked how the case was going. I told them, and they said they were sorry. Ellen had prepared a roasted chicken with green beans and mashed potatoes. I ate with them in the quilting room and listened to stories of Guthrie and Baltimore. I was very tired by the time I got to my room and crawled into bed.

Tomorrow would be a busy day.

10 DEATH AND REMEMBRANCE

I awoke to the sounds of my phone's alarm ringtone. I had slept soundly and didn't stir with the dawn as on previous days, something I've noticed happens when my investigations are not going well. Perhaps it's my brain's natural reaction to assist me finding solutions. As a matter of fact, I felt much more confident about my research that morning than I had the previous night.

All of the facts of the cases remained the same. The three cases whose samples had been analyzed each possessed similar significant concentrations of known — potent — carcinogens. Though I had not pinpointed the source of the chromium, beryllium, and the others, I had at least demonstrated the presence of sufficient cause with the first three. I had a feeling that Jim Dulaney would likewise possess these chemicals in his blood. Something linked these four together, something they were on the verge of telling me. I hoped Ron Widing would clear it up for me that day.

I turned on my computer and checked my email. No return yet from the database search.

After showering and shaving, I walked around to the front to greet Ellen. The sky was gray and the wind had picked up. Ellen was tending the porch begonias. "Morning, ma'am."

She smiled. "Morning, sir," she spoke in a hoarse whisper.

I cocked my head out of curiosity.

"Stacy's asleep on the couch in the living room."

I climbed the front steps, trying to stay quiet. Stacy was sprawled on the couch with a light afghan covering her. We tiptoed through the living room and into the kitchen. I closed the kitchen door.

Ellen explained, "When I threw in the towel about one this morning, she was still going strong. Looks like she completed Ferdinand's robes.

174

Judging by how much she did after I went to bed, Stacy must have been up until four o'clock or so. It looks good — very professional."

"I'll have to take a look in a bit."

"Yes, do." Ellen was frying hominy, starting with a generous dollop of butter.

"I'm glad to see other people like hominy. Most people turn up their nose outside of the South or Hispanic communities. I like it. So does Baylor."

She smiled. "The ancient Aztecs learned how to make it. Good way to make low-grade corn edible other than grinding it. It's cheap calories and it's bland in and of itself. You can add what you want to it. Kinda' like zucchini. I just fry the hominy in butter and pepper it when I'm fixing it for myself. I didn't want to presume on your tastes."

"Pepper away. That's how I like it."

She set out a bowl of strawberries on the table. They had been sliced and sugared, probably the night before. "More goodies from Faye. Lee Sisk keeps a big patch and shares with her more than they can eat, even with the grandkids visiting. Would you like some vanilla ice cream on them?"

"Oh, wow. I still amazing that this isn't a hot spot of atherosclerosis."

"Now, we talked about that. If you're active enough, you'll burn up the calories. And everything we've had is local. No processed fats, so no trans or industrial fats. Between my gardening and walking everywhere, there's not much left to settle in the arteries."

I thought about the different life style in Atlanta. "You're right."

She nodded. "Yup." She turned to me. "By the way, you seem more upbeat this morning than you did last night. Did you come up with something?"

"In a way. Everything seems clearer this morning. I'm quite sure I've found the cause of the cancer. I just haven't found the cause of the cause — haven't found where these four were exposed to the specific carcinogens. I have an uneasy feeling that those four know — or knew — something, yet aren't willing to tell me. I think it goes back to the football team and Coach Tatum. If he's still alive, I'll be visiting him and I will get the answer. I've got a national database search running right now."

"You seem pretty confident you'll find him."

"It's never failed me. If he's still alive, I'll be paying him a visit. If he's not, I may get some medical records to check."

She brought over the skillet of hominy and scooped half onto my plate, half onto hers. "Well, I've expressed my sentiments about him. Still, I'd like to know where he went and what he's done with himself. Sounds pretty un-Christian, but I think I'll be disappointed if he turns out to be successful somewhere. I think the German word is *Schadenfreude*."

"Yes, rejoicing in the misfortune of others. Even if we're not supposed to feel it, some people seem to earn the sentiment. To the extent that confidentiality allows, I'll update people on what I find," I assured.

"Put Doc Isabel at the head of the list. She's had so much cleanup to do with his football legacy."

I chuckled. "Yeah, she offered to help. Access to the database is under very tight control for obvious reasons. Every time there's a breach, it seems to make national headlines."

We finished our breakfast; I thanked her and headed for my room.

Ellen called behind me. "Can I lend you an umbrella? Forecast's calling for showers this morning. While I don't expect severe weather, I don't want you to get soaked."

I thought for a moment. "Yes, ma'am, I'll take you up on that."

She dug out a small travel umbrella. I thanked her again and promised to return it. I went to the quilting room to view Ferdinand's vestments. Ellen and Stacy had rigged some tables and chairs to approximate his dimensions. The nearly finished work was impressive. At last, I tiptoed back through the living room.

Just as I reached the front door, I heard a murmur. "Morning, Doctor P. What time is it?"

I looked at my watch. "Five after seven."

"Bleah. Thanks." Stacy turned over, facing the back of the couch, and looked as if she would return to sleep.

"Ferdinand's robes are magnificent!" I offered as I opened the front door.

"Thanks," she murmured again.

I checked my email again. Finding nothing, I picked up my samples and notes and headed for the post office and clinic. I followed Ellen's example and walked, waving to the neighbors along the way. There were other perks to walking beyond the cardiovascular benefits.

When I arrived at the post office, Mireese was leaning on the counter in conversation with Jack. On the counter were six or seven boxes waiting his processing. Mireese and Jack turned to me as I walked in. I sensed a glow of contentment and happiness in her face.

"Hey, Dr. Parker. Good morning."

"Good morning. How are you, Mireese of Guthrie?"

"Super fine. Jack says one of these will be my 500th doll." She pointed to the assembled boxes. "I think I'll choose this one. A little girl was helping her family clean out her great-grandmother's house after the old lady's death. The doll was in such bad shape that the girl's parents had thrown it into the dumpster. The little girl was inconsolable because she remembered playing with it whenever she visited the great-grandmother, so they agreed to save it and send it to me for fixing. Glad they did. I let them know right away that this doll fetches over a thousand dollars at auction.

Normally, I charge 300 for cleaning and restoration. I'm giving the service as a gift to the little girl."

"Nice, very nice. I totally agree. That should be number 500." I did some quick mental math. "That's quite a business."

She smiled a crooked smile. "Yeah. Who would have thought that doing something you loved would pay like that?" She turned to Jack. "Plus I get to visit my buddy almost every day."

Jack smiled as he worked on the registered mail forms. "What'cha got for me today, Doc?"

"Samples from Jim Dulaney for Atlanta."

Jack grinned and shook his head.

"And I've got a sample for the FBI database."

He looked up. "Whoa! That sounds more serious than we thought."

"No, this is a side thing that doesn't have anything to do with my mission here. There was a little girl who disappeared back in the 70s, and the forensics weren't very good at the time. I kept running across her story during my research and wanted to do what I could."

"The Jennifer Collins murder?" Mireese bit her lip.

I nodded. "Seems everyone's heard about it."

"You kidding? Back in school, any time there was a safety lecture about not going with strangers or letting your parents know where you were going, they'd bring up her murder. Think you have something?"

"No, it's just that having her DNA in the database might help some day. It's something I can do. I want to finish up on the cancers, which is my mission here."

Jack nodded. "How's that going?"

"I'm at a bit of a roadblock. The samples that I've sent in are all consistent for a set of known carcinogens for three of the patient … cases. The other family samples are clear. Today's samples complete the set, and I'll be shocked if they don't have the same chemicals. I just can't figure out the link among the four men. They've all traveled separate paths since they were part of the Five Demons back in high school."

Both Jack and Mireese were shaking their heads.

"Sorry. Before my time, Doc." Jack said.

"Ever hear people talking about chromated copper arsenate?"

They shook their heads.

"Beryllium?"

Still shaking. Mireese spoke up, "I've heard of beryl. That's a gemstone."

"Yes, ma'am, very good. Emeralds and aquamarine are both beryl gems. They're safe because the beryllium is bound up in their crystal structures. Free beryllium metal and soluble compounds are the problem."

"Haven't heard of those around here. Glad emerald's safe, though. It's my birthstone."

Jack looked up as he handed her the slips to sign. "I didn't know that."

She smiled a coy smile as she affixed her signatures. "Yes, you did."

The three of us continued our chat as he processed my two packages.

"I'm sending out more registered packages than Hopkinsville these days," Jack said.

"Well, these may be my last. I'm almost wrapped up. I'll be interviewing Ron Widing again today. I'll be doing some more interviews in the community to see if I can find the source of the contamination, the beryllium in particular. I think my boss is going to be wanting me back."

Mireese pouted. "Ah, you can't leave us, Doc. We're just getting to know you. You should come live here."

"You've got a great doctor already. As overworked as Doc Isabel is, there isn't work for two. I have to admit, though, it's so tempting."

I smiled as I left the post office. Amidst the backdrop of my grim task, there were stories of deep friendship, or perhaps more, and respect. I walked across the street to the clinic. Isabel's car was not in the lot, so I figured the clinic door would be locked, though I tried it anyway. I walked around to the front door, greeted Liz, and headed to my office. The stack of documents had dwindled to the point that I could hold them in one hand. I plugged in my computer and checked my email, appreciating that I was becoming compulsive about the checks. I wanted to find Reggie Tatum. Unlike most of the others, I wanted to find him alive.

A few minutes into my note-taking, I received a text from Isabel. "Roberta called. Ron is struggling. If you want to talk to him, best hurry." I put away my notes, closed the computer, and jogged back to Ellen's. I verified that I had a sampling kit for the final specimens if it came to that. I still remembered the landmarks along the Hadenville Road and drove into Ron's driveway a little before ten. Isabel's car was parked near Ron's tractor. As I approached the house, I found Roberta sitting on the edge of the porch. Though her face was tear-streaked, she seemed composed and calm.

"Ron was a fine man, Dr. Parker. One of the finest."

I sat down beside her.

"Some people said he was cold. That's not true. I knew him, maybe better than anyone else. He was just thinkin' all the time. And he didn't have much patience for stupid. Lord knows we have enough of that in this world. He fought for justice, and that's right. Like our pastor always says, 'You must speak truth to power.' Ron did that. Landed him in hot water more'n once. Of course, he'd always win in the end. Yes, speaking truth to power."

"I'm sorry I didn't have the chance to meet him earlier."

She nodded. "Umm huh. You two would have been quite a pair."

We sat in silence for many minutes. Even this close to Guthrie, the isolation from human sounds was dramatic. Maybe somewhere off in the distance I could pick up the sound of a tractor, so faint that it challenged my last good hearing test. On the natural side, I heard the low rumble of approaching rain from time to time and the rustle of leaves as the breezes picked up. Then I heard footsteps in the house. Isabel emerged, somber, wearing a heavy black scarf.

She addressed Roberta. "He said he'd put in a good word with God on your behalf."

Roberta smiled bravely through tears flowing free.

Isabel looked tired. "He was comfortable toward the end. The coughing was under control, and I cleaned up his face. Would you like Dr. Parker to do his tests now, and would you like me to call Bill Carson?"

Roberta nodded while struggling to speak. "Yes. Please. To both."

I reached around and hugged her. For a few minutes, she shook with sobs while I held her. Serenity returned and I relaxed my embrace while I kept my hand on her shoulder. Isabel sat down on the other side.

Roberta wiped the tears from her face. "Well, I know what Ron would say. He'd say, 'Done is done. I'll make a note of it and write another day. There's other work waitin'.'" She got up and Isabel and I followed her into the darkened room. In keeping with old traditions I had not observed in some time, some of the pictures had been draped in black and the one mechanical clock had been stopped at the time of death — 9:18. I sat down beside the body, donned my gloves, and began to lay out my vials, swabs, and label sheets. Roberta sat in a chair on the other side of the bed, while Isabel stood in the doorway, quiet.

As I moved through my checklist, Roberta asked questions.

"Do you ever get tired of this?"

I thought about her question. "No, can't say that I do. I know how important it is, how important it is to do it right. I can think of so many times when this routine has saved lives. Plus, ..." I looked up at Isabel. "... I'm pretty good at tedious and methodical."

Isabel grinned.

Roberta continued. "You must worry about catching the diseases. That's why you wear the gloves."

I smiled. "Oddly, that's not the reason for the gloves. I actually wear them to protect the samples from my touch. We're looking at the genes, the DNA, in Ron's tissue. To the best of my ability, I don't want to add any other DNA."

She nodded. "Very clever."

"It's enough of a routine now; I don't realize that I'm doing it. It's like walking — one foot in front of the other. There's thinking involved in that, just not in the brain." I took the last sample from the base of the brain and began packing the vials in the shipping case. "Our team has the whole sample flow worked out like clockwork. Each of us knows how to handle the samples, how to keep them clean, prepare them, and report the results. From the time they leave his body, they're shielded from contamination and, to the best of our ability, from errors."

Roberta smiled. "I think Ron's pleased to be part of this — his kind of mystery."

I returned the smile. "We'll do him proud. I promise." I continued by samples, ending with the brain, lung, and liver. Roberta was more curious than squeamish as she observed my technique.

I could hear the soft buzz of Isabel's phone, which was on vibrate, as usual. She looked at the number, shook her head, and excused herself.

I closed the armored shipping case. "Is there anything I can do for you, any way I can assist?"

"Naw. I've been doing everything around here for a long time already. Ron didn't do much to make a mess for the last few months." She looked into his face. "You know what he told me this morning, before he began the struggle?"

I shook my head.

"He said he'd left the place to me. He didn't have any family, no close relatives. I've never owned much beside my car. Now Ron's given me a real farm. Can you beat that?"

I smiled. "I think he wanted to leave it in good hands. You'll do well. First suggestion — get that lumber disposed of properly."

Her eyes grew wide. "Oh, yes. You can count on it. That's first on my list."

We got up and moved through the house to the front porch. She swept her arms around the rooms as we passed through them.

"I'll get the house aired out and get onto the painting. I had wanted to do that for a year. Amazing how much work it is to take care of someone who can't move around."

Isabel was talking on the phone, pacing the front yard just beyond the front porch. "I said I'll be there as soon as I'm able. I'm dealing with a death right now." She rolled her eyes. "As soon as I'm able." She grasped the phone and ended the call. Her jaw and free hand were clenched. "That …" She looked at Roberta and tempered her language. "… hideous woman."

Roberta could not help smirking as she turned to me. "Think she was talkin' to Donna?"

I nodded.

Scattered raindrops were beginning to fall. Isabel continued to pace, agitated. "She wants me to do something. She says he's coughing more blood. Says the medicine isn't working."

"Medicine?" I asked.

"Exactly. All he's on at this point is pain management." She sat down on the edge of the porch. "Sorry. She just gets under my skin so bad. I'll head out there in a bit and up the dosage. I may have some other things in my arsenal." She looked up at Roberta and me. "You know, though I hate to be so callous, I'm kinda glad this isn't going on much longer. Given his condition yesterday, I don't think he'll be with us this time next week." She straightened her doctor's coat. "Sorry." She reached out and took Roberta's hands. "I'll call Bill. I'm guessing he'll be out here by early afternoon. Anything you need?"

"No, ma'am. Like I told Dr. Parker, I've been doing everything already. I'll just keep on keeping on."

Isabel smiled and turned to me. "Did she tell you that Ron left the place in her good hands?"

I nodded. "Everyone keeps saying he was smart."

Isabel stepped back. "Well, I gotta go. Dr. Parker may need to calm me down when I get back to town." She walked away, got into her car and drove off.

Roberta was shaking her head. "Those two. It's a wonder they haven't killed each other. Donna's the only person I know of who doesn't just love the doctor."

"Yeah. I know that Ron held her in highest esteem."

"I'm sure glad she was with him when he passed. He was crying, real softly. Not like him. Do you see that often?"

I thought about her question. Both Faye and Gina had mentioned crying, yet I didn't recall such things in other cases I'd witnessed.

"Can't say that I have. He was privileged to have kind people around him at the end."

"I know you need to be on your way. Ron had something for you. Wait here."

She went into the house and returned with a CD in a white sleeve.

"Ron said that writing is never finished, you just stop writing. He was working on his last story on his computer through the afternoon yesterday. He said for you to read it in private when you get back to Atlanta. He was a good writer. I'm sure it's special."

"He said he'd have something for me. I'll treasure it," I assured.

We stood on the porch for a while as gentle rain began to drip from the edge of the porch roof. The air was fragrant with earthy smells.

"OK. I'm going to go now. You've got my card. I look forward to hearing what you do with the place — your place."

"Yes, sir. You drive safe now. These country roads can be dangerous when they're wet."

I went straight to the café. Lunch was spaghetti with meatballs, and I could smell as I walked in that they were going to be delicious. I had just finished placing my order when I sensed a presence beside me. I turned to see a smiling Eugene Gough.

"Mind if I join you?" he asked.

I smiled and opened my hand to the seat across the table. "Please. Good company on a rainy day is always a pleasure."

Cheryl came over to the table. "What can I get ya today, Mr. Gough?"

He pointed to me. "I'll have what he's having."

She smiled. "Good choice. Comin' right up."

After she left, he turned to me. "Sorry about the other day. I realize I was pretty rude."

I shrugged. "When you spend your whole life studying history, you can develop some strong feelings."

"Yeah, but I didn't give you the benefit of the doubt. I made some assumptions that weren't fair. You've done some good work here, Doc."

"Thank you, sir. Just doing what I can with what I know."

"You're too modest. I'm particularly grateful for what you did for my nephew."

I couldn't think of the connection. "Nephew?"

"Chris. I was up in the stands when he had that collision out on the field. I could tell from how you and the doc jumped into action and worked like you'd been a team forever that Chris was going to be all right. I talked with his 'wife' this morning." He grinned as he punctuated 'wife' with his fingers. "Gina says that he'll be coming home Thursday, and your doctor friend down at Vandy says he'll make a full recovery."

"I'm really happy to hear he'll be back so soon."

"Well, family's important to me. You did good. You're a true professional, and I wanted you to know I respect professionals."

"Thank you, sir. I'm honored that you feel that way. Does it mean maybe the government does a few things right?" I grinned.

He laughed a hearty laugh. "Don't push your luck! I'll grant you one temporary exemption."

Our lunch arrived, and it was delicious. He and I talked for about half an hour. He picked up the tab for lunch.

"No double-billing the government now, Doc."

"I promise. I keep scrupulous documents that are public records."

He laughed again, and left a small tip.

Cheryl watched as he left the café. She came over and motioned for the others to join her. She got out her cell phone and took a picture of the table.

"What's going on?" I asked.

"We've all been working here over ten years and Mr. Gough has never … never … picked up the tab. Mary's off today, and she's not going to believe it without proof." She turned to me. "This doesn't mean the Second

Coming is about to happen, does it?"

I grinned. "I don't think so."

I returned to my office at the clinic. I checked my email and felt a surge of excitement to see the first item.

```
"Global  search  has  returned  one  finding.
Log in to secure area to review results."
```

The secure nature of the Homeland Security site made for a long login process. As I entered the final credentials into my browser, I heard the clinic door open and then close. I looked up as Isabel came to my door. She looked exhausted.

"You OK?"

She shook her head. "I don't know. I won't even ask why God would create such a woman. In fact, I'm not sure it was His doing."

"What happened?"

Isabel looked at the floor. "I'm not sure I feel like talking about it. I think I just need to calm down and do some forgetting." She turned back toward her office.

I got up and followed.

She sat down at her desk and swiveled her chair toward the window. "The reason he's in pain is that the cancer inside is beginning to break through all the barriers. I guess you could say he's on final approach. I tried to explain that to them. I'm pretty sure Jim understands, though she's having none of it. I was in the process of giving him a morphine injection and she started screaming at me, and knocked the syringe out of my hand and across the room. We got into a knock-down, drag-out shouting match with Jim moaning and coughing for background. I left at last with her stomping after me. It was borderline scary."

I stood in her doorway for a while. "I'm sorry."

"Yeah, well. What'cha gonna do?"

I nodded in sympathy, and then brightened up. "I got a notice from our search system that it seems to have a match for Coach Tatum. I was just pulling it up."

She turned back to me and smiled a crooked smile. "That's good. So he's alive after all?"

"Don't know. The system searches the living and the dead. If this is the one and he's alive, I should have enough information to pay him a visit."

She gazed at her hands folded on the desk. My cell phone chirped. The number I saw had the local area code. "Someone calling me from the 487 exchange."

She frowned. "North County. Did you give Jim your phone number?"

"I gave him my card."

"Better answer then."

I pressed the receive button. "Hello, this is John …" I was cut off by a woman screaming into the phone.

"Jim says to get you up here right now. That woman didn't do him a bit of good and he just keeps repeating 'Call Dr. Parker.'"

I felt an unsettling mixture of irritation at Donna and sympathy for the dying Jim Dulaney. "I'm not his physician and I believe that Dr. Rodriguez was just out to see him." I looked at Isabel.

She closed her eyes and tilted her head back.

While I could hear Jim shouting in the background, I couldn't make out what he was saying.

I still had to hold the phone some distance from my ear as Donna shouted, "Yeah, I sent that bitch packing. She was trying to drug him. I think she's trying to get him to agree to something, and I won't stand for that. Now Jim is all agitated and says he needs to talk to you right now."

"OK. Can you hand him the phone, please?"

I could hear her offer him the phone. She was back on the line in a few seconds. "No, the stubborn ass insists on talking with you one-on-one."

"Just a minute." I put my hand on the receiver and talked to Isabel. "Jim Dulaney, or at least Donna, insists on a private meeting. I don't feel comfortable about that, him being your patient after all."

She waved her hand in dismissal. "Don't worry about it. I've seen all of those two I can stand for today. I don't sense that he has a tomorrow, and the shit's going to hit the fan big time when she understands that she's a penniless widow. Look, you missed witnessing the other three deaths. This may be your only chance. I'll warn you, it won't be pretty."

The situation still seemed awkward. I put the phone back to my ear. "Mrs. Dulaney, I can come out there, but there's nothing I can do for your husband."

I heard more heated exchange on the other end of the line. After a moment, Donna continued. "He says he'll 'tell you everything.' What's he talking about? What does he need to tell you?"

I now had a legitimate reason to pay him a visit. "There were some loose ends in the information about what he was exposed to. I think he may have remembered something for me."

"Why won't he tell me?"

"I don't know, ma'am. If I were you, I'd ask him. Do you still want me to come out there?"

"Bet your ass!" she shouted.

"OK. It'll take me about 20, 25 minutes. I'm on my way." She hung up before I could say anything else.

I looked at Isabel. "I'm still sorry. Do you want to go along?"

She shook her head vigorously. "Like I said, I've had as much of her as I can take in one day. I have some errands to run this afternoon. The car's full of donation stuff I need to deliver. You go and have a good time. If I were the drinking sort, I'd say that I'd have a big bottle of fine Kentucky whiskey to split with you when you get back. But I'm not."

I patted my pockets and felt my keys. The sample cases were already in the car. I walked out of the clinic past her car. The back seat was indeed filled with boxes, clothes, and the front seat with a cute basket, the kind Judy would make. I ran to my car as light rain continued to fall. 25 minutes might be on the optimistic side given the condition of the road now wet with rain. I hadn't traveled far from Guthrie when I experienced the first little skids. I kept my speed down to a safe limit, and the trip took just a little over 30 minutes.

I got out of my car and trotted to the front porch. Donna was waiting at the door.

"Why won't he tell me what he wants to tell you?"

"I don't know. Did you ask him?"

"Yeah. And he says it's none of my business. I'm about to be a widow. I say everything about this disaster is my business. And what was that horrid woman trying to inject in him?"

"Morphine. For the pain."

"She's trying to get him addicted. Bet she sells it on the side. First hit's free, they say."

"Mrs. Dulaney, your husband doesn't have time to get addicted."

I motioned to his room to suggest we get on with the business at hand. She gave a disgusted sigh and led me to his room. I approached Jim's bed while she remained at the door, arms folded. Jim looked much worse than he had looked a mere 20 hours earlier. His face had a definite gray cast, and the sheets were flecked with coughed-up blood.

When he saw me he gave a relieved sigh. He turned to Donna. "Leave us."

"Nothing doing. Anything you say to him, I have a right to hear."

Jim's face flushed red, and he leaned up on his elbow. "I said leave us. I'm not talking 'til you're gone. And if you don't go, I will come back as an evil spirit and haunt you all the days of your miserable life." He fell back, coughing violently.

"Fuck you!" She turned and left the room, slamming the door so hard that my ears hurt.

"Lock the door," Jim gave instructions between coughs.

I locked the door.

"Turn on the radio. It's tuned to WSM, country."

I complied. The radio filled the room with twanging guitars and songs of heartbreak.

"She'll be listening at the door." He had restored some calm and composure.

"I'm here," I offered.

His eyes grew wide. "Doc Parker, she's the devil."

I turned to look in the direction of the living room.

"No, no, no. Not her. Doc Isabel is the devil," he whispered, breath labored.

I must have exuded buckets of skepticism. "Uh ..."

He began to breathe rapidly, voice excited. "You've got to believe me, Doc. I don't have time left to say this twice. I'm not crazy. It's 2009, we're in Todd County, Kentucky, you're from Atlanta, the President is Barack fuckin' Obama — damn it — and Nashville's the capital of Tennessee. I'm telling you Doc — I'm not crazy. Doc Isabel is the devil. Only she's not Isabel Rodriguez. She's Jennifer Collins."

Despite the stale heat of his room, I felt a powerful chill. Goose bumps rose on my arms, and I only listened from that point on.

"When she was out here earlier, she got Donna to leave the room — said something to her about it was going to be messy and she would need some help. She knew that would get rid of Donna. Once the room was clear, she began to undo her scarf. She was wearing a heavy black scarf this morning. As she undid the scarf, I could see that most of the side of her face was missing, just a sheet of scars.

"She stared at me all serious and said, 'Do you remember the night of October 19, 1973, Jim Dulaney? Do you remember attacking a little girl on the side of the road? Do you remember Jennifer Collins? Do you remember how she cried, Jim Dulaney? And do you remember taking that rock and trying to crush her head?'

"I couldn't say anything, my heart was pounding so hard and my throat kinda closed up. She had her scarf off. There was no hair on that side of her head. Some of her ear was missing. She leaned in to me real close and said, 'My name is Jennifer Collins. I am the Angel of Death, and I've come to escort you to Hell, Jim Dulaney.'

"Doc, we were stinking drunk that night, the five of us. We'd just beaten the pants off Hoptown. Ron was at the wheel. Dale Liston had passed out — never could hold his liquor. We were stinkin' drunk and horny. Back then, around Coach Tatum, we were above being turned down when we were wanting it. That night, the girls wouldn't have anything to do with us 'cause we were so drunk. So we were just cruising out in the countryside when we saw this girl on a bicycle. Someone called out, 'target of opportunity,' I think. At first we talked to her nice and flirty. When she got nervous and tried to get away, we got aggressive, the four of us who were awake. Each took a turn. By the time I laid down on her, she was screaming, saying she was going to tell.

"I don't remember too clear. Somehow I picked up a rock and began hitting her in the side of the head. By then, Dale had come to; and just as I was about to deliver the final blow, he grabbed the rock from my hand and pulled me away. She lay there limp like a doll while Dale shouted at us and went half crazy.

"Before we could come up with a plan, we heard a car off in the distance and we froze. The car was getting closer, so we jumped back into our car and tore off into the night. We drove around for half an hour or so until we figured we'd have to bury the body somewhere before someone found out. We drove back to the place where we left her body, but it was gone, along with the bike.

"We didn't know what the hell to do. By then, we were horribly sober. We decided the only one we could trust would be Coach Tatum. That was a big mistake.

"The five of us met him at his office the next morning. We told him everything. And you know what he told us? He told us to shut up about it. He said no one had reported anything as far as he knew. He said that if we told anyone anything, the season would be over, and we'd be nothing. That's what he told us, Dr. Parker. He told us to shut up about it because it would ruin his damned season. And we've kept shut up about it all these years except Dale. He couldn't handle the guilt and killed himself.

"So this morning, Jennifer Collins is looking down at me, with her eyes all on fire, telling me she is the Angel of Death come to take me to Hell. Oh God, Doc, she's alive and knows everything. And I'm the only one she's taking to Hell."

I was numbed enough that I made no reply, only looking at a desperate man telling his tale.

"She told me how she had pieced the story together over the years, how she had come to the county to hand out the justice she had never gotten. She gave us all the cancer so that we would die miserable long deaths. And she watched us get the cancer and slowly, one by one, die disfigured and in pain. She was there for each one of us as we died.

"She forgave Dale because he wasn't part of her rape and tried to save her that night. But she was not going to forgive me.

"She said she forgave Frank as he died because he had turned his life around and tried to make up for what he'd done, especially rescuing his niece Stacy. But she said I had never done anything to deserve mercy and there would be no forgiveness.

"She said she forgave Walt as he died because he worked so hard to empower the women around him, especially Gina. She said that I had done nothing except evil and that I had raised a demonic whore in the likes of Jessie Belle. She said she'd had J.B.'s DNA tested and J.B. was not my offspring, yet I was still responsible for the way she turned out.

"She said she forgave Ron as he died because he had devoted his life to justice and helping with healing over a little girl's loss by being one of the 'troublemakers.' She said Ron saved lives and fought evil. But she said I had sown evil and she would not forgive me. She was going to personally take me to the doorway to Hell and leave me there like I had left her on the side of that road that horrible night.

"She had her syringe out with the pain killer. That's when Donna came in and slapped it out of her hand."

Jim broke down crying at that point. I now understood in full the reports from the others of crying at the end.

"What am I going to do, Doc? Am I going to spend eternity in Hell? You've got to help me, Doc. I don't want to spend eternity in Hell."

I shook my head. "I'm a doctor, not a priest. As a Baptist, all I can say is you'd better pray. That's all you have time for."

He rose up on his elbows. "You've got to stop her, Doc. You've got to talk to her. Tell her to forgive me, Doc. Tell her to forgive me." He fell back onto the pillow, coughing violently. The blood was coming now as large drops, not flecks. "Go!"

I strode to the door and unlocked it. Donna was just outside the door.

"What did he tell you?" she demanded.

"Your husband is dying. He's dying a horrible, painful death. Go in and be with him. He needs you."

I raced through the house toward the front door, with Donna in close pursuit.

"That bitch told him that J.B. wasn't his. She had no right to do that. I'm reporting her. Do you hear me? I'll sue!"

"Go be with your husband!" I shouted as I walked out the front door and off the front porch with a "thunk" as my feet met the ground, straight into the pouring rain.

"That bitch said tomorrow I would be a penniless wretch. What did she mean by that? Who's going to take care of all this? What about me?"

I got into my car and closed the door. I tried to gather my thoughts. Still in a daze, I turned the car around and headed toward the road. In the rear view mirror, I saw Donna raising her clenched fists at me.

I stopped at the end of the drive before the road and pulled out my cell phone. I pushed Sheriff Nolan's number into the phone. All I heard was an urgent beep. I looked at the phone — no signal. Half of my mind was desperately trying to construct a scenario where what I had just heard was all misinterpretation. The other half of my mind realized that Isabel had sent me out of communication range for over an hour. I punched in a text message to the sheriff, hoping that it would fly the moment I was in range of a tower.

I stepped on the gas and sped down the road, the windshield wipers on fast. My pace didn't last long. Rounding a bend deep in the wooded stretch,

I went into a terrifying skid. By the time I got the car back under control, both right wheels were off the road. Another foot and I would have been in a deep ditch, marooned out of touch with the rest of the world with no idea how close the nearest help might be. I started again, going only as fast as I felt I could maintain control.

Whenever I came upon a longer stretch of road, I pressed redial on my phone until Sheriff Nolan picked up when I was about five miles out of town.

"Hey, Doc, what's with this text?"

"Curtis, you have to go to the clinic and take Doc Isabel into custody. She's responsible for the cancers. She killed them."

"Whoa, Doc. That's a lot to swallow."

"It sounds crazy at first, but it all makes sense. If it's not true, she can explain it. Are you at the office?"

"Aw, shit! I think you're on to something. I got a call from her. She said there'd been an accident out in East County and needed assistance. I got out there, and she wasn't anywhere to be found and there was no accident. I've been gone about an hour. I'll be back at the office in ten minutes."

"Me too. See you there." I ended the call and concentrated on getting back in one piece and figuring out what to do when I got there. She surely knew that I knew everything by now. I wondered whether she would be surrendering or fighting. I was relieved to see Curtis approaching fast from the opposite direction at the same time as I came up to the clinic. Her car was gone.

We pulled up to the building and got out almost simultaneously. The sheriff drew his gun.

"I don't think that will be necessary. I think she was ready for us to learn what's been going on. I don't think she's dangerous."

"With all due respect, Doc, you're telling me she's Jennifer Collins, that she's killed four men and we didn't know it, and you think she's safe?"

I looked at him. "Good points."

Curtis pushed the clinic door open and leapt inside, sweeping his weapon around the room. The clinic was empty. I followed him to her office. Everything appeared intact. On her desk was a paper grocery bag with "Dr. John Parker" written in her neat hand with black magic marker. I tried to peer inside, but it was folded tight at the mouth. I pointed to a box of latex exam gloves. "Let me have a couple of those."

I put on the gloves, teased the bag open, and withdrew several bottles of chemicals from familiar laboratory suppliers. I found sodium dichromate dihydrate, ACS reagent grade; beryllium chloride, purified 99%; and a small vial of aflatoxin B2, research grade. A sticky note attached to the dichromate bottle read "You owe Ellen $50."

I looked at the sheriff. "Ellen bet me fifty bucks the cancers weren't caused by a virus. If you were trying to give a lab animal cancer, it would be hard to find a more potent combination than this."

There were other items in the bag. I withdrew an inkpad and fingerprint card bound together by a rubber band. She had provided a clean set of prints and signed the card both as Isabel Rodriguez and Jennifer Collins. The final items were two vials of blood, still warm, again signed with both names on the labels.

"She wanted no doubts left about her identity. I just sent your '73 forensics to the FBI ..." I looked up at Curtis. "Oh, no."

I raced from Isabel's office to mine with the sheriff just behind. My laptop was still open on the desk. I rounded my desk and my heart sank.

"What is it?" he asked, alarmed.

I pointed to the screen at a series of commands.

```
"WARNING:  CROSS-AGENCY  SCRUB  COMMAND  IS
IRREVERSIBLE
ARE YOU CERTAIN YOU WANT TO CONTINUE? Y/N"
"Y"
"Cross-agency   scrub   initiated,   please
wait…"
"Cross-agency  scrub  complete.  File  report
AE784r within 24 hours."
```

Curtis frowned. "What's this?"

"I had gotten a notice that a record was located for Reggie Tatum. In all the turmoil of the Dulaney call, I forgot that I was logged in. She took his information and then purged it from the databases."

"There must be backups."

"No, not for this. A cross-agency scrub is used when someone needs to vanish — like witness protection programs. If the backups weren't scrubbed, someone could still get to the person, in theory. As far as public records are concerned, he's gone, known only to God and Jennifer Collins."

"All right, Doc, let's find her. Where would she head?"

We returned to her office. Everything seemed normal, as if she would return at any moment. I glanced at the windowsill and saw her Mason jar, half-filled with water — nothing else. "I've got an idea. Let's head to the cemetery, to the Jennifer Collins headstone."

We raced out of the clinic and into his cruiser, since his tires were better suited to strenuous driving, and he had much more horsepower. We could have used his siren, though there was neither traffic nor any reason to alert Isabel. I had never been to this particular cemetery, yet I recognized the hallmarks of a classic Midwestern graveyard, flat and open with only a few trees.

"There's her car." The sheriff pointed to her Prius in the midst of the tombstones.

We pulled alongside.

"When I headed out to the Dulaney's, it was full of boxes and clothes. It's empty now. Where's the headstone?"

He pointed toward a spot near the edge of the cemetery and began walking in that direction. The rain had eased up by then into a gentle drizzle. As we approached, I saw another Mason jar, half filled with water only. Under the jar I saw a note.

Up close, we found it was an envelope in a zip-locked bag under the jar. The sheriff turned it over and read the address. "To the medical clinic board members of Guthrie, Kentucky. I'm on that board."

He opened the envelope and began to read. In a moment, he chuckled and handed the letter to me.

"To the members of the board. It is my honor to recommend for your consideration as the new physician for Guthrie and southern Todd County Dr. John Parker. Dr. Parker has demonstrated …"

I looked up at Curtis. "Unreal. She had this planned for today."

"Uh huh. And look at the date of the letter."

I looked down at the paper again. Saturday, May 23, 2009. "She wrote this the day of Frank's memorial service."

Curtis took the letter back, folded it, and returned it to its envelope and tucked the envelope into his shirt pocket. We left the headstone and walked over to her car. Another envelope lay on the front seat. The sheriff opened it.

"She signed the vehicle title over to Stacy." He looked around.

I rubbed the back of my neck. "I'm guessing she had a car or truck waiting here, transferred her stuff, and headed off. Maybe we can find something at her house."

Curtis wrinkled his brow. "This sounds bad — I don't know where she lives. Never been there. Come on."

We got back into his car and sped again to the city office. We went inside, and he headed to a file cabinet of county employee records. He pulled out her folder and put it on the desk, leafing through the contents.

He shook his head. "Only a post office box number. It's like a treasure hunt. Let's go see Jack."

We jogged across the street.

"Shouldn't we be alerting more law enforcement agencies?"

"Right now I'm figuring the time's better spent trying to get some hints as to where she's heading. At the moment, my call would be to search for a vehicle of unknown make or type driven by a woman or woman looking like a man traveling in an unknown direction — well within the speed limit. The driver will have a perfectly good story and spot-on ID. Not sure how seriously the other guys will take that, Doc."

We entered the post office. Jack was by himself. He looked up. "Hey, Curtis, hey, Doc. What's up?"

Curtis leaned on the counter. "We need to get the actual address of one of your box holders."

Jack frowned. "OK. You have a warrant? A federal warrant?"

"Not yet. Jack, time is of the essence. We need to reach Doc Isabel."

"While I'm ready to help, you must know that divulging that information requires a court order or permission of the owner. I can't just give it to you. I'm duty bound. I could go to jail for just turning it over."

The sheriff folded his hands, pleading. "Jack, it's a matter of life and death. She's left in a hurry; and by the time we get a warrant, she could be in another state or country. You know I wouldn't ask this of you if it weren't really, really serious."

Jack shifted his gaze between the sheriff and me. He bit his upper lip. At last, he walked into a back room and returned with a locked box. "I'm really sorry, Sheriff. I just can't do it. Anyone who would obtain that information without a warrant is breaking federal law." He unlocked the box and turned it around facing us.

The sheriff nodded. "I understand, Jack. I'm sorry to have troubled you. I'll come back with a warrant."

Jack opened the lid of the box revealing several hundred filed forms. "Now if you'll excuse me, I have to get the registered mail in the back ready for pickup. I'll be back with you in two minutes." He left the opened box on the counter and retreated into the back room.

Curtis flipped through the forms until he found the one. He held open the spot where the form had been and showed it to me.

I already had out my pocket notebook and wrote down the address – 1348 R 106. I wrote down the phone number as well. I nodded, he returned the form to its proper spot, and closed the box.

Curtis called to the back. "You're right, Jack. Sorry to have caused any discomfort. We're leaving now. I'll let you know what's going on when I know myself."

Jack emerged from the back room, looked at the box, and nodded. "Good luck, gentlemen."

"OK. Route 106 — Boulder Road. That heads northeast of here. You're responsible for tracking the numbers. That'll be about a mile and a half, two miles."

As we once again boarded his cruiser, Curtis's phone rang.

"Uh oh. Trouble." He put the phone to his ear. "Sheriff Nolan." Right away, he held the phone back from his ear. I could hear Donna's screaming voice. "Yes, ma'am, I'm sorry for your lo... No ma'am, I don't know where she is, but I hope to be seeing the Doc soon. Now, I don't think she's responsible for ... No, you're right. I don't know what you're going through. Say again? Yes, we can have the body picked up. Today? Of course. Let me make arrangements."

He lowered his head listening to her harangue. "Dr. Parker? Yes, I'll be seeing him today, too. Yes, ma'am. I'll tell him. Is there anything ...?" Curtis held the phone in front of him. "Can you beat that? She hung up on me." He turned to me. "I'm supposed to tell you 'to go to Hell if you were in league with that bitch.'"

I nodded. "Thank you. Was that verbatim?"

"Pretty much." He pulled out and headed north. "As you must have gathered, Mr. Dulaney has passed away. She wants someone to come and get the body. I'll call Bill Carson as soon as we get to that address."

"I've got Bill's number in my phone. I'll call if that helps."

"Yes, it would. OK. It's a little ways to Boulder Road. What was the number again?"

"1348."

"Well, we've got a ways to go. Give Bill a call."

I called Bill Carson and filled him in on the circumstances of Jim's death. While the Dulaneys had not made any arrangements for his funeral, an anonymous donor had given several thousand dollars to cover it. Bill would have his hearse at the Dulaney place in the late afternoon. He asked me how the cancer investigation was going, and I told him we might have had a break in the case — too early to tell.

We sped through rolling hills of pastures and fields interspersed with an occasional farmhouse.

"All right, John. We just passed 1290. Am I going too fast for you?"

"No. I'll get it. 1308 ... 1316 ... 1330 ... OK, slow down 1342 ... 1346."

He slowed down as we drove past a lush, well-trimmed, gated pasture and then to the next mailbox.

"1354. Did you see a driveway back there?"

As he drove a short distance farther, the numbers continued to rise. "No, let's re-check."

He turned around and we crept back to the gap in numbers. Mailboxes 1354 and 1346 bracketed the pasture. He turned in at the drive at mailbox 1346.

"This is the home of Thelma Cornette. She and her husband ran the office supply shop in Guthrie."

A gentle-looking lady came to the front porch at the sound of our tires on the gravel drive. She greeted us as we emerged from the cruiser. "Well, good afternoon, Sheriff, Dr. Parker. I think I'm up to date on all my county bills." She grinned.

Curtis returned her smile. "Yes, ma'am. Knowing you, you're paid ahead. We were looking for an address ..." He turned back to me.

"1348."

She shook her head. "That would be the field here." She waved her hand in the direction of the field next door. "There hasn't been a house there since we moved here 15 years ago. Actually, kinda like it that way. The only activity I see over there is several times a year the Waddail boy comes to cut hay."

I turned to Curtis. "I remember Gina telling me that Doc Isabel lets them cut hay on her property."

The sheriff saluted Mrs. Cornette. "Thank you for your time, ma'am. We'll just take a look over there. Mind if I leave my vehicle in your drive for a few minutes?"

She smiled again. "Go right ahead, Sheriff. Might provoke a little scandal. That'd be fun. Not much happens out here."

Curtis nodded. "Yes, ma'am. We kinda like it that way."

As we walked along the road, grasshoppers jumped away from us into the bordering growth. If this was her field, she had maintained it well. The fences were strong and tight. There was a huge lone oak tree at the crest of the rolling grass. On the shoulder ahead, I spotted a patch of orange. We approached and I picked up a bouquet of flowers, still quite fresh. "She stopped here not long ago. They're *Begonia boliviensis*. They would be the flowers that Ellen left in the Mason jar on the headstone this morning. Should we bring them back?"

He shook his head. "Naw. Any idea how long they've been there?"

"These begonias are succulent so they could have been left several hours ago."

The sheriff scratched his chin. "OK, then this is the timeline I'm looking at. She left the clinic right after she sent us off, drove to the cemetery, transferred things from her car to her current vehicle, left the note and title, picked up the flowers, laid the flowers here, and took off. Allowing for some other errands around town, she's been on the road for a little over two hours. She could be anywhere in a 30,000 square mile circle. Let's head back so I can make my reports."

I followed him, taking one last look at the field. It was beautiful and silent save for the sound of our steps on gravel and insects stirring in the grass.

Back at the office, I stared at the pile of file folders. A wave of fatigue washed over me as I thought about going over every note I had taken in light of the truth. I looked at the CD that Roberta had delivered to me from Ron Widing. I could imagine the opening lines in the file I was certain to find on it. "On the night of Friday, October 19, 1973 ..." Too weary, I couldn't look at it now. I remembered my promise to Ron that I would tell Jane that he loved her. I would keep my promise before she returned to

Baltimore. That conversation would be difficult. I thought about the Form AE784r I needed to file, the report of a cross-agency data scrub. I didn't have one. Never dreamed I would need one, and, professionally, it was going to cost me dearly. I'm sure it was available somewhere online as a PDF. I was too tired to look at the moment. I wondered what disciplinary consequences there would be. The lapse of leaving my computer logged in and unattended would almost surely cost a man his life — unacceptable regardless of the reasons.

I looked up at the clock. A little after six. I would get some sleep, get up early, and tackle all those tasks in the morning. I locked the door to my office and left through the clinic, stopping at Isabel's ... Jennifer Collins's ... door. Staring at the diploma on the wall, I figured I would suggest to Curtis that they alert the alumni office at Old Dominion in case they heard from their former student.

I drove back to Ellen's, parked, and trudged up her front steps. She was sitting silent in the porch swing, a box of tissues beside her. She picked up the box and put it in her lap, opening a place for me. I sat down in silence beside her. In the gathering dusk, I saw on the porch table a familiar basket, one I had last seen on the front seat of Isabel's — Jennifer's car. I was going to have to decide which name I was going to use going forward.

"Nice basket," I said.

Ellen's lips trembled as she explained. "She had Judy make it up. It's for a future wedding. It's the little packets with the throwing grain."

I reached forward and picked up one of the packets, tied with a neat white ribbon. I looked closer and smiled. "Bird seed."

"You know about that?"

"Uh huh. First day I was here. My first meeting with Gina and Doc." I looked closer at the basket and spotted an envelope. "I've seen a lot of envelopes today."

"It's the deed to her field. If Chris and Gina get married and agree never to build on the property, she's given it to them. George Boone worked up a binding covenant for them. 47 more acres for Gina."

"Curtis and I were out there about an hour ago. I think that was the last place she stopped."

She turned to me. "How do you know she'd been there?"

"There was a bouquet of *Begonia boliviensis* placed on the shoulder at the edge of the field."

Ellen began to sob.

I sat in silence.

After a while, she explained in a tear-choked voice, "That was the spot where they attacked her. That was the place on the road where they left her for dead. Our little Jennifer. The sweetest, smartest little girl you'd ever hope to meet."

I closed my eyes. "How long have you known she was Jennifer?"

"I made it a point to never know. A few years back, we were in some committee meeting. Someone said something funny, and she laughed that throaty little laugh that Jennifer did when she was my student. I turned to her fast and our eyes met, and without a word we just kinda agreed not to pursue it any further. She's been my best buddy all these years. I don't know what I'm going to do without her."

"You're not alone. The community has lost an amazing doctor." I turned to look at her and half-smiled. "She wrote a letter of recommendation for me to the clinic board."

"Well, you've got a unanimous vote if you'll take it. I'm on that board."

I shook my head. "Curtis is on the board too, he says."

"And Mireese and Eugene Gough."

"Mr. Gough? I'd think that would be a problem," I cautioned.

She laughed. "I heard he bought you lunch. That's practically a coronation."

"You heard that, did you?"

"Prairie dogs, John. Prairie dogs."

I got up and breathed in the moist and fragrant evening air. "I need to call Baylor. We have a lot to talk about."

"Remind her she can grow all the peonies she's ever dreamed about."

I smiled as I descended the stairs. As I rounded the front of the house heading back to my room, Ellen came to the edge of the porch. "You know what the last thing she said to me before she got in the car to go to the cemetery was?"

I shook my head.

Even in the twilight I could see fresh tears. "She said, 'Ms. Miller, you were my favorite teacher. Ever!'"

196

11 PATIENT

"I still say that I would have figured it out before that." My patient exuded confidence.

"Hey, you were there at the same time. You had almost all the facts that I had, and already at that point a better network than I had." Some patients are such fun to argue with.

"You'd been there longer than I had," she insisted.

"By a few hours!" I shook my head.

"I still say that I would have figured it out."

I finished my exam, removed the latex gloves, and tossed them in the sterile disposal bag. I went over to the assay analysis machine and tore off the output strip. Turning to Stacy, I smiled. "I normally wouldn't say this to a young single woman, but congratulations, you're pregnant."

She pumped the air with her fist. "Yes! Thank you, Dr. P! That means I don't have to go back for any more of those *in vitros*."

"Hey, this pregnancy took pretty fast. *In vitro* can sometimes take dozens of tries. I'd say you're pretty fortunate."

"Fortunate? The procedure's a real pain. Have you ever tried it?"

I laughed. "No."

"See?" She turned serious. "OK, now, you can't tell Gina and Chris yet."

"Uh. It is their child. As surrogate, you'll be doing the heavy lifting — literally. Ethically, though, they need to be informed."

She pleaded. "Please. Just two days. Gina's birthday is Thursday and I was hoping I'd have good news to tell her at her party."

I folded my arms without comment.

"Speaking of which, are those pee sticks safe?"

"What?"

"I got one of those pregnancy test kits when I started feeling different, the kind you pee on. Anyway, it came up with that little plus sign. I wanted to wrap it up as a present, and Gina would open it and find out at her party. Wouldn't that be cool?"

I nodded. "Hmm. Aside from maybe a little odor, it's probably safe. Urine is almost sterile unless there's a UTI. And you are ferociously healthy, for certain. I'm sure if you just wrapped it in some cling wrap, it would be fine."

"Awesome. Thanks, Doc. Please don't tell her 'til then. Please."

I pondered whether I should extract some concession for the delay, and then decided against it. "Well, it might take a couple of days to write up the results."

"Thank you, thank you, thank you." She thought for a while, a pattern I long ago learned was the prelude to something zany. "Don't you think it ironic that here she is, the major cattle breeder in this part of the state, and she can't get knocked up?"

I shook my head. "There are many reasons for infertility — it's not uncommon. One thing that's been observed is that the presence of an active child or other changes in environments will sometimes change the conditions of the womb, and women can get pregnant later."

"Still, I'd like to get pregnant the regular way some time."

"All in due time, all in due time. You are young, intelligent, and will some day find a soul mate worthy of you."

"I don't know. Kind of a guy desert out here compared to Baltimore."

"What about that young photographer from Nashville who's been flirting with you?"

She looked at me in surprise. "How did you know about him?"

I felt uncomfortably smug that I knew something she thought I didn't.

"You're not going to tell me, are you? He and I are doing a project. I'm body painting like a construction site on the side of my belly and he's going to take pictures of it as it grows. I'm calling it 'Womb with a View.'"

"I'd worry about things in the paint. I wouldn't want anything harmful passing the skin."

She laughed.

"I'm serious," I protested.

"I know. When we were making plans, Gina said that's just what you'd say. We already checked the paints. They're vegetable dyes and certified safe and organic."

"OK. You're wise, as I expected. I'd still like to take a look at them."

"Of course. Say, if this one goes well, maybe you and Baylor ...?"

I smiled. "I don't think you'll want to make this a career. And remember what I said. A change in environments can bring a change in fertility."

She cocked her head. "Oh, really? Are you saying ...?"

"Yours was not the only positive test today." I had already told Baylor, and Baylor asked me to tell Stacy just to see how long it took for the news to get around.

"Woo hoo! She and I can be our own support group."

"That's actually a great idea," I agreed.

She calmed down for just a minute. "This is amazing, Doc."

"Well, I hope you feel that way in six months. By the way, is the school administration OK with all this?"

"Oh, yeah. Didn't they talk to you?"

"Yes. I told them it was borderline heroic, and that you were taking your responsibilities very seriously. I just hadn't heard back from them."

"We're building a whole curriculum around me — us. My little art students are drawing pictures of what they want the prince or princess to be. Health is using me as a life lesson. Even the math classes are learning to budget for kids. So you're going to be a daddy. How cool is that?"

"Are your and Gina's plans for the hand-off developed?"

"Yep. She'll start lactation hormones so she can breast-feed from delivery day. I'll be backup in case it doesn't work. After that, I'll be 'Crazy Aunt Stacy,' the aunt every parent fears and every child adores."

I believed her. "You can get dressed now. I'm going to write you a prescription for prenatal vitamins. I know you know how important those are."

"Yep. Say, did you hear what happened to J.B.?"

"I don't listen to gossip." I was curious, however.

"Yeah, whatever. Anyway, she and that skunk Nick figured they'd get rich dealing in a little meth."

I put my hand to my face. The news was no surprise, yet still disappointing.

"Oh, it gets way better. They went down to Louisiana to pick up their deal, and, wouldn't you know, it was a sting. Their 'dealer' was a fed. The two of them turned on each other in a flash, and they're both looking at about ten years in prison."

"Wow!"

"Hey, guess who else is preggers?"

I gave Stacy my stern look.

"Right, right. Patient confidentiality. I know you can't tell me. But I know, so I'm telling you. Mireese. Hey, maybe she'll be in our support group, too. It's amazing. She and Janet agreed on the whole arrangement, almost like sisters. Jack was donor — that was Janet's idea. Now, that procedure's a whole lot easier on the pre-mom than this *in vitro* pain, believe me! Anyway, they used the clinic over in Clarksville just once, and — boom — another one on the way. They agreed that the kid will always know who his or her biological father is. It's kinda sweet. I may be just a touch jealous. I didn't exactly have a dad. And that little tyke will have a dad and two moms." Stacey pondered awhile. "No, no, I'm not jealous. I wouldn't trade this crazy life for anything. But you know what I do wish?" She grew quiet, fighting back tears. "I wish Uncle Frank could be around to see all this happening. I think he'd approve, and he'd be happy for just about everyone."

I nodded. "He's left a good legacy. You've done him proud, water hyacinth."

She looked at the wall of the clinic at Isabel Rodriguez's diploma. "So she really did graduate from Old Dominion?"

"Yep, top of her class. They'll be watching for any communication from her, though we all know she's too clever to do that."

Stacy bit her lip. "I wonder where she is now."

12 NEW AIDE

"What happened to Juanita?" he asked.

"Apparently you weren't very kind to her, sir. She asked the agency for a transfer. They send me for their problem cases," the new aide explained.

"Hey, I was just flirting with her."

The new aide did not appear amused.

"And what's with the scarf?" he asked.

"I keep my head covered out of respect for the Lord," she replied.

"You're not a ..."

"Muslim? Would that be a problem?" she inquired.

"No, I've just never had a Muslim aide before. I'll bet you're real pretty without the scarf."

"Touch it and you'll find out what bad injection technique feels like."

"Sorry!"

"I don't mess around, Coach," she scolded

"What did you call me?"

"Coach. You seem like an athletic coach. Strong build, short hair."

"Yeah, well that was a long time ago. And it didn't end well. Traitors, ingrates."

"People can be so intolerant," she sympathized.

"Yeah, well, let's just keep the coach thing between you and me."

"You behave and it's our little secret. Now, I see your tests show a little vitamin deficiency. We have some new multivitamins for that. I hear they don't taste very good, though. Are you man enough to take them?"

He smiled. "Anything for my little angel."

Her face was serene as she turned and gazed out the window at the fog rolling in from the Pacific. She murmured, "That's right. I'm your little angel."

COMFORT FOOD

Growing up in Western Kentucky, I was the beneficiary of tasty food traditions, with histories stretching back centuries. The meals that Dr. Parker enjoyed during his stay are a tribute to the culinary treasures of the Pennyrile region

Tuesday
Lunch (White Castle)
White Castle Hamburgers

> Our family is devoted to White Castles. Taxonomically, they are distinct from mainline hamburgers, in that they are smaller than common burgers and are cooked on a bed of onions. Once imprinted in one's youth, one carries a permanent craving. https://www.whitecastle.com

Dinner (Faye Johnson)
Fried Chicken
Green Beans
Potatoes
Mrs. Tinley's Coconut Cake
Sweet Tea

Wednesday
Breakfast
Country Ham with Red Eye Gravy
Cantaloupe

> One of the great gastronomic treats of Western Kentucky is the aged country ham. The robust flavor comes from a combination of smoking and aging. Perhaps the pinnacle of achievement producing

country hams would rest with Broadbent's:
http://www.broadbenthams.com

The best cantaloupes in my youth — maybe in the world — came from farmers in Posey County, Indiana. These melons are large and have a smoother skin compared to the typical grocery heavily netted skin. They possess a wondrous fragrance and have a taste that will bring tears to your eyes. The Posey County melons ripen in earnest starting in July.

Lunch (Ferrell's)
Fried Bologna
Sweet Tea

Dinner (Ellen's)
Roast beef
Potatoes
Green Beans
Glazed Strawberry Pie with Whipped Cream
    The family recipe for strawberry pie can be found at http://clarkriley.com/dots/. Aside from the crust, it has very few ingredients and the whole fresh fruits in the pie are one of the high points of the season.

Thursday
Breakfast
Cinnamon Coffee Cake
Oranges
    I've enjoyed this coffee cake as far back as I have a memory. The family recipe for this cinnamon coffee cake can be found at http://clarkriley.com/dots/.

Lunch (Hopkinsville Main Street Diner)
Locally Sourced Pork Chops
Vegetable Medley

Dinner (Ellen's)
Fried Chicken
Corn
Freshly Baked Cornbread
Peach Ice Cream with Peaches

Friday
Breakfast (Ellen's)
Goetta
Coffee
> Goetta is a breakfast meat dish, likely of German origin and probably designed originally to extend costly meat with grain. It is still a treasured breakfast dish in the Cincinnati area. The family recipe for goetta can be found at http://clarkriley.com/dots/. One excellent supplier is Glier's — http://www.goetta.com/.

Lunch (Ferrell's)
Hamburgers
Freshly cut potato fries

Dinner (Mireese's Concessions, the Game)
Duck à l'Orange
Chateaubriand
> These are examples of traditionally difficult-to-prepare dishes. With good organizational skills, it is possible to prepare close equivalents that capture the taste in an economical way at sufficient scale.

Saturday
Breakfast (Ellen's)
Scrambled eggs
Bacon
Biscuits
Cantaloupe

Lunch (Guthrie Baptist Church)
Community Pot Luck

Dinner (Johnson Farm)
Picnic at Johnson Farm after memorial service
Mrs. Tinley's Cake

Sunday
Breakfast (Ellen's)
Country sausage patties
Biscuits with sorghum molasses
> Again, it's hard to beat Broadbent's country sausages. Sorghum is the "sugar cane" referenced in the Kentucky State Song, "My Old Kentucky Home."

Dinner
Slow Cooker Chili with Grated Cheese
Crackers

Monday
Breakfast (Ellen's)
French Toast
Cantaloupe

Dinner (Ellen's, late)
Roast Chicken
Green Beans
Mashed Potatoes

Tuesday
Breakfast (Ellen's)
Hominy
Strawberries with Ice Cream

Lunch (Ferrell's)
Spaghetti with meatballs

ABOUT THE AUTHOR

Baltimore author Clark Thomas Riley has written and published non-fiction since the 1970s in support of careers at The University of North Carolina, Chapel Hill, the United States Navy, Graduate Studies at The University of Chicago, biomedical research, and information technology. He began writing fiction in 1994 and has five novels finished to the first draft level or beyond. *Dots, Cancer Sleuthing on the 21st Century Frontier* is his second novel, after *What If They Lied (just a little)?* Following this work will be a pioneer romance, a spy novel, a liberation adventure, and a commentary on building the 21st century hobby greenhouse.

Other interests include teaching Sunday School, growing and speaking about orchids, publishing services, teaching, and social activism. The author can be reached at ClarkTRiley@gmail.com. You can join a moderated discussion of *Dots, Cancer Sleuthing on the 21st Century Frontier* at http://clarkriley.com/dots.

90336280R00128

Made in the USA
Middletown, DE
21 September 2018